Jerry's Passion

AN INSURGENTS MC ROMANCE

Chiah Wilder

Copyright © 2016 by Chiah Wilder
Print Edition

Editing by Hot Tree Editing
Cover design by Cheeky Covers
Proofreading by Wyrmwood Editing

All rights reserved. This book or any portion thereof may not be reproduced or used in any manner whatsoever without the express written permission of the author except for the use of brief quotations in a book review. Please purchase only authorized additions, and do not participate in or encourage piracy of copyrighted materials.

Your support of the author's rights is appreciated.

Disclaimer: This is a work of fiction. Names, characters, businesses, places, events and incidents are either the products of the author's imagination or used in a fictitious manner. Any resemblance to actual persons, living or dead, or actual events is purely coincidental.

I love hearing from my readers. You can email me at chiahwilder@gmail.com.

Make sure you sign up for my newsletter so you can keep up with my new releases, special sales, free short stories, and other treats only available to newsletter readers. When you sign up, you will receive a FREE hot and steamy short story. Sign up at: http://eepurl.com/bACCL1.

Visit me on facebook at facebook.com/Chiah-Wilder-1625397261063989

Description

The first time Jerry saw Kylie, he was taken by her beauty and innocence, but he stayed away because she was too young. A member of the Insurgents MC, Jerry's life revolves around the club, his Harley, and easy sex. Women clamor for the rugged, tatted outlaw's attention, and he obliges, but his sights are set on the pretty, young blonde who is all grown up now—sweet curves and all....

Kylie fills his thoughts, and he dreams of his fingers tangling in her glossy hair, her legs wrapping tightly around his waist, her full lips quivering as she comes.

Only problem is he can't have her.

But... he can't stop himself from craving her, and if he acts, it'll surely cost him *everything.*

His resistance is waning....

Kylie McDaniels is the pretty daughter of Banger—President of the Insurgents MC. She grew up in the outlaw biker world, but her father shielded her from the dark side of it, and she still has an innocence he prefers she keep. Banger is very protective of his daughter, and he's made up his mind that she won't fall in love with a biker, especially Jerry.

She'd listen to her father, but the hot, muscular biker makes her want to do some not so innocent things.

Her insides melt, and her brain turns to mush whenever he looks at her with his hungry, brown eyes.

Damn. Why does he have to be so sexy?

As Kylie maneuvers her budding sexuality and attraction to Jerry while trying to stay on the good side of her dad, someone is out there watching her, waiting to make his move. He's come for retribution, and Kylie is the pawn in his scheme. Will Jerry be able to stop the madman before he strikes?

Can their forbidden love survive the chaos of the world around them? **The Insurgents MC series are standalone romance novels. This is Jerry and Kylie's love story. This book contains violence, sexual assault (not graphic), strong language, and steamy/graphic sexual scenes. It describes the life and actions of an outlaw motorcycle club. If any of these issues offend you, please do not read the book. HEA. No cliffhangers! The book is intended for readers over the age of 18.**

Previous Titles in the Series:

Hawk's Property: Insurgents Motorcycle Club Book 1
Jax's Dilemma: Insurgents Motorcycle Club Book 2
Chas's Fervor: Insurgents Motorcycle Club Book 3
Axe's Fall: Insurgents Motorcycle Club Book 4
Banger's Ride: Insurgents Motorcycle Club Book 5

PROLOGUE

Mid-March
Red Rocks University
Crested Peak, Colorado

HE STOOD IN the shadows behind a bush, staring intently at the second-floor window. A glimpse of her made his heart race and he licked his lips, ripping off the dry skin with his front teeth. She was so damn beautiful. When he'd decided to seek her out, he had no idea how pretty and innocent she was. Since she was the daughter of the president of the Insurgents MC, he'd figured she'd look tough and used-up. But she was an angel with blonde hair that touched the top of her ass, rounded tits that would fit perfectly in his hands, and big blue eyes that sparkled with innocence.

He inhaled sharply. Seeing her had changed his plans somewhat. Watching her come and go for the past several weeks, he'd grown attached to her. As crazy as it sounded, he wanted to get to know her, become a part of her world.

"Mary, come on up. Taylor and I aren't ready yet!" Kylie yelled out her dorm window.

The girl she'd called to bounced up the flight of concrete stairs, then entered the three-story, Gothic-style building. It had taken some time for him to find which dorm Kylie lived in. The university had more than fifteen thousand students, but he'd persevered until he found her. She lived with a dark-haired roommate—Taylor—in room number 222, on the second floor in the middle of the hall. A perfect location for him to watch her as she sat at her desk and studied, glanced down at her phone, or just stared out the window at the distant Rockies, a wistful glimmer in her eyes.

The man had been driven to find her, hate and retribution fueling him on, but then he saw her and his pants grew tight, and he knew his plan had changed. He buried himself further in the bush when the large wooden doors of the building opened and Kylie, Taylor, and Mary filed out, laughing and talking like young college students do. He breathed out when the trio passed by the greenery which hid him. The scent of vanilla, lavender, and patchouli lingered as they scurried down the brick path. Not knowing which aroma belonged to his Kylie—he'd started thinking of her as *his*—the young man made a note to find out.

Slipping out from his hiding place, he shoved his hands in his pockets, keeping his distance as he followed the women. Each time Kylie's hips swayed, his dick twitched more, and he willed himself to focus on his goal.

A broad-shouldered young man approached the girls. "Hey, Ricky." The slight breeze carried Kylie's sweet voice.

"Hey. What're you guys up to?" he asked.

"We're going to grab a burger at University Café, then check out the show for Thursday Thrills." Kylie moved closer to Ricky. Her stalker growled when he saw her arm rub against the college boy.

"There's a hypnotist. Everyone's raving about him. Want to join us?" Mary asked.

He watched as the three women flirted and fawned over Ricky, who kept staring at Kylie in a way that made his blood boil. *Note to self— Ricky's fucking history!*

"Sure, why not?" Ricky looped his arm with Kylie's and the four students ambled toward the café.

Wrapping his leather jacket tighter around him, the man leaned against the wall of the Student Center. He'd wait—he *had* to. He wanted to make sure Ricky Fuckface didn't spend the night with Kylie. She was his, and no one would take her away from him. Just thinking about running his hands through her silky hair and touching her skin— he imagined it would be soft as velvet—made his dick jab hard against his jeans. It wasn't time yet, but soon he'd have her legs wrapped around his waist as he plunged into her tight heat. Their fucking would be sweet and nasty, and she'd cry out his name as she came all over his cock.

Then he'd hurt her real bad. Maybe even cut her delicate throat.

He had to.

Retribution sucked sometimes.

Chapter One

April
Crested Peak, Colorado

JERRY LEANED AGAINST the trunk of the evergreen as he watched Kylie and her three friends amble on the sidewalk. Her hair shone in the moonlight like liquid gold, and he sucked in his breath when she threw her head back and laughed, covering her lips with her hand. He knew her lips well; he'd been studying them for the past three years. He loved the way she'd lick the sugar off them whenever she ate the donuts in the club's kitchen. So many times he'd wished he were those granules on her lips as her pink tongue had skimmed over them.

Kylie stopped and checked her phone, the glow of it casting a white sheen over her face. "Ari says she's going to meet us," she said, then giggled uncontrollably. The other two women started laughing with her, and then all three bent over, holding their stomachs, laughing and gasping for air.

A smile brushed over Jerry's lips. *She's fuckin' plastered.* His amusement quickly turned to anger when he saw the guy, who'd been walking with them, wrap his arm around her as she leaned in to him, swaying and stumbling. She didn't seem like she cared that the young man's hand slowly rode up her shirt, but Jerry cared. He cared a whole fucking lot.

Pushing off the tree trunk, he came up behind her. "Kylie," he said in a low, deep voice. From the way she jumped at her name, he knew he'd startled her. She whirled around and peered at him, her face blank, her eyes narrowed. Then a broad smile rolled over her mouth and recognition dawned on her face.

"Jerry! I didn't recognize you because… you're *here*. What are you doing on campus?" Her eyes didn't quite focus on his.

"I came up to visit some friends who live near the university. I thought I'd come by and see you." His gaze roamed up and down her body, and when it landed on the guy's hand, ferocity replaced softness. "How are you?"

"Great." She pushed the man's hand away and Jerry smiled, letting his eyes linger on her mouth. Her plump lips shone under the full moon, and he imagined her gloss tasted like cotton candy or watermelon. How he yearned to taste those lips.

"That's good." Jerry leaned in close and caught a whiff of lavender as it wafted around him, landing on his dick. With his fingers, he brushed her hair back from her face, soft like a whisper.

She looked up at him and blinked. "You're so sweet." She pressed against him. "You made a special trip to say hi to me." She curled her arm around his neck, pulling him down toward her. "Thanks," she breathed, her lips grazing his ear.

Fuck! Jerry looped his arms around her small waist and held her close, loving the way she felt in his arms. He'd fantasized about holding her for too long. With her long, silky hair, round tits, and curvy hips, she was his perfect wet dream. And what the hell was up with the way his nerves were sparking? He'd held a ton of women before, but he never felt this connected, this emotional with any of them. Then again, none of them were Kylie.

"Hey, are you coming with us?" one of the young women asked.

"Who's the hot guy you have wrapped around you?" the other woman said.

Kylie pulled away from Jerry, but he reached out and grabbed her as she nearly fell. "You've had too much to drink," he rasped against her ear. She giggled.

The other guy took hold of her hand and tugged her to him. "Let's go." He began walking away from Jerry with a swaying Kylie in tow.

Gritting his teeth, Jerry sprinted ahead of the group then stopped abruptly, causing the guy and Kylie to crash into him. Putting his arm around her shoulder, he glared at the young man. "I'm taking care of Kylie. Her dad would want it that way." The guy looked Jerry up and down then rushed over to the two girls, hooking an arm around each of them.

Jerry was such a bullshitter. He knew Banger would be livid if he saw his precious daughter snuggled against Jerry's chest. He knew she was off-limits because she was the president's daughter, and Banger had made it a point, on more than one occasion, to let Jerry know not to get near her. Hell, Banger didn't even want him to *talk* to her, but he couldn't keep himself away from her. He was drawn to her, and even though he knew it was wrong, dangerous, and all kinds of stupid, he'd wanted Kylie so bad for far too long.

"You want to come with us to the festival?" She looked up at him, her pretty face so innocent and tempting.

I want to kiss you hard, suck your pretty tits, and ram my cock in you. I hope you're not fuckin' that pansy-ass prick up ahead. If you are, I'll have to beat his ass. "Sure. Where's it at?"

"In the quad. It's the spring festival, and they have a band, beer, and everything." Her gaze was wide.

He laughed and fought the urge to kiss her. She was so damned adorable. *Fuck, I'm playing with fire.*

"Wait up, guys." Kylie gestured her friends to stop then looked up at Jerry. "I want you to meet some of my friends."

"Is the asshole a friend, or boyfriend?"

"Ricky? We're just friends. Anyway, so what if he were my boyfriend?" She raised her chin defiantly.

"I don't give a shit, but your dad would."

"You're not going to tell my dad about me being tipsy, are you?"

"You're more like drunk, babe, but no, I'm not gonna tell him." *There's no fuckin' way Banger's ever gonna find out I've got my hands all over his daughter. Shit.*

"Thanks," she whispered.

They caught up to her friends, and Kylie introduced them to Jerry while he stared impassively at them. His thoughts were only on Kylie, and if she continued drinking at the festival, he would definitely have to carry her back to her dorm room, tuck her into bed, and give her a long, deep kiss good night.

"It's kind of awesome you being here. I never pictured you at my college." Her soft voice interrupted his thoughts.

"How come?"

She shrugged. "I don't know. I just think of you as being at the club."

"So, you think of me?" he teased, clasping her shoulder tighter. "I like that."

She punched him lightly in his side. "You know what I mean. I just picture you and all the other guys as living and breathing the club. I guess I never imagined you outside the Insurgents' world."

"Yeah, well, I *do* step out sometimes. I wanted to say hi before I headed back to Pinewood." *I rode my ass up here to see you. Fuck, I go hard just thinking about you.* "You don't come to Pinewood Springs that often."

"I know," she groaned. "When I first got here, I was so homesick, but now I'm so busy with school, activities, and parties that I never seem to have time to go home and see Dad, and all of you." She held him tighter. "I'm fucked up. I drank too much."

"I'd have to agree, but hold on to me. I'll make sure you're okay." *I love the way she feels around me. Damn. I'm like a goddamned love-sick teenager.* "Are we almost at the quad?"

She nodded, pointing in front of them. Jerry saw a crowd and heard the whine of the electric guitars as they approached a large, grassy area. Floodlights were installed all around. Booths scattered around the perimeter of the area, the largest boasting a neon yellow sign over it with the words "Beer Tent" printed in black. All around, students talked, laughed, and drank beer out of red plastic cups. The scent of hickory wisped around the quad, and billows of smoke rose from some of the booths as burgers sizzled on the large grills.

"You want something to eat?" Jerry asked Kylie, who was still clinging on to him.

"Yeah, I better get some food. I haven't eaten since early this morning." She laid her head against his leather jacket. "I'm feeling real woozy."

"Drinking on an empty stomach will do that. Let's get a burger." He led Kylie—tucked under his arm—to the food booth, glancing around as they waited in line. There were so many drunk students, and he couldn't help but laugh aloud as he watched them stumble and fall. He wondered how many times Kylie and her friends went out drinking. It couldn't be very often; he knew from the bits of conversation he overheard from Banger that she was doing well in college.

"I want a lot of relish on mine," she said.

He looked down, and her gaze met his. They stood watching each other for a long moment. "I think you put your own on. I see a table with a bunch of packets."

The people manning the booth looked older than the ones at the event. "What would you like?" a man in his forties asked.

"Two burgers." Jerry pulled out his wallet and gave a twenty. After much maneuvering, he managed to sit Kylie down, put the food on the table, and turn over six packets of relish to her, for which he received the sweetest smile he'd ever seen. "You wanna Coke?"

Shaking her head, she said, "A beer."

"Don't you think you've had enough?"

She groaned. "Please don't act like my dad. Just be a friend, okay?"

He definitely had no intention of treating her like a daughter, so he just smiled. "Okay, I'll be right back."

When he returned to the table, a medium-sized guy sat next to Kylie, saying something to her, close to her ear. Jerry's jaw tightened. "Here you are." He placed the red cup in front of her, his steely eyes boring into the young man. The guy immediately jumped up and scurried away. "Who was that? Another admirer?"

8

"I don't have a clue who he is. He didn't tell me his name. He wanted to hang with me. I've never seen him before, but the school is really big, so that's not a surprise." She took a bite of her hamburger. "Yum." She wiggled in her seat.

Jerry loved the way she munched on her food—so delicately—and told him all about her classes. As she shared the funny stories about her friends and professors, he had a hard time staying focused on anything else but having her wrapped in his arms, kissing her deeply.

"There you are, Kylie. I've been looking all around for you. Where're Taylor and Mary?" A young woman with purple and pink streaks in her hair stood behind Kylie, her gaze lingering on Jerry's ink across his hard biceps.

Kylie turned away from Jerry. "Hey, Ari. Taylor and Mary are with Ricky in the beer tent. Did you just get here?"

"Not too long ago." She smiled. "Who's your friend?"

"Oh, sorry." Kylie placed her hand on his forearm, her touch soft and warm. "This is Jerry, and Jerry, this is Ari."

"Hi," Ari said thickly. "What year are you?"

Jerry tilted his head. "Year?"

Kylie giggled. "He doesn't go to school here. He's a friend of mine from home. He stopped by to say hi to me. Isn't that sweet?" She leaned her head against his shoulder, his jeans grew tighter, and Ari's gaze never left his face.

"Wow, I didn't know you had such a good-looking friend. Are all the guys this gorgeous in Pinewood Springs?"

Kylie nodded. "A lot of them are in the Insurgents." The simple comment pissed Jerry the hell off. *Who else is she looking at?*

"Insurgents? What's that?"

Another giggle. "My dad's motorcycle club. Remember, I told you he's the president?"

"Oh, yeah." Ari's leg rubbed against his knee. "So, you're a biker. Cool. Do you ride a Harley?"

Jerry jutted his chin out. "Of course."

"Only Harleys are worth riding, right?" Kylie poked his side in a teasing way, and a low growl vibrated in his throat. Damn, she was fucking turning him on, and she didn't even know it. "Jerry has a real badass Harley that's electric blue. I love it."

"Sounds cool. I've never been on a motorcycle. I'd love to take a spin," Ari hinted.

"It's the color of your eyes," Jerry whispered, his lips brushing against Kylie's ear as he breathed her scent in deeply, felt her hair against his forehead. She turned toward him, his lips skimming across her cheek, and smiled. For one long moment, it was just him and Kylie, and the urge to capture her mouth overwhelmed him. He was so close. All he had to do was move his head a tiny bit and he'd be on—

"So, will you take me for a ride on your Harley?" Ari's nasally voice cut into his thoughts.

Jerry shook his head, his lips pressed together. "I don't take bitches on my bike."

Ari's gasp mingled with Kylie's peals of laughter. As Ari opened her mouth, Kylie said, "No, don't rip his ass. He's not calling you a bitch in the way you think. In the biker world, all women are 'bitches.' It's their word for 'women.' Don't take offense."

Throwing him a dirty look, she said, "That's fucked up."

He shrugged then turned away. He was done with this woman's idle chatter; he wanted to have Kylie all to himself. Wrapping his arm around her shoulder, he said, "You wanna get another drink?"

"Earlier, Ricky said he'd bring me a beer."

Jerry grunted. "I can get you a beer. You don't need any prick doing that when I'm here."

"Stop." She scrunched her face, trying to appear angry, but then she laughed. "He's not a prick. We're good friends, and he's always helping me out."

"I bet he is," he muttered under his breath. "You just watch yourself with him. He looks like he wants more than friendship. He's not for you."

"Why do you say that? Who *is* for me?"

Jerry could swear he saw a shimmer of lust in her blue gaze. "I just know *he* isn't." How could he tell her he was the best one for her, that he'd treat her real good in and out of bed? *I have it bad for her. Fuck!*

"Here you go, Kylie." A smiling Ricky placed a plastic glass of beer next to the one Jerry had brought. Taylor and Mary, smashed off their asses, laughed behind him.

"Thanks." Kylie's lips curled into a flirty smile, which made Jerry's insides boil. He leapt up, pulling her with him. "What the fuck?" she said as beer spilled over the table.

"Let's go dance. I'll get you another one."

Before she could say anything, he was tugging her behind him, marching over to the area in front of the band. The music was not the hard rock beats he preferred—it was alternative music in the vein of Imagine Dragons—but he didn't give a shit. As long as it placed Kylie in his arms, he'd dance to beating conga drums. Whirling her into his embrace, he moved to the music, loving the easy swing of her hips. His fingers inched down until they landed just under her rounded ass and he pulled her closer to him, chuckling when he saw her gaze widen as his hardness pressed against her.

"Uh… I think this song is more for freestyle dancing instead of couple," she said, pushing him back with her hands on his chest.

"You don't like dancing with me?" Jerry cupped her chin in his hand. "That's too bad, because I'm enjoying dancing with you," he said in a low voice, smiling at her discomfort. He liked the way she darted her eyes everywhere but on him and licked her lips repeatedly. He fucking *loved* that he was getting to her. *Oh, yeah.*

"I do, but I think we should dance freestyle." Her voice was breathless, and she bet if he placed his hand on her chest, he'd feel her heart pounding away.

He squeezed her tightly, loving the feel of her. "Okay, whatever you want." She pulled away quickly, her gaze still everywhere but on him.

They danced apart for a few songs, and then she and her friends made several trips to the beer tent. Jerry chugged the red cups of beer she brought him, even though they tasted like piss. He couldn't believe how everyone was guzzling it down like it was premium shit. He guessed that's what they thought beer tasted like. After the third cup, he was done with it, and he watched in amusement as Kylie and her friends became even more smashed than they already were.

After she almost fell for the fourth time, Jerry decided it was time to take her to her dorm. Pulling a protesting Kylie away from her friends, he wrapped his arm around her and headed back. Stumbling and stopping along the way provided many opportunities for his hand to skim across the side of her breast and brush against her ass, lighting a fire within him.

Finally managing to find her key on the ring of over two dozen—why the hell she had so many, he couldn't figure out—he opened her door and lay a giggling Kylie on her bed. "Babe, I can't believe how drunk you are. I hope you don't do this every weekend."

"No, just every night," she slurred, bursting out in uncontrollable laughter.

"Fuck, I hope you're joking." He took off her biker boots and tugged the sheet and comforter down from under her. Tucking her in still clothed—he didn't trust himself to take off her jeans and tight knit top—he stared down at her, mesmerized by the way her hair spread around her head on the pillow, like a halo. Her breasts heaved gently, and he wanted to feel their softness in his hands. He was sporting a major hard-on, and he knew he could have her, but he didn't want to take advantage in her drunkenness. It wasn't that he was a gentleman—if it were any other girl, he'd already have his dick inside her, licking and sucking her tits—but *this* beautiful, vulnerable girl was Kylie. If and when he fucked her, he wanted it to be her decision as well as his. He wanted her to know every single dirty thing he'd be doing to her. Right then wasn't the correct time.

Jerry sighed and pushed up to leave when a gentle touch held him back. As he bent his head, Kylie put her hand on the back of his neck and drew him to her. With their lips inches from one another's, she strained forward, hers catching his. Her kiss was soft and warm, and the barriers he'd erected collapsed with that one, solitary kiss.

She drew back a little and Jerry crushed her to him, his mouth seizing hers, knowing he was going to regret it—and not giving a damn. He tangled one hand in her hair, the other one cupping her jaw. It was like he'd never kissed before; it was wild and desperate, and he didn't know if he'd ever stop. Her tender lips moved in rhythm with his, parting slightly. He slipped his tongue into her welcoming mouth, eager to consume her. She tasted like beer and honey, and the hesitant stroke of her tongue on his sent him reeling. He plunged his tongue harder and deeper, losing himself in her sweet scent and panting breaths. He closed his eyes and the world faded around him.

Then she rubbed her soft tits against him, and it was as if a hot poker jabbed him. His cock strained against his jeans. "You're killing me, Kylie," he muttered against her mouth.

"Am I?" she whispered back, her breath scorching his skin.

He was ready to slam her onto the bed, peel off her clothes, and lavish kisses all over her ripe and tempting body. Remembering she was his president's daughter, who was very drunk, he reluctantly broke away. Jerry's eyes locked with hers as he rose to his feet. "You don't know how fucking hard this is, but I gotta leave. Now." His gaze rested on her lips, swollen from their kiss, and he ached to return to her arms. "You gonna be okay?"

She nodded, and in the moonlight he spotted the heated flush from her arousal. Swallowing hard, he rasped, "See you next time you come to Pinewood Springs. Take care of yourself." He grabbed the jacket he'd thrown on her desk chair and dashed out of her room, making sure the door was locked. His hard-as-shit dick punched against his zipper, and he knew it'd be a fucking long four hours before he'd be back home. Slipping his hands into his leather gloves, he revved up his Harley and zoomed out of the university's parking lot.

Chapter Two

Kylie woke up the following morning and groaned when she moved her head. The pain was like a jackhammer plunging through concrete, and it was relentless. When she opened her eyes, another wave of piercing pain like shards of glass poking the backs of her eyeballs assaulted her, and she licked her dry lips, hating the way the desert had overtaken her mouth. *Why the fuck did I drink so much of that cheap, shitty beer?* She laid her arm over her throbbing eyelids, trying to block out the light in her dorm room.

The previous night, she'd drunk more than she ever had since coming to the university. Whatever had possessed her to have had so much beer? She groped the nightstand next to her bed, searching for the bottled water she always kept on it. Finding it, she sat up, her body screaming, unscrewed the cap, and swallowed a long gulp. Relief coated her parched mouth and throat. Setting the water back down, she glanced at Taylor's bed. Small snores filled the room as her roommate slept.

Easing back down, Kylie covered her eyes again, the pressure making them feel a tad better. She replayed the previous night's events in her mind, and she knew the reason she'd drunk so much—Jerry. She'd been shocked when she'd seen him in her space, and at first she'd thought he'd come up just to see her, but when he'd told her he had friends in the area he was visiting, a tinge of disappointment had weaved through her. She'd chided herself on her silliness. After all, they'd known each other for many years, and he was used to older, more experienced women. But during the night, she'd caught him looking at her as more than a friend, and when he'd danced close to her, his hardness pressed against her, pleasure had battled with the urge to flee far away from him.

Then he'd helped her back to her dorm, patiently putting up with her nonsensical chatter and giggles she hadn't been able to control. When he'd tucked her in bed, she'd been so overcome with tenderness that she'd kissed him gratefully, never expecting his response. It was like she'd unleashed a powerful caged beast, and she'd loved it. The way he kissed her still made her flush heatedly and her toes curl. And just when she'd thought her heart was going to burst, he'd broken away and left her. She winced as she recalled the punch to her pride. He'd probably been drunk the previous night as well, and when he realized he'd been kissing her instead of one of his slutty women who knew how to fuck, he'd recognized his mistake and freaked out. Her chest hitched and she rubbed her temples in a vain effort to banish those thoughts.

With a sigh, Kylie forced herself up and into the bathroom. She jumped into the shower, resting her forehead against the cold fiberglass wall. As the cool water washed over her, she began to feel better, gripping her stomach as it growled. Thinking a donut and a cup of strong black coffee would hit the spot, she finished getting ready then headed to the snack bar at the Student Center.

The snack bar was quiet, with only a few students scattered at the different tables. Sundays were usually like a ghost town during the morning and afternoon hours, only coming to life in the evenings after a night of partying had worn off. Kylie sat at a table for two, a few feet away from the window and the bright sunlight. Sipping her coffee, she leaned back, feeling much better. She took out her phone and noticed a text. Opening it, her stomach lurched when she saw it was from Jerry. She'd plugged in his phone number a couple years back when he'd called on her dad's phone about club business. For a split second, she racked her brain trying to remember if she'd given him her number the previous night. It was such a jumbled puzzle, bits and pieces fitting in different spaces of her memory; it was very possible she'd given it to him. Looking back down, she read his text.

Jerry: *How're u feeling?*

Kylie: *Like shit. Drank 2 much!*

Jerry: *U think???*

Kylie: *Cute. Don't tell my dad. K?*

Jerry: *Now I have something to blackmail u with.*

Kylie bit into her donut, loving the burst of deliciousness from the icing. She licked the small flakes off her lips, took another sip of coffee, and returned to texting.

Kylie: *Blackmail? What do u want from me?*

A very long pause ensued. She laid her phone on the table and promptly finished her donut and coffee. A ping drew her attention back to her phone.

Jerry: *Sorry bout last night. I drank too much too. I didn't mean anything by it.*

Kylie sucked in her breath as fluttering butterflies made her stomach queasy. *I knew he probably thought I was someone else.* Her skin crawled and bitterness invaded her thoughts.

Kylie: *What did u do? I was so drunk. I remember u helping me to my dorm, but nothing past that. Am I missing something?*

Another long pause. Her insides quivered.

Jerry: *Nah.*

Kylie: *Thx for helping me. :)*

Jerry: *Ya. So u don't remember anything after getting to your room?*

She pressed her lips together and reread his text a few times before replying.

Kylie: *No. Did I do something embarrassing?*

Jerry: *Not at all. No worries.*

Kylie: *I gotta go. It was fun hanging with u. See ya.*

Jerry: *Later.*

Kylie let out a long breath, having held it in since he'd alluded to their kiss. Oh, that wonderful, sexy, panty-melting kiss. No boy had ever kissed her like that, not that she'd had many guys around. With her dad being so protective, she was surprised she'd even been allowed to date in high school. She had Cara to thank for that. Her dad had a soft spot for the woman because she was such a good cook, and she'd been the one to catch Hawk, so he'd listened to her when she told him to let Kylie go to the school dances. If it hadn't been for Cara, she never would've been able to convince her dad to let her come to Red Rocks University.

She smiled when she thought of her dad. They'd been through a lot after her mother's death, and during her teenage years, but they were super close and she loved him dearly. Now that he was married to Belle, she hoped he'd ease off on being her guard dog when it came to men, especially the Insurgents brothers. Belle had already stood up for her twice when Kylie came up during President's Day weekend and had been at the club, flirting with Jerry and Rock. Banger had been livid, but Belle had convinced him it was only natural for Kylie to feel comfortable with the brothers since she'd grown up with the majority of them. He'd softened under Belle's soothing voice, but Kylie knew her dad still had his eyes on her and Jerry.

And Jerry had always made her insides melt, ever since she'd first laid eyes on him when he came to the MC as a prospect. How could she *not* notice him? He was a powerfully built man of over six feet, with sandy hair, large brown eyes, muscles that could rival any Greek Adonis, and enticing tattoos curling around his biceps, forearms, and ripped chest. Looking at him made her drool, and with the way the club and party girls checked him out, she knew they were drooling as well. Jerry had been a patched member for a little over two years, and he'd told her during one of their talks at the clubhouse that he was saving his back for the Insurgents logo—the one a member earned after being with the brotherhood for ten years.

If Kylie were honest, she'd had a major crush on Jerry since he'd first walked through the doors of the Insurgents' clubhouse. It became worse when she entered high school, and when she'd hit sixteen, she'd noticed *him* noticing *her*. Fantasizing about him had filled up many teenage nights. When she'd turned eighteen, his flirting and roaming eyes had gone into full gear, and she'd find as many excuses as her dad would believe to go to the clubhouse.

The times she'd come into the great room to see one of the club whores—usually Wendy or Rosie—wrapped around Jerry, his face stuffed in her tits, ignited a burning in the pit of her stomach. Then she'd go home, cry, and start comparing herself to the women who held his attention. She'd always come to the same conclusion—he liked women who had big breasts, hardly wore any clothes, would screw him on command, and worked their mouths, hands, and hips like a pro, and she was *so* out of his league. But even when he was lip-locked with a woman, he'd stare at her as she padded through the great room, and within five minutes, he'd stroll into the kitchen, flashing her a big smile, and their flirtation would begin anew.

She'd lost count of how many times her dad had told her that Jerry was nothing but a man-whore, and he didn't like the way he looked at her one bit. A funny feeling twisted her insides when Banger would tell her about how Jerry was crushing on her. One afternoon, when she was eighteen and a senior in high school, her dad had caught her flirting with Jerry, her crossed leg touching his. He'd gone ballistic, throwing the biker against the wall before lashing out at her. When he'd lifted himself off the floor, Jerry had zipped out of the kitchen. For the next week she'd been grounded, and Jerry had been made off-limits for her natural life, but it didn't stop her fantasies over the sexy biker.

Kylie shuddered, thinking about what her father would do to Jerry and her if he could see the way she'd shamelessly enjoyed his kiss the previous night. She knew her dad trusted her, and she didn't want to betray him, but the way Jerry kissed and held her made her want more.

"Hey," a male voice said behind her.

Withdrawing from her musings, Kylie pivoted to see who the bearer of the penetrating voice was. A man of medium height and dark brown hair and eyes came into view. She glanced at him, trying to determine if she knew him, but her mind was a blank.

"We met last night. At the spring festival." He plopped into the empty seat across from her.

She frowned. "I don't remember." Then she turned away, dismissing him.

"Sure you do. You were eating a burger, and I came by and told you how pretty you looked. I've seen you around campus. You're in my political science class." He smiled, and she noticed his bottom teeth were crooked.

Poking her tongue lightly into her cheek, she inhaled a long breath. "Sorry, I don't remember. I had too much to drink."

He snorted. "Yeah, seemed like it. How do you like Dr. Reagan's class?"

"It's okay. I'm not that interested in the subject, but I wanted to get the requirement out of the way. What about you?"

"I spend most of the class staring at you, so I'm not sure what the fuck is going on."

She squirmed in her chair. The guy looked older than a sophomore, and he was definitely giving out creep-vibes. She didn't want to chat or get to know him. She scooted her chair back, trying to create some distance. "Nice talking to you, but I gotta do some homework. See you around."

The man extended his hand. "I'm Marcus. I'll see you in class tomorrow."

Ignoring the offer, she rubbed her neck. "I'm Kylie," she muttered.

He stared at her. "I know."

"Gotta go." She whipped around and strode out of the snack bar, quickly crossing the grassy area to the West Hall dorms.

When she walked into her room, she saw her roommate sitting up on the edge of the bed, elbows braced on her knees, head in her hands. "That was me this morning," Kylie said as she shrugged off her black cardigan.

"I got so fucking wasted last night," Taylor moaned, motioning to the water bottle on her desk. "Can you bring it to me?"

Kylie handed her the bottle then sat on the bed opposite her friend. "It was fun, though."

"I had a fucking blast." She took a big gulp of water, groaning when she tipped her head back. "Do you have any aspirin?"

"Yeah. Wait a sec." Kylie padded to the bathroom, spilled out two tablets from the aspirin bottle, and placed them in Taylor's hand.

"Thanks." She swallowed them with another gulp of water. "So, who the hell was that hot guy you were attached to all night? He was so damn good-looking. Is he a senior?"

Laughing, Kylie said, "He doesn't go here. He's a friend from back home."

"Where have you kept a hunk like that hidden during the times I went to Pinewood Springs with you?"

"He's actually a member of my dad's motorcycle club. I've known him since I was like, twelve. We chat and stuff when I'm at home."

"What does 'and stuff' mean? Have you guys had sex? I'll be super pissed at you if you have and didn't tell me about him."

Kylie waved her hand. "No. No way. I could never do that. My dad would fucking kill him then send me to a convent for the rest of my life."

"Seriously? Damn, the story gets better all the time. Why does your dad care if he's a biker? I mean, your dad's one too, so what's the big deal?"

Kylie shrugged. "I don't know, but my dad doesn't want me to hook up with a biker, especially Jerry. He thinks he'd do me wrong because he's always chasing women."

"Isn't that pretty much the norm with most bikers? I mean, the stories you've told me make me wonder why your dad cares about *this* one."

"My dad's just looking out for me." Kylie reached over and grabbed her water from the nightstand. "He's overly protective. I'm his only daughter."

"Maybe your dad's crazed about this one because this Jared has the hots for you."

"It's Jerry, and he doesn't have the hots for me. It's just a dad thing. Who did you hook up with last night?"

"Nice try at changing the subject. I didn't hook up with anyone. So, why was Jerry at the university?"

"He was visiting some friends and came by to say hi. My dad probably told him to check up on me."

"It didn't look like that to me. The way he was holding and squeezing you told a different story. Anyway, I'm sure your dad would've been pissed if he saw the two of you attached at the hip." She rose from the bed. "Damn, my head is pounding. Why the fuck did I drink so much? I've got a paper about civilization versus the wilderness in *The Scarlet Letter* for Dempsey's class on Tuesday, and I haven't even begun to research it. Shit."

"I took her class last semester. I got an 'A' on my paper on the same topic. Do you want to check out my resource list? It'll cut your research in half."

A wide smile broke over Taylor's face. "Definitely. I'm going over to the library to start the damn thing. You wanna come?"

"No, I'll study here. I got all my heavy-duty stuff out of the way yesterday."

"You going to tell your dad you bumped into Jerry?"

"Hell, no. You think I'm a glutton for punishment? My dad would've been pissed if he'd seen the way I was acting. It's better to just file last night away as a blissful memory. It'll never happen again."

Before closing the bathroom door, Taylor shook her head. "The way you two were carrying on, I wouldn't bank on it."

The door shut and Kylie stared blankly at it, the rush of water filling her ears. She touched her lips, remembering the way they felt with Jerry's mouth on them. A shiver ran up her spine as her stomach clenched. She had to forget about last night. And Jerry. She couldn't disappoint her dad.

Jerry was just a handsome, funny guy she talked to whenever she went to the clubhouse. Nothing more.

Yeah, right. Try and convince yourself of that.

She was on a tightrope, and one misstep meant disaster. She had to be good. Her dad depended on it, and Jerry's life did too.

Chapter Three

Jerry reread Kylie's texts, honing in on the smiley face she sent him. She was so fucking adorable. Who the hell sent smiley faces? He didn't know any chick who'd ever sent him one. He motioned for Blade to give him another beer, even though he knew if he didn't stop, he'd have to crash at the club. Jerry had a three-bedroom apartment near downtown Pinewood Springs, wanting the extra space because he was always puttering around with his tools and supplies, making front and back fender ornaments for motorcycles. He'd sold several to Hawk for his bike shop, and had just received an order for six dozen assorted ornaments for a motorcycle vendor in neighboring Silverplume. His hobby was becoming a business, and he was happy to have the space to accommodate it.

Blade plunked down the beer on the counter in front of Jerry. Curling his fingers around the cold bottle, Jerry gulped it down then gestured for another. The softness of Kylie's mouth on his invaded his thoughts. He never should've gone to see her. And he certainly shouldn't have tasted her sweet lips. Before the previous night, he'd only imagined what it would feel like to kiss and hold her. Now he *knew*, and he was fucking hooked.

I should just walk away. Cherish the memory then lose it in Rosie's tits and Wendy's pussy. There'd be plenty of hoodrats to help him forget how fantastic it felt to hold Kylie and breathe in her lavender-powdery scent. He had to let it go… but how in the fuck could he? He needed to touch and kiss her one more time, and then he'd be done. *What a fuckin' mess you've gotten yourself into. You shoulda left her alone. You knew she was off-limits. Damnit!*

He didn't believe for one minute that Kylie didn't remember their kiss. She was probably reeling from the memory of it the same as he was. She knew the score, knew her dad was a no-nonsense type of guy. Jerry's unbridled passion for her made him seek her out at school, just so he could see her, hear her voice, be with her. Now, he'd put them both in the danger zone. He'd just have to make himself forget her and move on.

"Fuckin' good shot." Banger's baritone voice punched him in the gut. Turning his head toward the pool tables, he saw Banger and Bear smoking weed, downing shots of Jack, and playing a game of pool. A large stack of bills sat on a nearby table.

"You ready to pay up?" Bear joked as he inhaled his roach.

"Not a chance." Banger chuckled.

Jerry watched his president's every move. Guilt assaulted him before tension grabbed at his insides. Banger would beat the shit out of him for touching his little girl, maybe even kill him. He was positive that if Banger ever learned about his antics, he'd lose his patch. Jerry had worked damn hard to become a patched member of the Insurgents MC, and he'd be a goddamned fool to throw it away on a pretty face and some wicked curves. But then there was the lavender scent, and the way her hair felt in his hands, the softness of her skin, her silly laugh, and her incredible lips with the flavor of watermelon on them. *Fuck!*

"Hey, what's up? Missed you at the party last night," Throttle said as he slid onto the barstool next to Jerry.

"I had shit to do." He gulped down the new bottle of beer the prospect placed in front of him.

"Like what?" Throttle threw back a shot of tequila, then squirted a wedge of lime in his mouth, his lips puckering.

"Just shit. I gotta fill that order I got for the fender ornaments."

"Oh, yeah. Man, this must've been the first party you missed since you've been patched."

"Really? Why the fuck are you keeping count?"

Throttle shot him a quizzical look. "What the fuck's your problem? Just making conversation."

Steady, man. Why are you ready to rip Throttle's head off just for mak-

ing small talk? "I'm just tired. I didn't get much sleep last night." He put his lips against the bottle, wishing Throttle would either get the fuck away from him or shut the hell up and drink in silence.

"I gotta get one of your ornaments. I saw the ones Hawk bought for his shop when I was helping out last week, and they're wicked. How much you selling them for?"

Jerry gritted his teeth. "Depends on the style, but they go from fifteen bucks to two hundred fifty big ones."

"Do you think you can bring some?"

Clenching his jaw, he swiveled on the stool and faced Throttle. "Why the fuck don't you go to Hawk's goddamned store and check them out?"

Throttled narrowed his eyes. "I fuckin' told you I did, but I wanted to see what else you had. Fuckin' change your attitude before I beat your ass."

Jerry leapt off the barstool, quickly followed by Throttle. Both men stood rigid, staring at one another, nostrils flaring, chests rising up and down.

"What's going on here?" Rosie asked as she came up beside Jerry.

Lola followed suit, only she stood next to Throttle. "You guys look like you're out for blood."

"Stay the fuck outta this," Jerry growled at the women.

Rosie curled her hand around his arm. "I missed you last night, honey."

"Get the fuck away," he hissed, shaking her hand off him.

Her face fell as she stepped backward. "Why you mad at me? I didn't do anything."

"I'm not mad at you. I'm mad at—" He stopped short. He was fucking mad at *himself*. Throwing his beer bottle across the bar, he walked to the front door. Before he stepped out into the sunshine, he heard Throttle say, "I just fuckin' asked him if I could see his damn fender ornaments. All he had to say was no."

He jumped on his Harley and fired up his engine, ignoring Chas as he pulled into the parking lot, and rode away from the club.

Chapter Four

THE FIRST FEW days of the week were a blur of studies and parties. Final exams were fast approaching, and Kylie threw herself wholeheartedly into her studies. She hadn't heard from Jerry since they'd texted the previous Sunday. At the beginning of the week, each time her phone would make a noise, she'd jump, hoping it would be him. But there was nothing from him; it was as if that night hadn't happened. She imagined he'd screwed a few club women by now, and the thought of him kissing another woman the way he'd kissed her made her insides ache. She was being silly; it was just a kiss. It wasn't like he was her boyfriend or anything, but Kylie had hoped—in a romantic, unrealistic way—that Jerry would've been so blown away by kissing her that he wouldn't want any other women. But it was better this way because she didn't have to worry about her dad and all the drama associated with that.

Kylie sat on her favorite comfy chair, highlighting passages in her economics book when someone knocked on her door. Thinking it was Ricky coming to work on their psychology project, she yelled, "It's open!"

Expecting to see her friend come in, she smiled widely then frowned when Marcus entered her room, his small eyes staring at her. She gripped the side of the chair, swallowing her gasp. "I thought it was someone else," she said as she tried to keep her voice steady while her insides quaked. "What do you want?"

"To see you." He took a few steps closer to her.

She stood up. "You here to talk about poli-sci? Did you know what was going on today? I swear, half the time, I'm so bored that I zone out."

She kept talking, hoping it would stop him from coming any farther into her room. *What is he doing here?*

As she babbled on about their class, he stood still, his eyes on her mouth. *Why is he just standing there staring at me? Ew....* She wanted to push him out, then take a shower so she could scrub his gaze off her.

Marcus licked his lips. "I'm not here to talk about class. I want to know why you act like you don't know me while we're there."

Shit! "I don't know what you're talking about."

"You never sit next to me, and afterward you run out, like you're avoiding me."

"Do I do that?" She crossed her arms. "I don't think I do. I have another class right after and it's in another building, so I have to rush to get there on time. I've been sitting in the same seat since the semester started. I'm kinda OCD that way—I don't like changing seats each time."

He inched closer, his eyes fixed on her face. She tried to read him, but she couldn't tell anything except that he was definitely giving off some whacked-out vibes. His brown eyes bored into her and his face was tight, like he was clenching his teeth.

He continued to approach her. Each time he took a step, she moved back until she was pressed against the wall. *If he comes any closer, I'm going to scream.* He took another step. She opened her mouth, but before she could make good on her promise, Ricky came in through the open door. Relief washed over her and she let out a long breath. She saw him check out Marcus, who was only inches away from her, then look at her, eyebrow raised.

She pulled away from the wall and waved. "Hey, Ricky, you ready to do some psychology?" Kylie placed her hand over her wildly beating heart. Marcus craned his neck and, seeing the six-foot Ricky, mumbled something incomprehensible before scurrying out.

Ricky watched him as he left, then closed the door. "Who was that?"

"Some weird guy who came up to me at the spring festival and has been acting like we're friends ever since. He's in my poli-sci class." She wrapped her arms tighter around herself. "He definitely gives me the creeps. Have you seen him around campus?"

He shook his head. "I've never seen him. He's not in any of my classes, but I can find out who he is. My friend has work study, and he has a job in the registrar's office. He can look up anyone. Do you know the creeper's last name?"

"No, but I can find out. I'll give it to you when I do. I just want to know what he's up to. I mean, it's like he just appeared and now he seems to have some fucking bug on me." She shivered.

"If he bothers you again, let me know. I'll talk to him." Ricky stared at her, not like a friend, but in a way a man does when he's interested in a woman.

Kylie grabbed her psychology book and pulled out her desk chair. She motioned to Ricky to sit down. "Thanks for the offer, but I think it'll be okay. I guess I'm just nervous about finals and getting through all the projects and papers due in the next two weeks." She didn't want to think about the way Ricky looked at her.

He shrugged, flopping down in the chair. "Just let me know."

She smiled and went over to the mini fridge in the corner of the room. "Want a Coke?"

"Sure. Do you have any munchies?"

"Chips and salsa good?"

"Yeah."

She brought them over and set them on the desk. They opened their books and notebooks and began working on their school project.

Two hours later, Kylie stood and stretched. "This is going to blow Dr. Reddle away."

Ricky followed suit, yawning as he did so. "It better. Damn, I need to raise my grade in the class. I'm glad he paired me with you. You understand all this crap. I'm a math guy, and this touchy-feely shit just doesn't make sense to me."

"Next year I have to take my math requirement, so you can help me. It all works out."

He nodded, his gaze running the length of her body. She crossed her arms over her chest, suddenly conscious of her breast size. "So, you going to eat at the cafeteria or off campus?"

Darting his eyes from her hips to her face, he answered, "The cafeteria. I'm broke until I get paid on Friday."

An awkward silence surrounded them, and Kylie pretended to be busy arranging her books on the desk.

"Are you and Taylor going to the cafeteria?"

"Not sure what she's going to do for food. Right now, she's at the library freaking out." Kylie smiled. "I ate so many chips, I'm not hungry. I may just pick up a salad at the snack bar."

"Yeah." Ricky bent down on one knee and untied, then tied, his shoelaces. "I guess I better get going." He picked up her retractable pen and pushed the button over and over with his thumb. The clicks filled the silence as she watched him play with it.

"So, I guess I'll see you in class tomorrow." She walked to the door and opened it.

"Yeah." He placed her pen on the desk and sauntered over to the door. Stopping in the doorway, he rubbed his chin and cleared his throat. "You want to go to a movie and dinner with me this Saturday night?" A slight sheen appeared above his upper lip.

Kylie's eyes widened. *He's asking me on a date. Holy shit!* It was ironic because, before Jerry's visit, she would've been ecstatic about going out with Ricky. Since the second semester had begun, she'd been hoping he'd ask her out, but since she'd kissed Jerry, everything had changed.

"I hope I didn't stick my foot in my mouth. You aren't going out with that dude you were with on Saturday, are you? I thought he was just a friend."

The truth was she *wasn't* going out with Jerry. He hadn't even called her. It was like he had a good time groping and kissing her, then he went back to the real women at the club. *I bet he's fucking Rosie and Wendy right now.* Bitterness crept through her. "No, Jerry and I aren't dating. He's just some guy I know who's in my dad's club. No big deal. I'd love to go to the movies on Saturday."

"You would? Great!" Ricky's face lit up like a lantern, and she couldn't help smiling. He was cute, with his light brown hair that fell across his forehead and his shining hazel eyes. He'd also been a great friend while she'd been at the university. "I'll find out what time the movie is and let you know. Are you into action stuff?"

"I am. I heard *Deadpool* is good. Are you into seeing that?"

"Yeah, I've been wanting to see that movie. I'm stoked you want to see it too. Awesome."

The way he gushed made her laugh. This would be fun. She couldn't care less what Jerry did, or with whom. "Sounds like a plan."

"Yeah. I'll see you in class tomorrow. It was fun hanging out with you, even if all we did was school work." Red streaked his cheeks.

"It was nice. See you, Ricky."

She closed the door and leaned against the wall, wishing it were Jerry who'd asked her out. *You're fucking hopeless.* She liked Ricky a lot, but he didn't make her insides melt or her breath stop when she saw him like Jerry did. *Why did he have to go and kiss me?* It would've been better if he'd never come to see her on campus.

Touching her lips, Kylie knew that wasn't true. Even if she never spoke to him again, she'd always have the memory of their first kiss. It was hot, wet, and amazing. But Jerry wasn't the one asking her out—Ricky was. If they'd kissed like that, she was pretty sure Ricky would've been calling and coming around to see her. Not like Jerry, who'd probably forgotten all about it.

She walked to the window and gazed out at the Rocky Mountains. *I need to just let go of this and give Ricky a chance.* Jerry's half-smile flitted across her mind. Resting against the window pane, her feelings were more mixed up than ever.

Chapter Five

By the time Friday rolled around, Kylie was so antsy she wanted to jump out of her skin. She *had* to get away from campus and people. She and Taylor worked well together as roommates, and they'd become good friends, but after being an only child and having a room to herself for all her life, sharing a two-hundred-thirty-square-foot room with another person was pretty damned cramped. Sometimes, she just needed to be by herself.

Jerry hadn't contacted her since the previous Sunday, and even though Kylie acted like she didn't give a damn, there was that miserable part of her brain that imagined he was so grossed out by what had happened that he didn't want to talk to her anymore. She tried not to dwell on it, but it'd creep up when she was studying, or in a lecture, or even hanging out with her friends. More than anything, she wanted to stop thinking about him. So she did what always cheered her up—she shopped.

When she returned to campus after her shopping spree, the two parking lots closest to her dorm were full. Cursing under her breath, she parked in the third, securing the numerous packages in her hands. "This is such a pain in the ass," she said under her breath as she trekked toward her building. From behind her she heard the hum of a motor, and she moved closer to the side of the lot to give more room for the car to pass her. Out of the corner of her eye, she saw the car next to her, its engine sounding like a sewing machine. She picked up her pace and the vehicle matched it.

"Hey, where're you going?"

Kylie turned her head and saw a purple Corvette with a white racing stripe over its hood, roof, and trunk. The windows were tinted, and even though the driver's window was halfway down, she couldn't make out his features. Ignoring him, she continued walking, fully aware of the car's proximity.

"I know you heard me." The driver clucked his tongue. "Don't be that way, Kylie." His voice was smooth and mellow.

She stopped in her tracks. Facing him, she bent down slightly, trying to see his face. "How do you know my name?" she asked.

His chuckle sent shivers up her spine. "I know a lot of things about you, Kylie."

She peered at him, but the glare from the western sun made it difficult for her to see his face clearly. He wore sunglasses with a thick, shiny gold frame; his face appeared dark, like he stayed in the sun a lot; dark brown—maybe black—hair; and he was clean-shaven. She couldn't quite tell, but judging by his voice, she guessed him to be in his late twenties. The golden orb's blaze hid most of his features and left only a smudgy glimpse of him.

"Do I know you?" she asked.

"You do now."

"What's your name?" She could hear her father's voice telling her to get the fuck away from this guy. Though she could sense a thread of danger weaving around her, she remained there, talking with him, as though they would become friends.

"That's for later."

"It isn't fair that you know my name and I don't know yours." She shielded her eyes from the sun, bending down lower to see him better. He pulled his head back into the shadows of his sports car.

"Life isn't fair. Haven't you learned that yet?" A hard edge slipped into his voice and her blood ran cold. "Let me take you back to your dorm. You've got too many packages."

Fear seized her. She shook her head. "Thanks, but I'm good."

"Come on, get in the car. It's too far for you to walk." His idling engine threw off hot waves of exhaust. "Come on." His voice rolled over her as he coaxed her.

Swinging her hair over her shoulders, Kylie shifted the bags in her hands. "I'm good." She started walking again. He followed her. Her heart racing, she looked around the parking lot, but no one was there except for this man with the suave voice and the mirrored sunglasses. Beads of sweat formed on her forehead. *I'm all alone. This guy could grab me, and no one would have a damn clue what happened to me.*

Gliding her hand into her tote, she felt around until her fingers wrapped around her pepper spray can.

"You're not gonna make me beg, are you, Kylie?" His voice was too calm, laced with a sinister undertone.

He unnerved her, and she quickened her pace, her pulse throbbing. If only she were back at her dorm.

"Kylie. Sweet Kylie, come into the car. You know you want to. I'm not gonna hurt you. Is that what you think?"

Shaking her head, she said, "I like walking. I'm good. You can go."

He chuckled again. "You like my car?"

"It's cool. It's a Corvette—1982, right?"

"You're pretty *and* smart. You know cars."

"I used to help my dad fix cars and bikes when he had his shop." She walked while she spoke to him, keeping him in her sight with sidelong glances.

"I love motorcycles."

"Do you have one?"

"Not yet. Do you?"

"No, but my dad promised to get me one once I graduate."

"You a Harley girl?"

She stopped and turned to him, smiling broadly. "All the way."

He licked his lips, and she saw her reflection in his sunglasses: small and distorted—like she were looking in a carnival mirror. He let out a long breath then said huskily, "What else do you do all the way?"

Her scalp prickled as clamminess rode the length of her spine. Swallowing hard, she said, "Please go. I don't want to talk to you anymore."

"Is that right?"

"Go."

"What are you gonna do if I don't?"

She picked up her speed, her stomach twisting in knots.

He sped up a little. "You're so beautiful. I just want to get to know you. What's the harm in that?"

Gulping air, she stumbled over the cracks in the parking lot, cursing the university for not having enough parking close to the dorms.

"I can see you're tired. Your arms must be aching, carrying all your packages. I can drop you off."

"Leave me alone," she said breathlessly.

"You're not afraid of me, are you?"

His soothing voice was scaring the shit out of her. *How am I going to get away from him?* Then she spotted the security vehicle in the distance, cruising through the parking lot. Kylie dropped her bags, raised her hand, and called out to the two security guards in the car, grateful they had their windows rolled down.

His head whipped to the right as if to see to whom she was gesturing. He turned to her. "You shouldn't have done that, Kylie." The hardness was back, slicing through her like a razor. "I'll see you soon." His car lurched forward as he sped away from her. She strained to see his license plate number so she could memorize it, but there wasn't one.

"Can we help you, miss?" the security officer asked as his vehicle came beside her.

She nodded. "Some creep was bothering me. He was in the purple Corvette. Did you see him?"

Shaking his head, the officer turned to his partner and asked if he'd seen the sports car. He hadn't either. "Did you get his plate number?"

"I looked, but he didn't have any plates. At least not in the back."

"Would you like an escort back to campus?"

"Yes, thank you."

She climbed in the back of the car, settling down on the cloth seats. Rubbing her sore wrists, she replayed her encounter with the man, and it made her insides tingle with fear.

Several minutes later, the security patrol car stopped. "Here you are." Kylie hesitantly looked at the back of her dorm building. "Do you want one of us to escort you inside?"

"I do, thanks." She slid out of the vehicle, scanning the parking lot. There wasn't any sign of a purple Corvette, just a few students exiting from their cars. She sprinted up the stairs, thanked the guard, and breathed deeply when she entered her room. Locking her door, she checked it twice, afraid *he* may know where she lived, especially since he knew her name. She shuddered, then began hanging up the new clothes she'd purchased, the fun of shopping overshadowed by her strange encounter in the parking lot.

Half an hour later, Kylie heard a key turning in the lock. Taylor walked in with an armload of books. "What's up with bolting all the locks?" She threw the books on her bed, grabbed a Coke from the mini fridge, and slumped in the cushy chair by the window.

"I was sorta freaked out. This guy came up to me when I was trekking back to the dorm from parking lot C." Kylie then recounted what had happened while she walked back to the building. "Sometimes he seemed cool and sincere, like he was a pal or something. He made me feel unafraid until he'd stare at me like he was undressing me, or a hard edge would slip into his voice. I've never had an experience like that before with a total stranger." She took a sip from her bottled water. "He knew my name. Too scary."

"He sounds like a perv who wanted to pick you up. If he goes to the university, it's not hard to find out a girl's name. Maybe he's been crushing on you from a distance. Was he good-looking?"

"I couldn't see him clearly. He wore these big mirrored sunglasses with really thick, gold frames. They looked like something a pimp would wear, or someone back in the 1970s." She shook her head. "He wanted me to get in the car, but I got the vibe he'd hurt me. I hope I don't see him again."

"Remember last year when that guy kept trying to pick up girls in the parking lots behind the dorms? When the university got a lot of complaints, they finally beefed up security, and he went away."

Kylie pulled her hair in a low ponytail. "Oh, yeah, I remember now. I totally forgot about that. I wonder if he's back, and that's who the guy was. What kind of car did the women say he drove? I can't remember."

"Me neither. You should file a report with campus security."

"The two guards told me that, as well. I plan to."

"The guy from last year just got his kicks out of talking to the women. Fucking fantastic that we have to watch out for pervs on top of everything else."

"I know." Kylie wanted to believe the guy was just some weirdo who got his jollies from talking to women in parking lots, but her gut told her he'd targeted her. He wanted something with her. Something dark, perverse, and terrifying. She knew she should tell her dad, but she was afraid he'd overreact and make her come back to Pinewood Springs, and she liked being on her own. She was probably reading more into the encounter than there was; the guy was probably some jerk who thought he was super cool. When she didn't wax up to him, it bruised his ego. Some men were like that.

"Let's go eat. I'm starving."

Shaking off the dark feelings, Kylie grabbed her wrist wallet. "Me too. Cafeteria or café?"

"Cafeteria. I'm low on money until next week when my dad puts my monthly stipend in the bank."

Opening the door, Kylie said, "Let's go."

The two women walked down the hall.

"THE MOVIE WAS great," Kylie said as she entered the restaurant, Ricky's hand on the small of her back. "It was so fast-paced I held my breath through most of it."

"I know what you mean. I loved it. It was the anti-hero at his best."

The Burger Shack was teeming with young people. The eatery served up fat, juicy burgers, fries, onion rings, shakes, and fountain drinks at an affordable price, so it was little wonder that it was a favorite weekend hangout for college students.

Kylie and Ricky sat in a small booth next to the window, and the din of video games, laughter, conversation, and the ever-present tunes from the digital jukebox on the wall filled the eatery. She picked up a piece of chalk and wrote on the blackboard tabletop, "What are you going to eat?"

Ricky laughed and placed his hand over hers. She stiffened slightly, causing him to slide his hand away. "It's not that loud, is it?" He looked at the one-sheet menu. "You want some wings to start?"

"Sure."

For the next hour, they laughed and talked, and when Ricky excused himself to go to the bathroom, Kylie realized she was having a good time. She knew several people in the place, so she chatted with them until he came back.

After he paid the bill, they left, the reduction in noise immediately apparent. "That was so good. I'm more than stuffed. I'm going to have to work out even longer tomorrow," Kylie said.

"Do you work out at the school's gym?"

She shook her head, tugging her leather jacket tighter around her. "No, I go to a martial arts studio. I work out there before class."

Ricky stopped. "You know martial arts? Damn, I better be good around you." He laughed and gripped her hand, pulling her to him.

She licked her lips. "My dad insisted that I take classes to learn self-defense. When I was in high school, I couldn't go to the mall or movies with my friends because I had a class, or practice, or a tournament, and I'd be so pissed at him. Now I'm glad he made me go. It's empowering, you know?"

"I'm still trying to come to terms with you being some sort of ninja."

She laughed, poking him with her fingers. "Silly."

"How long you been studying martial arts?"

"Since I was about ten. I stopped for a couple of years when my mom got real sick and died. I don't go to classes every week. It's a great workout."

"I bet." He wrapped his arms around her and lifted her chin up. "I had a great time tonight," he murmured.

She nodded. "Me too." As he bent his head, she lightly pushed away from him. "Isn't the moon beautiful?" she said, her head tilted back.

He came up behind her, placing his hands on her shoulders. "You're beautiful."

She bit the side of her cheek. "Thanks." Kylie sprinted forward. "I'll race you to the car." Then she was running, the cool night wind caressing her cheeks. The rush of adrenaline was the jolt she needed. She didn't want to cross the line with Ricky. She liked him a lot, and she'd had a great time, but the flutters in her stomach weren't there, and there was no slow burn heating her body like there'd been with Jerry. It didn't react to him the same way. She wished it did, but there was nothing there.

"I win!" Breathlessly, she leaned against the car, hearing Ricky's soft chuckle as he came over to her. "You let me win."

He smiled, unlocking and opening the door. As she slid into the passenger's seat, Ricky leaned in, brushing his lips against hers. She jerked her head back, squeezing his hand when she saw his crestfallen face. "Let's go slow, okay?"

"I really like you." His eyes fixed on hers.

"We've been friends for a while. I don't want to jeopardize that. Finals are around the corner, and then school will be out. You'll be going to Denver and I'll be in Pinewood Springs. Let's not rush into anything, okay?" *I wish I felt for you the way I do for Jerry. It would make my life a helluva lot easier.*

Ricky nodded, his face glum. He closed her door and slipped into the driver's seat, switching on the ignition. "Do you want to listen to 96KIX?"

"I love that station." She touched his forearm. "You're not mad at me, are you?"

Shaking his head, he said, "No. Disappointed, but not mad."

"We still good?"

"Yeah. I'm not giving up, though." He turned to face her. "I want you to know that."

"Okay," she whispered.

As they drove out of the eatery's parking lot, Kylie spotted a purple Corvette across the street, the beam from the streetlight bouncing off the driver's sunglasses. She gasped, the hairs prickling on the back of her neck. As Ricky drove past, her gaze locked with his mirrored one.

It's him. He's watching me, and he wants me to know it.

Her heart skipped a beat.

Chapter Six

"What the fuck are you looking at?" Jerry pushed his chair back.

"I don't like the way you're gawking at my girlfriend," a tall man said as he took a step toward the biker.

"I'm not looking at her, but if you want to start something, asshole, I'm all in." Jerry leapt to his feet. At six-foot-two, he made an imposing figure.

The guy turned to his girlfriend, a blonde woman who had a small smile on her face. "Are you sure he was staring at you, baby?"

The blonde's close-set blue eyes widened. "Yeah. He was making me feel uncomfortable."

Jerry heard the man blow out a long breath and rolled his eyes. "I wasn't staring at your bitch. She was the one staring at me. I can't help it if she'd rather be with me than you."

"Fuck, Jerry, take it down a notch," Chas said as he rose from his chair. "We're not in a biker bar; we're in a citizen's bar. Banger won't like it if you hurt this jerk over a bitch who isn't worth it. Come on." He placed his arm on Jerry's, who jerked away.

"So, you want something or not?" Jerry snarled, his hands forming into fists. Out of the corner of his eye, he saw the bartender pick up a phone. "Let's take this outside, asshole." He marched to the door.

"Aren't you gonna follow him?" he heard the blonde ask her man. "You ain't chicken, are ya?"

"I just don't want to have the cops called. I got enough trouble with them. I'm on probation, remember?"

"That didn't stop you from punching out that old man who leered at me the other day. You ain't nothing but—"

The door slamming behind Jerry tuned out the bitch. He slammed his fist against the metal newspaper stand on the street corner. "Fuck! I should go back in there, drag the sonofabitch out here, and beat the shit outta him. Asshole!"

He whirled around, heading for the bar's door when Chas pulled him back. "What the fuck's your problem? You don't want to start a fight with a citizen. The fuckin' badges will be all over it."

"He's an asshole."

"Agreed, but he's an asshole who backed down. If you go back in there and beat his ass, you're going down on it, and Banger will be beyond pissed."

"I don't give a shit about Banger. He's president of the club, not my goddamned life."

Chas threw his friend against the wall. "Whoa, man. Just fucking calm down. You need to cool way the hell off before we go to church. You can't be saying shit like that about Banger. You know damn good and well that if you mess up this citizen, it puts heat on the club. And *that* is Banger's business." Chas rubbed his hand over his face. "What the hell's going on with you? You've been in fight mode for the past week. What the fuck?"

Jerry pushed off from the wall. "I'm just tired of the way Banger thinks he can tell everyone what to do in their personal lives. I'm getting sick of that shit. And that asshole in there—" he gestured to the bar "—needs my fist in his face for starting something and not finishing it." He walked toward his Harley.

Chas followed. "You know, the asshole was right. You *were* staring at his bitch."

Swinging his leg over his bike, Jerry shook his head. "She's not even my type. If I was staring, I didn't realize it. I wouldn't have had anything with her, but if I wanted to, I know she would've fucked me in an instant. These sluts are all alike."

Chas nodded. "You heading to the clubhouse?"

"I'll be there for church. I got some things to do. See you." Jerry pulled away from the curb and headed out of Pinewood Springs.

As he rode on the backroads, he sped up, loving the rush of spring air around him. When he was on his Harley, it was as though he were alone in the world, just him and nature. During his solo rides, he became one with the earth, the sky, the trees, and the wind. It was the most liberating feeling he'd ever known.

He veered off onto an old path that wound around the side of Pine Mountain. Finally, he stopped and stretched his legs. To his right, he heard the gush of water and he walked toward it, his boots sinking into the soft ground littered with pine needles and dandelions. As he rounded a curve, he saw a creek coiling around the mountainside, its water cascading over the rocks in haste. Moving closer, he stared at the fish darting through it. Ribbons of sunlight spilled into the alcove, and from where he stood, he could see the creek bed's smooth-edged stones glowing amber and bronze. With ease, he sat on the ground, a cool, spring wind ruffling his hair. He leaned his head back, listening to the trees creaking in the breeze.

Jerry needed to be there, by the water, surrounded by the mountains, trees, and wildflowers. All of it was like a salve for his soul. He'd come real close to beating the shit out of a guy who had every right to be pissed at him. He *had* been staring at the guy's woman, but not in a sexual way. When he'd come back from the bar with another beer, she'd had her back to him and he'd noticed her long, blonde hair. For a heart-stopping second, he'd thought it was Kylie, but then she'd turned around. He'd stared through her, Kylie's sweet smile filling his thoughts and punching him in the groin. He hadn't been able to get her off his mind since he'd hung out with her two weeks before. The way she'd felt in his arms, and her lips on his, were burned in his brain and his dick. He had to see her again, hold her, breathe in her lavender scent, and kiss the softest, sexiest lips he'd ever tasted.

He picked up a stone and threw it in the creek, watching the current engulf it and take it away. He had it bad for Kylie, and not being able to have her the way he wanted made him crazy. Jerry knew he'd been in a mood since he'd come back from Crested Peak, but he couldn't help it. Knowing how she tasted and felt made his lust simmer, and the fact that she was off-limits made his blood boil. He was so damn pissed he'd started at least four fights with a couple of the brothers and some other bikers at a bar he'd gone to the previous Friday.

Jerry stretched his denim-clad legs and took out his phone, scrolling until he found Kylie's number. For a long while, he stared at the blank screen, debating whether or not he should text her. He wanted to, but then he remembered that she'd told him she had no memory of anything except him taking her to her dorm room. She'd been dead-drunk, so it could've been anyone or anything kissing her and she wouldn't have known anything different. If he contacted her right then, he'd start something he knew he shouldn't. If he didn't text her, she'd be none the wiser, but he'd end up with a hard-on for a while. The club whores could relieve that, but since he'd tasted Kylie's lips, he didn't want any of the other women. In time, that would pass—he was sure of it.

Jerry sat on the ground, staring at his phone, while nature played its music all around him. When the sun dipped further in the western sky, he pushed himself up, jammed his phone in his back pocket, and sauntered over to his Harley. Normally he'd feel refreshed and calm when he'd leave his favorite spot, but right then, he was horny, pissed, and confused. He revved his engine and began the journey back to the clubhouse for church.

THROWING BACK HIS fourth shot of Jack, he knew he'd be crashing at the clubhouse. Jerry had lived at the clubhouse for a couple of years after he'd patched in, but he'd craved a place of his own, so three years before, he'd rented an apartment. He only crashed at the club if he were shit-faced or having too much fun with the women.

"You look like you need some company," Wendy said, wrapping her arm around his neck as she gave him a small nip.

"I'm good, Wendy," he deadpanned, wishing she were Kylie.

"You've been avoiding all of us. What's up? You not feeling well?"

"Something like that." He gently unwrapped her arms from his neck. "Go have a good time. I'm not up for anything tonight." A dull vibration pulsed against his leg. Pulling out his phone, his blood pumping when he saw Kylie's name flash across its screen, he turned his back to the crowd and faced the bar.

Kylie: *Hey.*

Jerry: *Hey.*

Kylie: *Whatcha doing?*

He motioned for another shot. Blade placed it in front of him. *I'm thinking about you like always. I want to be with you, feel your naked skin against mine, taste your sweet lips again.* He threw back his Jack, the whiskey smooth and scorching.

Jerry: *Doing shots at the club. What bout u?*

Kylie: *U're at the club? Who's with u?*

He smiled. She wanted to know if he was with a club girl. *Oh, yeah.*

Jerry: *Most of the guys & women r here.*

Even though it was true, technically, he knew she'd think he meant he was with one of the whores. Making her sweat gave him a perverse pleasure. He knew he was acting like a bastard because he couldn't have her; he wanted to punish her for her dad's edict.

Kylie: *Oh. Rosie or Wendy?*

Jerry: *All the whores r here.*

Kylie: *U're outdoing urself. I gotta go.*

He'd gone too far. He didn't want to lose the connection to her.

Jerry: *Don't go. Like talking to u.*

Kylie: *Ricky just came in. We're going to a concert. Bye. Have fun with ur women.*

Then she was gone. He'd fucking blown it. She'd reached out to him, and he made her feel like shit. And why the fuck was Ricky in her room? Jerry didn't like *that* one bit. That kid was trying to get in her pants. He'd seen it that night, and he'd be damned if he'd let Ricky anywhere near Kylie's pussy. Narrowing his eyes, Jerry decided he needed another road trip, and Crested Peak was the perfect destination.

He had to rid his mind of Kylie, and the only way he knew how to do that was to drink himself to oblivion.

He motioned for another shot.

Chapter Seven

Kylie flung her phone across the room, not giving a shit if it broke. Grinding her teeth, she stomped over to her closet and shoved her clothes aside, searching for her jean jacket while she cursed Jerry under her breath. The asshole could fuck whoever he wanted. *Dad's right—he's such a man-whore.* He didn't even say anything nice to her, like he missed her or he'd been thinking about her. All he did was tell her he was with a bunch of women. *What a bastard!* She'd bet he was annoyed when he saw it was her texting him. He still thought of her as that twelve-year-old girl who had a crush on him.

She tossed her jacket on the bed and slammed the closet door shut. Pacing back and forth, Kylie berated herself for texting Jerry. She'd been missing him so much, and all she wanted was a tiny connection to him, so she'd weakened and contacted him. And he'd acted like she was a nobody! Red streaks crept across her cheeks when she replayed their "conversation." Her stomach dropped when she pictured Jerry with Rosie's lips around his dick and Wendy's boobs pressed against him. He probably couldn't wait to get rid of Kylie. That was probably why he told her about the women—he was *busy* when she'd texted. Her ears and face felt impossibly hot.

She wasn't stupid—weak, perhaps, but not dense. She learned her lesson: never contact Jerry again. No matter how vulnerable she felt, she'd rather die alone than ever call or text him again. She pounded her fist on her desk. *Never again.*

Knock. Knock. Knock. Kylie opened the door and Ricky, in blue jeans and a Megadeth T-shirt, smiled at her, raking his gaze over her form. "Hiya."

Still fuming over Jerry, she grunted her hello and with a quick wave of her hand, gestured him to come in. With a quizzical look, he came in and leaned against her desk. "You okay?"

"Yeah. Why?" she snapped.

He shrugged. "You just look really pissed. Did I do something to make you mad?"

Ricky's earnest face melted her frosty anger. It wasn't fair to be mad at him because of the way Jerry treated her. If she were smart, she'd forget about him altogether and concentrate on Ricky, who actually liked her and treated her well. But she was pulled to Jerry—the bad boy. And why not? All her life, she'd been surrounded by them. They were exciting, sexy, and dangerous, and she'd grown up in the biker life, even though her dad shielded her from a lot of the violence and darkness that was a part of his world.

"Well, did I?" His question brought her back to the present.

She shook her head. "No. I'm sorry. I'm just having a bad moment, but it's over. I'm ready to rock. This concert's going to be so much fun." As Kylie feigned an enthusiasm she didn't feel, Ricky's wide smile replaced his furrowed brow. "Are your friends meeting us?" She picked up her jean jacket on the bed and slid it over her black crop top.

"In the parking lot next to my car. I'm driving."

Bending over to pick up her phone, she inspected it to see if it had broken during her fit of anger. No, it was still intact. "I'll text Taylor, Mary, and Ari to meet us. It's parking lot A, right?"

He nodded. "Right next to the laundry room."

As they ambled to the car, Ricky took her hand in his. She wanted to pull away, but she didn't want to hurt his feelings, especially since she'd been bitchy to him when he'd come to pick her up. They walked hand in hand, and as they approached their group of friends in the lot, Kylie's skin prickled. She had the strangest sensation that someone was watching *her*. Looking around, nothing seemed amiss, but she couldn't shake the feeling.

"Are we ready to rock?" Taylor said as she lifted her arms in the air and shook her hips. They all laughed. Then the six of them climbed into Ricky's SUV, and they were off.

The Black Sheep was in the middle of the block on Prospect Ave. in downtown Crested Peak. Its capacity was six hundred people, and when popular bands played at the venue, it was usually sold out. That evening was no exception. Black Stone Cherry was a popular band and had never performed in Crested Peak before, so when the group got there, a long line had already formed. Since it was standing room only, they'd arrived early, hoping to be among the first in so they could secure a good spot on the floor.

Black Stone Cherry was one of Kylie's favorite bands; she loved their hard-edged, southern metal songs. She'd waited a long time to see them, having missed them two years before when they'd performed in Denver. She should've been excited to the max, but thoughts of Jerry with Rosie, Wendy, Lola, Kristy, and the other club women dampened her exhilaration. As hard as she tried, she couldn't shut out the images, and it pissed her off because she was sure he wasn't thinking about her at all. *What a fucking jerk.*

"This is going to be awesome," Ricky said as he tugged her close to him. "Are you feeling it?"

Even though she was overwhelmed by a hollowness in her chest, Kylie smiled. Ricky had purchased the tickets as a surprise for her. Taylor had told him how much she'd loved the band, and it was sweet that he'd done that. She didn't want to ruin his night, so she leaned in and whispered in his ear, "I can't believe you made all this possible for me. You're a good person."

He skimmed his lips over her cheek. "I'd do anything for you. I'm happy we're here together."

Turning her face away, she gave him a quick hug, wishing she were as into him as he was into her. Before she could muse further, the doors opened and the group of them moved forward, following the crowd.

The venue was packed, and Kylie and her friends found their spot right in front of the stage. Telling the guys to guard their territory, the girls went up to the bar to order sodas. "This is a great show so far," Taylor yelled over the music. "The local acts are kicking ass."

"They are. It's a great lineup," she agreed as she grabbed several cocktail napkins. Kylie hated holding a plastic cup that dripped water as the ice melted down. It was one of her pet peeves. "You want a Diet Pepsi? They don't have Coke products here."

Ari and Mary nodded, and Kylie placed their order. As she waited for their drinks, she watched the local band rocking out, the lights flashing on the stage. From the corner of her eyes, a flash sparked in the darkness. Turning in the direction of the gleam, she spotted him, the strobe lights bouncing off his gold frames. A cruel smile stretched across his mouth, and her stomach turned to ice.

Grabbing Taylor's arm, she spun her friend toward her. "He's here. The guy with the purple Corvette is here." She competed with the thunderous bass and hard rock vocals bouncing off the venue's walls.

Taylor shook her head as she pointed to her ears. Kylie jerked her thumb in his direction, yelling, "There he is!" Taylor's eyes shifted from Kylie to the spot where she pointed, then she shrugged again. Wild-eyed, Kylie looked over, but he was gone. She desperately searched the crowd, on alert for a glimmer of anything. But nothing. It was as though he was never there, and maybe he wasn't. Maybe she'd imagined the whole thing.

By the time Black Stone Cherry took the stage, Kylie was a bundle of nerves, seeing sparking flashes everywhere, but none of them were from gold-framed sunglasses. When the concert ended, all she wanted to do was go back to her dorm and shut out the images of scantily-clad women all over Jerry and mirrored sunglasses. Of course, the group wanted to munch on pizza and talk about the concert, so she went along, laughing, talking, and eating even though her nerves were in overdrive.

When they arrived at the campus, Ricky walked her, Taylor, Mary, and Ari to their buildings. When they reached her room, Taylor opened the door and went inside, lightly closing it behind her. Kylie and Ricky stood in the brightly lit hallway, the fluorescent lights buzzing overhead.

"I had a great time tonight. I hope you did." Ricky shifted from one foot to another.

"Oh, yeah. It was awesome. Thanks again for taking me. The band was totally cool." Silence spread over them, and she brought her hand up and nibbled on her thumb. He clasped her hand and pulled it away from her mouth then leaned in, his hand tilting her head back. Placing her hands on his chest, she pushed him away, her heart lurching when he winced then sagged against the wall, his shoulders hunched. "I'm sorry." Her voice hitched.

"What's wrong? You don't like me?"

Sighing, she leaned against the door. "It's me. I adore you as a friend, and I'm not ready to shift our friendship to something more. I hope you understand."

A bitter smile swept across his lips. "I do. I guess I was hoping you'd feel what I feel."

"I know you're frustrated with me, but I don't want to lead you on. I think you're fun, witty, totally smart, and very handsome, but I enjoy our friendship immensely. I hope it isn't in jeopardy."

He shook his head.

"Please, don't be mad at me."

"I'm not. I'm just disappointed. I really like you a lot, Kylie."

Her heart pulled. What the fuck was she doing? Pushing away a normal guy for the chance that the asshole in Pinewood Springs *might* like her someday? *How fucking stupid and pathetic.*

"I gotta go." He kissed her quickly on the cheek and walked down the hall. She waited until he turned the corner before she went into her room.

"So, did you guys make out?" Taylor stretched out on her bed, her elbow propping her up, searching Kylie's face.

"No. I gave him the 'I just want to be friends' speech." She groaned and flopped on to her bed. "Why can't I be normal? Ricky's a great guy."

"But you like the bad boy who's treating you like shit. I'm sure you'll cover that section in your psychology class."

Kylie laughed dryly.

"It's usually that way—the ones we want we can't have, and the ones we *can* have we don't want. I give you kudos for not settling. You know who you want, so go after him."

"No way. I texted him today, and that was a fucking disaster. I just need to put some space between us. I'm probably the only one who's happy finals are coming up. I can lose myself in my studies."

"It was a great concert, though, right?"

"It was. I just wish I wasn't feeling so weird tonight. That fucking jerk was there. You know, the one with the purple Corvette. I tried to tell you when we were getting the drinks, but you couldn't hear me over the music. I only saw him once."

"Are you sure it was him? I mean, you told me you don't really know what he looks like."

"It was his sunglasses—they're very distinct."

"So, what *did* he look like?"

"I still couldn't see him real clearly. It was so dark. I only saw his teeth twisted in a mean smile. Under the lights, they glowed an eerie blue." She shuddered. "I'm sick of his shit."

"Tell your dad. He'll take care of the asshole in no time."

"You're right. He'd also make sure his prized Corvette is reduced to a nice cube." The two women laughed. "I should tell my dad, but I know he'll overreact and not let me come back next year. He'll definitely put me in lockdown. I've told you what a hard time I had convincing him to let me come here in the first place. If it hadn't been for Cara, I'd be at a community college in Pinewood Springs. No, I think this jerk's game is in scaring me. Next time I see him, I'll be on the offensive. He's probably just a bully."

"I don't know. I wouldn't do anything foolish. Do you think it has anything to do with your dad and his club?"

"No. If it did, I'd already be toast. Bikers don't fool around and play games like this asshole is doing. He's probably doing it to me and a few other women."

"You're probably right, but I still think you should tell your dad, but in the meantime, file another report with security tomorrow."

Kylie nodded then pulled herself up from her bed and checked her phone. One text from Ricky saying if all he can have is a friendship with her, he's all in. She smiled. He really was sweet. Nothing from Jerry. She sighed heavily then went into the bathroom to wash up before crashing.

The next morning, Kylie gathered her books for her morning classes and was just about to leave the room when Taylor turned over on her side. "You want to come with me to Durango for my grandmother's birthday?"

Durango was in the southern part of the state, and since they didn't have classes on Friday or Monday, many of the students were taking advantage of the last free weekend before the final weeks of classes and tests began. Ricky and two of his buddies were headed to Las Vegas, and Mary and Ari were staying at Mary's parents' condo in Scottsdale. Kylie had thought about going to Pinewood Springs, but she didn't want to bump into Jerry. Plus her stepsister Emily was causing another bout of drama with her drinking, and Kylie wasn't up for the bullshit that all entailed.

"Thanks, but I'm good. I'm going to take advantage of the quiet and get started on the final term paper in my English Lit class. I have a ton of crap to do for psychology and sociology. It'll be good to just hang and take it easy."

"Do you think it's wise to be here alone when you got that creep bothering you?"

"I'm not alone. A lot of people on our floor and in the building are staying. Also, I'm going to talk to security after my classes. I'm good." She glanced at the clock. "Oh, shit, I gotta run. I'm late for poli-sci. Later." She closed the door behind her then dashed off to class.

After her classes, Kylie filed yet another report with security and then decided to go to the grocery store to stock up on some food for the upcoming weekend. An hour later, she swung into Parking Lot A, happy to have found a space close to her building. She had overbought, and now regretted it as she hauled out the grocery bags and water, trying to carry them all in one trip.

She slammed down the trunk and lugged her bags, her head bent down when the familiar sewing machine noise made her jerk her head up. The purple Corvette blocked her way, and the sun reflected off the mirrored lenses of the flashy sunglasses. Her stomach churned and she clutched her bags tighter.

"Hi, Kylie." His smooth voice made her skin prick with goose bumps.

"What the fuck do you want?"

His face was still hidden in the shadows of the car, but she could see his full lips and his bright white teeth. "Such ugly language coming from a beautiful mouth." He shook his head.

"I don't have time for your shit."

"You mad at me?" He smiled flatly.

"I don't appreciate you following me, and if you don't stop it, I'm going to tell my dad, who isn't going to like it one bit. And believe me, you don't want to make my dad mad." She jutted out her chin in defiance.

His smile disappeared. "You threatening me? I thought you were a big girl, Kylie. I didn't know you were a baby who had to run to her daddy for everything." He leaned further back into the shadows of the car. "Go ahead and tell your daddy. I'm not scared of him."

"You would be, if you knew who he was."

"I do. He's president of the Insurgents MC, and I don't give a fuck. You got that, pretty girl?"

She heard the edge in his voice and knew she'd gotten to him. She wasn't sure how he knew who her dad was, but he was probably too stupid to truly understand what Banger was capable of. Kylie cocked her head.

"I'm tired of your stupid, bullying games. What's the matter, you can't get any women who want to go out with you?"

He bared his teeth and she swore she heard a low growl, but then his smooth, suave demeanor was back. "I'm not playing a game with you. I just want to take you for a ride. You're so pretty."

"Fat chance." She took several steps backwards and sprinted around the car parked next to hers.

"Are you dating Ricky?"

Kylie stopped in her tracks, her mind reeling. He fucking knew *everything* about her. *What the hell does he want?* "It's none of your business what I do. Stay the fuck away from me."

"You're wrong, pretty girl. Everything about you is my business. Stop dating Ricky. You are *mine*."

Coldness crawled over her skin. "Campus security is on to you."

"Is that supposed to scare me? Those clowns are a joke." She heard a click from his car, like he unlocked the doors. "Get in the car. Now."

She bolted through the space between the two cars a few yards away from hers. When she crossed behind his vehicle, she saw the reverse lights right before the car moved, nearly hitting her.

"Hey, what the fuck are you doing?" someone from the parking lot yelled. Then there were several other students, who'd seen what he'd done and ran over, yelling and trying to make him stop. His car sped off, the tires squealing as he rounded the curve, and then he was gone.

"Are you okay?" A guy she recognized from her Spanish class stared at her.

Shaken, Kylie nodded. "That guy's a jerk. Did anyone get his license plate number?"

"I didn't see one," her classmate said, and the other students gathered around her nodded in agreement. "You need to report this. I'm Luke. I'm in your Spanish class."

"I'm Kylie. I recognize you."

"If security wants to talk to me, I'm in Highland Hall." The other students gave her their information, each one eager to tell security about the man in the purple Corvette who'd tried to hurt her.

After she'd filed her report with security, Kylie made her way to her building, the grocery bags still dangling from her wrists. She wondered if she should go home for the long weekend, after all. *What if he tries to hurt me? He seems to know my every move, so won't he know Taylor won't be with me and I'll be alone?* She really didn't want to run away, like a victim; she should be able to live her life and not let some fucking asshole bully and intimidate her. By the time she reached her room and opened the door, she'd made her decision to stay on campus. Security promised they'd keep an eye on her throughout the weekend, and if she saw him again, she'd call and tell her dad. Then he could make the boogeyman with the flashy sunglasses disappear.

Chapter Eight

He hurled the chair against the wall, bits of plaster flaking off. He'd slipped up. The six-pack of beer he'd bought the previous night crashed against the wall with a thud, green glass shards flying as yellow liquid trickled down the white walls. Ripping the sheets off the mattress, he tore them with his hands, spittle forming in the corners of his mouth. With flaring nostrils, he toppled the nightstand and smashed the lamp, and was in the middle of putting his fist through the television screen when a loud bang sounded on his door.

"Management. Open up."

Standing erect, he inhaled and exhaled deeply several times, even as the door groaned. "I'm okay. I just had an epileptic seizure. I knocked some things down, but I'm straightening it out. Thanks for your concern." His hands clenched into fists as he placed his ear against the door.

"You trashing the room?"

"No, of course not. I told you, I have a medical condition. I had a seizure, but it's passed. I just need to lie down." The man could hear the manager's feet shuffling on the concrete. "Thanks again for your concern." The smoothness had returned to his voice.

"Uh… sure. If you need help, call the front desk."

He waited several minutes by the door, making sure the jerk had left, then padded over to the bed and sat on it. He'd slipped up. The sweet bitch had snaked her way into his blood. He'd become careless—witnesses in the university parking lot and garnering attention at the motel. The brown-eyed man ran his long fingers through his wavy, black hair. He was too wrapped up in her, and her lavender scent drifting around him whenever he approached her was making him sloppy. *How the fuck does she have such an effect on me? This isn't the way it's supposed to play out.*

For the past eight months, his every waking moment had been spent planning how he'd make the president of the Insurgents suffer. Two simple goals drove him: make Banger pay for what he'd done, and make the president's life a living hell. The black-haired man had thought about it until it'd driven him almost crazy, knowing retaliation would be the only thing that would bring him peace. Bitterness and anger had been his only friends for months, and imagining the suffering he'd bestow on Banger made him salivate.

It was easy: take the one thing the president loved more than anything—his daughter. He'd planned it so well, proud of his meticulousness on the way he would exact his revenge. And then he saw Kylie, and his elaborate plans took a backseat as he became consumed by her. She should've been dead by now, and Banger should've already opened the box containing her head, her blue eyes frozen in terror. Instead, the bitter man was watching Kylie, compelled to make her his no matter what. Had he betrayed his loved one with this diversion? Perhaps, but the pull the blonde-haired vixen had on him was too much. He had to possess her; he couldn't resist. All of her belonged to him—her body, her love, and her life. If he had to kill everyone in his path to conquer her, so be it. The vengeful stalker had even stopped visiting his mother, yet the guilt he felt about that still wasn't enough for him to break away from Kylie.

And his poor mother—a miserable lump of a woman—had never wanted anything more in life than a good husband and children. But her husband had regularly beaten her to a pulp, and her two sons were loyal to their brotherhood. When she'd asked him to come see her, she'd pleaded with him to find out what had happened and to make it right. The dutiful son promised he'd exact vengeance for her—it was the least he could do.

But he hadn't planned on Kylie. Sleepless nights were filled with fantasies of her ivory-white skin against his tanned body, his hands running over her curves, his mouth on hers, his hard cock poking at her pussy while lavender swirled around him, caressing and intoxicating him.

Fuck! His hand rubbed against the hardness in his pants. Cursing, he grabbed the remote, thankful he'd been stopped before he smashed the television screen, and switched on a porn film. Propping the pillow against the headboard, he reclined against it, unzipped his pants, and let Kylie take center stage in his mind as he watched a big-titted woman stuff a massive cock between her red, shiny lips.

He gripped his dick firmly in his hand then moved it up and down rapidly, the sound of his ragged panting filling the room. With the pressure building, his whole body clenched as he crossed the threshold, grunting as satisfying spurts shot out. *This is for you, pretty girl. Only for you.*

Chapter Nine

Kylie wheeled Taylor's fuchsia suitcase down the stairs to the parking lot. "Tell your grandmother I said happy birthday."

"I will." Taylor stopped in front of a blue Mazda and popped the trunk. "I wish you were coming with me. I worry about you." A frown creased her forehead.

"Don't spend your weekend worrying. I'll be fine. Besides, security is keeping an eye on me and Ricky asked Andy to watch over me too. Have a good time. I really do need to catch up in some of my classes."

"I should be staying and catching up," Taylor groaned. "I'm so fucking behind in Ashcroft's class. I'll be pulling a lot of all-nighters for the next couple of weeks." She hugged Kylie. "I'll be back Monday afternoon. I'll call you, and you better answer your phone, otherwise I'll be freaking out."

Kylie pushed her affectionately. "Go. I'll answer my phone. See you on Monday. Drive safely, and call me when you get to Durango."

Taylor waved and backed out her car, Kylie watching her drive away until she exited the parking lot. Swinging around, she sprinted up the stairs, happy to have the room to herself for a few days. She made sure her door was locked then cranked up Twisted Sister's *We're Not Gonna Take It*, thinking how the sentiments of the song fit her situation. She'd decided she wasn't going to take anymore shit from the jerk in the Corvette. It'd been so liberating when she'd told him off, and she was pretty sure she wouldn't see him again. Bullies thrived on fear, and she'd shown him she wasn't afraid.

As she took out *Wuthering Heights* to begin her paper for English Lit, she thought she'd heard a knock on her door. Turning down the music, she waited and listened. *Knock, knock.* Taking a deep breath she shuffled to the door, her pulse pounding in her ears. What if it was Marcus, or worse, the Corvette guy? Not wanting to invite trouble in, she asked, "Who is it?"

"It's me." Jerry's voice was a husky whisper, sending a surge of adrenaline through her. She flung the door open and bit her inner cheek as she saw him standing before her in his tight jeans, black T-shirt that showed off his ripped chest, and black leather jacket. He had a goofy, lopsided grin on his face, and his silver earrings caught the fluorescent light. "Are you gonna invite me in?"

"Oh, sure." She jumped back, making room for his broad physique to pass through the narrow doorway. Crossing her arms over her chest, she leaned against her closet door. What was *he* doing here? Butterflies battled each other in her stomach, and she gripped her arms to steady herself.

"Aren't you happy to see me?" He slid his eyes over her, his gaze scorching her skin.

"I'm more surprised to see you. Did you come to see your friends?"

Shaking his head, his gaze lingered on her mouth. "I came to see you."

"Really?" Tingles chased up her spine.

For a long moment, he looked fixedly at her. "Really," he said in a low voice.

His voice, deep and sensual, sent a ripple of desire through her. She shifted in place, her mouth dry. "Can I get you something to drink?"

"You got beer?"

"No. Diet Coke, bottled water, orange and cranberry juice." Kylie exhaled forcefully. She could do this, act like it was normal to have Jerry in her room. Handsome, buff Jerry, who exuded sex from every damn pore on his body. It was cool; she'd be nonchalant, like the club girls who didn't know the meaning of "shy" or "nervous as hell."

He chuckled. "Gimme your car keys and show me the way to the nearest liquor store."

Twenty minutes later, Jerry was popping the top of a twenty-two-ounce beer bottle, his brown gaze on her blue one. Taking a long pull, he wiped his mouth with the back of his hand. "Fuck, I needed that. Want one?"

"Okay, but I want the smaller size." When she took the bottle from him, their fingers touched and strange twists churned in her stomach. "Why didn't you tell me you were coming to Crested Peak?"

"I wanted to surprise you."

"Well, you succeeded." She took a small sip. "I'm glad you're here."

"That's good. For a while there, I thought you may have been pissed about me comin'."

"No. Why did you want to see me?"

He moved one shoulder in a shrug, lit up a joint, and inhaled deeply. "Want a hit?"

Kylie took it from him, the weird sensations hitting her again when his fingers grazed hers. The weed calmed her down; she should've thought about smoking some when he'd first come into her room. Mellowing out, she put some music on from Shinedown and they began to chat easily. "How're things in Pinewood Springs? You know, I almost went home this weekend, but changed my mind at the last minute. I have a shitload of stuff to do for school, so I thought it'd be nice to have the room to myself. Taylor went to Durango to see her family. Wouldn't that have been funny if I went to Pinewood and you came here?"

Hunger filled his brown gaze. "You're alone for the whole weekend?"

"Yeah." Insecurity nipped at her weed-induced confidence.

"I'll be damned."

"Most of my friends went somewhere. I almost went with a couple to Scottsdale. Mary's parents have a condo there. It'd be nice to lie by the pool and get drunk on Mai Tais." She giggled.

"Sounds like fun. Why didn't you go?"

Kylie pointed to the stack of books on her desk. "Too much to do."

"Am I bothering you by being here? I could go and hang with my friends. I don't want to keep you from your work."

"No," she said quickly. "You're not bothering me at all." *Smooth, Kylie. Can you sound any more desperate?*

"If I am, just say the word." Jerry narrowed his eyes. "Is Ricky on campus?"

"Ricky? No, he went to Vegas with some of his buds. Why?"

"Did he ask you to join him?"

Was he jealous? No, it wasn't possible, because that would mean he *really* liked her. And if he did, why would he fuck the club girls? "He did. Can you open another beer for me?"

"You dating the dude?" He handed her the beer. That time, his hand covered hers and he didn't pull away.

Holding the beer in mid-air, loving the small jolts of pleasure his hand on hers caused in her core, she shook her head, her mouth too dry to answer without making an ass of herself. He let go and leaned back in the chair, lighting another joint. After taking a gulp of beer, she mumbled, "We're just good friends."

"Keep it that way." His tone was velvet, yet edged with steel. The smoke from the weed drifted around him.

She cleared her throat. "Smoking pot always gives me the munchies. You want something? I went to the store yesterday and bought a lot of stuff. I have Cheez-Its, chips, pretzels, Chex Mix, roasted peanuts—I love those—and string cheese."

"Let's grab some dinner."

"Yeah, we can do that too. What do you feel like eating?"

"You choose. I'm just having a good time being with you."

She swallowed hard. "Let's go for Mexican. I can drive. Let me just freshen up."

Several minutes later, she came out of the restroom, her makeup touched up and grungy jeans swapped for a short black jean skirt and a white lace crop top. "Ready?"

"Fuck, you look beautiful."

The way his gaze boldly assessed her body made her blush. Kylie quickly grabbed her keys and opened the door. "Come on."

Jerry rose to his feet and brushed past her so his chest grazed her breasts, her nipples hardening on contact. When she gasped, he laughed. "Give me the keys, babe. I'm driving."

"I can drive. I know where the restaurant is."

Cupping her chin in his hand, Jerry dipped his head and breathed against her ear, "As long as I'm here, I'm in charge, and I'm driving. Let's go." He gently pressed his lips against her neck, his warm breath caressing her before he grabbed her hand and started down the hall. Fearing he'd see her clenching her thighs, she coughed and then followed his lead.

Casa Moreno was buried in the corner of a strip mall on the northeast side of Crested Peak. Its burnt red-tiled floors and earth-toned walls contrasted strongly with the bright pink, yellow, and lime-green of the booths and décor. Large terracotta pots with bold and vivid geometric patterns housed various cacti arrangements. The upbeat rhythm of ranchera music filled the cantina, and the packed place lent an accompaniment of noisy chatter to it.

Munching on a chip, Kylie studied the menu. She and her friends had been there a ton of times so she knew it by memory, but by looking at it, she was able to avoid Jerry's eyes. Every time they met hers, her heart turned over in response.

"Are you ready to order?" The waiter's heavily accented voice made her jump.

"I am. Are you?" She looked up, meeting Jerry's gaze. It was blazing with a hunger that made her all squishy inside.

Without taking his eyes off her face, he said, "Steak fajitas, medium rare, corn tortillas, and another Corona."

"Very good. And for you, miss?"

"A cheese enchilada with a side of rice. I'll have some more iced tea." As she spoke, Jerry watched her mouth, his chest rising and falling in short succession.

The waiter took their menus and Jerry leaned back against the booth, his brown orbs traveling in little circles around her face before landing on her blue ones once more. "Do you come here often?"

She took a big sip of iced tea in a vain attempt to cool the heat between her legs. "Yeah. It's always packed."

"Am I making you nervous?"

Shaking her head vigorously, Kylie squeaked, "No. Why would I be nervous? I've known you for a long time."

"You seem nervous."

"I'm just still surprised that you're here. I didn't think I'd be having dinner with *you* tonight." She stuffed a chip in her mouth and looked around the restaurant. Anything to stop the havoc his voice, his eyes, and his nearness were playing on her emotions.

"We have known each other for a long time, but a lot of it was when you were younger." The waiter placed the bottle of Corona in front of Jerry, and he took a long pull. "You're all grown up now." His glance dropped from her face to her neck then to her breasts. "Yep, all grown up."

Thankful for the quick service, Kylie pushed her fork to the side as the server put her steaming dinner on the table. "Smells good. I didn't realize how hungry I was."

"Me neither," Jerry said hoarsely.

She darted her eyes to his, her neck flushing when she saw untamed lust in them. Clasping her hand on her neck, she tried to hide the red splotches, but he noticed and gave her a smile that sent her pulse racing. The *dink* of her fork hitting her plate pulled her away from him, and she giggled softly while she placed a large bite of rice in her mouth.

As they ate, Kylie made it a point to steer the conversation to club matters; bringing her dad up seemed to be the weapon she needed to cool down Jerry's ardor. She had to put a little bit of distance between what she wanted and what she feared. She wanted him to crush her into his embrace and make love to her, but she feared she'd be just another woman he bedded. After all, look how he'd acted after he kissed her. But she was a grown, mature woman and needed to experience sex. At nineteen she was still a virgin, and losing it to Jerry was very tempting. What better way to experience her first time than with someone she'd known and had been crushing on for a long time? If it was an isolated coupling, that would be fine. She was a woman on her own, and she could handle it. It'd actually be better if it were a one-time thing, because she wouldn't have to deal with her father's rage and disappointment.

When the bill came, Jerry paid and slid out of the booth. He offered his hand to her, helping her up. With his arm around her shoulders, they walked out of the restaurant, got into the car, and drove back to campus.

Opening her door, Kylie looked over her shoulder at him. "Do you want to come in?"

Nodding, he followed her. Instead of turning on the overhead light, she went over to her nightstand and turned on her small lamp. "Do you want another beer?"

Jerry was twisting open the bottle of Jack Daniels he'd bought earlier. "I'll have a few shots. You like whiskey?"

"I like the flavored ones, like cinnamon, apple, and berry punch." Laughter burst through her lips when he shuffled back a step or two, his eyes widening.

"Fuck, baby, that's downright sacrilegious." He reached out and swatted her butt.

"To each his own. I'll have another beer. You want to listen to some music? I know you like Aerosmith."

"Fuck, yeah. They rule."

After she turned on the music, Kylie kicked off her short black boots and eased down on the bed, crossing her legs. Jerry sat on her desk chair and stretched his legs in front of him, a plastic glass full of whiskey in his hand. A comfortable silence enveloped them as they listened to the music, drank, and stared at each other. When Aerosmith's *Angel* came on, Jerry rose and came over to her, yanking her to her feet with his powerful hands. Crushing her against him, he wrapped his arms around her and swayed to the music. Stiff at first, she relaxed in his embrace as she listened to him sing along with the song.

Laying her head on his chest, she placed her hand on top of it, letting her fingers trace the lines of his muscles. He smelled like soap, leather, and whiskey, and she breathed in deeply, loving it. Under her ear, she heard his heart thumping; its fast beat matched hers, surprising and delighting her. As his hands trailed up and down her back, slowly dipping further toward her ass, her insides jangled with excitement. His heated desire was like a magnet drawing her closer to him, making her resolve to keep it casual quickly dissolving.

"I like the way you feel in my arms," he rasped, the sweep of his lips against her ear like a caress. He danced her over to the wall, pinning her against it with his warm body. "You have no idea how fucking crazy you make me." He moved his mouth along her jaw, lavishing it with kisses.

His touch sent a shiver through her and she breathed lightly through parted lips, a tiny moan escaping. When he cupped her chin, their breaths mingled, and his hand skimming over her ass made her arch her back, pressing her body closer. Gentle fingers glided under her skirt, and when they dug into her soft, naked ass cheek, a feral groan ripped from his throat. Before she could react, he took her mouth with a savage intensity, forcing her lips open with his thrusting tongue. His kiss sent the pit of her stomach into a wild swirl, and Kylie curled her arms around his neck tightly, giving in to him.

They held each other, their lips, teeth, and tongues crashing, biting, and tasting with reckless abandon. It was as if all this passion and desire were unleashed in that one kiss, which neither of them wanted to end. Jerry thrust his hips against Kylie's belly, his hardness pressing at her core. She parted her legs and he rubbed her throbbing mound with his knee, swallowing her gasps of pleasure.

He captured her bottom lip between his teeth and gently tugged and sucked it. "You're amazing," he said, his words smothered on her lips.

Then her phone rang, interrupting their moment of impulsiveness.

Kylie glanced at it on her desk as it flashed. "I should see who it is," she whispered against his neck.

"Are you fucking serious?" He didn't lessen his embrace.

"I promised Taylor I'd answer if she called. I don't want her to worry." She brushed her hair out of her face. "And it could be my dad. He doesn't like it if I don't pick up."

The mere mention of her father made Jerry release her in a flash. She suppressed a laugh and went over to pick up the phone. It was Taylor. In her peripheral view, she saw Jerry pour another shot in his cup then sit on her bed. The two women spoke for a few minutes, then she put her phone down. With her back to him, she said, "Taylor was just making sure I'm okay. She worries about me like a mother hen." She laughed, then heard him rise from the bed, the springs squeaking.

"I better take off," he said. "I texted my friends I'd be there about ten o'clock, and it's way past that."

Her insides lurched. "Can you ride? I mean, you've had a lot to drink."

"I'm good." She heard his heavy footsteps on the linoleum floor. "I'll see you around."

She pressed her lips together, her body still burning from their kiss. She didn't want him to leave; she wanted him to stay, to make love to her. Even though she'd burn in Insurgents Hell for it, she wanted Jerry more than anything else at that moment.

He opened the door, the hallway light flooding in. She slowly turned around and walked to him. Grasping his jacket, she said softly, "Don't leave."

He groaned. "Baby, we're playing with fire. If your dad finds out what I've been doing to his little girl, fuck, he'll have my head. I know the rules. I don't want to cause problems for you, and I can't disrespect my president."

"Don't you want to stay?"

"Yeah, I fucking wanna stay, but what we want and what we should do are two different things." He rubbed his hands on his jeans.

"We're not in Pinewood Springs, and no one's going to find out. Tonight, it's just you and me. We're both adults and—"

"You better be damn sure you know what you're telling me, because if I go back in the room with you, there's no way in hell I'm stopping." He stared at her, his gaze heated.

"I know exactly what I'm saying. I want this, and I'm pretty sure you do too." Kylie lowered her gaze. "Don't you?"

"Fuck, babe, I've wanted this for a long time."

A warm glow flowed through her. "I want you."

He ran his fingers through his hair, his eyes on her face. Tugging her to him, Jerry pressed her close and guided her back into the room.

Chapter Ten

THE MUSIC WAS still playing and a soft breeze from the open window fluttered around them, making Kylie shiver despite the heat raging inside her. Jerry dipped his head, his tongue tracing the outlines of her full lips. She clasped her hand behind his neck, urging his mouth on hers. Slowly, he kissed her, threading his fingers through her hair. His kiss intensified and she responded with the same passion.

Breaking away, he brought his hand up and stroked her cheek with the back of his fingers. "You're so beautiful," he murmured as his eyes bored into hers. He trailed his hand down her cheek, skimming over the soft skin on her neck and shoulder until it landed on her breast. He cupped the underside of it, squeezing it gently. "I like that. You like the way it feels?"

Like it? She fucking *loved* it. Her nipples were hard as marbles just from his touch. Sucking in her breath, she nodded and looked away.

"Babe, I want you to look at me. I want to see the desire in your gaze. You have the prettiest eyes I've ever seen." He leaned in and kissed her eyelids, her nose, then her lips, all the while holding her breast. Dampness formed between her legs and she squirmed, her gaze moving upward until it locked with his.

Callused fingertips traced the neckline of her top, teasing her as they slipped inside, then moved out. The anticipation of those wicked fingers flicking her nipples drove Kylie wild, and when they slipped down under her neckline for the fourth time, she placed her hand over them, stopping them in their tracks.

"Are your nipples aching?" He smiled devilishly.

She moaned and pushed his hand further down her top until it hit her bra. In two small movements, Jerry pulled and tweaked her nipples, sending a wave of pure pleasure straight to her wet sex. It was exquisite. Nothing like the too-hard pinches the high school boys were famous for. Since she'd been at the university, she'd had a few dates, and the guys who'd groped her while they made out squeezed her breasts like they were sponges. But not Jerry; his touch ignited a fire in her like nothing she'd ever experienced. It was demanding but gentle, and the way he awakened her passion blew her mind.

Wrapping his arms around her, he pushed Kylie until the backs of her legs hit the mattress then eased her down. He kicked off his boots, threw his jacket on the desk chair, and moved on the bed, her legs between his knees. "I want to see your tits." The slide of his skin against hers as he pulled her crop top over her head made her tremble. He reached behind her and unclasped the hooks on her bra, then glided his hands down her shoulders, his thumbs hooking under the straps. Reclining back on his heels, she heard him suck in his breath and saw his dark gaze devour her exposed breasts. Cupping them, he raised them up and pushed them together.

"Delicious tits. Fuck," he rasped, then lowered his head until his mouth covered her nipple.

Her body jolted as he tugged her nipple with his teeth, the surge of pure lust hitting her right between her legs. "That feels real good," she murmured, her hand tangled in his hair. Each time he flicked, sucked, and bit her reddened buds, she pulled harder on his hair and bucked her hips against him.

Jerry ran his hand down to her silken belly and pulled at the zipper on the back of her skirt. "Take it off," he growled.

Kylie sat up and he pressed her to him as she unzipped her skirt, lifting her butt off the bed while she shimmied out of it. He pushed her back down, but she resisted and slid her hands under his T-shirt, bunching it up as she pulled it off him. She caught her breath at the sight of his sculpted, inked chest. With her fingernail, she traced the dark lines around his colorful tattoos, marveling at how flat and toned his belly was. "God, you're built."

He chuckled and pulled her head back by her hair. He gave her a searing kiss, leaving her breathless before he eased her onto her back again. Peppering kisses over her neck, he trailed his tongue down to her breasts and laved attention on them until she was a quivering mess.

"I love playing with your tits." His hand inched lower until it landed on her thong, and he glided his fingers under the fabric, burying them in her folds. "Fuck, you're soaking wet, and it's all for me. Love that, babe." Jerry stippled her inner thighs with hot kisses as his finger stroked the side of her nub.

Before she could enjoy it, a spasm deep in her pussy quaked and pleasure ripped through her, erupting across every nerve and muscle in her quivering body. Her thighs held his arm like a vise as she panted, waiting for her pulsing body to calm down. He gently pushed her legs apart and kissed her belly. "You must've needed it bad, baby." His chuckle vibrated against her skin. Pushing off the bed, he unzipped and peeled off his jeans and boxers.

Apprehension weaved through her when she saw his hard dick. How would he ever fit *that* inside her? It was huge. She gulped and noticed he'd taken a condom from the back pocket of his jeans. For a fleeting minute, she wondered if he'd planned on seducing her, or if he always carried a condom in case he spotted someone he wanted to fuck.

The bed bounced a bit as he climbed back on. Tearing open the package, he rolled the sheath over his dick. "I can't wait anymore, babe. I gotta be inside you."

He hovered over her and kissed her deeply, the tip of his cock rubbing against her slit. "Do you like it hard and rough?"

Cringing, she avoided his gaze. Could she fake being experienced? His dick was so big she was afraid he'd hurt her.

"Hard and rough it is."

With trembling hands, she pushed against his chest. "I've never done this before," she said in a barely audible voice.

His eyes widened. "You're a virgin? Well, I'll be damned."

"I want to do it, but I'm scared it'll hurt."

Jerry blew out a long breath, the warmth of it fanning over her face. "It may hurt a bit, but I'll go slow and stretch you. You gotta relax." He pushed the tip of his cock into her wet slit and placed his hands behind her thighs, bringing her legs closer to her body. "The good thing is you've already come, so you'll be nice and wet. It helps. Just relax, it'll make it easier for you."

Jerry pushed his dick in a little more, and Kylie felt herself stretching to accommodate him. "You doing good?" he asked. She nodded and he bent down, kissing her as he pushed deeper. When he was more than halfway in, she moved her hips, pivoting toward him. He gritted his teeth, sweat forming on his hairline.

"What is it? Am I doing something wrong?"

"You're doing something right. Fuck, babe. Don't move or I'm gonna lose it."

"It feels good when I move," she whispered, arching her back slightly.

Shaking his head, Jerry surged in, and she cried out as a stab of pain seared through her. He lay on top of her, inside her, until it subsided. She ran her fingernails over the back of his shoulders. "You can move now, if you want to," she said.

"You sure?" He kissed her when she nodded then pushed in and out, his hips moving in quick jerks. "Tell me if I'm hurting you." After several thrusts, he buried his face in her neck and slammed his cock inside her with such power that it took her breath away. He grunted and collapsed on top of her. For several minutes, they lay together—Jerry spread over her, Kylie with her legs open, holding him close.

Finally, he rolled off and hopped out of bed. "I'll be right back," he said as he went into the bathroom. She sat up and scooted over, grimacing as she saw spots of blood on the bedding. Embarrassment washed over her and she jumped up, hoping she could change the sheets before he came back. As she began to strip the bedding, he came behind her and wrapped his arms around her waist, flattening her back against him. "You look sexy, jiggling in all the right places." He nuzzled her neck.

"I just wanted to change the sheets." She craned her neck to him and kissed him on the chin.

"I brought you a warm washcloth. It'll help the soreness."

She blushed. "Thanks."

After they changed the sheets and Kylie washed up, Jerry drew her to him, tucking her under his arm. "You amaze me, babe." He kissed the side of her head.

Tracing circles on his chest with her index finger, she asked, "Did I do all right?"

"Oh, yeah." He tightened his hold on her. "You did awesome." He tipped her chin up, his gaze capturing hers. "Did you like it?"

She nodded.

"I'm sorry for going so hard at the end. The way you were moving made me fucking lose it."

"I liked it, and it didn't hurt so much." Happiness skated through her. *She* had made him lose control. *Yes!*

He kissed her again then closed his eyes, his breathing growing heavy. She knew he'd be asleep soon, but she couldn't begin to sleep. Her whole body was a circuit of live wires, and she replayed everything he'd done and said to her since he'd first knocked on her door earlier in the day. She was no longer a virgin, and she was thrilled beyond words that Jerry had been her first. Kylie felt like a bursting star, showering glitter on the world.

Best night ever!

Chapter Eleven

JERRY STARED AT the ceiling tiles, the water from the shower sounding like a rainstorm. He hadn't heard Kylie wake up. For the first time in a long time, he'd slept deeply through the night. *I can't believe I fucked Kylie. I can't believe how damn awesome it was.* How could he have been so weak? He should've kept walking down the hall, but he had to be inside her. She was so sweet, sexy, and soft; how the fuck could he resist her? It would've been too much for any man. And she'd been a virgin. Jerry groaned aloud. He never figured she'd be a virgin. It kicked ass that he was her first, but it made everything more complicated.

I fucked Banger's virginal daughter. Shit! He had to get away, chalk it up to being drunk and being too stupid to live. Kylie would understand. She was probably regretting it just as much as he was. It was best to get his ass on his Harley, head back to Pinewood Springs, put all this behind him. They'd both been drinking and things had gone too far. *Who the fuck are you kidding? You came to see her with fucking on your mind. You knew exactly what you were doing.* But a virgin? *Shit!*

He rose in one fluid motion and picked up his boxers and jeans from the floor. Finished zipping his pants, he searched for his T-shirt, finding it crumpled under the sheets and blanket of the twin bed he'd shared with Kylie. She was so fantastic, her body soft in all the right places. She'd been so ripe and he had been so turned on that he hadn't even had the chance to taste her pussy, but he'd get around to that another time.

Wait, what the fuck am I thinking?

There could never be another time. This was an isolated mistake. But damn, it was one of the most exciting and fun mistakes he'd ever made too. *Fuck, man. Get a grip.*

As he pulled his shirt over his head, the bathroom door opened and steam hit him like a wave. The intoxicating scent of lavender and patchouli teased his nostrils, and he gritted his teeth. Kylie's warm arms wrapped around his waist as her soft lips kissed the nape of his neck. He tilted his head back and the scent of her hair—fresh and clean—woke up his dick. He spun around and pressed her close to him, loving the way she felt in his arms. She only wore a pale blue towel around her, and his jeans were so damned tight he thought his zipper would burst open. Standing on her tiptoes, she pulled his face toward hers and kissed him softly on the lips, her fingertips skating over the aching bulge in his jeans. Without hesitation, he responded, taking hungry possession. His tongue pillaged the sweetness of her willing mouth.

The only thought reeling through his mind was how wonderful it was to finally hold and kiss Kylie—the woman who'd given him a hard-on for the past three years. He'd never felt such an explosion of emotion with any other woman. Overcome with need, he tore away her towel and ran his hands all over her nakedness. Pushing her down on the bed, he stripped off the clothes he'd just put on after making the resolution to leave and never touch her again. Like a starving man, Jerry feasted on her lips, neck, shoulder, and tits, knowing he could never have his fill of her. He wanted to taste her everywhere, but his desire was too much, so he slipped on a condom, stroked her clit—her wetness coating his fingers—and sank into her, trying desperately to go slow. Her cry that time was from pleasure, and he moved at a calculated pace in and out as he bent down and plundered her mouth. With soft, rhythmic movements, he stroked the side of her hardened nub, and when he swallowed her gasps, he felt her heated wetness clamp around his cock as she climaxed, bucking and panting beneath him. Unable to hold on any longer, his legs tightened and his balls shrank as the pressure released through his dick, his hot seed spilling into the condom.

Burying his face in her neck, he nipped it, loving the softness and the intoxicating scent that was Kylie. He kissed her lips again and chuckled when he saw her large smile, flushed cheeks, and sparkling eyes. She looked the way he felt, and he hugged her close before he rolled onto his side and scooped her to him. "You're so fucking beautiful. Damn, Kylie. You're killing me."

She giggled. "Is that a bad thing?"

Jerry sighed. "Not for me, but it could be for others."

"Like my dad?"

He nodded.

"Then we'll have to keep it a secret until the time is right. My dad will come around, you'll see." She slid her hand over the stubble on his face. "I like the way your face feels."

He smiled and caught her fingers in his mouth, nibbling them. Unlike Kylie, he didn't share in her optimism that Banger would accept him fucking his daughter. Jerry wasn't a fool, but he also couldn't keep his hands off her. He should've left before she'd come out of the shower, but he didn't and they were naked in bed again. Staying for the weekend couldn't hurt, and he didn't like Kylie being all alone in her dorm, especially since a lot of the students had left. He knew Banger wouldn't want her by herself under the circumstances. *Yeah, that's a good way to rationalize what you're doing to Kylie. Fuck, I almost believe my own B.S.*

"I love being with you. I knew making love would be good, but I didn't think it'd be *this* good." She kissed his smiling skull tattoo on his bicep. "I'm glad you came to visit me."

He squeezed her. "I am too."

She paused. "Are you staying for the weekend?"

I should get my ass on my bike and get the hell outta here. I know that's the best thing I can do for her, and for Banger. He's the goddamned president of my brotherhood. I owe him my loyalty. "Yeah, if you want me to."

Her head bobbed up and down. "I'm so happy."

And I'm so fuckin' screwed. "Let's go for a ride. There're some cool backroads around here. You ever explore them?"

"No. I've wanted to, but they're not so easy to do with a car. You really want me to ride bitch on your bike?"

"Yeah."

"You never let women ride bitch."

"I don't, but I want you to." He raised himself onto one elbow and trailed his finger down her arm, smiling when goose bumps popped up. "I gotta wash up. We'll head out in half an hour." He dipped his head and kissed her, then pushed up from the bed, gathered his clothes, and padded to the bathroom. Kylie lay on the bed naked, the sunlight streaming in from the window casting a peachy glow on her skin. She was gorgeous. His dick twitched as he closed the door.

THEY SPENT THE day laughing, talking, and kissing more than Jerry had ever kissed any woman in a twenty-four-hour period. Everything was perfect, and he decided to let go of his guilt and enjoy the time he had with Kylie because once he returned to Pinewood Springs, he'd have to forget about her. He'd have to fuck her out of his system with the whores and hoodrats. But for the time being, he was having the best time he'd ever had with a woman.

Women to Jerry were there for fucking, giving pleasure to the brothers when they needed it. The concept of having anything with a woman outside sex never occurred to him. Even when he'd made the decision to come to Crested Peak to see Kylie, fucking was the goal. He thought he'd bang her a few times and be back at the club in time for a rowdy Saturday night party. It never entered his mind that he'd have a good time with her beyond screwing. So the fact that he was enjoying her company enormously shocked and scared the shit out of him at the same time.

The Banger problem was always present when it came to her, but the truth was he didn't want a relationship with any woman, including Kylie. He liked the freedom of fucking different women, and he didn't want a woman around trying to change him. Women were like that; they acted like they were cool with the way a man was, but then, when the guy got hooked, they'd try and change him. He wasn't down for that. He also hated women who nagged, and it seemed like all women took that route at some point in a relationship. No, he wanted to stay a free agent without any attachments. And having a good time with Kylie disturbed the hell out of him.

"What are you thinking about? You have such a serious look on your face." She looped her arms over her bent knee as they sat on the blanket she'd brought. They'd turned off the backroad an hour earlier, stretching out the blanket on the ground to rest before they headed back to Crested Peak.

"Nothing much. Just drifting a bit. I like it here. It's different sitting here without being in the mountains. I mean, they're nice in the distance like this, but I'm used to being *in* them, you know?"

"I do. When I first got here, it was so weird not being surrounded by the mountains. You get used to it. I'm so glad my room faces west, so I can see them every day." She pulled out a few blades of grass and put them between her teeth, chewing lightly.

"You like it here, huh?"

"I love being at the university. I also love being on my own. I'm so glad my dad let me come here. I was afraid I was never going to leave Pinewood Springs or live on my own." Her laugh fell on his ears like the tinkle of wind chimes on a summer day.

"It's good to be on your own. You have to learn how to survive, 'cause you never know what shit the universe is gonna throw your way."

She smiled. "You're too somber. Are you ticklish?"

He frowned. "Nah."

"Sure?" She inched closer to him, moving her fingers, a sly grin on her face. Reaching out, she dug her fingers into his sides, tickling him.

"Is that how you want it?" He pretended to be perturbed then grabbed her and tickled her stomach and sides, triggering a bout of laughter as she tried to wriggle away from his grasp. She collapsed on the ground, her eyes watery, knees bent. Then he smothered her laughs with his mouth, running his hands over her full breasts. He unzipped his jeans and placed her hand on his throbbing dick. "Hold it hard," he murmured against her lips.

Kylie curled her fingers around his hardness tentatively then squeezed it gently. "I like it hard, baby," he whispered in her ear.

"Won't it hurt?"

He chuckled and hugged her. "Nah. You ever touch a cock?"

"In high school a few times. Having a dad who is president of an outlaw MC doesn't get a girl many dates, you know?"

"What about in college?"

"No. I haven't been that interested in anyone here."

He was panting, his dick aching for relief. "Have you ever given a blowjob?"

"A few times."

"Wrap your lips around my cock."

"I don't know if I'll do it right."

"I'll tell you what I need. Right now, I need my cock in your mouth."

Kylie opened her mouth and he put his dick inside, and she closed her lips around it. He held her head between his hands and told her to grab the base of his hardness real tight while she moved her mouth and tongue up and down. With his instructions and her willingness to comply, he came hard in her mouth. When she swallowed his seed, a weird sensation ran through him but he quickly pushed it down, not liking where it was taking him.

Stuffing his dick back into his jeans, he watched her as she discreetly took out a tissue and wiped her mouth. "That was great, babe."

She shook her head. "I don't think I did it right. I've only done it a few times."

"The way I feel and the shit you just swallowed tells you that you did great." Red streaked her cheeks, and he thought she looked too cute. "Next time, it'll be better. I like that you aren't a pro at it." *Why am I talking about 'next time?' I gotta end this, but she's too—fuck! No buts. I gotta finish this.* "You wanna eat something?"

"Yes. I'm starving."

"Let's get back to town. You pick the restaurant."

Kylie picked up the blanket and folded it neatly then placed it in his saddle bag. Hopping on behind him, she wrapped her arms tight around his waist, her head against his shoulder. He'd never had a woman on his bike, but Kylie was the exception. She'd always be the exception for everything in his life. Turning the bike around, they took off toward Crested Peak.

At the Grizzly Saloon, Jerry watched as she scarfed down the rest of the fries they'd ordered. She was more animated than usual, and a small pang of guilt pricked him. *He* was responsible for her laughter and sparkling eyes, and he'd also be the one to turn her laughs to sobs and her sparkle to tears. He never denied he was a bastard, but he was sorry he had to hurt her.

"Am I talking too much?"

He shook his head. He liked hearing her voice, the way she grew excited when she told him about the things she did at school with her friends. For being raised by a hardcore outlaw biker, Jerry was surprised how sweet and innocent Kylie was. She wasn't even rough around the edges. He never knew her mom, Grace, but he supposed it must have been due to her influence and the fact that Banger went out of his way to shield her from the darkness of the MC outlaw world.

Kylie stopped talking in mid-sentence, her eyes narrowing as she stared over his shoulder. He looked behind him and saw a guy of medium height, brown hair down to his neck, and very intense eyes approaching their table. "Who's that?" he asked.

Before she could reply, the man was at their table. Jerry thought the guy seemed nervous, with all his fidgeting—hands at his side, hands on the table, hands back at his side. It was annoying the hell out of Jerry.

"Kylie." It was a statement. The man glanced at Jerry then back at her.

"Hey, Marcus. You didn't go away for the long weekend?"

"No. I thought for sure you were gone. You're so popular."

The way he was checking out Kylie was pissing Jerry way off. *If he doesn't move his eyes from her tits, I'm gonna smash his face in.* He clenched his fists in anticipation.

"I had too much to do. You ready for finals?"

"You look pretty. You always look pretty." Marcus licked his lips, blinking rapidly.

The fucker has a death wish. "Who the fuck are you?" Jerry sat up straighter in his chair.

The guy turned his head and looked Jerry in the eyes. "A friend of Kylie's. Who are you?" He hissed out the last question, and Jerry began to rise from the table.

"Jerry, this is Marcus. I should've introduced you. We're in the same political science class. Jerry's my real good friend." Pink flushed up her neck, making Jerry smile.

His smile turned to a sneer when he addressed Marcus. "She's with me, and I don't like guys coming up to the table chatting with her and checking her out. You get my drift?"

Marcus narrowed his eyes and a hard edge tinged his voice. "I don't like guys who have more muscle than brains telling me who I can talk to. You get *my* drift?"

For a split second, shock punched Jerry in the gut. *The guy* does *have a death wish.* Noticing Kylie's tight face, he reacted before she could say anything to him. With one punch, Marcus went down with a thump and a loud groan, blood spilling from his mouth.

"What the fuck, Jerry?" Kylie asked in a hushed voice.

A man ran up to their table and looked down at Marcus who was lying flat on the floor. The fellow was in his thirties and wore a tie, so Jerry presumed he had to be the manager.

"What happened here?"

"He tried to grab her tits. I don't go for that shit."

Kylie jumped in. "He was bothering me, and he did accost me. If I were by myself, I would've been terrified." Jerry smiled. She was a biker's daughter; she knew loyalty always lay with the club.

Marcus stumbled to his feet and swayed a bit. "I didn't do anything to her. I know her from school. This asshole got jealous and belted me."

The manager looked between the three of them. "Well, sir, I have this man and woman corroborating each other and you don't have anyone to back up what you're saying." He turned to Kylie. "Do you want to press charges?"

"Press charges? This is ludicrous!" Marcus removed the blood-stained napkin a patron had given him from the corner of his mouth. "I should be the one pressing charges against him." He pointed to Jerry, who stared blankly at him.

"No, I don't want to press charges. I just want to forget the whole thing," Kylie said.

"Okay." The manager looked at Marcus. "Sir, I'm going to have to ask you to leave."

Marcus's face turned dark red and he stared at Kylie. "You'll be sorry for this."

Loud enough for Marcus to hear, Jerry hissed, "Don't fuckin' threaten my girl. You don't want me as an enemy." He saw the guy's eyes dart to the manager, but the man was already assuring patrons that everything was fine and everyone should go back to their tables. Marcus glowered at Jerry then walked toward the exit.

With the excitement over, diners went back to their own lives, and soon everything was as it had been before Jerry had decked Marcus. Looking at Kylie, he smiled broadly.

"I'm so glad you did that. I've been wanting to do it for the last few weeks." She grinned at him and he laughed his ass off, causing a few patrons to glare at him.

"Who was that fucker?"

"Some guy who came up to me at the spring festival. I don't know if you remember him—I barely do—but we were eating when he came up to me. Anyway, it turns out he's in one of my classes, and he's been creeping me out ever since. All he does is stare at me. He came to my room out of the blue, and he seems to always be lurking around. I think he wants to go out with me, but he rubs me the wrong way."

Jerry could see the trepidation in her eyes as she talked about the jerk, and he didn't like it one bit. He had half a mind to finish what he'd started, and he was pretty sure he would before he headed back to Pinewood Springs. No one messed with Kylie.

"I'll make sure he doesn't bother you anymore." He reached over and grasped her hand.

"I don't want you to do anything stupid. I think he got the point."

"I'm not so sure. Leave it to me."

"I'm glad school will be over soon… for a lot of reasons." She stroked the top of Jerry's hand with her thumb.

The flickering candle in the holder cast an amber glow over her face, and she looked stunning. He stared at her lips, the way her front teeth bit into the corner of her lower one. He wanted to lean over and lick and kiss her delicious mouth. It felt good being with her, just eating and talking.

"You're staring at me. What are you thinking about?" she asked.

"That I want to come inside you," he said huskily. He brought her hand to his lips and kissed it tenderly.

"Let's go," she murmured.

He paid the bill, and in less than thirty minutes, he had her pinned against the wall, her tits exposed, her jeans off, and her legs wrapped around him. As he kissed her hard and deep, he played with her breasts, making her nipples into rigid peaks. When his fingers slipped under her panties, she gasped, digging her nails into his shoulder. Since she was new to fucking, she wasn't very adept at screwing against the wall, so he carried her over to the bed and hovered over her.

It was still early—the sky had just turned dark, and dancing stars glinted in the sky. In the distance, an owl hooted. The radio played a sultry tune by Barry White, and Jerry kicked off his boots and stripped naked. He loved the feeling of his skin against hers. Hours stretched before them, and he vowed she'd be purring and exhausted before the sun rose.

Chapter Twelve

Jerry looked at his phone as it vibrated and he stiffened, the muscles in his jaw twitching. He brought the phone to his ear. "What do you want?" he asked sharply.

"I just called to see how you've been. I haven't seen you in a while. I've missed you," a shaky voice said.

"How much money do you want, Wanda?" He rubbed his brow.

"Why do you think I want money? Can't your mother call you to see how you're doing?"

"Yeah, she could if she was normal, but you're not. Tell me how much you want or I'm hanging up."

Her breath crackled over the phone. "Five hundred bucks."

"Fuck. What did you do with the thousand I gave you a few weeks ago?"

She coughed fitfully, then rasped, "I got bills to pay. Your sister's an expensive one. Anyway, five hundred is nothing to you."

He narrowed his eyes. He should tell this sorry excuse for a mother to fuck off, but he knew he wouldn't. "I'll be over in an hour."

"Can you come over later? I got to go over to Vicky's. She's having man trouble and wants my help."

He laughed dryly. "That's a joke. I'll be there in an hour or I won't come. You choose."

Another wheezing cough. "You're a hard one." He heard her inhale—either weed or cigarettes.

"I learned from the best. One hour." He broke the connection. Clouds of dust rose up from the dirt as he kicked the ground. He didn't know why he bothered with Wanda. She hadn't given a damn about him, his brother, or his sister since the day they were born.

Pete was the oldest of the three. At twenty-seven, he was two years older than Jerry. He'd graduated from college and lived in Anaheim Hills in California. He was married, had a two-year-old son, and he wanted nothing to do with Wanda, Jerry, or their half-sister, Kelsey. Jerry was fine with that because he didn't really know his brother, and what he did know he wasn't eager about. His brother worked for the corporate world, and Jerry had no use for his high-paying job, overpriced house, or conventional life.

Wanda had been a meth addict who'd used before, during, and after her pregnancies. The state came into the home after his little sister had been walking around the neighborhood barefooted and dressed in a bathing suit in thirty-two-degree weather, and several neighbors called the police. When the cops had knocked on the door, his strung-out mother had refused to open it. Jerry had waded through trash on the floor to answer it. The wave of putrid stench assaulted the officers, and they'd pushed their way into the abode.

Jerry remembered reading the report where the badges described the living conditions as being the worst they'd seen. The only thing in the refrigerator had been a gallon of spoiled milk and cans of beer. Jerry and his siblings had eye infections so bad they had oozed yellow discharge. Of course, all three had been promptly removed from the house.

They were separated and placed in foster care. Pete lucked out and had a good family who actually wanted to try and help the traumatized young boy. Jerry had ended up with three different families over the course of nine years. Each one was greedier than the next, until the last family let him do whatever the hell he wanted as long as they received their check. They were the best because they didn't pretend to give a shit.

He rounded the corner into the Cedars Trailer Park on the northwest side of town. It was a rundown rat hole, and a favorite for dealers cooking up meth. The perfect place for his mother to wallow in her addiction.

When Wanda had first reached out to him, he hadn't wanted anything to do with her. But when he'd been reunited with his sister, he'd softened a bit and decided that he shared the same blood as Wanda, so he'd give this family shit a try. Deep down, he felt sorry for the used-up woman who'd sired him. She'd been abused by men her whole life, and she never had anyone in her court before. He hated what she was, but he felt sympathy for who she could have been.

Kelsey had moved back with their mother a couple years before. She'd be graduating high school, if she ever bothered to attend. She'd been removed from her last foster home because she'd accused the foster dad of messing with her. As far as Jerry knew, nothing came out of it, and she'd been placed back with their mom. At the time, their mom had stopped using, but Jerry suspected she'd been lured back to the drug.

He kicked a rusted wash basin off the step, then opened the torn screen door and walked into the trailer.

"There's my boy." Wanda sat on a ripped recliner. She was skinny as a rail and oxygen ran from her nose to the tank behind her chair. "Clear those papers off the couch and have a seat. I haven't had the strength to clean, and that lazy-ass sister of yours is always whoring around instead of helping me out." She wheezed and broke into a coughing fit. Jerry watched her as she wiped the spittle from her lips. "What have you been up to?"

"Nothing." He walked over and dropped seven one-hundred-dollar bills in her lap. "I gave you extra to buy groceries. I shoulda bought them, though. I'm pretty damned sure you're gonna use the money for crank."

"I told you, I stopped using. I'm clean." She smoothed out her floral housecoat.

"Bullshit. All the sores on your pasty face tell me otherwise." He shook his head, glancing at the dirty dishes piled in the sink. Wanda was definitely using again. "Why did you let Josie go? I paid her to come and clean this place once a week. She told me you fired her. What the fuck?"

"She was taking your money and not doing shit. She was stealing from me too."

"Josie wasn't stealing from you. Your addiction's got you all messed up in the head. Anyway, she refuses to come back. She told me you were always yelling at her and calling her a slut."

"Well, isn't she? Isn't she one of those who spreads her legs at your biker club?"

"Whatever. Where's Kelsey?"

"Whoring around. She's always at Brian's trailer. She thinks he's the best thing around. I told her nothing good comes outta trusting a man. All the men I've ever had in my life knocked me up and left me with no money. Good-for-nothing motherfuckers." The excitement brought on another coughing fit, and Jerry stood up and walked over to her.

"You want some water?" he asked.

She nodded and he went to the kitchen, cussing as he tried to find a clean glass. He opened the refrigerator to see if there was any bottled water, and saw nothing in it but beer, olives, pickles, and orange juice. He slammed it shut, washed out a glass, and brought the water to his mother. After she took a large gulp, she placed the glass on the tray next to her. He picked up the money from her lap and took out two hundred dollars.

"What the fuck are you doing?" she cackled.

"Buying groceries for you and Kelsey. I'll be back later. I'm also getting someone over here to clean this goddamned pigsty, and if you don't like it, I'll fucking disappear. Not that you'd miss me, but the money goes too."

The screen door groaned when he slammed it, Wanda's curses bouncing off his back. Jerry walked over to one of the nearby trailers when he spotted his sister's Honda Civic. He pounded on the door and a burly man in his late forties opened it, a scowl on his face. "What the fuck do you want?"

Jerry pushed him aside and entered the trailer. It was neat and a breath of fresh air from the dirtiness inside his mom's place. "Where's Kelsey?"

"Who?"

Jerry loomed over Brian, his face inches from the older man's. "I'm in a fuckin' pissed-off mood, so you don't want to mess with me. Get my fuckin' sister now, and I better not find out you've been banging her."

The man moved away from the biker. "Kelsey. Your brother's here."

A girl of eighteen bounced out of one of the rooms, tugging down her tight T-shirt. She wore Daisy Dukes and flip-flops, her brown hair cascading down her back. "Jerry." She ran over and hugged him. "It's good to see you." She leaned closer and whispered in his ear, "Did you bring me any money? Mom never gives me any. She takes everything you give her and uses it just for her."

"What the fuck are you doing here with a guy who's older than Wanda?"

"Talking."

"And playing a video game," the man added.

Jerry turned to him and pointed his finger in his face. "You. Shut the fuck up. Kelsey?"

"I already answered. I like it here because it's clean and Mom's not around hacking her brains out or yelling at me."

"Come on." He grabbed her wrist and yanked her to him, dragging her out of the trailer.

"Stop. Jerry, stop! You're not my fucking father."

He plopped her down in front of Wanda's residence. "Why the hell aren't you in school? If you don't want to go, then get a damn job. I don't like you hanging out with that fucker."

"You mean Brian? He's nice. He buys me stuff and takes me to Burger King and Royal Inn. Have you been there? It's all you can eat for fifteen bucks. Sometimes he takes Mom with us. He's really nice."

He ran his fingers through his hair. "He's too old for you. Have you fucked him?"

From the way she looked down at her feet, he knew she had, and he wanted to beat the shit out of the guy.

"I haven't done anything with him except talk, go to dinner, and play video games. Mom doesn't care. She likes Brian. He gives her money sometimes."

So Wanda was pimping out her daughter. Another great moment in his fucked-up family album. "If you need something to do, clean up the trailer. It's disgusting."

"Why bother? Mom just makes it dirty again. I'm sick of not being appreciated."

In the background, he heard Wanda hacking away, and he suddenly wanted to get as far away from them as he could. *No wonder Pete moved to California. I don't fuckin' blame him.* "I'm outta here. I'll be back later, and your ass better be here to help unload the groceries."

"You gonna give me any money?" she asked in a low voice.

He blew out a long breath. "When I come back. Be here. I'm not joking." He straddled his bike, gripped the throttle clutch, and took off without a backward glance.

When he returned, night had already fallen. He hopped up the wooden stairs and entered Wanda's home. Kelsey was stretched out on the couch watching TV, and Wanda was dozing in her recliner.

"I'm back," he said in a hushed tone.

Kelsey leapt from the couch and followed him out. "Did you bring me any potato chips? You know I like the sour cream and chives."

"I bought them." He grabbed seven bags of food, and she grabbed the rest.

In silence, they put the food away, Kelsey's occasional squeal when she saw something she liked pricking the quiet. After everything was neatly stacked in the fridge and cupboards, Jerry handed her a hundred-dollar bill. She clapped her hands and stuffed it in her bra.

"If you clean the place and keep it neat, I'll pay you eighty bucks a week."

Her eyes widened. "Are you serious? Make it a hundred and you have yourself a deal."

"Eighty bucks. I'm not negotiating." Her eyes rolled up and her lips pressed together like she was trying to figure out how much that would amount to on a regular basis. "It's three hundred and twenty dollars a month."

"Wow. Okay. Deal. When do I start?"

"Tomorrow. The hundred is your first payment. I threw in a twenty-dollar incentive bonus. I'll do that from time to time. And I have no qualms about firing you if you do a shitty job. Remember that." He brushed past her and glanced at Wanda, who was still sleeping. He jerked his head toward her. "Don't tell her about our arrangement."

"I'd never do that. She'd want me to turn all the money over to her."

He opened the screen and stepped back in when he saw a man in his early twenties with platinum spiked hair and tattoos on the side of his face and neck, wearing jeans, black leather jacket, and biker boots. Jerry watched him as he walked to one of the trailers, trying to make out the logo on the back of his jacket. He definitely belonged to an MC, but Jerry couldn't read the name. The guy jumped up the stairs, opened the door, and closed it behind him. Jerry noted the trailer number was 72.

"You know him?"

"Uh-huh."

"How long's he been here? And who's he stayin' with?"

"He's been here for about ten days. He's with a couple of other guys, and they're staying with Randy and Dolores. Randy and his girlfriend keep to themselves a lot. They're not friendly at all."

"Ever notice funny smells coming from their place?"

"Yep. It kinda stinks." Kelsey wrinkled her nose.

"Do the guy's two buddies wear the same type of jacket?"

"Yeah. How'd you know?"

"Ever notice what it says?"

"Something with skulls. There's a big one in the middle and it looks like its head is split open on one side. I don't know. I don't see them often. Why you asking all these questions?"

"Just want to make sure I know who's around here so I can keep you and Wanda safe. Gotta go. Stay in tonight and lock the fucking door."

"Okay. Thanks for the food and money." She waved from the door as he started up his truck. He was glad he didn't have his Harley; the asshole would've spotted it in a second. Jerry was positive the three men staying with Randy and Dolores were from the Skull Crushers MC. *They're back in our territory selling meth. Sonsofbitches.* They were probably selling the homemade crank the couple was cooking up. It was pure luck he spotted the fucker that night.

He bypassed going to his apartment, instead racing to the clubhouse to share the news with the brotherhood.

Chapter Thirteen

Kylie rushed down the hall to her room when she heard her phone ring. Still riding a high from the previous weekend with Jerry, she held her breath as she picked up the phone from her bed, not daring to look at the screen in fear of jinxing herself.

"Hello?"

"Hey, babe." Jerry's deep voice covered her like a warm blanket on a wintry day.

"I was hoping it was you. What're you up to?"

"Same stuff—working, drinking, smoking too much weed." His chuckle danced on her skin. "What about you?"

"Studying and more studying, and even more studying. Ugh, I am *so* ready for the semester to end. You know, I'll be home in three weeks, and we'll have the whole summer together. I can't wait to see you. You excited to see me?"

"Uh… sure. Yeah."

Kylie frowned. "Don't overexcite yourself," she snapped.

A jagged breath pushed through her ears. "You know I fucking want to see you… and be with you. We just gotta be extra careful."

"Way to kill the romance."

"Babe, you know we're both skating on thin ice with this, right?"

She rolled her eyes. "Of course I know. I'm not stupid. I was just excited about seeing you soon, that's all. I didn't want to talk about anything but that." She paused, hoping he'd say something. He didn't. "Whatever. I have to go to the library. I should have been there an hour ago."

"Don't be that way. I really can't wait to see you and spend time together."

"Whatever. I'll talk to you later." After his good-bye, she clicked off the phone, tears springing in her eyes. She knew she was overreacting, but she wanted him to tell her that he couldn't wait until she came, and they'd have the whole summer to make passionate love, ride the backroads, and lie on the ground, staring up at the twinkling stars, their hands clasped together. She didn't want to hear the hesitancy in his voice, the warning about being careful, and all the other shit he left unspoken.

"You going to the library?" Taylor walked into the room, interrupting Kylie's musings.

"Yeah. You planning on going?"

"Fuck no. I've lived in that damn place for the past five days. I'm beat. Tonight, it's junk food and a juicy reality TV show." She took her lollipop out of her mouth, her purple tongue licking her lips. "Want a sucker? They got a whole mess of these at the front desk downstairs. I picked up a handful."

Kylie shook her head then flopped onto the bed with a long sigh.

"Trouble with your hot guy?" Taylor sat on the desk chair and scooted closer to Kylie's bed.

"No. Yes. I don't know. He was so different when we were together over the weekend, but now that he's back home, he acts reserved and hesitant. It pisses me off, that's all."

"Didn't you say your dad would go ballistic if he knew you were having an affair with Jerry? And he is in your dad's club. I mean, when he was with you last weekend, it was like he was on vacation. No club. No pissed-off dad. Just the two of you."

"I get that, I really do, but does he have to remind me every time that we need to be careful, or what the consequences are if we get caught? I want him to tell me he'll fight for me, no matter what."

Taylor nodded. "I'd want that too. Maybe he's not ready for that, though."

"As the time passes, I'm starting to think he just wants some fun for a while, and there's no reason to get on my dad's bad side if what we have is going to fizzle." Her voice hitched.

Taylor looked at her, softness lacing her eyes. "Guys are like that. They think with their dicks, and we think with our hearts. Do you love him?"

"No," she replied quickly. "I'm all in for the fun too. I don't know. I guess I'm worn out with all the studying and stress of the upcoming finals. And my period is starting. I always get so sensitive during that time of the month. It's fine with Jerry. No biggie at all." She pushed herself up and slung her backpack over her shoulder. "I better get going. It's going to be a long night."

Crunching on the bits of sucker in her mouth, Taylor grasped and squeezed Kylie's hands. "It's going to be okay. I could tell by the way he looked at you at the spring festival that he's crazy about you."

"Thanks," she said with a half-smile. She shuffled out of the room and made her way to the library.

A few hours later, Kylie walked out into the fresh twilight air, inhaling deeply the scents of spring. Along the tree trunks and brick borders, daffodils and multi-colored petunias added punches of color to the college's landscape. As she headed back to her dorm, she heard a male voice call out her name. She paused and turned toward it, a warm smile spreading across her face as she saw Ricky coming toward her. "Hey."

"I'm glad you heard me," he breathed between gulps of air.

"Did you run over here?"

"Yes. I saw you when you walked down the stairs. I was at the science building. I'd know your walk anywhere." His eyes shifted down to her hips encased in her tight jeans.

Uncomfortable, she pulled her backpack closer to her side. "How's studying going for you?"

"Terrible, except for my math and science classes. I know I blew the English paper I had to do in Jansen's class." He shrugged. "Want to grab a sandwich at University Café? I'm paying."

"Sure, but I can only stay for an hour because I have to finish my paper for English Lit."

Taking a shortcut, they crossed through the thicket of pine trees and, in no time, opened the glass doors of the college eatery. Even though she and Ricky knew the menu by heart, they stood reading it, their arms crossed over their chests. "What do you want?" he asked as he approached the counter.

"A grilled cheese with extra tomatoes and pickles."

"You want to share a basket of fries?"

"Sure. I also want an iced tea with lemon. I'll grab us a table." She spotted a corner table for four near the window and dropped her backpack on one of the extra chairs. Several minutes later, Ricky came over holding a tray of food. She helped unload the tray, placing several napkins in front of him.

As they ate, he said, "I found out some information on that Marcus dude." Kylie leaned forward, her eyes wide. "He's from your town, Pinewood Springs."

She sat back. "No. Really? *He's* from Pinewood? I wonder where he went to high school."

"Registrar records show he was homeschooled."

"Oh. Maybe he found out I'm from there, and that's why he's been in my face."

"Maybe. He's definitely weird."

"Damn, I never knew he existed until the past few weeks." She took a bite of her French fry. "You're right—he's an odd one. I bumped into him over the weekend at the Grizzly Saloon. He came up to the table and just stared at me. It sorta creeped me out."

"Were you alone?"

Kylie took a gulp of iced tea. "No. My friend Jerry was there."

"Jerry? Who's that?"

"A friend from home. I love the grilled cheese sandwiches here. They always toast the bread just right."

"Is that the biker dude who hung out with you at the spring festival?"

"Um… yeah. I'm eating all the fries. Don't you want any?"

"Did he spend the weekend with you?"

"We hung out, yeah. I'm serious about finishing up the fries. Last chance." Kylie wished he'd stop asking her questions about Jerry. She didn't want to tell him that she had the best weekend of her life. That her years of dreaming about him didn't compare to being with him. That she gave herself up to the man she'd been holding out for. That was for her girlfriends to know, not Ricky. And she hated the way each of her answers made his shoulders drop a little more.

"Are you dating him?"

Dating? No, she didn't think Jerry thought of her as his girlfriend. That thought made her eyes sting. "No."

He slumped back on his chair, a relieved grin cracking his face. "I'll order another basket of fries." He rose from the table and headed to the counter.

Kylie looked out the window, staring at the headlights of the cars as they turned into the parking lot close to the café. Her phone pinged.

Jerry: *I fuckin' think about u all the time.*

Her insides danced, and a burst of joy coursed her body.

Kylie: *Is that a bad thing?*

Jerry: *Guess it depends on who u ask.*

Kylie: *I'm asking u.*

Jerry: *It's a good thing. Wish u were here now.*

Kylie: *Me 2.*

Ricky placed the basket of fries in the middle of the table. "I got some more ketchup." He plunked down the bottle. She looked up and smiled, grabbing a fry.

Jerry: *U being good?*

Kylie: *Define good.*

"That should get him going," she muttered under her breath.

"What?" Ricky asked.

"Nothing." She shoved the basket closer to him. "I *cannot* eat all of these. I already killed the first basket. Keep them next to you."

He laughed. "Who're you texting?"

"A friend. We should plan on a day to go over our in-class presentation for the psych project."

Jerry: *Not fucking anyone but me. Not hanging out with asshole prick or any other fucker. Only thinking about me.*

Kylie: *Check on the first. Having fries with Ricky. And a HUGE check on the third. 2 out of 3 isn't bad.*

Jerry: *Fries and what else?*

Kylie: *Just fries. Talking about psych class. U being good?*

Jerry: *Thinking about u, so yeah, real good.*

Kylie pressed her lips together. Should she ask him if he was still fucking the club women? Would she sound too possessive?

Jerry: *Gotta go. Church called.*

Kylie: *Say hi to my dad for me.*

She knew that was a low blow, but he deserved it; he purposely didn't bring up that he wasn't with any women. In a perverse way, he wanted her to think everything was okay with him. Maybe it was. She guessed she didn't have any right to tell him not to screw the club women, but then he didn't have any right to tell her which guys she could hang around. Typical biker—no, *male*—double standard. She gritted her teeth.

"You okay? Your friend must've said something that made you mad. You look pissed."

She shook her head. "You about done? I really have to get started on my paper."

He seized the last fry and plopped it in his mouth. "Done." They pushed away from the table and headed back to their dorms.

THE NEXT MORNING, after her psych class, Kylie approached Marcus. His head was bent down as he rummaged through his backpack.

"I didn't know you were from Pinewood Springs," she said, gasping when he jerked his head up and she saw his bruised face. It seemed like there were additional bruises besides the fat lip Jerry had given him the previous Saturday. "What happened to your face?"

His beady eyes narrowed. "As if you didn't know, you bitch."

Taken aback, she took a couple of steps backward. "I don't know what happened. Why would I?"

"Because that fucking goon you were with paid me a visit. Don't tell me you didn't know. I wouldn't believe anything you told me. You've turned out to be like all other women." His lip curled, and his cold eyes took her in. "I thought you were different, Kylie. I was wrong." The tone of his voice turned her blood to ice.

"I didn't mean for any of this to happen."

"Well, it did. You lied at the restaurant. You chose him over me." He rose to his feet. "You'll find out I don't forgive easily. You'll find out I can be very cruel when someone disappoints me." He pushed against her so hard that she lost her balance and had to grip the back of the chair to keep from falling down. "I'll see you in Pinewood Springs, very soon," he hissed as he walked away.

She watched him leave, cursing Jerry for not controlling his temper. She'd lived among bikers her whole life—they all wanted to beat their chests and pummel whoever looked at their woman, then come home and expect a good meal and a helluva fucking. Sometimes it was too much. Jerry had made his point when he'd belted Marcus at the restaurant; did he really have to go back for seconds?

She whipped out her phone and found a bench outside her classroom.

Kylie: *Did u have to beat Marcus up? Wasn't 1 time enough?*

Jerry: *Who the hell u talking about?*

Kylie: *The guy at the restaurant. Remember?*

Jerry: *That asshole? So what?*

Kylie: *He looks awful. Really…?*

Jerry: *He better. lol*

Kylie: *He's pissed.*

Jerry: *He threatened u and had an attitude with me after I belted him. No way I'd let that go. He gives u trouble u tell me. I'll take care of it for good.*

Kylie: *U should've told me.*

Jerry: *No reason to. U wearing tight jeans and a sexy top that hugs ur tits?*

She giggled.

Kylie: *Maybe.*

Jerry: *Come on. I need to picture u in something. I got a hard-on just hearing from u.*

Kylie: *U're being a bad boy. I gotta go to class.*

Jerry: *Babe, when u come home, I'll show u just how bad and dirty I can be.*

She read his words several times, each time hitting harder between her legs. She couldn't wait to find out.

Kylie: *Sounds fun.*

Jerry: *It will be. I got a whole lot of nasty things to teach u.*

Kylie swallowed, getting turned on just thinking about his lips on her private parts. She knew he'd wanted to lick and kiss her there, but she'd come so fast each time that he didn't. She didn't want him to know that she was scared about him kissing her sex. Taylor told her she'd never had a boy do that to her, but she read in *Cosmopolitan* that if a guy knew what he was doing, it was mind-blowing. Kylie knew Jerry wanted to do that to her. She clenched her thighs tighter.

Kylie: *Gotta go. Later.*

She clicked off, the power and sexiness of his words making her feel funny and achy, especially between her legs. Jerry was so experienced, and he routinely screwed women who knew how to please a man the way he wanted. She was so inadequate. How could Jerry ever be satisfied with her only when she barely knew what the hell she was doing?

Her phone pinged again. She groaned, but then her face lit up when she saw it was her dad.

Banger: *How're you doing?*

Kylie: *Good. Studying a ton. Glad to hear from u.*

Banger: *I miss you, honey. When you finished for summer?*

Kylie: *Three weeks.*

Banger: *You need me to come up and help with your shit?*

Kylie: *No. I can fit it all in my car.*

Banger: *If you change your mind, let me know.*

Kylie: *Will do. I gotta go to class, Dad. We'll talk soon.*

Banger: *Ok. I love you.*

Kylie: *Me too. Always. :)*

She hurried into the classroom. She should've asked about Belle and her pregnancy, but she didn't want to. Kylie liked Belle enough, but she still wasn't used to her being in her and her dad's lives. Knowing her father wasn't alone anymore did bring an enormous amount of relief to her, and he was happy. She just needed time before she embraced Belle wholly. She liked her stepbrother, Ethan, and Emily, her stepsister, was all right as long as she wasn't drinking and being a pain in the ass. The one thing Kylie was thrilled about was the baby. She'd always wanted a sibling, and she couldn't wait to hold the little baby in her arms.

The professor walked in, and all talking or texting ceased. Kylie put hers in her purse and focused her full attention to the front of the room. Taking out her notebook and pen—she preferred taking notes by hand—she began scribbling as her instructor lectured.

She recalled Jerry's text, and the ensuing, sweet throb between her thighs felt good.

I can't wait to see him. Three weeks can't come fast enough.

Chapter Fourteen

HER LIPS SOUGHT *his, pressing hard against them before she drew his tongue into her mouth. He ran his hands down past her shoulders and came up under her round, soft tits, cupping them. She groaned, crushing against him. He trailed his mouth past her jaw, kissing down her neck and slowly across the top of her chest. Dragging his tongue lightly, his warm breath left goose bumps on her skin and he inhaled deeply, breathing her in. With his thumb and forefinger, he pinched her hard, erect nipples as she squirmed, her hand palming his throbbing dick.*

"I want to suck your big, pulsing cock. I want it down my throat," Kylie whispered as she slowly unzipped his jeans. He sucked in his—

"Where the fuck are you?" Banger's irritated voice broke in on his daydream. Jerry's chair scraped against the floor as he moved it closer to the table. No reason for the brothers to see he was pitching a helluva tent. "I've been asking you the same damn question for the last minute. Fuckin' pay attention." He scowled at Jerry. All thirty pairs of eyes in the room were on him.

"Sorry about that. I was trying to figure out how we can flush the fuckin' Skull Chasers out of their rat hole."

"That's what we been talkin' 'bout. Fuckin' keep up." Banger spread his hands out on the table. "So, Jerry says they're staying at the Cedars Trailer Park. Word on the street is three guys are selling crystal. Now Jerry's confirmed the assholes are in town."

"I couldn't read the fucker's rocker, but from what my sister told me about the way it looks, it's them for sure." While speaking, Jerry stared at Hawk, avoiding Banger's eyes.

"I can find Rodney and see what he knows," Axe said. Rodney was an informant they used from time to time.

"Sounds good. Let me know what you find out as soon as you do. We gotta move fast on this one. The last time they were here, they got wind we were looking for them and they split before we could 'talk' to them. This time, we'll show them what they missed." A hard smile formed on Banger's lips. "No one fuckin' moves in on Insurgents' territory. We'll crush their skulls." He laughed and the brothers joined in.

Jerry joined in as well, but his mind was on Kylie and the way her soft fingers explored his body. She was new to being with a man, and he loved the way she let him guide her on how to please him. When she came home for summer break, he'd block off a whole day to explore her fresh body, taste her pink pussy, and show her what her holes were made for.

He shifted in his seat and watched the brothers shuffling outside the room. He'd been so wrapped up with his thoughts of Kylie he hadn't even heard Banger adjourn church. Breathing deeply for several minutes, he calmed down and waited for his dick to grow limp. Thinking about the blonde sweetheart wasn't helping, so he concentrated on the Skull Crushers and bashing their faces in. That did the trick. He rose from his chair and headed to the great room.

The brothers were milling around, drinking beer and having some fun with the club whores when he entered the room. He saw Rosie sucking Rock's cock, and Wendy was bent over his lap as he fingerfucked her with one hand and played with her tit in another. Jerry's dick twitched—he wished Kylie were there. He walked toward the bar, his eyes glued on Rock and the bitches, and he slammed right into Banger.

"Shit. I'm sorry, man. I wasn't watching where I was going."

"Fuck. Your head's been up your ass all afternoon," Banger said.

Jerry stared at his president. *I'm fuckin' your daughter. Damn. I'm sorry I disrespected you like that.* "I got a lot on my mind. Sorry again." With his head down, he moved quickly away, but he heard Banger tell Hawk that something was going on with him. He had to play it cool. He couldn't let the man ever know that he'd had his daughter.

He watched as Banger and Hawk took off, then he let out a breath and ordered a beer and two shots of Jack, his gaze fixed on the wall behind the bar. After he'd come back from his weekend with Kylie, he'd made a half-hearted vow to himself to leave her alone, but he knew he couldn't. He was hooked, and he craved the time they'd be together again. *You really got yourself into a fuckin' mess.*

"Where did you go last weekend?" Axe asked as he slipped onto the barstool next to Jerry, motioning to Puck for a beer.

Chas and Jax joined the duo. "What's up with you? Baylee still keeping you in line?" Chas asked, chuckling.

Axe's jaw clenched. "No woman keeps me in line."

Jax slapped his hand on his buddy's shoulder. "Yeah, right."

"Women have a knack of getting what they want from us, but letting us think it was our idea and we're in charge. Fuck, Addie does that to me a lot. I can't figure out how she does it." Chas took a pull on his beer.

Axe laughed. "Baylee too. Fuck, we're screwed." He turned back to Jerry. "You got someone?"

Jerry choked on his beer. "What the fuck?"

"Where were you last weekend?"

"Here. I was busy with one of my inventions, and I had shit to do for Wanda."

"Really?" Axe cocked up one eyebrow.

Jax grinned. "You know something. I'm gonna guess everything Jerry just said was a crock of shit. Am I right?"

Jerry scowled while Chas and Jax guffawed. "You're fuckin' right, man," Chas said.

"So, you weren't in Crested Peak?" Axe said as he brought the beer bottle to his lips.

Jerry froze. *How the fuck does he know?* He didn't look at his brothers, just continued drinking and staring at the back wall.

"You pleading the Fifth, dude?" Axe nudged him in his side. "I don't give a shit where you were. I just want to know who the blonde was you were with. A charter brother in Crested Peak told me he was at a Mexican restaurant on Friday night, and you were with a knockout with a great rack."

Jerry turned and stared at him icily.

Jax pretended to look somber, but the corners of his mouth kept twitching upward. "Looks like you've been found out. Time for you to confess. Who's the woman, and why are you keeping her hidden?"

"She must fuck real good if you're willing to drive four hours for it when you got it only a few steps away here. You didn't even drop by the charter club. Did you fuck her all weekend?" Axe asked, his eyes twinkling.

"Hey, guys, isn't that where Kylie goes to college?" Chas smirked.

Jerry cracked his neck from side to side then slammed his beer bottle down on the bar, the sound making a few brothers look his way. "Fuck off. Do I have to report everything I do to you? Stay outta my personal life." He shoved Chas aside and began to leave when Jax and Axe grabbed him and pulled him back.

No longer joking, Chas said in a hushed tone, "Are you fuckin' crazy? Kylie?"

"You're fooling around with Banger's daughter? Do you have a goddamned death wish?" Jax chimed in.

Jerry jerked out of their grasp and scrubbed his face with his fist. "Kylie and I are the only ones who know. And now you guys, but I can trust you."

Axe whistled low and shook his head. "Bro, you're a fuckin' dumbass if you think this shit you're doing with Kylie is gonna stay in Crested Peak. And thinking Banger's not gonna find out? Well, that's just stupid."

"You need to cut if off now before anyone gets hurt. Think with your brains, not your dick. Fuck Lola, she's got blonde hair. Damn, you owe respect to your president." Chas stared hard at him while the other two nodded in agreement.

Jerry nodded. He knew they were right, and he also knew the one who would be hurt the most was Kylie. He was in over his head. If he broke it off with her right then, she'd be hurt, but he couldn't treat her like a slut. For God's sakes, she'd been a fucking virgin, and *he'd* popped her cherry. How would she feel if he never touched her again? How would *he* feel? He'd had feelings for her since she was sixteen. Every time he fucked a blonde, he pretended it was her.

I'm so damn mixed up. I never should have touched her.

Relationships weren't for him. A nice girl like her didn't just give herself to any man, and when she *did* give herself, she expected a loving, traditional relationship. It was something he couldn't give her. Banger was right—he was the worst guy for her. The last thing he wanted was to be tied down, let alone endure the fireworks that went along with dating Banger's daughter.

"So, you gonna break this shit off?" Axe asked, snapping Jerry back to the conversation.

He blew out a deep breath. "Yeah. You guys are right. I fuckin' lost my head."

Jax grasped his shoulder. "Women have a knack of making us do that." He gestured to Puck to bring another round.

Jerry would break it off. Kylie would be upset in the beginning, but in time, she'd understand it was best for both their sakes. She'd never really be happy with him. She needed a guy who wanted to settle down, be faithful. A guy who'd have all his limbs.

THE FOLLOWING EVENING, Axe and Jerry met with Rodney in a warehouse off old Highway 85. It was a moonless night, and the shadows covered them as they rolled their SUV behind the locale. Rodney, a nervous, small guy who was always sniffing, confirmed that the Skull Crushers were dealing meth in Insurgents' territory. For the moment, they were confining themselves to Pinewood Springs proper.

"Set up the buy. I'll meet with them," Jerry said.

Shaking his head, his mop of curls moving all over the place, he said,

"That'll never work. They'll make you as a biker the minute they see you. None of you guys can do it. You all look like bikers, and not one of you could pass for a user of crystal."

"You got a point there," Axe said. "We'll figure this out. Just set up the buy for Sunday night. We'll take care of the rest."

"Dudes, I'm risking my reputation by doing this."

Jerry snorted. "*Reputation?*"

Rodney darted his eyes back and forth between Jerry and Axe. "Yeah. I can't be known as a snitch. I won't be able to help you if I'm found out."

"You're not gonna be found out. We don't leave fuckin' evidence." Jerry lit up a joint. "Want one?" he asked when he saw Rodney's hungry eyes. He handed him a roach.

"So, what're you getting at?" Axe asked.

"I need more than the usual five hundred and a couple of pounds of weed." He licked his lips continuously, shoving his hands in and out of his pockets.

"Go on." Axe's voice was steely.

"I been good to you guys, right? We been working together a long time now. I've always been straight with you."

"How fuckin' much?" Axe said.

Blinking rapidly, he blurted, "A thousand bucks."

Axe looked at Jerry. "Do you wanna beat the shit outta him, or should I?"

"Let's both do it." They took a couple steps closer to Rodney.

"Okay. What about seven hundred?" They continued to walk to him. "Six...?" Closer. "Okay, five hundred sounds good." They stopped in their tracks.

"Sounds fair," Axe said, as Jerry stared at the sweating man. "Sunday night at nine o'clock in the back of the alley by Wesley's Ironworks. Got it?"

Bobbing his head up and down, Rodney wiped the sweat from his face. "I got it. I'll set it up. Thanks, guys."

The two bikers left the trembling informant in the middle of the room, holding the bag of weed they'd brought him as a down payment. Driving back to the clubhouse, they discussed who they could trust to execute the buy.

"What about your sister?" Axe asked.

"No way do I want Kelsey mixed up in this. Anyway, I wouldn't trust her to keep her mouth shut. Besides, having meth around her is like giving an alcoholic a bottle of booze. It wouldn't work." Jerry looked out at the inky blackness.

"Let's see if Hawk or Banger have any ideas."

Back at the clubhouse, Banger pulled at his beard as he, Hawk, Jerry, and Axe discussed possible buyers for the transaction.

"We can't get a user 'cause users can't be trusted," Hawk said.

"Maybe an old lady?"

Banger shook his head. "Don't want the old ladies knowing the club's business. Anyway, something could happen, and most of us seem to have old ladies who don't come from biker backgrounds."

"It could work if we use an old lady who's tough and been around," Axe suggested.

The four of them fell silent until Hawk said, "What about Emma?"

Emma was the manager of the club's strip bar, Dream House, and she was Danny's old lady. She had been a hoodrat for years before hooking up with him. She didn't put up with any bullshit. Emma had also been a meth user about eight years before, so she could play the part well.

Banger nodded. "That may work. I'll talk to Emma and Danny. If they're good with it, we'll take a vote tomorrow. Then we'll get ready to smash some skulls."

The following day, the vote came in unanimous. Emma and Danny had agreed to the setup the previous night when Banger had paid them a visit. Axe contacted Rodney to confirm the Sunday night buy. All the brothers had to do was wait and make sure their weapons were in order.

Chapter Fifteen

Every time Ricky saw Kylie, he'd get excited, and he went out of his way to talk and spend time with her. He thought about her too much, and if he didn't see her or speak with her, his day would seem pointless. He liked her a whole lot and was more than dismayed that she didn't return the sentiment.

Each time he tried to take their friendship to a different level, she'd give him one of her smiles that made his pants tight, and then remind him that they were really good friends. Problem was he didn't feel like a friend anymore; he wanted much more from her, but she kept rebuffing him. Ricky knew she had the hots for the muscle man who'd shown up to the spring festival just by chance. He never believed that flimsy story, but from the way Kylie looked at the biker and the way he looked at her, he knew it'd be a long haul to steer her away from the tatted guy and over to him.

How could he compete? The guy lived in Pinewood Springs and could see Kylie every day. Ricky lived in Denver, a good three-hour drive away. And he was almost positive she'd slept with him the previous weekend. He'd asked his buddy, Jonas, to keep an eye on Kylie while he was in Vegas. When he came back, Jonas told him a tough-looking guy in leather, denim, chains, and tats spent the weekend in her room. It was like Jonas had shoved him into a brick wall. He was crushed and jealous that the badass had a love session with her, and he, the nice guy, only had a friendship.

Shaking his head, he realized he was doing *it* again: thinking about her. He rushed across the street to Lot C, swearing he was done with all that for the rest of the day. A dentist was waiting to fill a couple of cavities, and he was already running late. He hated parking in Lot C; it was too far when he was in a hurry. The night before, he'd come back to campus too late and the other lots had been full, so he'd had to park in No Man's Land.

As he approached his car, his face fell and he groaned: the rear passenger's tire was flat. He didn't need this. Now he'd never make his appointment. With his remote in hand, he pressed open the trunk and rummaged through it, retrieving the jack then rolling out a spare tire.

Upon closer examination, Ricky realized the tire hadn't gone flat on its own—it'd been slashed. Standing up, he looked at the other cars to see if any other tires had befallen the same fate. He spotted a few. Figuring someone had gotten his jollies by vandalizing the cars, he crouched down and began to loosen the lug nuts.

Faint music punctuated the stillness of the afternoon. A warm, dry breeze curled around him as he cursed under his breath. Concentrating on placing the jack in the right spot on his car, he wasn't aware of thumping bass and hard, loud beats until they were almost right on him. Ricky tilted his head up and saw a purple Corvette slowly cruising the lot. Relief washed over his face and he rose to his feet and waved the car over. The sports car stopped in front of him, heat emanating from the engine.

"What's wrong?" a guy with a baseball cap pulled low asked.

Ricky noticed the driver had on a pair of gold-framed sunglasses with mirrored lenses. They looked like something people would've worn in the 1970s. "Someone slashed my tire."

"That sucks. Need some help changing it?"

Ricky glanced at the time on his watch. "Damn, I'm going to miss my dental appointment." The dull ache in his mouth reminded him that he couldn't concentrate for finals without having his cavities filled. "I was getting ready to change the tire, but I really have to keep my appointment. What year are you?"

"I'm a senior. Where's your dentist at?"

"On Thirteenth and Washington."

"I'm going right by there. I can give you a lift, if you want."

Ricky beamed. "Cool. That's a big help. Let me just put the spare and jack away. I'll deal with it when I get back."

A couple minutes later, he was settled into the passenger seat of the Corvette. "I can't tell you how much I appreciate the ride."

"No worries," the driver said as he looped around the parking lot. "You have a ride back?"

"I'm texting a friend right now." Ricky looked down at his phone.

Kylie: *Hey.*

Ricky: *Hey. Can I impose on u? I need a ride back to campus. My tire was flat and I got a ride from a senior to my dentist. U cool with picking me up?*

Kylie: *What time?*

Ricky: *Bout 4:30.*

Kylie: *Sure. Where?*

Ricky: *1340 Washington St. On the west side. Brick building. Second floor.*

Kylie: *Got it. Be brave. ;)*

Ricky: *Thx. :)*

He put his phone in his pocket, laughing.

"What's so funny?" his ride asked.

"My friend cracks me up, that's all."

"Is your friend gonna pick you up?"

"Yep. She said she'll be there."

There was a long pause. "What's your friend's name?"

"Kylie. Why?"

Ricky heard the guy suck in his breath. "Kylie. I know a Kylie. Beautiful, blonde, perfect pair of tits. Is that the same Kylie?"

Ricky jerked his head back. "What?"

"Is that the Kylie you're talking about? She's a sophomore and her roommate is Taylor."

He detected a hard edge to the guy's voice, and his hands gripped the steering wheel so tightly his knuckles were turning white. "How do you know Kylie?" Ricky asked.

"We go back a while. Her dad is someone I've known of for a long time." He glanced in Ricky's direction, and he noticed the guy was clenching his jaw real tight. Ricky was definitely getting a weird vibe from him. He stared back, his face reflected in the man's mirrored lenses. "You fucking her?"

"What?" Ricky gasped. "I don't like the way you're talking about Kylie. She's a nice person."

"I didn't ask if she was nice. I want to know if she's nasty." He rounded the corner at Thirteenth Street. "While you were in Vegas, she fucked her brains out with an asshole Insurgent. I'm sure you know that. I didn't think she'd do anything that slutty, did you?"

When the driver passed right by Washington Street, Ricky looked behind him. "You just missed the street you were supposed to turn on."

The man kept driving. "Did I? Huh."

As the Corvette sped further away from where his dentist was, Ricky turned to the man. "What's going on here? How do you know Kylie?" Then snippets of Kylie's conversation about the creepy guy who'd been stalking her came to the forefront of his mind. "Are you the one who's been creeping her out?"

A dry laugh filled the space between them. "Is that what she said? I don't know if I like that."

"You *are* the jerk."

Without warning, the guy punched Ricky in the side of his face. "Have respect. You're in my car."

Ricky, rubbing his face, searched for the door handle. He had to get out of the car. He felt around the door, and when he couldn't find the handle, he looked down. It was missing.

"I'd say that right about now, you're thinking you're fucking screwed, and you'd be right. I don't like you hanging with Kylie. You're so damn transparent. All you want is to shove your pathetic dick in her.

I'm making sure that doesn't happen."

Cold sweat broke out all over Ricky as he tried to figure out what to do. He settled back, pretending to give in to the idea of going with the crazy jerk, and it seemed to have calmed Kylie's stalker. Ricky could see him loosen the grip on the steering wheel. By now, the Corvette was well out of the small county and heading further into the countryside.

When they turned down a dirt road leading to the state park, Ricky lunged at him, punching him and trying to throw the car into neutral. The guy, taken by surprise at first, shoved him aside. Ricky was startled by his powerful arms. From underneath his seat, he saw the guy bring out a large security flashlight, and he tried to wrestle it away. Slamming on his brakes, the driver swiveled around and pounded Ricky in the head with the weapon. Black spots floated in front of his eyes and he slumped back into the seat.

"Don't fucking try that shit again." He clobbered Ricky again, then pushed down on the gas pedal and sped down the road.

Dizziness accompanied a mind-numbing pain in Ricky's head, traveling down to his stomach where nausea consumed him. Everything was closing in on him, and he couldn't breathe; it was like all the air around him had been sucked into outer space. He couldn't think straight, his mind a foggy mess of blurred images. Ricky was pretty sure his skull had been cracked.

The car came to a sudden stop. The driver jumped out and ran around to the passenger side, opening the door and dragging Ricky from the car. He couldn't fight back, his head was like a balloon that had been blown up too much then popped. He could barely keep it upright. The man threw him on the ground and pummeled his fists against his helpless body, adding kicks to his sides, head, and face. Ricky knew if he didn't pretend to be a goner, the man would beat him to death. And all because he was friends with Kylie—it was incomprehensible.

"You weak asshole. I knew you'd be done in no time. Kylie deserves a man, not a fucking mama's boy." He delivered an incredibly forceful blow, and Ricky felt himself slipping away.

His attacker dragged him across the dirt, the sharp pinecones and stones scratching and ripping his skin. Ricky didn't think he would survive. He didn't even know where the hell he was. Strong arms picked him up, and for a few seconds he felt like he was soaring in the wind, the breeze cooling his aching body. Then he rolled down a small hill, feeling every bump until he slammed against a large rock which ended his short ride. The way the pain shot up his arm and rippled through his body, he knew it was broken. Then deep, maniacal laughter echoed in his ears before he heard the man's crunching footsteps retreat, leaving Ricky's bruised, bloodied, and broken body to wither away.

Chapter Sixteen

Jerry hid in the shadows of the alley, watching as three men approached. It was a dark, moonless night, and pinpricks of light pierced through the sky's black canopy. The hour was late, and the town's lights ebbed to a mere glimmer. Twenty Insurgents manned their posts, waiting for the sign from their president to move in and take care of business. The three men stopped at the entrance, glanced around, and slowly walked into the alley, the echo of their footsteps slicing through the stillness of the air. From where he'd positioned himself, Jerry could see the Skull Crushers logo on the backs of their jackets, and his fists instinctively tightened. One of the Skull Crushers took out a cigarette and lit it, the glow from its tip making his face appear ghoulish.

"She's fucking late," one of them said.

"I got a bad feel 'bout this." The member blew out smoke.

"You're just fuckin' jumpy 'cause I interrupted you when you were bangin' that slut at the trailer park. You can have at her when you get back. She'll be waiting for you. These sluts love biker cock." The tallest member laughed, shaking his head.

Jerry's insides clenched. He hoped to hell he wasn't talking about his sister, but a part of him knew he was. It took all his will to stand motionless, listening to them, and not rushing over and bashing their heads in. He had to be patient; there'd be plenty of time for him to beat the shit outta the dude.

Light, hurried footsteps made the three bikers retreat into the shadows, hugging brick walls with their backs. A dark-haired woman in her early thirties entered the alley, her head moving from side to side as if looking for someone. The tallest Skull Crushers member came out of the darkness. From the way she jumped, Jerry knew Emma had been startled. He was the closest to her, hidden in the doorway of a garage. She did a good job with her makeup, and all the acne and angry sores she'd placed on her face, arms, and neck, made her look like a major meth user. He wondered if she'd transformed her teeth too. Emma actually had all her teeth capped a couple of years after she'd stopped using. The crystal had rotted and discolored them, so Danny had coughed up thousands of dollars to fix them up. Jerry knew Emma would be livid if she found out Danny had shared that fact with his brothers.

"You alone?" the tall biker asked.

Emma turned and twisted, appearing nervous and anxious as she nodded. Jerry smiled. She was playing the part perfectly.

"You got the money?" As he spoke, his two comrades came out of the shadows.

With shaking hands, she took out the money from the pocket of her hoodie. "You got the crank?"

"Yeah. First the money."

She handed the tall member a wad of bills. He took out his Kill Light—a large industrial flashlight, favored weapon among outlaws—and switched it on as he counted the money. "All here," he said, pocketing the cash. He stared at her. "You want it bad, don't you?"

Nodding, Emma ran her hands up and down her arms, her body shaking.

"How bad?" he asked, taking a few steps closer to her.

"Bad enough to fuck and blow us, bitch?" one member said. Jerry recognized him as the one he'd seen at the trailer park the week before.

"What?" Emma's voice trembled.

She's good at this. Jerry smiled, aching to bash the skulls of the three assholes who were only a few feet away from him.

"You heard us." The taller one reached out to touch her, but she jumped back.

"Leave me the fuck alone. You got your money, now you owe me what I came for. Do you even have it?"

"Show it to her, Gamble." The tall guy stepped closer to her as a shorter member took out a baggie of clear, chunky crystals. "See, we got your stuff. You just need to give us what we want and you can be high in no time." He grabbed her arm, yanking her to him.

Emma twisted out of his grasp, her steel-toed boot kicking him in the shin. "Fuck!" He bent down and rubbed his leg. "You fuckin' bitch. I'm gonna beat your ass." Emma ran out of his reach, and the two other men lurched toward her. "Get the bitch," the tall member said.

"The only ones getting the shit beaten outta them are you sorry motherfuckers." Banger stepped out from the shadows, his deep baritone voice sizzling with danger. The three men stopped, their postures stiffening. Banger lightly pushed Emma away. "You go on now. You did good." Emma's clacking heels on the pavement cracked the mounting tension.

"Who the fuck are you, old man?" the tall guy said as he eyed Banger. The three Skull Crushers looked to be in their early twenties.

"I'm the one who's gonna teach you fuckin' punks respect. You don't fuckin' deal in Insurgents' territory."

The three men circled Banger. "The shit you're spewing was for the old days. Times have changed. The Skull Crushers don't give a shit what the Insurgents think. We'll do what the fuck we want." He spat at the ground, narrowly missing Banger's boot. Jerry gritted his teeth, ready to leap out to protect his president if one of the fuckers laid a finger on him.

Banger looked at where the punk spit then at him. "Problem is you fuckers don't know shit about the brotherhood. Respect never goes out of style, and I'm about to show you what happens when you don't give it." He took a step and Jerry held his breath, already in his fighting stance.

"And you're gonna do that all by yourself, asshole?" They laughed.

"I could, but I don't wanna have all the fun. I brought along some brothers." With a wave of his hand, twenty men stepped out of the shadows and formed a circle around the three Skull Crushers.

Jerry smiled when he saw the fear creep into their eyes, his hands clenched into fists just itching to be used.

"It's time to teach you young boys some respect," Banger said before his fist landed in the tall man's gut. He groaned and fell to his knees. In one fell swoop, the Insurgents were on them, showing no mercy. For ten minutes, the lives of the three Skull Crushers were pummeled, kicked, and stabbed out of them… until they were no more.

Jerry wiped a bloodied knife on his black skull bandanna, stuffing the blade in his boot and the kerchief in his cut's inside pocket. Banger came up to him. "We're taking the bodies to the hole."

"I thought you wanted me to make sure nothing was left."

"Bear is gonna stick with the prospects and make sure the bleach and peroxide wipe out all traces. I need you back at the hole. You're pretty handy with a chainsaw." Jerry chuckled, and Banger clapped his hand on his shoulder then walked away.

Puck, Johnnie, and Blade silently stood back, holding large containers of both bleach and peroxide. Jerry nodded to them and walked to the end of the alley, then jumped into Axe's SUV. No one rode their Harleys because the noise of their cams would've sounded like a thunderstorm. They preferred to operate in the stillness of inky black nights, like all outlaw MCs did.

Rock, Bruiser, Axe, Throttle, Rags, and Jax threw the battered bodies of the former Skull Crushers MC on the floor of the hole. The Insurgents had constructed it many years before, a concrete room built under the barn on their property. It was where people who messed with them met painful deaths, and where bodies were dismembered to make burial, cremation, and annihilation easier.

Against the thick walls, steel tables decked out with knives of varying sizes and various tools of torture lined the room. Above some of the tables, chainsaws hung on hooks mounted on the walls. A pulley suspended above a steel beam was used for various forms of "persuasion."

"Give me their wallets," Banger said gruffly. "I'm gonna send them as a reminder to their fucking president not to fuck around in Insurgents' territory. I should send him their hands, but it gets to be too damned messy." The brothers in the room chuckled along with their president. Banger nodded at Jerry. "You know what to do." Holding the bloodstained wallets, he walked out with Hawk, closing the steel door behind them.

Jerry took down a chainsaw, placed it between his legs, and pulled on the starter rope a couple times. The saw jumped to life, and the whirring buzz bounced off the walls. Dropping to his knees, he began the arduous task of cutting up a human body. Rock and Throttle each grabbed a chainsaw, and soon the hole was filled with the roar of the spinning saw blades as they cut through fibrous tissue, fat, and bone, splattering blood against the gray walls and floor. Once the job was done, all the brothers in the room picked up the body parts and dumped them in a large machine against the back wall of a small room attached to the hole. The room resembled a large walk-in closet. The machine looked like an enormous pressure cooker, and the boiling lye would dissolve the bodies, leaving the liquefied remains which could be poured down a drain. A perforated basket caught any small bone fragments that remained, which were crushed into a fine, white powder and scattered. The Insurgents preferred to keep the law out of their club business, so lye was the preferred choice for disposing bodies. It was easily purchased without any questions asked, whereas strong acids were closely monitored due to their use in bomb-making.

Three hours later, the men exited the hole as three prospects entered, ready to clean up all traces of blood. After the lye cooled, the fragments would be crushed, and all physical presence of the three young Skull Crushers would be blown away.

Covered in blood, Jerry went to his old room in the basement of the clubhouse and jumped in the shower, scrubbing the now-black blood from under his nails. His clothes would be burned along with the other brothers', and he was glad he hadn't worn the AC/DC shirt he'd bought the previous year at the band's concert in Denver. It was one of his favorite band T-shirts.

Fresh and clean, he slipped on a black T-shirt that molded around his chiseled chest, blue jeans, his cut, and another pair of biker boots. Putting on his silver earrings—a small hoop, a knife with a black crystal handle, and a skull—he combed his hair and ambled out of the room, the party sounds from the great room filling his ears.

When he entered the hub, he headed straight for the bar, thirsty for some whiskey neat. He stopped and chatted with some of the brothers from the Wyoming chapter who were passing through on their way to a charity run in Utah. They'd spend a few days at the national club then head over the Rockies into Utah. Jerry hadn't seen many of them since the previous summer's Sturgis. A couple of them were busy with some hot-looking hoodrats, so Jerry decided to talk to them later in the night.

He leaned against the bar and swirled the amber liquid in his glass, breathing in its woodsy scent that only came from seven years in an oak barrel. He took a sip, savoring the light scorch on his tongue and the smoky taste as it hit the back of his throat, warming it as it slid down to his stomach, the heat spreading all over. *Fuck, that's good.* His goal that night was to get good and drunk. The moments he'd spent with Kylie were on fucking replay in his mind, and the only way he knew how to stop them was to get plastered. He ordered two more double shots and a couple of beers. It was a start.

"You wanna have some fun tonight?" Rock asked as the muscular Sergeant-At-Arms sidled next to him. "I got my eye on a hot-as-fuck brunette, and she's with a blonde friend who's busting out at the seams. I thought we could have some fun with them. I know you like blondies, and it'd be fun to share. It's been a while since we did that." Rock threw back his tequila shot. "There they are." He pointed to two women, who kept throwing glances their way. "What do you think?"

Any man would think the two women were hot with their barely there tops and tight-as-hell skirts, the curve of their rounded asses peeking out, but Jerry wasn't interested in anything more than looking at them. "Not feeling it," he said to Rock.

"Why the fuck not? Don't you think they're delicious?" Whenever Rock was drunk or horny, his Cajun accent became thicker. "And the blondie, she's your type, *non*?"

No. Kylie's my type. "Just wanna drink and zone out tonight." Jerry saw Throttle smoking a joint a few feet away. He whistled, and the biker turned his head. Jerry waved him over.

"What's happening?" Throttle asked.

"Rock wants to bury his dick in a pair of hot babes, but he wants a buddy along to join in on the fun. You in?"

Throttle scratched his chin. "I got a bitch whose pussy I'm aiming for. She's taking a piss."

"Bring her along." Jerry threw back his shot and motioned to Puck to give him another.

"So the three of us and the three babes?"

"Jerry's only zoning tonight," Rock said, raising one of his shoulders.

"What the fuck does that mean?" Throttle stared at Jerry.

"Means I'm not into fucking right now."

"You shittin' us?" Throttle narrowed his eyes. "What's going on with you? You got some secret babe stashed somewhere? You know, Axe acted like this when he was banging Baylee on the side before any of us knew about her. Lately, you've been pretty low-key with the club whores."

"It's not like that. Just tired and want to zone. Do you wanna join Rock or not?"

Throttle tilted his head back and stared at Jerry as though he were studying him, then he said, "Where're the women?"

Rock laughed. "The one shaking her big tits on the table is the brunette. She's mine for the first round, and the blondie with the perky tits is her friend."

Jerry saw the brunette doing an impromptu strip show as the other men hooted and hollered, her eyes gazing in the guys' direction. "I'm in," Throttle said. "Come on, Rock. Let's get a closer view. I'll get my bed warmer and the five of us can have a fuckin' good time." The two men left Jerry at the bar.

After a few hours of heavy drinking, Jerry had more than a buzz going on—he was damn drunk. Long fingernails scratched his back, then landed on the nape of his neck, squeezing softly. "Want some company?" a sultry voice asked.

Turning his head slightly, he saw a blonde, blue-eyed woman pressing against him. She scooted over to his side, and he saw that she was stacked just the way he liked. He smiled. "Aren't you pretty," he slurred as she giggled and ran her fingers through his hair.

He leaned toward her and the stench of too much cheap perfume assaulted his nostrils. "You're not wearing lavender. Why'd you change your perfume?" He swayed and lost his balance, his face landing right between her breasts.

Holding his head on her chest, she said, "You want to buy me some lavender perfume? I'll wear it for you. You're real handsome and sexy. And I like this." She placed her hand on his crotch and pressed down hard. "Feel good?"

"Yeah, Kylie, it feels fucking good."

"I'm Haley. You got a room we can go to?"

Jerry pulled back and looked at her through bleary eyes. *Kylie looks harder and older. Maybe she studied too much.*

"Come on, handsome," Haley said as she hooked her arm around his waist. He stumbled to his feet then wrapped his arm around her shoulders and yanked her to his basement room. As he lurched down the stairs, he kept catching the whiff of her musky perfume. Confusion set in as he wondered why Kylie was wearing perfume that stunk and not her delicate one.

Struggling with the lock, the blonde took the key from Jerry and opened the door. In his room, he flopped on the bed and watched as she stripped off her spandex dress, leaving only her red lace thong. The room spun and he closed his eyes, his body moving a bit as the mattress sagged. Then he felt thin lips on his, and he tried to figure out why Kylie's lips had changed. When her urgent tongue plunged in his mouth, her hand unzipping his jeans, his eyes flew open and he saw the woman up close. Shoving her away, he bolted up. "You're not Kylie. What the hell?"

Kissing his jawline, she said, "I told you, my name is Haley, but I can be Kylie if you want me to." She nuzzled his neck and her perfume surrounded her. It was like she'd bathed in it.

Gently, he pushed her away. "Sorry, sweetheart, I made a mistake." He stood up and the room spun around him. He flopped back down. "Go on, go back to the party. You're an attractive woman—you'll find another brother in no time."

She walked her fingers down his chest. "I don't want anyone but you."

"Not gonna happen. I'm fucking trashed, and I only want a lavender-scented angel in my bed."

He closed his eyes and heard her frustrated sighs as she put her clothes back on. "I thought bikers loved to fuck," she snapped.

He opened his eyes. "We do, but when a man's got a woman on his mind, no one else will do. Have a good time."

She slammed the door, the noise splintering his head. Jerry listened to the beat of the bass and he thought of Kylie. He missed her too much. He had to taste her one last time before he broke it off. He shouldn't. He wouldn't. He couldn't. *Oh, fuck!* He picked up the phone and dialed her number.

"Hi, Jerry." Her sweet voice was the balm his throbbing cock needed.

"Hey, babe. Whatcha doing?"

"Nothing much. I studied most of the day, so I'm wiped out. What are you doing?"

"Listening to you. I'm pretty sure I can hear your heart beating." *Fuck, that's corny shit. I'm too wasted.*

"That's romantic. What were you doing before you called? I'm going to guess belting down shots."

"How'd you know?" He leaned back against the headboard.

"Your boozy voice gave you away. Are you at the clubhouse?"

"Yeah."

"Is there a party going on?"

"Yeah. Some members from the Wyoming chapter are here. It's crazy."

A long pause. He could hear her breathing, and then, in a small voice, she asked, "Are you being crazy?"

"Like?"

"Partying with the club women and party girls. I hope…" Her voice trailed off, and he imagined she was sitting cross-legged on her single bed, the lamp light on her nightstand encasing her in a lovely golden glow.

"No. The only one I want to party with is you. When you coming home?"

"In about ten days, but I may stay longer."

"Why?"

"My friend Ricky is missing. You met him at the spring festival. I was supposed to pick him up at his dental appointment Friday afternoon, but when I went, he wasn't there. He'd never shown up. I found his car and it was in Lot C. The tire was slashed, but no sign of Ricky." Her voice hitched. "I'm worried about him," she whispered.

In his drunken state, Jerry tried to make sense of what she was saying. "Maybe he met someone and is shacking up with her for the weekend. Guys do shit like that." *I've done my share of waking up in different apartments with women I never remembered meeting.* "I'm sure he'll be in class tomorrow. Probably wanted a good lay before school ended." He laughed.

"Maybe… It just isn't like him to do this, but he did mention meeting a girl last week. I hope you're right." He heard her swallow like she was drinking something. "I miss you. Wish you were here with me right now."

His dick stood at attention. "I fuckin' miss you too, babe. I want to feel your lips on mine, and hold you tight in my arms, breathing in your scent. Do you know your hair smells amazing?" *Damn. I can't call Kylie while I'm plastered. It makes me say pansy-ass, hokey shit.*

"I like this sweet and romantic side of you. You'll have to call me when you're drunk more often." She laughed, each note hitting him in his cock.

"I want to be inside you."

"I want that too," she murmured.

The room was spinning faster around Jerry, and sweat trickled down his back. "I gotta go. I'm ready to crash. I'll see you next week."

"Sounds good. And Jerry? Thanks for calling."

A funny feeling squiggled in his stomach, and he knew it wasn't the alcohol. Pushing it down, he answered brusquely, "Yeah. See ya." Then the connection between them was gone. His whole body buzzed. What was she doing to him? The beautiful angel was a devil in disguise, and he loved every wicked inch of her.

I'm so fuckin' screwed.

Then he passed out.

Chapter Seventeen

Kylie's eyes stayed glued to the classroom door, watching each person who walked through, hoping Ricky would soon come in, flashing her his boyish grin. But he didn't. The professor closed the door and her psychology class began. As the minutes ticked by, her insides began to quiver as ice flowed through her veins. Her eyes darted from the clock to the doorway repeatedly, as though she were watching a tennis match. A sense of foreboding weaved around her, and images of worst-case scenarios tormented her. *Something's happened to him. I just know it.*

When the class was over, Kylie packed up her computer, realizing she had no clue as to what had transpired during the past hour. She slung her backpack over her shoulder and heard a soft groan as it thudded against something. Whipping around, she uttered, "Sorry. I didn't know anyone—" Her gaze scanned Marcus's face and arms, which were covered in red scratches and a couple of small abrasions.

"Hello, Kylie." He stared at her mouth, his voice hard and mocking.

"I didn't see you," she mumbled. "Sorry. What are you doing in the class?"

"I sat in to see if I want to take it next year. I'll walk out with you." Marcus moved close to her and the hairs on her arm stood up. Inching away, Kylie walked toward the door.

"You look like you had a rough weekend," she said lightly.

"I did." His small eyes bored a hole through her.

"How did you get so banged up?"

"It's not any of your business. We don't have that kind of relationship." He held the door open. "Yet," he whispered as she brushed past him.

"Uh… I gotta go to my next class. It's in another building. See you around."

His cold hand grabbed her wrist, and he yanked her back to him. "Let's meet up for coffee later."

Jerking out of his grasp, she said, "Can't. I have a lot to do before finals next week."

"Then I'll walk you to your next class."

"I thought you had Statistical Methodology."

He blinked rapidly, his tongue darting out to lick his upper lip like a snake. "I'll be late."

"Okay." She rushed across the campus, hoping he couldn't keep up. Much to her chagrin, he did.

"I'll come by and pick you up."

No, you fucking won't. "I have to go to security after class. Thanks, though. I'll see you around."

"Why're you going to security?"

She smiled sweetly. "Can't tell—we don't have that type of relationship, remember? See you." Kylie walked into the classroom, still feeling the anger radiating from him.

After class, she headed over to the university's security office. She'd gone immediately after Ricky hadn't shown up the previous Friday, but the security personnel acted like it was no big deal, as did the Crested Peak Police Department.

"You again?" the older security supervisor said as she walked into the office.

"That's right. My friend didn't show up for class, and there's no way he'd miss the last class before our presentation. Something is wrong, I know it."

After a half hour of going over all the details and making her plea for help, security said they'd look into it, call his parents, and see if they could find anything out. Kylie pleaded with them to call the police, but they said they didn't have enough to go on at that point.

"So the fact that Ricky never showed up for his dental appointment, even though he was in pain, his car is still in a parking lot with a slashed tire, and no one has heard from him since Friday afternoon means nothing to you?"

The supervisor narrowed his eyes. "I don't like your attitude."

"I'm just trying to figure out what you need that would convince you that my friend is in danger. Maybe his dead body?" With flushed face, pulsing veins in her neck, and hands clenched, she stormed out of the office. Wiping the tears from her cheeks, she headed back to her dorm, dialing Ricky's number for the hundredth time. *Please pick up. Please be okay. Please.* No answer, just his voice mail with his familiar, cheerful voice. The message was wrenching, like a punch in her gut.

After splashing cold water on her warm face, she fell into the chair by the window and stared out at the Rocky Mountains. It was a beautiful day and the breeze carried summer on it. Several blue jays and cardinals chirped outside in the large oak tree next to the window, and the steady whir of lawnmowers blended in with their songs. The smell of newly cut grass danced on the breeze and wafted through the open window, and Kylie broke down and sobbed. How could it be so calm and lovely outside when Ricky was missing? It was a distorted slice of life—it should be cold, gray, and miserable.

With tissue in hand, she blew her nose, then called Jerry.

"Hey, babe. Good to hear from you." His deep, smooth voice caressed her.

"I'm so worried about Ricky. He wasn't in class this morning." She sniffled.

"You crying?"

"I know something's happened to him, and no one will believe me or try to help." Her voice broke.

"Calm down, okay? Did you talk to the police? Fuck, I wish I was there."

"I need you to be. Can you come?" His pause was like a crack on her heart. "If you can."

"I'll leave in an hour. Don't do anything stupid like try to find him. Make sure you get the fuckin' badges involved."

"They didn't seem interested when I went to them over the weekend."

"Go now. They'll take notice now that he didn't show up for class and no one's heard from him. I gotta finish what I'm doing then I'll take off. I'll see you in five hours or less."

"Thanks." She hung up, a huge weight lifted from her shoulders. Jerry would know what to do. Having him there would make everything much easier. She wiped her eyes with a tissue. Dialing Ricky's number again, she crossed her fingers then uncrossed them when his voice mail reached her ears.

The door swung open and Taylor walked in with an armload of books. "I'll be studying for the next week nonstop." She tossed the books on her bed and shook out her arms. "Hey, what's wrong? Is Ricky—" She placed her hand over her mouth, her eyes wide.

Shaking her head, Kylie said softly, "God, I hope not. He wasn't in psych. I'm so fucking worried. You know this isn't like him. I went to security *again*, and they acted like this is normal. They are such incompetent assholes! I'm going to the police. You wanna come?"

"Sure. Let me brush my hair first."

"Jerry's coming up. I don't know what he can do, but I need him right now."

Taylor came over and hugged Kylie. "I'm glad he's coming. This is so hard, and I know out of our group you were the closest to Ricky. Every time I remember that he's missing, I feel like someone kicked me in the stomach."

"I know what you mean. He has to be found. He just does."

Taylor pulled away. "Let me freshen up then we'll go." Kylie turned back around to the window, staring out at a normal spring day as it unfolded before her.

As Kylie tried to concentrate on writing her English Lit paper, her thoughts kept drifting back to where Ricky was and if he were in any pain. Why would anyone want to hurt him? A small part of her was relieved that the police department finally took her fears seriously, and they'd opened an active investigation. She pushed her desk chair back and stretched out her legs. How would she ever finish anything as long as Ricky was missing? She pulled her hair up in a high ponytail and secured it with a neon green twisty. A knock on the door brought her to her feet.

As she shuffled to it, she prayed it wouldn't be Marcus. Something just wasn't right with him. She'd told the cops about all the scratches on his face and arms, and had added that they'd appeared after Ricky had gone missing. He definitely hadn't had them the class prior to Ricky's disappearance.

She opened the door and let out a huge breath as all tension flowed out of her. Jerry, in his tight blue jeans and black T-shirt stretched across his toned chest, crushed her to him, cocooning her in his strong arms. Tears formed behind her eyes, and she clung to her inked rescuer like a drowning person beneath a wave.

"Shh… I'm here now." The movement of his fingers rubbing small circles on her back fused her connection to him. "I know you're upset, and I feel like shit that I can't do something for you."

"You have," she said against his chest. "You're here."

He walked her back into her room and over to the cushy chair by the window, sitting down and settling her onto his lap. Warmth spread throughout her as he held her close. Nestling her head under his chin, they sat like that until twilight erased the colors of the day. Sitting upright, she looked at Jerry, whose eyes shimmered with tenderness. His brown orbs pulled her in and she pressed her lips to his, kissing him fervently, never wanting to break away. He responded, and his tongue swirled around hers in a frantic dance which ignited sparks of desire through her.

"I want you so bad," she murmured against his wet lips.

"You sure? I mean, you're upset and all that." His hard-as-granite bulge prodding the backside of her thigh told her he wanted it as much as she did.

Knowing how hard he was for her made the ache deepen between her legs. She wanted to block off all thoughts and only *feel*. She craved to be lost in his arms, feel his lips on her body, and explode into a million pieces with his dick inside her. She needed to forget about Ricky, if only for one breathless night. "I'm sure." She kissed him deeply, and his guttural moan shimmied from her hardened nipples down to her curled toes.

Leaning back, Jerry gazed at her lustfully. "Let's get a room." His mouth trailed down her neck, peppering it with light kisses that tickled and teased her skin.

"I just have a couple things I need to do before we can leave. I want to call Taylor and give her the heads-up that I won't be home." As she finished an assignment for her Spanish class, he watched an episode of *Beavis and Butt-Head* on his phone, his low laughter twining around her.

After finishing her homework, she went to the bathroom to take a quick shower. She turned the water on while she began to undress. A knock on the door startled her, and she opened it. Jerry leaned against the doorframe.

"Whatcha doing?"

"Taking a quick shower."

He pulled her to him and buried his face in her hair. "We can do that at the motel," he rasped. Sucking in her breath, she simply nodded, butterflies swarming in her stomach.

She swallowed. "Okay. Just need to pack a few items then I'm good to go." He kissed the top of her head and sauntered back to the chair. *We're going to take a shower together? Oh, my God!* For a second, a pang of guilt pricked her heart as she thought of Ricky and where he might be at that moment. Then she heard Jerry's voice, muffled by the closed door, asking if she were almost ready. Pushing down all thoughts and feelings of guilt, she ran a brush through her hair and went out to meet her lover.

The sign for the Silver Spruce Motel was neon blue and had a flashing pink arrow under the name, pointing to the parking lot in front of the lobby and the two stories of rooms. Tourists loved the motel because of the large pool, the all-you-can-eat breakfasts, and the friendly staff. The university students' parents stayed there when they visited, but when the college students wanted a place away from the scrutiny of campus security, they stayed at the inexpensive and tacky Wildflower Inn by the interstate.

Jerry pushed the card key in the door, and Kylie scratched at a dry patch on her forearm as her stomach kept rolling over. The cold air from the AC blasted out from the dark room, and it seemed like she was walking into a cave. Jerry flipped on the light switch and a yellow glow bathed the room, a king-sized bed set in the middle. Glancing at it, her stomach rolled again. Stiffly, she walked over to the dresser, set her purse down on it, then just stood there, rubbing her hands down her jeans' legs.

"This is a nice room, huh?" Jerry said, picking up the remote and turning on the TV. He kicked off his boots and sat on the edge of the bed. Kylie saw him look at her, and she averted her eyes and stared at a stain on the carpet that was half-hidden by the dresser. She jumped when his arms wrapped around her; she hadn't heard him come over.

"No need to be nervous." He tilted her head back and gently kissed her lips. "Let's sit down for a bit, okay?"

"I want to wash up first. I'll be right out." She twisted out of his embrace and scurried to the bathroom, closing the door. Leaning her forehead against it, she breathed heavily, chiding herself for being so foolish. *It's not like you haven't slept with him. What's the matter with you? You want to be with him.* She didn't want him to think she was acting like a child. He was used to experienced women who knew how to make a guy feel great, and she *was* inexperienced.

"Kylie?" His low voice outside the door made her jump.

"Yeah?"

"You okay?"

"Yeah."

A short pause then she heard the door knob jangle. "Open up."

"Why?"

Another pause. "Because I'm telling you to."

She placed her hand on the knob and froze.

"Babe, come on and let me in. I want to see you. This is crazy."

Even though she agreed, her stomach was doing major gymnastics, and a cold sweat had broken out over her skin. "Kylie, come on." His voice was as soft as a feather, and she slowly turned the knob. He stood on the other side, concern covering his face. "What's going on, babe?"

She shrugged and looked down, fascinated with the herringbone pattern on the tile floor. His hand cupped her chin and he brought her head up, his eyes staring intently into hers. "Tell me what's wrong. You can't get your friend off your mind?"

Turning away, she shook her head, then nodded, then shrugged. Jerry drew her close to him. "You have second thoughts about us being here?" Her head waggled while she pulled at a hangnail on her pinky. "You don't want to be with me?"

"I do," she said in a barely audible voice.

"Well, that's good, because I want to be with you too. You know I'd never hurt you, right? We can go real slow, if that's what you want."

"I want to be just like the women you fuck at the club. I want to please you the way they do."

He shook his head. "You're nothing like they are. I like you the way you are, and baby, you please me real good. Better than all the club whores put together."

"You're just saying that."

"No, I'm not. Damn. I wouldn't want you to be like them. I like that I'm your first man. Haven't you been thinking about me?"

"A lot."

"Me too. And isn't this what you've been imagining while you've been sitting through your classes?"

She nodded.

"This is what you and I have been wanting since the last time I was here."

"I know." Silence spread around them.

He cleared his throat. "You're too tense." He rubbed her small shoulders with his large hands, and she moaned in pleasure as he massaged her stiff muscles. After several minutes, he whispered in her ear, "You want to take a long, hot shower? It'll make you feel better."

She bobbed her head up and down then watched him walk over to the tub and turn on the water, checking the temperature with his hand. "Nice and warm." He smiled and she melted. He padded over to her and kissed her then tugged his T-shirt over his head, his broad chest adorned with colorful ink, enticing her. When he unzipped his jeans, his biceps flexed and the ink on them danced. Kylie sucked in her lower lip when he slid his pants down over his tanned skin, around the curve of his hips, his ass, and past his corded legs. In the bathroom, with the mega-watt lightbulbs across the mirror, he looked like a sculpture she'd seen photos of in her European renaissance history class.

Without thinking, she reached out and traced his toned muscles with her fingernail, grazing across his erect nipple. She leaned over and licked the small peak then circled her tongue around it. "Fuck," he rasped under his breath. She ran her hands down his chiseled arms, coming up under them then lightly scratching his sides until she landed on his perfectly round and firm ass. Grasping his cheeks, she squeezed them, her nails digging into his taut flesh. He groaned and pushed into her, his hard, thick dick jabbing her in the ribs. When she twined her hand around it, she was surprised how warm and hard it was, like a hot poker. She moved her hand up and down and he growled, gently untangling it from his pulsing hardness.

She blinked rapidly. "Did I do something wrong? You didn't like it?"

His brown eyes smoldered as he slowly looked her up and down, lingering on her mouth. "I like it too fuckin' much, and I don't wanna come yet. You got me all fired up, babe. Now take your clothes off for me." The water was still running, so Kylie hurriedly whipped her top off. "Slowly," he ordered.

Kylie undid her jeans and lowered them inch by inch, her eyes never leaving his. A hazy lust shone in his as he watched her peel off her clothes. She stood before him in a sheer green bra and matching bikini panties, her smooth lips straining against the fabric. "Touch your tits," he breathed. She cupped her breasts, loving the way his hard dick twitched and throbbed because of her. Her stiff nipples pushed against the sheer bra, and Jerry whistled softly under his breath. "Take your bra off. Nice and slow."

She unhooked her bra, and before she could slide it off, he was next to her, his fingers looped around the straps on her shoulders, his hardness poking her. With deliberation, he slipped it down her shoulders and arms then bent down, took an aching bud into his mouth, and sucked it. *Holy shit!* Jolts of pleasure zigzagged through her body as she felt dampness in her panties.

He reached down and kneaded her quivering pussy. "I can feel how wet you are. Fuck."

Her body tightened, and she willed herself not to come. It seemed that every time he touched her she went off like a rocket, and she wanted to slow it down and savor their bodies touching one another's, skin to skin. "The water's still running," she said against his shoulder.

"Turn around and take off your panties," he ordered.

With her back to him, she slid them down her toned legs and they landed on the floor, pooled around her ankles. "Open your legs a bit, then bend down and pick them up." She complied, and her ass cheeks spread open as her wet pussy was fully exposed. "Fuckin' beautiful," he said huskily. She picked up her undies and turned around, his hungry eyes making her blush.

"Give them to me." Jerry held out his hand, and she placed her crumpled panties in it. Bringing them to his nose, he breathed in deeply. "So sweet and tempting," he said as he placed them on the fake marble counter and tugged her to him. Kissing her deeply, he nudged her toward the tub. She saw him bend down and take a foil package out of the pocket of his jeans before parting the shower curtain and helping her into the bathtub.

The warm water felt good, and Jerry stepped in behind her and drew her back against him, reaching for the soap. After unwrapping the package, he lathered up his hands and rubbed them over her neck, shoulders, and tits, tweaking her hard beads each time he massaged the soap over her breasts. It felt amazing, and all the doubts she'd had earlier dissolved. She leaned back and let herself enjoy the sensations coursing through her. His soapy hands kneaded under her tits, then down to her ribs and belly, and all while his hard dick pressed against the small of her back. To her disappointment, he bypassed her pussy, instead washing her thighs in a slow, circular pattern. She dropped her head back, pillowing it against his shoulder, and moaned.

He kissed her jawline while his hands continued soaping her body. Pushing her forward a bit, he kissed and nipped the back of her neck for several seconds, then moved to her shoulders as he soaped her sides. She was in shower heaven, and thought she'd never be able to take one again without reliving every moment she was experiencing with him.

Jerry ran his hands down her back until they landed on her rounded ass. He grunted when his soapy hand massaged her cheeks, his fingers digging into the soft flesh. He ran a finger down her ass and she jumped, not expecting him to touch her in such an intimate way. "You don't like that?" he whispered in her ear as his finger played with her crack.

"I don't know. It feels funny having you touch me there."

"I'll stop if you want me to."

She didn't want him to. For reasons she couldn't articulate, she *loved* him playing with her ass, but she was shy to tell him. It was too nasty. What would he think of her? He'd told her earlier he was glad that she wasn't like the club girls, so if he knew she loved what he was doing to her, he'd think she was slutty. "Okay. Maybe we can do that another time." Much to her disappointment, he moved his finger away.

He turned her around and kissed her passionately under the shower as the water ran along their faces. Breaking away, their gazes locked and he ran his hand down her neck, brushing his thumb against her collarbone. Cupping her tit, he said hoarsely, "You fucking turn me on. I can't get enough of you."

Smiling, Kylie took the soap from the dish and lathered her hands, skimming them over his pecs, abs, and the defined "V" that led to his impossibly hard dick. "Don't touch it," he said as he moved her hands in another direction.

"Why?"

"We're not ready for that yet." He guided her hands onto his back, and she marveled at how sculpted it was.

She'd always thought Jerry was hot, but she'd never imagined he'd look like this. She knew he did martial arts, something they'd had in common when she'd started training in high school, so she figured he was fit. Kylie had the training to thank for her toned body, but she never thought he'd look like a damn Greek god. She'd only seen him once without his shirt before they'd slept together, and it was when she'd walked into the great room one day looking for her father. Wendy had been on his lap, running her talons down his bare back while he sucked on one of her big breasts. When he'd heard Kylie bump into the barstool, he'd looked over, his face turning white when he realized it was her. He'd shoved Wendy off his lap and jumped up, and that's when she'd seen his magnificent chest. She'd ogled him, barely able to keep the drool from running down her chin. From the way he'd smiled and winked, he'd known the impact his body had on her. Embarrassed, she'd muttered something stupid and stumbled away. For a very long time, Jerry and his naked chest had been the fodder for her fantasies and explorations of her body.

Kylie smoothed the soap over his firm butt, and the urge to bite his taut, round cheeks surprised her. *What is it with me and the ass tonight? Damn.* After several minutes of touching him everywhere but his dick, she rinsed him off then let him rinse her. Her body was humming and desire bubbled just below the surface of her skin. He turned the water off and helped her out of the tub, then wrapped a large towel around her. He dried her down, and each time his hand grazed over her nipples or pussy, she held her breath. She was on fire, and she needed him to put it out.

He kissed her deeply, holding her hand as he guided her over to the sink. Removing her towel, he nipped the back of her shoulder blades. "Put your hands on the counter and bend over," he said in a low voice.

Placing her hands on the cool surface, she obeyed. "Like this?" She looked at him in the mirror.

"Spread your legs more."

She complied, her pussy twitching from excitement. He rubbed his hands all over her back and ass then slipped over her throbbing sex before he cupped it tightly. And it felt *so* good. Her head dipped down and she moaned, gasping when he buried his fingers into her slick folds. *This feels incredible.* She clenched her sex and rolled her hips, causing a sweet ache, which heightened her pleasure.

"You like that, babe?"

"Mmm… It feels real good."

"It only gets better."

In the mirror, she saw him drop to his knees. Then her legs bucked when his warm tongue swiped her clit in one long, slow lick from just above her puckered tight hole all the way to her sweet spot. He lapped over and over, and she squirmed with each lick. He chuckled, the vibration going right up her pussy, and she whimpered in response. Spreading her legs wider, he separated her swollen lips and sucked her clit into his mouth. She gasped—it was divine. She looked at herself in the mirror: her face was flushed, her skin dewy, and her eyes burned with arousal.

Jerry deftly played with her clit, stroking the side of her hardening nub with his tongue. Then he swirled it around her sensitive spot in teasing circles, then back to the stroking, then the slow, long licks. Kylie was beside herself with passion and burning lust. When his tongue lightly laved her wet opening, she reached behind her, grabbed his hair, and pushed his face against her pussy, urging him on.

"You want me to tongue-fuck you?" He laughed softly, and the sound of it made her crazed with desire. She never knew she could feel this way.

In one movement, his stiff tongue entered her and he shoved it in and out, his index finger gently stroking her sweet spot. The pressure built deep inside her and all her muscles tensed, clenching until a huge jolt of raw pleasure ripped through her. Dropping her head down, she drew herself closer to the counter, her knees weakening. "Oh. That's so good. Oh!" Her moans and cries echoed off the bathroom's tiled walls, and Jerry flattened out his tongue and covered her trembling mound as she flew over the top of the world. In all the times she'd touched herself, or had a few men fumble with her during major make-out sessions, Kylie had never experienced anything as intense as that.

As a shattering euphoria morphed into a pleasurable warmth spreading through her, Jerry stood up, his smoldering eyes connecting with hers in the mirror. He licked her juices off each finger, his gaze never leaving hers. Then he moved her hair to the side and kissed the back of her neck, trailing his lips down her spine to the small of her back. Leaning over, he grabbed the foil packet, ripped it open with his teeth, and took out a condom. Kylie watched him roll it over his stiff dick.

Placing his knee between her legs, he spread them out more then took his sheathed cock and ran it up and down her wet arousal, bringing it to her heated slit. Gripping her hips, he inched in. "Does it feel good?" he asked as he looked at her in the mirror.

"Yeah," she breathed.

"Doesn't hurt?"

"No."

"You're so fuckin' wet, baby. That's good. You're gonna love it this time." He pushed further into her until he filled her up. Her walls closed around him like a clamp. "You're so damn tight. I fuckin' love it." He pulled out then pushed in, following the same pattern for a while.

Kylie, picking up on the rhythm, ground her ass against him as he thrust into her. "Raise up more on your arms. I want to see your tits bounce while I fuck you."

She pushed up, her breasts suspended a few inches above the counter. Then he shoved his cock in her hard and she yelled.

"Did I hurt you?"

"No, it's good. Do it again."

"You sure?"

"Yeah."

He pulled out and shoved back in hard and fast. As he banged her, her tits swayed, and Kylie watched Jerry's face contort as the pressure built inside him. "It's so fuckin' hot watching your tits bounce. I love watching me fuck you." He bit his lower lip and she kept his gaze as he came, his eyes rolling back, his fingers digging into her hips. "Fuck!" He stood silent for several minutes, then bent over and kissed the side of her face. "That was awesome."

Kylie was consumed with joy and tenderness. This man, about who she'd been fantasizing, was with her at that moment, and they'd just made incredible love. It was better than anything she could've ever imagined.

Jerry pulled out of her, threw his used condom in the trash can, and kissed her deeply. "You're really something, you know?"

"Am I?"

"You know you are. My sweet Kylie." He kissed her again. "You want some food?"

She nodded. All of a sudden, she was ravenous.

"What's good around here?"

"I don't feel like going out. Let's order pizza and salad and watch a movie."

He smiled. "Sounds good to me."

An hour later, the empty pizza box and salad containers sat on the small table near the window. Kylie and Jerry decided to watch *American Ultra*, and as she snuggled in his arms, she realized this could be one of the happiest nights of her life. If only Ricky weren't missing. Tears sprang to her eyes, and she kissed Jerry's chest and stared blankly at the moving images on the TV screen.

Chapter Eighteen

Ricky's still-swollen eyes fluttered open as best they could. The pounding in his head had been nonstop since the sinister guy hit him the first time with his heavy flashlight. He had no idea what day it was or how long he'd been at the bottom of the hill, but he knew if he stayed there much longer, he wouldn't survive. His throat was so parched that the only thing that came from it was a deep croak.

The first night, he'd just laid on the ground, too sore to move, but the following day he'd been able to pull himself up in a sitting position, despite the immense pain from his broken right arm and left ankle. His ankle was as big as a watermelon, and he wasn't sure if he'd broken or just sprained it. All he knew was that it hurt like hell, and if he didn't get help soon, he'd die of dehydration.

He'd been lucky it had rained on and off. Even though the rain was cool, the temperatures remained temperate. Since his clothes were drenched, he was able to suck the water out of the fabric, but it hadn't rained in a while and he was becoming weaker. He'd lost his cell phone when he fell, but he doubted if he'd have any reception in the desolate and hilly part of the Crested National Park, anyway.

Ricky knew keeping calm was imperative to his survival. He'd munched on dandelions which carpeted the ground that time of year. He'd read in a trivia book once that the yellow flower was edible and a good source of food if ever stranded in the wilderness. The many grasshoppers and spiders that jumped and crawled around him would be his next choice, but if he didn't get more water soon, he wouldn't have to worry about feasting on insects. The problem was he was so tired, and all he wanted to do was close his eyes and sleep for a hundred years.

As he began to drift to oblivion, a couple of male voices rose above the sounds of the meadow. Panic seized him and a shiver of fear wrapped around his spine. *What if he's come back to make sure I'm dead?* Ricky realized he couldn't do a damn thing about it. Maybe if he tried to move to the brush, he could conceal himself until his attacker left.

He pushed with his good arm, but it collapsed from weakness, and he fell back hard against the tree trunk. The voices were getting closer and his heart raced. When it seemed like the chatter was right above him, he discerned a female voice. He'd thought the tones belonged to two males, but he was wrong. He tried to yell, but his parched throat wouldn't let him. Desperate to gain their attention, he picked up a small rock with his good arm and threw it against a larger rock. In quick succession, he pummeled the large stone with smaller ones.

"Do you hear that?" the female asked.

"Yeah, I wonder what it is. I've never heard that before when I've been up here."

"There it is again."

Fueled on by their attention, Ricky grabbed handfuls of pinecones, stones, and whatever else he could find to maintain a steady stream of noise that didn't fit in with the cacophony of chirping birds, scurrying critters, and rustling leaves.

"I think it's coming from down there. I'm going to take a look."

The woman said, "I don't think you should. You don't know what or who's down there."

A small laugh. "You wait here, I'll be right back."

Ricky was weak from throwing the stones at the rock. He didn't think he could do it anymore, but he pushed himself on, until he saw camouflage pants breaking through the bushes. A man in his late thirties stared incredulously at Ricky before he shuffled back a step or two.

"Gayle, call 911 ASAP." The man came over to Ricky. "Don't worry, you're safe now."

"Nate, the dispatcher's asking where we're at," the woman—Gayle—called out.

"Tell her we're at the ten-mile mark above Aspen Meadow." The man took out a water bottle from his backpack and helped Ricky guide it to his dried and cracked lips. "Easy, kid. You can't have too much. How long you been out here?" Ricky shrugged. "That's okay. Help will be here in no time."

Ricky nodded then closed his eyes, tears trickling down his bruised face.

WHEN KYLIE RECEIVED the call on Tuesday morning from the police department informing her Ricky had been found, Jerry had already left for Pinewood Springs. Elation coursed through her, and she said a silent prayer of thanks that he was alive. It was torture sitting through her back-to-back classes, and when she finished with her last one, she sprinted to her car, anxious to see him.

Peakview Hospital was only a fifteen-minute drive from the university, and Kylie made it in ten. She passed through the automatic glass doors and approached a shiny black counter with an elderly woman behind it, staring at a computer screen.

"May I help you?" the woman asked cheerfully.

"Which room is Ricky Lanning in?"

The woman's fingers flew over the keyboard, and in a few seconds she'd provided the room number and directions for the elevators. Kylie rushed over to them and punched the key to the third floor. When she exited, she walked slowly down the hallway, the polished linoleum tiles shining like glass. Locating his room, she softly padded in, passing the first bed. She quietly pulled the flimsy curtain back that separated the room in half. Ricky lay on the hospital bed encased in brilliant white bedding, his head elevated and IV fluids flowing through his veins.

She came close to him and placed her hand over his. His eyes flew open, the swelling still apparent, although lessened by the ice pack treatment the nurse administered throughout the day.

"Hey," Kylie said, her lips trembling. She couldn't believe how horrible he looked. Who the hell had done something so vicious to him?

"Hey," he said hoarsely, a small smile playing on cracked lips.

"I'm so glad they found you. I was so worried." She wiped away the tear that escaped down her cheek. He squeezed her hand. "If you wanted some alone time, you should've just told us." She smiled and ran her thumb across his rough skin.

"You're in real danger, Kylie."

"What are you talking about?"

"The guy who did this to me drove a purple Corvette, and he knows you."

A sudden sense of terror ran through her like the chill of an icy wind. She felt weak in the knees and collapsed on the chair near the bed. The color drained from her face. "*He* did this to you? How awful."

"Do you know who he is?"

Kylie shook her head. "No. I thought he was just a jerk who got off on intimidating women. But he did this to you because of me. It's my fault you're here."

"Stop it. I'm here because the guy is a goddamned psychopath. You have to tell the police."

"I'm going to tell my dad. He'll take care of the fucker." Anger crept into her voice.

"Oh, yeah. He said he knew your dad, and that they went back a long time."

"A long time? How old was he?"

"I couldn't see his face so well because he had on these sunglasses with mirrored lenses. Every time I looked at him, I saw my reflection. It was bizarre. He told me he was a senior. I believed him at the time, but now I know it was a lie."

"Did you tell the police everything?"

"Yeah. I'm sure they'll be contacting you." He brought her hand up to his mouth and kissed it. "The guy's obsessed with you. He kept telling me you're his. I don't want to lose you."

"You won't. My dad will know how to handle this. You look tired. I should go."

Holding her hand, he said, "Don't go. Stay with me until I fall asleep. The meds I'm taking make me so tired.

"I'll stay, don't worry. You just get better."

She stayed long after he'd fallen asleep, the image of the guy in the purple Corvette haunting her thoughts.

The nurse came in to replace Ricky's empty IV bag with a new one. She smiled at Kylie. "He's a lucky man. Are you his girlfriend?"

"No, we're just really good friends. I'm so glad those hikers came across him. I don't know what I would've done if I lost him." She didn't add that what had happened was her fault because her stalker thought she had something with Ricky. She couldn't let the asshole get away with it. Being raised with a dad in an outlaw club, she knew the guy would slither away for a while. He hadn't planned on Ricky surviving, so he'd lay low. She'd even bet he was long gone from Crested Peak.

"Your friend is going to be fine. A couple days in the hospital for observation and to get his fluids back, and he'll be able to go home."

She nodded. The nurse made some notes on a clipboard that hung on the foot of the bed, and then left the room. Kylie stood up and stretched her arms above her head. Leaning over, she placed a kiss on Ricky's forehead. "I'll be back tomorrow," she whispered.

As she gathered her purse and car keys, a couple in their forties entered the room. The dark-haired woman had Ricky's eyes and mouth. Kylie guessed they were his parents, so she extended her arm. "Hi, I'm Kylie. I'm a good friend of Ricky's."

Mrs. Lanning shook her hand and scanned Kylie's face. "Ricky speaks highly of you."

She blushed. "The nurse just left, but she said he's doing real well and will probably leave the hospital in a couple days. I'm so glad."

His mother nodded as his father cleared his throat. "Do you know who the man is who hurt our son?"

"No. I wish I did. I'm sure the past several days have been rough for both of you."

"You can't even imagine," Mrs. Lanning said as she stroked Ricky's forehead.

An awkward silence spread around them. "Where are you staying?" Kylie asked.

"The Silver Spruce Motel," Mr. Lanning said. Kylie bit the inside of her cheek to keep her wicked smile from her lips. "It's very nice."

"I heard it is." Kylie slung her purse over her shoulder. "I was just leaving. It was nice meeting you. I'll be by in the morning to see Ricky." She walked out of the room and made her way to the elevators.

Back in her dorm room, she updated Taylor on Ricky's condition. When she told her who'd done this to him, Taylor's mouth dropped open. "Girl, if you don't tell your dad, I will. This is some real scary shit like you see in the movies, only this is real life. What a sick fuck. It's a damn good thing school's almost out. At least you'll have the distance for the next three months."

"I know. And I'm calling my dad straight away. I just have one more week then I'm home. Ricky's parents are here, so they'll take him back to Denver when he's released from the hospital."

"I wonder what'll happen with his finals. The whole thing sucks."

"The school is giving him an Incomplete in his classes for now, and he can take the finals when he feels better over the summer. What a fucking drag. I'd invited him to come see me in Pinewood during the summer. I hope he will. And you have to come see me too."

"I plan to. I'm taking it easy this summer. What're you doing?"

"I'm looking for a job. I want to earn my own money, and I'm still not all that comfortable with Belle being my stepmom. It still seems weird, but I pretend it's cool for my dad's sake. I mean, it *is* cool—for him. I'm happy he found someone. He's not as grumpy." She laughed.

"It took me a long time to get used to my stepdad, but now we get along fine. He'll never replace my dad, but he doesn't want to, and when I really understood that, everything just fell into place. Give it some time."

"I am. It'll be nice when the baby comes. I never thought I'd be a big sister."

The two girls chatted well into the late-night hours. Later, as Kylie lay in her bed, staring up at the ceiling, she let herself be happy. For the past several days, anxiety took center stage, but Ricky had been found, so she could cherish and linger on the memories of her awesome night with Jerry at the motel. It was the happiest she'd been in a very long time. She felt a deep connection between them, and the way she'd catch him staring at her when he didn't know she was looking told her he felt it too.

She was beginning to fall hard for him, and she knew that was dangerous. She'd been around bikers her whole life, and they were "fuck 'em and leave 'em" type of men. Kylie was lucky to have a wonderful dad who'd never cheated on her mom, and she knew he would be true to Belle, but he was quite the anomaly in the outlaw biker world. The way the men played musical pussy with the club women made her head spin. She had no business even entertaining the notion of falling in love with Jerry. He was a runaround, a man who liked easy sex and a lot of it. She was his fantasy come true, just like he was hers. But after the novelty wore off, he'd move on.

Her insides lurched when she thought of him with the club girls. She'd hoped he wasn't screwing them, but she didn't have any claim on him. He was a free agent. *Stop doing this to yourself. You're having a great time with him. Take it for what it is.* Kylie covered her eyes with her arm. *But I want more. I want all of him. I want him to fall hopelessly in love with me, and never want anyone but me. Stop it! You're acting like you're still in high school.*

Jerry was a womanizer, and she'd given her body to him—and was loving every minute of it. But she was determined not to give him her heart so he could trample on it.

After all, she knew how bikers were with women.

Chapter Nineteen

"This fucking dead man drives a purple Corvette and, according to Kylie's friend who this asshole beat up, he has a big-ass cobra tat on his right arm. He's been scaring my little girl, and the way he's acting tells me this isn't some random shit. He's targeted her, and I want the fucker dead, but not before I have a 'talk' with him." Banger's blue eyes flashed, waves of anger emanating from him.

"How long's this been going on?" Jerry asked tightly. He tried to act pissed in the same way all the other members were, not in the way a man crazy over a woman would be. He was one step ahead of Banger, because he was gonna cut the sonofabitch's balls off and stuff them in his goddamned mouth.

"Apparently for about a month or so. I wish Kylie would've told me right away. The fucker would be nothing more than dust. Damn, she should've known better than to keep this to herself."

"The asshole's probably gone underground with that kid pulling through. There's no way he's gonna hang around with all the heat on him." Hawk rubbed his face. "But we know that's not gonna stop him, right?"

"He's obsessed with my little girl, and it seems he's got something against me. He's not gonna stop until we stop him." Banger turned to Hawk. "Find out how many damn purple Corvettes with a white racing stripe there are in the state. I want to know the profile of each and every damn owner."

"I'll also check Nebraska, Wyoming, and New Mexico, just to be sure. I'm with you—this isn't any random shit."

"It's sounding like some fucked-up vendetta," Throttle said. "Now that's gonna be hard to figure out who you pissed off, Prez. It'll be easier to find the owner of the damned sports car."

"You're right. I've pissed off a shitload of people, but I don't want my Kylie suffering for shit I've done." Banger took a gulp of beer.

Jerry narrowed his eyes. "We know the fucker's a coward. Going after a beautiful young woman to get back at her dad is chickenshit." Jerry looked away when Banger threw him a quizzical look when he said "beautiful" to describe Kylie. It just slipped out.

Still staring at Jerry, Banger said, "Let's put it to a vote, because I'm gonna need everyone in on this. I'm gonna ask you all to keep an eye out for the bastard, and for Kylie. I want to find him, and this may be my personal problem, so if some of you don't want any part of it, I'll understand. No worries."

"Kylie's like our own daughter," Bear said. Several of the older members nodded in agreement. "Count me in."

Many voices echoed Bear's sentiment, and when all was over, the membership voted to find out who was targeting Kylie and snuff him out. When the gavel hit the table adjourning the emergency meeting, the brothers made their way to the great room to unwind. Jerry started to walk out when Banger called him over.

"What's up?" Jerry shoved his hands in his jeans' front pockets.

"You don't need to get too involved with this situation. You're busy at the grow store, and I want you to keep your eye out at that trailer park and see what's going on with that couple the Skull Crushers were staying with."

Jerry wanted to tell Banger that there was no fucking way he wasn't going to be involved in finding the SOB who'd been scaring Kylie, but he just nodded. He knew Banger was testing him, especially since he'd slipped and called Kylie "beautiful" a few minutes before. *It could've been worse. I could've called her a "hot babe."* He sniggered under his breath. "Okay. Whatever you want."

Banger's eyes hadn't left his once. Staring back, Jerry said, "Are we done here?"

A long pause ensued, neither man making a move until Axe came into the room. "Hawk said you wanted to talk to me."

"I do." Banger's steely gaze shifted to Axe. "Jerry and I are done."

Jerry tilted his chin and left the room. As he stood guzzling his beer, he made a vow to find the asshole on his own and make him pay for what he'd done. Leaving the empty beer bottle on the bar, he walked out into the bright sunshine. He rode in the direction of the trailer park; he wanted to make sure no more Skull Crushers were lurking around. He was pretty sure the couple the other guys had stayed with was cooking meth. He'd check it out and let Banger know.

As he rode, he thought about Kylie. It had become a habit to think about her most of the time. In a few days, she would be home for the summer. He couldn't wait to hold and kiss her; he'd missed her too much, and that was a first for him.

Jerry had trouble getting close to people. He chalked it up to being bounced around in foster care for most of his childhood thanks to a drugged-out mother, and a father who was in prison more than he was home. After Jerry and his siblings were taken out of Wanda's house, he'd heard that his dad killed a woman he'd been shacking up with. He'd been incarcerated ever since he'd pled guilty to second degree murder.

A couple years back, Jerry had received a letter that was postmarked Cañon City. It was from his old man, who'd been sitting on his ass in prison for the previous eleven years. In all the time Jerry was dealing with growing up in the foster care system, he hadn't heard anything from his dad. It was like the man had forgotten his kids existed. He'd thrown the letter away—unopened—never to receive another one, which suited him just fine.

He'd never belonged to anyone or anything until he began prospecting with the Insurgents when he'd turned twenty. Even though it fucking sucked to be a prospect, and the brothers treated you like you were a piece of shit on their boots, he still felt the tie that bound the members together. It was something he'd never seen, and when he'd received his full patch, he couldn't believe the camaraderie and closeness the brothers had for each other. It was the first time he understood what it felt like to have a family. Loyalty, love, and trust were integral to the brotherhood, and he embraced it wholeheartedly. He'd been craving it and he didn't even know it.

The light feeling he experienced when he thought of Kylie coming home for the summer dissipated as he reflected on the club. Him fucking her wasn't just about Banger and how pissed he'd be; it was about losing the only real family Jerry ever had. It wasn't so easy to think of walking away. Besides, he'd never forgive himself if Banger and Kylie drifted apart.

Rounding the corner, he rode through the open, rusted gates, parked in front of Wanda's trailer, and went inside. It was definitely in better condition than it'd been when he was last there, but there were still magazines, empty pop cans, and a few dishes in the sink. Kelsey came out of her room and smiled when she saw him. "Hi."

"Hey." Jerry frowned at her too-short shorts and tight tube top. "How've you been?"

"Bored. My boyfriend's gone."

"Who's that?"

"The guy who was staying with Randy and Dolores. He just up and left with his friends. They think the cops were on to them because they just left all their shit behind."

"That asshole I saw the last time I was here was your boyfriend?"

"Not at that time, but we got friendly and started hanging out. I miss him."

"I'm sure you'll get over it."

"She always does," Wanda interjected. "She's got a different boyfriend every week. I tell her to enjoy it while she can because when them wrinkles start in, the men don't want you. Can't blame them. Who the hell wants to fuck a dried-up prune? You wouldn't, would you? I bet the whores you screw are real pretty with their made-up faces, high heels, and low-cut clothes that show off their boobs." She laughed and took a sip from her cup. "This is such good coffee."

"Bet it's a hundred proof." Jerry shook his head.

Kelsey came close to Jerry and said in a low voice, "Did I do a good job? Do you have my money?"

"What's she whispering to you? Don't you believe a damn thing she's saying. Last week was the only time I went to the casino."

"I'll talk to you in a bit," Jerry said as he went over to Wanda. "I've heard you been going to Casanova's Nightclub and losing a lot of money. You realize if you can't pay those guys, they're not the patient or gentle type. How much are you in over your head?"

"Who told you I been going there?" She rose up slightly in her recliner and gave Kelsey a hard stare. "It's the little whore who's spreading those lies. She's always been jealous of me."

"I didn't tell him nothing! Why you so quick to blame me for everything all the time?"

"Will the two of you shut the fuck up? Damn, you're giving me a headache. A couple of the brothers saw you when they went to bet on the roosters."

Casanova Nightclub was across Aspen Lake. From the outside it looked like a respectable place, but once inside, all respectability was left at the large steel doors. Ecstasy was readily available, and the staff turned a blind eye to what the patrons did. Underneath the colored lights flashing on the dance floor and the pulsing beats of the music, people gathered—mostly men—to place bets on a pair of roosters who were raised for stamina and strength to duke it out in the cockpit. Metal spurs were attached to the birds for the sheer enjoyment of the spectators. The Berrios family owned and ran the club and illegal fights, and the police raided them about once a month, although they were never shut down, much to the dismay of the upstanding citizens of Pinewood Springs.

"So what if I was? My gentleman friend took me out for a drink. We decided to check out the fight."

"If you gamble with his money, I don't give a fuck what you do, but if you're using mine, that's gonna make me real pissed, Wanda."

"It was all his. I swear it."

What the fuck am I doing here? Each time he visited his mom and sister, he swore it'd be the last time, but he kept coming back. Part of him felt bad that he couldn't have helped his sister when they were younger, before the state separated them. He was nearly seven years older than her, and he tried his damnedest to take care of her, but what was a ten year-old boy supposed to do?

"You gonna give me some money? The bills are coming and I don't have nothing to give 'em," Wanda said.

"You gonna spend it on paying the bills, or you gonna drink, gamble, and snort it away? I'm not about to support your fuckin' habits. Why did you let Kelsey drop outta school?"

"Don't you go lecturing me. I can't control the little bitch. How the fuck can I make her go to school if she don't want to? I didn't finish high school. I had to drop out to have your brother."

"Yeah, I see how great that worked out for you. Kelsey needs to get her GED. I'll talk to her 'bout it."

"Don't bribe her with money. She's so money-hungry it makes me sick."

"And you're not?" Before she answered, he walked out the door to see Kelsey talking with Randy and Dolores. "Kelsey!"

She turned around, the two meth dealers taking him in. He swung over the bannister and sauntered over to her. "Come on." He jerked his head in the direction of Wanda's trailer.

"I'm talking right now. Oh, Dolores, Randy, this is my brother Jerry."

He noticed how Dolores checked him out, her lusty gaze lingering on his crotch. As if he'd ever fuck her. She was in need of a good scrubbing from head to toe. Her thin, greasy hair stuck to her scalp, and she smelled like ammonia—a telltale sign she and the short man were cooking shit on their burners. He saw aggression in Randy's gaze. The guy was a good five inches shorter than Jerry's six foot two, and he wished like hell the loser would try something so he could beat the shit outta him. Randy grabbed Dolores's hand possessively, and Jerry shook his head and gave him his "never would be interested" face.

"I told you to come on. I'm not fucking gonna tell you again." The sharpness in his tone silenced Kelsey, and she headed back to the trailer.

Jerry turned away and Randy said, "You an Insurgent?"

"Yeah."

"Wow, that's cool. I love your Harley. Can I get a closer look?"

"No."

"What about me? I'd love to feel how powerful it is." Dolores smiled and ran her tongue over her upper lip. Jerry ignored her and walked away.

"You're not too friendly, are you?" she asked.

Jerry swung around and marched right next to Randy. "Let me tell you what the fuck I am. I'm goddamned pissed that you're cooking meth in your shitty house next to my sister and mom's. I'm also gonna warn you to fucking stop it. Now." His face was inches away from Randy's, and Jerry could smell the fear seeping through his pores.

"We're not making meth." Randy stepped back a few steps.

"You are. The Insurgents don't want that shit in their territory, and believe me when I tell you that you do *not* want to get onto the club's radar. This is your first and last warning. Get rid of the shit, or you won't have anywhere to cook it. You don't want to fucking get on the Insurgents' bad side."

Dolores and Randy stood silently while Jerry sneered at them before finally walking away. He wasn't making idle threats; when he told Banger what the hell these two jerks were doing, the Insurgents would beat the shit outta them and torch their trailer. He was nice enough to have given them fair warning.

Kelsey waited by the porch stairs. "What did you say to them? Now they won't talk to me. What's your problem, bro?"

"I don't want you hangin' with them anymore. And since you're so bored, your ass is in summer school preparing for the GED. No way are you sitting around all summer getting into a shitload of trouble."

"You're just a big bully. You come around here wearing your jacket with your logo, scaring the hell outta everyone. Pretty soon no one's gonna talk to me. You fixed it with Brian—he won't look at me—and now you're doing it with Randy and Dolores."

"You don't need to be friends with them or that old asshole. Stay away from them, or I'll make sure you do. And you won't like it."

"You're so bossy. So, where's my money for cleaning the place?"

He handed her sixty dollars. She counted it and he saw a frown crease her forehead. "You said eighty"

"If the place was clean."

"It was. So give me another twenty."

"Dishes in the sink and magazines and paper strewn around isn't clean. It was better, but for eighty bucks it needs to be cleaned well. We'll see how next week goes."

"Asshole," she muttered under her breath. Jerry let it go.

"You coming back in?" Wanda wheezed.

When he came back in the trailer, Wanda was in the kitchen pouring herself another cup of "coffee" from the vodka bottle. She glanced up, and Jerry observed guilt etched all over her face. He walked over to her, threw down two one-hundred-dollar bills on the Formica counter, and left the trailer. Wanda came out on the porch, and the moment she opened her mouth, he revved his engine, shattering the trailer park with 90 ear-splitting decibels from his customized pipes. The noise sounded like a barrage of fireworks going off all at once, and several people came out of their trailers shaking their fists, their mouths moving in anger. Jerry put on his sunglasses and sped out of the trailer park, his middle finger high in the air. He needed to ride hard and fast, to be a part of the wind, the sunlight, and the earth. For him, the only true peace was in the ride.

Riding hard.

Riding free.

Just fucking riding.

Chapter Twenty

Flashes of lightning cracked the sky, followed by ominous rolls of thunder. The blue sky from earlier in the day was now a sheet of steel gray, and the white clouds had turned into darkened charcoal smudges against it. The clubhouse windows creaked as the gusting wind pushed against them, the trees bowing to its strength. Jerry watched the raindrops as they tumbled from the graphite sky, pelting the dry ground and trees, their leaves drooping on the curved branches. The door opened and a rush of air blew in, bringing a fresh, earthy scent with it.

"Damn, it's really coming down out there," Rock said as he wiped his rain-soaked face. He grabbed the shot the prospect had placed on the bar for him and went over to Jerry. "The two assholes you told me about at the trailer park where your sister lives are connected to the fuckin' Skull Crushers. I'm on my way to tell Banger. You wanna come?"

"Nah, I'm just chillin' right now. I don't get to do that very often. You can fill me in on what he says."

"Okay. I know he's stoked 'cause you found that out." Rock set his shot glass on the table and walked away.

Jerry motioned Puck for another beer and, in less than a few seconds, the prospect had it delivered. He took a long drink, loving the way the cool liquid slid down his throat. His cell phone on the table lit up and he picked it up, a tickle of desire teasing his dick when he saw Kylie's name. He opened her text.

Kylie: *I want 2 see u.*

He smiled, took another long drink, and stretched out his legs.

Jerry: *Wanna see u 2, babe.*

Kylie: *Real bad?*

Jerry: *U know it.*

Kylie: *Do u wish I were in PWS?*

Jerry: *Oh yeah… Want u here with me now.*

Kylie: *Great! I'm on my way.* ♥

Jerry sat up, his elbow knocking his beer bottle on the floor. *What the fuck?* Puck rushed over, placed a new bottle of Coors on the table, cleaned up the spilled beer, and ambled back to the bar.

Jerry: *U driving back home now? The rain is bad.*

Kylie: *No. I'm here. Almost at clubhouse. :)*

Jerry: *Ur dad's here.*

Kylie: *Figured he was since he wasn't home. See u in a bit.*

Why in the hell was she coming to see him at the club when she knew Banger was there? Damn, he wished she would've told him she was coming sooner, and he definitely wished he wasn't sporting a hard-on just thinking about her being near him again. He groaned inwardly. He had it so bad for Kylie that he couldn't fucking believe it. Even though he'd fantasized about her and figured it would be awesome to fuck her, he never counted on the emotional pull she'd have on him.

"Hey, you drinking alone?" Axe asked as he pulled out a chair and plopped down on it.

"Not anymore." Jerry stared at the front door. "What're you up to?"

"Just hanging. Baylee's got a dinner meeting with some business people. She's trying to get them to come onboard with the firm. She really wants the Gilpin Mall Complex. So, I'm solo tonight. Want to get barbecue later?"

"Sounds good, but I'm not sure I can make it."

"You guys going out for barbecue? Count me in," Throttle said as he came up to their table.

"Me too," said Chas as he motioned to Puck for a round of drinks.

Addie's hanging with the old ladies on their night out bullshit."

"You don't seem too happy 'bout it," Throttle said.

"Belle started it. It started off with them getting together when we'd have a club party that they couldn't go to, but now they're doing stuff on days their men are home. Damn, it pisses me off. All I think about is if someone's checking out my woman."

Jerry laughed. "I think that's the point of the ladies' night out gatherings. They want their men to think about them the way they do when you guys are at a club party with all the bitches. And from the scowl on your face, it's working." He clapped Chas on the shoulder.

"So I'm guessing Jax will be available as well as Banger, Hawk, Bear, and Danny?" Throttle took a sip of his drink.

"Pretty sure they'll be at the club tonight," Axe said. "It was a bitch riding in the rain."

The brothers all gave stories about the worst weather they'd ever ridden in, and Jerry half-listened. His ear was tuned in to the parking lot and the hiss of tires on the wet gravel. Soon couldn't come fast enough for him. He couldn't wait to wrap Kylie's small body in his large arms, kiss her deeply as her scent circled around them. He had to stop thinking like that or else he'd have to stay pushed in at the table, hiding the bulge in his jeans.

The squish of wet rubber on damp gravel hit his ears, and his jeans got even tighter as a current of joy zinged up his spine. He wanted to jump up and meet her in the parking lot, give her a big hug and kiss, murmur against her silky hair that he'd missed her and thought of her too much. But Banger's office faced the parking lot.

Cool air skimmed his back, and he knew she'd entered. He could sense her, smell her, *feel* her. Her soft footsteps padded over to him, and her hand on his shoulder burned away the wind's chill. She bent down low and breathed in his ear, "Hey."

Her subtle floral scent made his muscles tighten with desire. Jerry took her hand, squeezing it then letting go. "Hey," he replied hoarsely.

Kylie dragged a chair next to him and sat down. She smiled at the guys who stared at Jerry. "How's everyone doing?"

"Good," said Rags. Jerry didn't miss the way his eyes ran over her body, and it made his blood boil. He slipped his hand under the table and placed it on her thigh, clutching it lightly.

"What about the rest of you? Oh, Puck, can you please bring me a Coors?"

Puck looked like a deer caught in the headlights. Jerry chuckled. "Do you think you should have a beer with your dad around? I mean, you don't want to cause any grief for Puck if he serves you and your dad goes fucking ballistic." Puck's face relaxed.

"I don't think my dad would mind, but I don't want to get anyone in trouble. I'll just take a Diet Coke, no ice." She moved her hair behind her shoulder. "How's Addie been?"

"Good." Chas rubbed his hand over his face.

"So everyone is just good?" She smiled at the prospect when he set her pop down in front of her. "Thanks, Puck." He scurried away to the safety of the bar. After she took a sip, she turned to Jerry, her voice soft. "And how have you been?"

"Okay." His gaze lingered on her mouth, her full lips begging to be kissed or wrapped around his cock. He shifted his eyes upward, locking onto hers, and he sucked in his breath when he saw longing in them. In that moment, it was as if they were the only ones in the room; the physical awareness of each other was that acute. Seeing her, being so close to her, made him crave her like an addict. He'd tasted her mouth, and he couldn't forget its flavor.

"I need to talk to you." Throttle's gruff voice broke the connection between them.

"What about?" Jerry asked, his gaze still on Kylie's face.

Throttle stood from the table and jerked his head to the area where the pool tables were. He started to walk away. Jerry rose from his chair and followed him to the corner of the room. Before he could say anything, Throttle shoved his face a couple of inches from his and snarled, "What the fuck is going on between you and Kylie?"

Jerry stepped back. "What the hell are you talking about?"

"Don't fuckin' lie to me. I see the way you're looking at each other."

"We've always talked and flirted with each other. It's no big deal."

"Bullshit. This is different. You both seem too familiar with each other. Shit, man, you're fucking her with your eyes. Do you know what a goddamned idiot you are for messin' with her?"

Jerry shoved Throttle away. "Keep outta my business." He stormed off, but paused in the doorway. "I got shit to do. Tell me when you guys are ready for dinner. It was nice seeing you, Kylie." He turned around quickly and left the room, taking the steps two at a time. There was no way he wanted to see the hurt look in Kylie's eyes. They'd talk later, but he had to get away from her before he did something he'd regret.

He closed the door to his old room, where he'd been crashing for the previous three nights since the landlord had decided to paint all the apartments in the complex where he lived. He stared at the rain as it soaked the ground, his body aching from unfulfilled desire.

Jerry didn't hear her come in, only felt the brush of nails against his lower back. Wendy and Rosie often came down to pay him a visit, and he was so not in the mood to explain why he didn't want to fool around. "Wendy, not now." Then a sweet, familiar scent drifted around him and he spun around, crushing Kylie against him. He wanted to be part of her—not just inside her but all around her. Twisting in his arms and arching her body, she sought to get free. "Why you pulling away from me?" he said as his mouth tried to capture hers.

"You thought I was Wendy? Does she just drop by your room all the time? Fuck, why wouldn't you think it was me? You're still with all the... girls, aren't you?" Her blue eyes clawed at him like talons.

"No," he said simply as he struggled to keep his hold on her.

"Liar. Let me go!"

"Never. Now calm down and listen. I haven't been with any woman since I first came to Crested Peak and you dragged me to that lame-ass festival." He swallowed her retort with his demanding mouth, plunging his tongue in deep, savoring her taste and feel. After a few seconds, her squirming stopped and she looped her hands around his neck, pulling him even closer to her face.

His hands glided down over her hips and cupped her ass, her small moan hitting him right in the dick. Each step they took moved them closer to his bed, until his calves hit the side of it and he eased her down on top of the mattress. "Don't you know I'm fuckin' crazy about you? The smell of your hair, the softness of your skin, the way you taste—all of it drives me crazy. I can't get enough of it. I missed you, babe."

They lay on his bed, the rain spattering against the window, and they kissed. Deeply. Passionately. They clung to each other's mouths—their lips raw with desire and want—not daring to let go for fear that the moment they shared would flitter away before they could hold on to it. Just when his finger slid under her T-shirt and skimmed the underside of her soft breasts, someone knocked on the door.

Raising his head up, Jerry said, "I'm busy."

"I need to talk to you." Banger's baritone voice was somewhat muffled through the wood door.

Jerry bolted up from the bed as Kylie leapt up, pulling her T-shirt down. "Where should I go?" she whispered as panic replaced her glaze of arousal.

"Fuck," he muttered under his breath as he yanked her behind him into the bathroom. "Stay here. And don't fucking listen. It could be club business. Damn, what a fuckin' mess."

She giggled and pulled him back to her, kissing him, her soft tongue tickling the roof of his mouth. He groaned and squeezed her butt. "Babe, you're killing me. I can't face your dad with a damn boner." He pulled away and closed the door.

"Are you opening up, or what?" Banger's voice had an edge of irritation.

"Coming at you." Jerry smoothed down his hair, thought of Banger breaking his neck—which helped his hard dick go limp—and opened the door. "What's up?" he asked as nonchalantly as he could muster.

Banger walked in and leaned against the wall. "You did good with the Skull Crushers. You spotted them then figured the two dirtbags they were staying with had some connection, and no one suspected shit."

"Thanks, but the credit goes to Wanda for living in such a shithole." They both laughed.

"We're gonna pay the couple a visit, just so they know your warning wasn't idle." Banger looked around the room. "How long is your place gonna take to be done?"

"It's finished now. I'm gonna move back tonight. It'll be good to get back."

"Yeah. Living at the club can be a helluva good time. Easy pussy, brothers all around, booze twenty-four-seven, but it can be too much after a while. It's good to have a place you call your own."

Normally, Jerry would sit back and shoot the shit with Banger. He knew the prez was killing time because Belle was doing the girls' night with all the old ladies, but he had Kylie in the bathroom, and he wasn't in the mood to pass the time with him. "You want to join us for barbecue at Big Rocky's? A group of us is going. Mostly brothers whose old ladies are out." He smiled.

"Hell yeah. That beats sitting at home wondering what they're doing. Even though Belle is good and pregnant, I still can't stand thinking 'bout a man coming on to her. Fuck. See what women do to your head? You got time, though. You're young, and trying new pussy all the time is fun. What time are you all going?"

"In about an hour. I'm sure Hawk's going too."

"Oh, yeah. He can't stand being without Cara. I gotta admit I never saw that one coming. I figured him as being single his whole life." He chuckled.

"Yeah. Everyone's still surprised on that one." *Why the fuck did Banger have to pick tonight to talk up a storm? Fuck!*

"I don't want to stay too late. Kylie's back for the summer, and I want to spend some time with her tonight. She's supposed to have come here. Have you seen her?"

Shaking his head, he said, "Not really. I think I saw her in the great room earlier. I'm sure she's around somewhere."

"Yeah? Good. I'll go find her."

Jerry breathed a sigh of relief. Now all he had to do was get Kylie out of his room and upstairs without Banger seeing any of it.

Banger turned toward the bathroom and took a few steps.

Oh, shit! "The bathroom's off-limits," he blurted.

"Off-limits? What the hell does that mean?"

"Toilet's plugged up."

"Did you fill out a work order?"

"Gonna do that before dinner."

"Make sure you do. I'll leave you to that. See you in an hour."

When Jerry shut and locked the door, he rushed over to the bathroom. As he opened the door, Kylie came out. "Damn, that was too close. I'd have died if my dad found me in your room." She curled her arms around his neck and gave him a quick kiss. "I better go. He'll be looking for me."

Jerry unlocked his door, opened it slowly, then popped his head out, looking around to make sure no one was lolling about. Before Kylie left, he hugged her tight and kissed her. She broke away, waved, and shuffled down the hall. He shut the door, resting his forehead against it for a moment, then pulled back. Shirking his T-shirt, he walked to the bathroom and turned on the shower. He needed a hot one, but he wished Kylie were there so he could soap up her lush body. Thinking of how her skin glistened under the falling water when they'd showered together at the motel, his dick woke up. Shedding the rest of his clothes, he stepped into the steamy water.

Chapter Twenty-One

One Thursday night a month, the Insurgents came together at Steelers Bar and Grill to have a few beers, talk about Harleys, and play some pool. It was one of the activities that old ladies were invited to. Club women stayed sequestered behind the walls of the clubhouse. Old ladies and club girls never mixed at any functions. They'd bump into each other sometimes at the clubhouse if an old lady came by to see her man, or if the old ladies were preparing food for one of the family gatherings or a special occasion, but they never acknowledged each other. The club whores knew their place, and they respected the property patch the old ladies wore, secretly wishing they could one day wear that patch themselves.

Steelers Bar and Grill was a local bar that served great wings, burgers, and roast beef sandwiches. It didn't start out as a biker bar, but when Moe Hampden inherited it from his dad, he changed things up a bit: hard rock and metal music, Harley memorabilia, waitresses with tight white T-shirts, and the best brews on the east side of town. Bikers began flocking to the place, and soon they outnumbered the citizens.

Citizens still came by, but by and large, Steelers was known as a biker bar. The citizen women came to ogle the bikers and try to get a ride on one of their powerful bikes, and the citizen men who came around were usually in their twenties who figured the bar attracted hot women. Some were weekend bikers, and in the warm months their Japanese or German bikes would be parked out front, a source of much disdain and criticism from the Insurgents, who were Harley men to the bone.

On that Thursday, all the old ladies were there and the girlfriends of a few of the Insurgents brothers who didn't have a property patch. Kylie had often gone to Steelers with her dad before, and that night was no exception. She sat at one of the tables, her white crochet crop top showing off her toned belly, the dangling citrine stone drawing attention to her belly button. Her short jean skirt and four-inch wedge sandals earned many lookovers from the men in the bar—bikers and citizens alike. Every so often, she'd throw her head back and laugh, then glance over in Jerry's direction.

He stood by the tall counters against the wall, holding a bottle of Michelob. He couldn't believe how beautiful and sexy Kylie looked, and his fingers itched to sink into her soft flesh, or tangle around her silky hair. Each time she stole a glance his way, he was waiting for it with lust brimming in his gaze.

Sidling up to him, Jax leaned over and said in a low voice, "You better fuckin' cool it, dude. You're being too obvious with Kylie. It's only a matter of time before Banger catches on. You don't want that shit to go down, do you? Especially here. Just chill. There're other women who are damned hot in here. Don't set your sights on something you'll never be able to have forever."

Jerry bristled but heeded his friend's warning for Kylie's sake. The last thing she needed was for him to make a scene over her—again. He glanced at Banger, who was beaming every time he looked at his very pregnant wife. *Banger's a good guy and a helluva president.* Guilt pricked at him as an image of him and Kylie writhing under the sheets flashed in his brain. Banger trusted him to be respectful of his daughter and his wishes, and he'd failed miserably on both counts. But how could he resist his pretty, blonde angel who was so sweet and nasty in bed? How was he ever going to make this work? It seemed no matter what he did, someone was going to get hurt.

The beer bottle clanked against the counter when he put it down hard, drawing a few glances from the brothers. Kylie smiled at him, but he pretended to be engrossed in a conversation with Jax, Rock, and Throttle. Out of the corner of his eye, he saw her staring at him, a small pout forming on her lips when he didn't turn to face her. How he wished he could cover that pout with his mouth and suck on her delicious lips.

"That one is a beauty. She's wearing her top real low so we can see her titties. I like what I see." Rock clapped Jerry on the back as he nodded in the woman's direction. She sat at the table next to Kylie with two of her friends. "Why don't we go over there and join them? My cock's hard just looking at her."

Rock was a pretty basic man: he loved his Harley, Cajun food, whiskey, hard rock, beating the shit out of men, and pussy. He wasn't interested in going the way of some of his brothers. "Commitment" wasn't a word in his vocabulary, but he was apparently a good lover and always made sure the women enjoyed themselves. Jerry knew the Sergeant-At-Arms was surprised that he was passing on a lot of hotties both in and out of the club, but Kylie was the only one he wanted to be inside. He couldn't tell that to Rock, so he dodged out early or made lame excuses about why he wasn't able to randomly fuck like he used to. He and Rock had had great times sharing women, so he knew the big guy was wondering what the fuck was going on with him.

"Let's go." Rock flashed a big smile to the redhead, who kept pulling her top down further. "The blonde with her is just your type. They look like they'll be fun."

Jerry glanced at their table and saw Kylie turning around to see what he and Rock were looking at. When she noticed the women, he knew he'd receive the death glare and, sure enough, she delivered it promptly. He shook his head as if to convey he wasn't interested in the women.

"So, you don't want to? Man, what the fuck's wrong with you lately?"

"I got a lot on my mind with the shit about the Skull Crushers, my sister, and the patent I'm trying to get for one of my inventions." *Not to mention I can't get Kylie outta my mind, no matter how wrong I know it is.*

"That's why it's good to fuck. You get rid of all the tension, and you don't think of nothing but how good you and the bitch are."

"You got a point." *That's why I'm planning a fuckfest with my Kylie after Steelers.*

"So, you in?"

"Nah."

"Okay, brother. It's your loss. I can handle both, just thought you'd like in on it." The muscular man sauntered away, and Jerry saw him say a few things to the redhead, who laughed and brushed her hand against his. He was in. Jerry smiled, remembering how fucking had been so much easier just a few short weeks before. No complications. Just in and out. Easy. Fun. Simple. But not Kylie. He feared he'd never get over her. Sighing, he pushed away from the counter and walked down a small hallway to go to the restroom.

Upon exiting, Kylie lounged against the wood-paneled wall, waiting for him in all her fresh, sexy splendor. "Are you ignoring me?" she asked.

"Nah. Just been super busy with club shit, that's all."

"I've been home for three days, and except for our encounter at the club—which *I* instigated—I haven't seen you. I don't like that." She paused. "And I don't like you ogling the women at the table next to me whose tits were on display for any man in the bar."

"I wasn't ogling anyone but you. Shit, Jax had to tell me to tone it down."

"You were looking at those women. I saw you."

"Rock was talking 'bout them. He wanted me to go with him to see if they were worth fucking later on. I didn't want to because the only woman worth fucking is you." He reached out and trailed his finger from her bottom lip, down her throat, past her collarbone, and straight down her cleavage.

"If you feel that way, then why have you been avoiding me?"

"I told you, I had a bunch of club business to do. I want to be with you." *The devil's gonna pull me to Hell, but I crave her and need to taste her again.* "What about you coming to my place later tonight? Can you get away?"

"Yes. What time?"

"I'll come by at eleven o'clock. We should be done here by then. I don't want you coming over by yourself, not with that fucker fixated on you."

"The purple Corvette creep? I doubt he's in Pinewood. I haven't seen him in a while. I think he's moved on. Probably bullying another poor girl. I'll just come to your apartment on my own."

"I'm picking you up, woman. Don't argue with me. Drive your car around the corner from your house. I'll meet you there."

"Okay. Crap, my dad's headed this way." Kylie moved back from him and began walking down the hall. "Hi, Dad."

Banger glanced at Kylie, then at Jerry, who saw a hard glint for a split second before it was gone. "Hi, honey. What're you two doing?"

"Talking martial arts. I've signed up to take more classes this summer."

Jerry noticed Banger's face relaxed, and he breathed out while Kylie and her father spoke. "Well, I'm gonna head back out. See you." He brushed past Banger, and when he went past Kylie, his fingertips grazed hers lightly. He went back to his space by the counter, inserting himself in a discussion about bikes.

A couple hours later, he was wiping the wings' hot sauce off his thumb when he noticed Kylie wasn't at her table. Glancing around, he saw her at the bar placing an order. He also saw a fraternity-type guy standing too close to her, talking and laughing. From Kylie's face, Jerry could tell she was uncomfortable. Two of the guys' buddies came over, and they had her enclosed in their circle. When the frat boy's hand ended up on her ass, Jerry saw red, and he rushed forward like a bull charging the matador's moving cape. "Take your fucking hands off her." He broke through the circle and tugged her to him.

"Who the fuck are you?" the frat guy asked, puffing up his chest.

"I'm the one who's gonna kick your ass for disrespecting her." In his peripheral view, he spotted Banger coming toward them. Moving Kylie behind him, Jerry slammed his fist into the guy's jaw, then lowered the man's head and kneed him smack in the face. Blood gushed out, and the frat boy's two buddies started cussing at Jerry, trying to hold his arms back, twisting him around so he faced the bar. Behind it, Moe watched, a bored expression on his face. Bringing his leg up and front, Jerry kicked one of the guys in the kneecap and he fell to the floor. The other let go of Jerry's arms, who then kicked him full-on with his steel-toed boot. The man yelled in pain and collapsed. Jerry bent down and was ready to slam his fist in his face when Hawk pulled him back. "It's over. Leave it alone."

Jerry grabbed Kylie's hand. "Come on." He led her away from the downed men. As he approached the Insurgents group, Banger blocked his way, a scowl on his bearded face. Jerry stared back, a glint of defiance in his gaze.

"Why the fuck did you jump in like that for Kylie? I had a handle on it." His blue eyes narrowed. "You got something with her?"

"Some fucking jerk has his hand on your daughter's ass, and that's what you ask me? You should be glad I did something to help out. I'm tired of your goddamned questions."

Tersely, Banger said, "You're making a lot of noise, but you haven't answered my fuckin' question yet."

"You know, I don't have to take this shit. I'm outta here." Jerry whirled around and headed for the door, the murmurs from the old ladies and the brothers filling his ears.

He opened the door, and as he went through it he heard Banger's gruff voice. "Kylie, in the back room. Now. We gotta talk."

Then the door closed behind him.

Chapter Twenty-Two

Kylie stood in the back room, picking at her nail polish. Her dad's anger was palpable as he stood boring a hole through her. After what seemed like forever, he asked in a low, hard voice, "You got something with Jerry?"

She shook her head, dread weaving around her nerves.

"Look at me when I speak to you. I want to see your eyes."

Kylie's muscles tensed and a small stab of defiance jabbed her. She wasn't a child anymore, and she should have the right to choose whomever she wanted to date. Her mother and father certainly did, and her grandpa couldn't stand her dad, but her mother continued seeing him because it felt right. If her parents had the freedom to choose, why couldn't she?

She fixed her eyes on her dad's and jutted her chin out. His flashing eyes chipped away at her new feeling of independence, and she lowered her gaze.

"So, are you?" Banger glowered at her, and she shifted uncomfortably in place.

"I think Jerry's real cute, and it was nice that he stood up for me. Those guys were jerks, but I was ready to knee the one who had his hand on my butt in the balls and pop the other one behind me in the ribs with my elbow. I didn't need you or Jerry to help me. I had it covered."

Banger's eyes softened and he chuckled. "You're my girl all the way. I saw fuckin' red when that fucker touched you, but I'm your dad. Jerry's the only brother who charged over. All the rest knew I had your back. It was something a guy would do for his woman."

She shrugged. "I think any of the brothers would've come to help me."

"If I weren't there, for sure, but none of them did because they knew I owned it." He sighed and came closer to her. "I know you're young, and flirting with a good-looking guy is fun, but Jerry isn't for you. He's the type who'd break your heart. I know you can't see that because you haven't been around a lot of guys—"

"Whose fault is that? You made sure every guy in high school knew you were the president of an outlaw MC. The boys would look at me, but they were scared to death to date me."

"Maybe I was overprotective, but I didn't have your mother around to tell you 'bout boys and all that girl stuff. I didn't want you to end up pregnant and dropping outta school. I did what I thought was best."

"I know, and I'm good with that."

"You're in college now and meeting all sorts of guys. I'm sure there're some you like. All I'm saying is that I don't want you to give your heart to a biker who knows how to sweet-talk you. Jerry's a good brother, but he'd make a shitty boyfriend. He chases too many girls, and he's not interested in settling down with one woman. He's a fucking player, and every time I see him, he has another woman or two around him. I don't want you with a man like that. I don't want no man breaking your heart."

She smiled softly. "I don't think you can protect me from ever having a broken heart. I have to find my own way, Dad. I love you, but you have to let me fall so I can learn how to get back up on my own. Losing Mom taught me that the people I love aren't always going to be around my whole life."

"I'll always be there for you, honey. No matter what happens, I'm there for you."

"I know, and it makes life easier to maneuver knowing I have your support and unconditional love."

Softly, he said, "I want the truth from you. Is something going on between you and Jerry?"

She took a deep, pained breath and looked down at the floor. She couldn't lie to her father, even though she knew he'd go ballistic and end whatever she had with Jerry. But how could she let Jerry get hurt? She had no doubt in her mind that her dad would crush him, and he'd lose his patch, something which was more important to him than his life. She knew what the patch meant; she grew up understanding that the brotherhood and life were entwined, and a member couldn't have one without the other. How could she destroy Jerry? How could she lie to her beloved father?

How the fuck can I choose?

"You gonna answer me?"

Nodding, she opened her mouth, but before she could say anything, Hawk burst into the room. "You gotta come quick. Belle thinks the baby's coming."

Banger's face paled and he rushed to the door. Kylie intercepted him, hugged him, and whispered, "It'll be okay." He nodded at her then dashed off.

The Insurgents and their women watched as Banger's SUV sped away from the bar. Kylie offered to go along, but Belle asked that she take Ethan home and watch him. When she and Ethan arrived home, she called her dad on his cell phone. He told her that the doctors said it was a false alarm, but Belle's blood pressure was very low and she was a bit dehydrated, so the doctor wanted to keep her overnight for observation. She offered to come to the hospital, but he told her he was good, and he needed her home to watch Ethan. Kylie hung up and said a small prayer that Belle and the baby would be okay. Nausea rippled through her stomach and she stretched out on the couch, staring out the French doors.

The summer night was warm and breezy. She'd been so happy a few days before, thinking about coming home and having a romantic summer with Jerry, but at that moment, guilt assuaged her. Why did it feel so wrong when they weren't together, but so right when they were? If he wasn't any good for her, why was he such a sweetheart to her? No matter which way she went with her tie to Jerry, she'd end up losing out.

Her phone vibrated and she grabbed it, hoping all was well with Belle.

Jerry: How's it with ur dad?

Kylie: Not sure. Belle had a false alarm. He's with her @ the hospital. That part is ok.

Jerry: Shit. I still want to see u. U?

She sighed, knowing she should stop whatever they had before it consumed her, but she wanted his strong arms around her, his whispered voice telling her she's the only woman for him. She needed his warmth and desire.

Kylie: Ya. Emily will b home soon. So 11:00 around the corner.

Jerry: Can't wait, babe.

Kylie: ♥

The minutes ticked by and she finally heard the front door open, the jangle of her dad's chains as he stepped on the marble foyer floors. "Is Belle okay?" she asked.

"Yeah, she's good. We just had a scare. Her blood pressure is doing good, and she's got some fluids going in her. I gotta make sure she drinks more."

"How are you?"

"Fuckin' beat. I'm gonna head upstairs. You in for the night?"

"Margo wanted me to come over. We haven't seen each other since Christmas."

"Have a good time. You gonna be late, or just stay at her house?"

She held her breath. "Just crash."

"What time you going? I'll take you."

"I'm good, Dad."

"No fuckin' way I'm letting you drive alone until I nail this fucker who's been giving you grief."

Damn! "At eleven. Is that good for you?"

"Yep. I'm gonna wash up, then we'll go."

She picked up her phone and texted Jerry the change in plans: he'd pick her up at Margo's house.

Heat radiated through her when she saw Jerry roll his bike out right after her dad's taillights disappeared. Butterflies fluttered in her stomach when she thought about spending the night with him. Her body craved his touch, and already shivers rode her spine as she saw the rugged biker pull up beside her, his inked arms lit up by the streetlight.

She hopped on behind him, and he turned around and kissed her firmly on the lips. With her arms wrapped around his toned waist, she leaned her head against his upper back and relished the warm night air as it caressed her.

Fifteen minutes later, they were at his apartment complex, and he helped her off his bike. Closing the garage door, he hooked his arm around her shoulder and murmured against her hair, "Glad you're here, babe."

Tingles coursed through her body and she tucked herself tighter against his side. He led her up a flight of stairs into his building. As they waited for the elevator, his mouth captured hers and they kissed deeply until the bell pulled them apart. Inside the elevator, he tugged her to him again, kissing her and whispering, "I wanted to kiss you the minute you came into Steelers. Fuck, babe, you taste and feel so good."

When she stepped into his apartment, she noticed the freshly painted white walls and prints of different Harleys hanging on them. The place was neat and functional, and he had the generic bachelor pad color scheme of brown, black, and beige. "Nice place," she said.

"Thanks." He continued to trail kisses down her neck, tugging down the strap on her crop top so he could nibble her shoulder.

She giggled. "That tickles. Do you have any beer?"

He nodded, his eyes smoldering. Then he went to the kitchen and brought her a can of beer, which he opened for her. "No hard feelings?"

She took a large gulp and wondered if she'd ever stop being nervous when they were alone. Walking to the couch, she squealed when he pulled her back. "We're going in this room." He led her to his bedroom, kissing her as they walked inside. He switched on a small light on the nightstand then whipped off his T-shirt. He took the can of beer from her hand and placed it on the dresser then yanked her to him and whispered in her ear, "I want to make you feel good." Small nips on her sensitive skin sent a cluster of shivers up her spine, and she whimpered and pressed closer to him. Tugging on her top, he said, "Take this off."

She lifted it over her head and arms, her lacy periwinkle bra encasing her round, heavy breasts. A low growl from Jerry's throat startled her, and the feel of his face between her cleavage made her tingle. With her fingers, she stroked his sandy hair, bending down to kiss it. As she did so, he raised his head, his lips covering hers hungrily. With urgency, his tongue jabbed into her willing mouth, and his kiss sent spirals of pleasure through her.

"You make me think a shitload of dirty thoughts, babe." His lips brushed against hers as he spoke. His hands slid across her silken belly, his finger flicking against the dangling piercing in her navel. Then he trailed his hand up her skirt to the sweet ache between her legs. Slipping his finger under her panties, he buried it between her wet folds as she moaned and pushed her hips forward against him.

"Fuck, baby. Look how wet you are for me. I like that a lot." With skill, Jerry tweaked her trembling clit and she cried out. "You like that?"

"Yeah. It feels so good." Desire raged inside her and she dug her bright blue fingernails in his back, dragging them down, wanting to leave marks to brand him as hers. She sank her teeth into his neck and sucked his skin hard, wanting every club woman, hoodrat, and citizen to know he was taken.

He chuckled. "You marking me? You're an outlaw's daughter."

"When you're with me, you're mine. When you're not, my marks tell women to fucking stay away." The possessiveness that coursed through her was so strong it frightened her, but she'd have another time to think about it. That night, all she wanted was to feel him on her and in her, fusing their bodies together as one.

Kylie broke away from him and slid her skirt down, and he knelt and placed his mouth against her damp panties. With slow movements, he rubbed his lips over her mound through the fabric. She threw her head back and let the shudders of desire consume her.

He pulled the silky fabric away from her pulsating pussy, muttering "fuck" under his breath before his tongue dove between her swollen lips, stroking them slowly. With each lick, he brought her closer to ecstasy until her knees buckled and her body began to vibrate with liquid fire. The single, hooked thrust of his finger deep inside her unleashed a hot tide of passion, and moans of ecstasy slipped through her lips. She sank to the floor and curled up, quivering as spasms of delight coursed through her. As she rode the wave, Jerry stroked her damp skin and trailed kisses down her arms and legs. When she was left with a warm glow, he scooped her up and lay her on his bed then kicked off his boots, jeans, and boxers.

She lay naked but for her panties, and his hungry gaze ate her up. Gently, he glided her undies down her smooth, taut skin, past her high wedged heels. She reached down to take off her sandals, but he moved her hand away. "I want you to keep these on. I want to feel you dig them into my ass when I fuck you."

In her fantasies, she'd imagined he'd be a dirty talker, and she was thrilled that he was. Each nasty word he uttered tingled deep inside her. Hovering over, he kissed her deeply then crushed her against him; skin to skin, they were as one. Pulling back, his gaze slid downward, slowly and seductively. "You're so fuckin' beautiful," he murmured, and her heart turned over in response.

"I've missed you so much," she whispered as she buried her face against his throat. Lightly, his hand outlined the circle of her breast, his touch sending currents of desire through her. She moaned softly as his tongue teased her rosy buds to pebble hardness then squirmed beneath him when he sucked each rigid peak. Each kiss and touch made her body tingle, and she drew herself closer to him.

"I fuckin' can't get you outta my mind." Jerry ran his tongue over her ribs then down to her stomach. "I fuckin' crave you." While he licked around and in her belly button, he reached under her and grabbed her ass cheek, his fingers digging into her flesh. He nipped a trail to her inner thighs, and as he teased the soft, sensitive flesh, Kylie arched her back. Moving his hands from her ass, he ran them up and down her legs, drawing closer and closer to her pussy, but never quite touching it. Then he moved his hand up to just beneath her sex, lightly whisking his fingers around her mound but not touching it, all the while his mouth peppering kisses across her sensitive skin.

"It feels so good." She reached down and caressed the strong tendons in the back of his neck, then dug her nails into his taut flesh. When his tongue inched closer to her throbbing sex, she sucked in her breath in anticipation, but then he returned to nipping her inner thighs. Back and forth his tongue tormented her, and her nerves were sparking like live wires on the verge of short circuiting.

He began stroking, kissing, and licking her swollen lips, returning every so often to her inner thighs and belly button. When she whimpered, his soft laugh vibrated against her, manifesting a jolt of pleasure only he could conjure. He moved her thighs further apart, and a cool rush of air covered her wet mound. With his finger, he pressed against her heated opening, moving his digit back and forth. "You like that?" Instead of answering, Kylie grabbed his hair and pushed his face into her, trying to move it up to her engorged clit. "Patience, baby," he said in a deep, sensual voice, his eyes locking with hers. Then he slid a finger through her slit, and her moans filled the room.

"Touch me. I'm aching for you. Please," she whispered. Kylie thought for sure if he didn't touch her throbbing clit soon, she'd go insane. Every fiber and nerve inside her shivered and sparked. "Jerry. Touch me. Now," she rasped in a deep voice she didn't recognize.

With a mischievous smile, he rubbed all around her pussy, his finger going in and out of her partway, but her clit was left untouched. It created a vacuum of sensation that made her yearn for his strokes on her sweet spot more and more. Was he ever going to give her what she was so deeply craving?

Jerry buried his nose among her wet folds, sniffing loudly as she looked on. He raised his head and locked his gaze with hers. "You smell fuckin' awesome, and I bet you taste just as good." Withdrawing his finger from inside her, he slowly placed it in his mouth and sucked her juices off it. "Hmm… fucking fantastic. Now I need a deeper taste."

Kylie's ass jumped off the mattress when Jerry slid his tongue over her clit, then licked her over and over as though that was the only thing in the world he had to do. It felt amazing. The sound of his lapping drove her crazy as he consistently stroked her sweet spot, taking her to higher levels of euphoria than he ever had before. She cried out for release, then shattered into a million glowing stars, yet he still licked her until it tickled and she laughed. Shimmying up her body, he kissed her. She tasted herself mixed with his minty flavor.

"I can't believe how great that was," she gushed.

He smiled and kissed her again. "You're something else. You turn my fuckin' world all around."

She felt his hardness poking between her legs and reached down to grasp it, loving the way he grunted from deep in his throat. "You want me to lick it?" she asked, loving the way it was smooth and warm in her hand.

"I want to plunge it inside you. I want to fuck you hard and deep." Feathering a trail of kisses down her body, he leaned back on his heels. "Open the drawer and take out a condom for me, babe." He pointed to the nightstand and she rummaged through the drawer then handed a foil packet to him, but he shook his head. "You put it on me."

Rolling it on, she marveled how something so small could fit over something so large. Before she secured it all the way down, she ran her tongue over the base of his hardness and he groaned. Kylie loved the effect she had on him. He gently pushed her down on her back and spread her legs open. "Can you take it rough and deep?" he asked hoarsely.

"Yeah. I want it that way." She placed her hands on his hips.

"If it gets to be too much, tell me and I'll slow it down. It's just that

I need you so fuckin' badly." He entered her and she gasped, her tight walls immediately closing around him. "Fuck, it feels so good. You're so damn tight. I love it. And your heels digging into my ass turns me way the hell on." He slowly moved in and out, and her body met his rhythm fairly quickly.

"I like you inside me," she said.

He smiled, bent over, and kissed her lightly on the lips. "Lift your legs," he commanded. She brought them upwards and pressed her knees to her chest. He took off her sandals, each of them thumping on the bedroom floor. "Put your feet on my chest." She did as she was told, and when Jerry leaned over her, she raised her hips. "Fuck, I'm so deep in you, it feels fantastic. You like that, honey?"

She absolutely loved it. As Jerry pounded into her, she pushed him back out with her feet, and soon they were moaning and sweating, their bodies fused together in a fiery dance of sex. He wet his finger between her folds and ran it over her small puckered opening as he continued to thrust in and out of her. The way he touched her ass cheeks and rosy opening drove her over the top, and she came hard, her pussy clenching his dick like a clamp. "Oh, Jerry. Oh…" Ecstasy overtook her and Kylie cried out, not caring who heard her through the thin walls of his apartment.

Jerry followed her with throaty growls, his body rigid one minute and draping over her knees the next. After a few moments, he pulled back, placed her legs to one side of him, then fell back on the mattress, tucking her next to him, her back against his spent dick. "That was fuckin' incredible," he said, lightly running his fingers up and down her arms.

She pressed her butt closer to him so no space separated them; it was as though they were joined as one. "I'm very happy. You make me happy." She turned her head sideways and her mouth grazed his jawline.

He dipped his head and captured her lips, and they kissed for a long time. Patting her ass, he slipped his arm around her. Soon, Kylie heard his even breaths and knew he'd fallen asleep, but she was still on a high plane of emotions, and sleep eluded her. She stared at the generic white curtains as they billowed in the cool, summer breeze, and replayed the whole evening in her mind.

I'm hooked on him.

Oh, shit.

Chapter Twenty-Three

For the past week, Jerry and Kylie had fallen into a routine: texting during the day, fucking at night. Sometimes he'd pick her up at her friends' houses or around the corner from her dad's house. He spent his whole day waiting for it to end so he'd be with her. He hated like hell that he couldn't touch or hold her in front of the brothers, but he knew Kylie wanted it that way for now, and he supposed he did too.

Each time he saw and spoke to Banger, he'd beat himself up for inflicting his president with such disrespect and betrayal. Something had to give with the situation. He'd promised himself numerous times that it would be the last, but it never was. He wanted all of her: her taste, the feel of her skin next to his. His compulsion to kiss and touch her consumed him, and he craved feeling her from the inside. She had become his everything, and as hard as he tried to push his feelings away, he couldn't. It was like she was what he'd been looking for his whole life. But he knew it was too much, and even though he wanted her, the thought scared the shit out of him. He prided himself on having self-control, but this thing he had with Kylie was out of control, and he didn't know how to rein it in.

The phone ringing intruded on his thoughts. "Hey, Kylie."

"Hi. Whatcha doing?"

"Not much. Just hanging at the club until church. How did the job interview go today?"

"I think I did all right, but I've thought that for the past two weeks. I can't believe I'm having such a hard time finding a job. I applied to a few more today. One of them is with the Wildlife Preserve Association, and I *really* want that job. It has full benefits and it's right up my alley."

"Full benefits with a summer job?"

She paused, and he was ready to repeat himself when she said, "No. It's a full-time job. The last two interviews I had were full-time jobs."

"You just gonna quit when school starts?"

He heard her cluck her tongue then take a deep breath. "I decided to stay in Pinewood Springs. I'm not going back to school."

"What the fuck? Why not?"

"I want us to spend more time together. I'd miss you too much."

Jerry's head spun. She was dropping out of school for him? "I never asked you to do that."

"I know, but I want to."

"Does your dad know 'bout your decision?"

"Not yet. You don't seem happy about it."

He blew out a long breath. He wasn't sure how the hell he felt about it. Having Kylie around full-time would kick ass, but that would mean a major commitment, and he wasn't there yet with her. Their fucking was all-consuming, but the *relationship* part of it scared the shit out of him. "I don't want you screwing up your future for what we have."

"And what do we have?" He picked up a tremor in her voice. *Shit.*

"A helluva good time. But good times don't last forever."

"Is that all I am to you—a good time?"

"Yeah," he lied.

"I don't mean anything more to you than all the other women you've fucked?"

He couldn't let her change her life for him. Hell, he couldn't promise her the type of relationship she deserved. He was confused about his feelings, and blown away at the intensity of the connection they had. *Fuck, I know I have to push her away. I can't let her do this.*

"We're having a good time. Let's leave it at that. You told me you love college, and now you want to throw it away for me? I can come up and see you sometimes, and when you come home on breaks we'll hook up. You need to go back to school."

"I thought we had more between us. I'm willing to go to the community college in town so I can be with you, and you're telling me not to bother?"

"Pretty much." His insides clenched with the knowledge he was hurting her.

"So, to you, I'm just another fuck?"

No, Kylie. You're so much more than that to me. You're in my system, and no woman has ever been with me the way you have. But I can't destroy your life. You deserve better. "I wouldn't say that. You're by far my favorite."

"Thanks for *that*." Her voice was brimming with unshed tears, and he wished he could hold her and tell her he was a poor liar. "Can we get together after church?"

He gritted his teeth. "Won't work. I've got a ton of shit to do at the club. I'll call you. Maybe tomorrow."

"You said that yesterday."

"What can I say? I'm busy. Gotta go now, they just called church. See you."

She mumbled something he couldn't quite make out. He hated the hurt feelings he brought her, but he didn't want to be responsible for her quitting school. He should never have started anything with Kylie, should've left it in his head as he had for several years. But since he'd taken the plunge, it was up to him to stop it. He never should have led her on, but after the first taste, he couldn't let go. Quitting school was just the sign he needed to tell him to back the fuck off.

Over the next few days, Kylie called him asking why they hadn't met up. He always told her he was too busy with club business, but he knew she didn't believe him. It'd been almost a week since they'd last spent time together, and his body ached for her. He was deliberately pushing her away, and he knew it had to be hurting her, because it was killing him. After some distance, she'd get over him; he'd snap out of it too, as soon as his cock made it back into easy pussy. The last two times they'd spoken, it'd ended with her hanging up on him.

As he sat at the clubhouse thinking about her, Axe plopped down on the chair next to him. "Hey, buddy."

"Hey."

Puck rushed over two beers for them then walked away. In a low voice, Axe said, "I gotta talk to you about something." He took a long pull on his beer. "You know how Banger's been flipped about this fucker in the purple Corvette? Well, he asked me to tail Kylie, so I've been doing it for a few weeks. He wants me to report to him what's going on, if anyone is following her, and pretty much all that goes on with her." He fixed his gaze on Jerry's. "He wants to know *everything*. You know what I'm sayin', dude?"

Axe's words punched him full on, and Jerry just nodded. What could he say? Since Axe was tagging Kylie, he saw all the times he and she met, spent the night, and even kissed. Once Banger found out, it would be hell, so it was just as well he was pushing her away; he didn't want her to see him get his ass kicked by her dad and lose his patch. "What're you gonna tell Banger?"

Axe ran his hand through his hair. "Damn, you two been fucking up a storm. Shit, I don't know what to do here. If I tell Banger, you're as good as dead, but if I don't then I'm betraying the brotherhood and our prez. Fuck, man. Help me out here."

Jerry shrugged. "Do what you have to do. I knew the risk, and I deserve the punishment."

Axe stared hard at him. "You know I don't wanna do this. I shouldn't be tellin' you, but we're brothers and friends, so I wanted to give you the heads-up. No hard feelings, but I have to tell Banger."

Jerry finished his beer then held Axe's gaze. "None taken. I'd do the same thing if I were in your position."

"I noticed you guys haven't been together for the last week. She break it off with you?"

"No, but I'm breaking it off with her. I've been trying to avoid her, but it's fuckin' hard to do."

Axe nodded in agreement. "Maybe you can work this out. Go to Banger and tell him how you both feel. Fuck, he was young once. I'm sure he'll get it."

"She wants to quit college to stay in Pinewood Springs."

"Damn. Now *that's* not gonna fly with Banger."

"I know. Besides me fucking the prez's daughter, you find out anything about the asshole?"

"Nah. There was a guy watching her. Found out his name was Marcus Westman."

"I know that fucker. I beat his ass when I was in Crested Peak and he was bothering Kylie. I warned him. What the hell's he doing in Pinewood?"

"He lives here."

"I'll be damned. Does he have anything to do with the other fucker?"

"Not sure. Right now, it seems like he's acting alone. He follows her around a lot, but only when she's alone or with her girlfriends. I'm gonna check with Banger on how he wants me to handle this asshole."

"I'd like to be in on the fun with this."

"Not sure what Banger's gonna want me to do. I'm meeting him in a bit to tell him about this Marcus jerk. I won't say anything about the two of you, but I'm gonna have to tell him at some point."

"Appreciate it, man."

"Hey." Banger's voice startled Jerry.

He turned around and watched as the president approached their table. "How's it going, Banger? How's Belle?"

"So ready to have the baby." Banger chuckled.

"You know what it is yet?" Jerry asked.

"A boy." Pride shone in the president's eyes. He cleared his throat. "You got the routine down on the couple at the trailer park?"

"I do. They didn't heed my warning."

"Guess we'll have to show them we mean business." Banger turned to Axe. "Let's go in my office. I don't have much time, gotta take Belle to the doctor." Axe stood and the two men left the room.

After a half hour, Jerry heard Banger's powerful Harley leap to life as

Axe came by the table. "He wants me to 'talk' to Marcus, but not kill him… yet."

"You need help?"

"I'm good. Kylie's coming soon. Banger wants her to file a bunch of shit on his desk. I'm outta here. Be smart, bro."

Jerry nodded then watched Axe leave the clubhouse. Kylie was coming, and he'd have to hurt her real bad so she'd hate him. He could deal with her hate, just not her disappointment or pain. He stared out the window, waiting for her car to swing into the parking lot. A while later, he spotted it.

"Wendy. Get over here," he called out to the club girl who was seated on a barstool. Before he'd been with Kylie, Wendy and Rosie were his favorite club whores, and he knew they were confused as to why he'd stopped asking for them.

Wendy squealed with delight and slid off the stool, marching over to him. She wore a low-cut tank top and a short, pink spandex skirt. "You want something, handsome?"

Grasping her hand, he yanked her onto his lap, facing him. She moved her face closer to kiss him, but he turned away. "No kissing."

"Okay. I'm just glad you want me. It's been too long." She leaned closer to him, her tits pressed against him.

When he heard the door open, he placed his hand behind Wendy's neck, pulled her close, and whispered in her ear, "You gonna get me a beer soon?" The effect he intended was successful, and he heard Kylie gasp. When he turned to look at her, his heart lurched. She was so beautiful in her gingham sundress and strappy sandals, her lush hair flowing around her. For a heartbeat, he locked his gaze with hers; when he saw the hurt tearing in it, the guilt churned like gasoline in his guts. She rushed down the hall, the slam of a door echoing.

Once Kylie left, Jerry gently pushed Wendy back. "Be a good girl and get me a beer."

She wiggled off his lap. "You want it here or in your room?" Her eyes sparkled.

"Here. I've changed my mind."

Her eyes widened and she cupped her breasts in her hands, squeezing them together. "You turning this down?"

"Yeah. Another time. Now, go on and get me a beer."

When she brought it over to him, she bent down low, her tits rubbing against him as she raked her fingernails up his arm. "Need anything else?"

He picked up the bottle. "I'm good. Thanks." He guzzled it down, his cock hard from knowing Kylie was only a few yards away. His sweet, perfect Kylie.

After a while, his stomach grumbled and he decided to go in the kitchen to make a sandwich. He knew he should get his goddamned ass on his bike and leave, but he wanted to hang around. He wanted to see her again before he left.

On his way to the kitchen, he bumped into her as she exited Banger's office. The softness of her skin against his arm made him want to haul her on his bike and take her with him in search of their own private island.

"I need to talk to you. Let's go on the back porch." She pushed past him and he followed her outside, shutting the door behind them. He leaned against the railing, watching her.

"Why are you being mean to me?" she asked softly, her bottom lip trembling.

He wanted to pull her into his arms and cover her mouth with his, but he knew he had to be the strong one. He was older, a patched member of the Insurgents; he owed his president loyalty, and he couldn't let her fuck up her life because of him. He inhaled deeply. "I'm not being mean."

"You keep making excuses not to see me, and I find a club girl in your lap when I come in? Have you been fucking them again?"

"You and I had a good time. You were a challenge I enjoyed conquering, but it's time you find a younger guy. You know, a college kid who doesn't know much about a woman."

"You don't want me anymore?" Her eyes glistened.

I fuckin' crave you. "It's just that I'm used to experienced women who really know how to pleasure a man." Pain shot through his heart when he saw her wince at his words, her finger wiping at an unshed tear. "There're plenty of them. I'm not the type to settle for one woman. I like easy pussy and a lot of variety—you knew that. Not looking for anything long-term. Sorry if I gave you the wrong impression. You're better suited for a guy who wants the boyfriend shit." He paused, then dealt her the final blow. "You're not for me." *You're the only one for me. I can't fuckin' get you out of my mind and heart.*

Kylie sniffled, shifting from one foot to another. "So, that's it then?" She looked down at the floor.

"Guess it is. You'll find someone. You'll get over me."

She glanced up, her eyes brimming with defiance. "I know I will. It's much easier to get over the jerks than the nice guys. I'll be over you in no time. As a matter of fact, Ricky's coming to visit me this weekend. He's been wanting to date me for a long time, so this all works out. I can tell him I'm free."

He gritted his teeth as sudden anger at her being with another man pricked at him. He couldn't blame her for hating him. He wanted it; it made it easier for her. "Sounds like you got a handle on it." *I'm sorry, Kylie. I'll cherish you forever.*

"Yeah. I do. I gotta go." She pushed past him, her arm brushing against his. That accidental touch went straight to his dick as he watched her hips swing from side to side until she disappeared into the great room. A thickness formed in his throat. She was gone. It was finished. He'd done the right thing, even if it'd cost him her love. He turned around and placed his forehead against the doorway. Behind him, he heard footsteps.

"You look like you lost a friend," Wendy said, rubbing her hand over his back.

"I did," he said softly. Walking away from her, he headed out into the night, the darkness mimicking his heart.

Chapter Twenty-Four

H E WATCHED AS Kelsey slurped her Dr. Pepper through her straw, the noise grating on his nerves. She glanced up at him and smiled widely. *Fucking cunt thinks I'm into her.* He leaned back in the chair and pushed away his half-eaten sandwich, wishing the skinny girl with the bad complexion was Kylie. He'd had to lay low ever since Ricky had been found. The black-haired man was pissed as hell that he'd made a stupid mistake in thinking he'd killed the asshole. If the punk hadn't survived, he'd have Kylie with him already, but all his plans had gone askew. He was in Insurgents territory, and he knew there was no way she wasn't being watched by the damn brotherhood. And she'd been fucking one of the bikers. He'd found out Jerry was his name, and he had a sister—Kelsey. So he sat, watching her in disgust.

"How often does your brother come by to see you and your mom?"

Kelsey finished slurping her drink then said, "'Bout once a week or so. Depends. If my mom needs money, she calls him."

"Does he have a set day when he comes by?"

She shook her head. "You're not hungry?" She pointed at his dish.

"No. You didn't answer my question."

"What was it?"

The man spoke through his teeth with forced restraint. "Does your brother come by on the same day each week?"

She shrugged.

He bared his teeth. *What a stupid bitch.* "You using?"

"No," she said too quickly, her eyes darting to the side. "Why you ask me that?"

"You got the signs on your skin. Your brother give you the money to buy the shit?"

"Why're you asking so many questions about my brother? Since you're so interested in him, you should be on a date with him rather than me." She laughed.

The man narrowed his eyes. "Aren't you the funny one." He motioned for the waitress to bring the check. After he threw a twenty-dollar bill on the table, he scooted out of the booth. His dick was hard—not from Kelsey, but from thinking of Kylie. He hated that she was fucking Jerry, so he'd fuck the biker's sister until he was tired of her, then throw her away. "Let's go." He walked out of the restaurant with Kelsey trailing behind him.

In his car, he turned to the young woman. "You look like someone who wants to be fucked." She giggled, and he wanted to smack her real hard, but that was for later. "Do you want it?"

"What do you have in mind?" She leaned toward him, running her fingertips up his arm.

"You strike me as someone who likes more than a vanilla fuck. Am I right?"

"I like a lot of things, but I can't do half of what I think you want because my mind isn't into it right now. I'm too worried about money." She slid her eyes up his face until they met his.

"I like it rough and real nasty. You up for that if I can give you something for your effort?"

A wide smile broke out across her face. "I can manage that. Are we going to your place?"

"A motel. A fucking seedy motel, to be exact. That's the way I like it."

Kelsey settled in the passenger's seat. "Let's get going."

The Fallen Star Motel made reservations by the hour, and he booked three hours in one of the rooms farthest from the small lobby. The room was shabby, the sheets dingy white, and the curtains were dust mite central. A scratched table with a metal folding chair was in the corner of the room. The guy set his black doctor's bag down on the table.

"What's that? We spending the night here?" Kelsey asked.

A cold smile played on his lips. "It's my bag of toys. We're going to have a real good time, Kelsey. And if you do well, I'll give you a bonus. For the next three hours, you're mine. You do what I tell you, and you'll be fine. If you don't, you'll be punished. Do you understand?"

"I guess. Are you into that bondage shit?"

"Yeah, and a lot more."

"I'm okay with it as long as you don't get too rough."

"No promises." He unzipped the bag and took out a paper towel, a spoon, a lighter, a syringe, and a baggie of white powder. "You want some?" He waved the baggie in front of her face.

Licking her lips, Kelsey's eyes lit up and she nodded. "I've never injected."

"You've been missing out. I can show you how good it'll make you feel." He poured a small amount onto the spoon and lit the lighter underneath it. "You're gonna love the rush."

Three hours later, he untied Kelsey's hands and feet. She'd been trussed up like a hog, and the angry red marks on her ass and back made him go tight in his pants. She lay still on the mattress marked with her blood and his semen. "Our time is up." He placed the ropes, wrist and ankle cuffs, collar, and paddle in his bag. Out of the corner of his eye, he spotted the leather crop he'd used earlier on Kelsey's clit. It was his favorite way of disciplining a bitch, and when he was whipping her clit, making it red and swollen, he was punishing Kylie for fucking the goddamned Insurgent.

Flexing his wrist, he flicked the crop against her reddened ass cheeks. "I said, let's go." Kelsey groaned and turned over, grimacing as she pushed herself off the bed. He'd placed her clothes next to her, and she slowly dressed. Under his breath, he chuckled, his dick growing hard once more just thinking of all the things he was going to do to his Kylie when her time came. And it would be soon. He had to have her.

"You got anymore crystal?" Kelsey asked as she walked stiffly toward him.

"You had enough. Next time, I'll give you more."

The guy opened the door and walked out without a backward glance at Kelsey. Once she got in the car, she sat sideways, and he figured it was because her ass was too sore. He fucking loved that.

"Here we are," he said as his car idled in front of her trailer. The purple Corvette was locked away in a storage unit, since fucking Ricky had managed to live. He didn't have a choice, so now he was driving a sensible Buick. He ought to seek out the little shit and finish off what he'd started.

He leaned over and pulled her to him by the hair. She yelped and he covered her mouth with his. She moaned softly, pressing closer to him. Bitches were all the same. They'd tell a guy they didn't want to do the hard shit, but then they ended up fucking loving it. It happened all the time to him. Cunts were so predictable.

"Don't tell your brother we're going out."

"Why?"

He twisted his hand in her hair and yanked it until her eyes teared and a painful whimper emitted from her throat. "Don't fucking question me. Just don't tell him shit about us."

"Okay," she gasped.

"You can go now." He shoved her back toward the door. She slowly slid out of the car, groaning as she moved her legs.

"What about the money you promised me?"

He opened his wallet and took out four one-hundred-dollar bills. "Three hundred for the fucking, and one hundred for having such a great ass." He threw the money on the ground. "Close the door." She complied.

As he was leaving, he glanced in the rearview mirror and saw her struggling to bend down to pick up the bills before they blew away. *What a dirty slut.* If the Insurgent weren't her brother, he wouldn't even spit on her. While he banged her rough, each time he came, he saw Kylie's pretty face. He needed her badly, and he couldn't wait much longer.

Chapter Twenty-Five

KYLIE WAS FULL of sadness, as every other emotion was pushed away. Where there once was passion, laughter, and light, it was now just an aching emptiness. When Jerry had told her he didn't want to be with her anymore, her heart had broken into tiny pieces, and she'd had to leave before she broke down in front of him. She'd wanted to wrap her arms around him and beg him to stay with her, but he'd made it clear he was bored of her already. What they had hadn't even lasted the whole summer, only seventy-two days—nothing more than a blink of an eye in a person's life.

She pulled her knees closer to her as she sat on the front porch, watching summer unfold. Her dad was right—Jerry was nothing but a macho, asshole man-whore. She was well rid of him, and she shouldn't have ever let her feelings get the better of her. From the beginning, she knew becoming involved with him was a risk, but deep down, she'd hoped he would've fallen for her, realizing she was the only one for him. But he hadn't. He'd had his fun, and now was bored with her inexperienced fumbles when they screwed.

How could he leave me when we had a connection stronger than anything we'd ever felt before with anyone? How am I going to survive the summer before school starts? She'd made up her mind that she wouldn't go to the clubhouse for the rest of the summer and would limit family gatherings with the club.

The glass tabletop rumbled softly, and she looked at her phone's screen as it started blinking.

Ricky: *Just touching base re this weekend. We still good?*

She'd forgotten he was coming this weekend. At that moment, though, she was grateful he'd insisted on coming to see her.

Kylie: *Yes! Can't wait. When u coming?*
Ricky: *Friday good? I'll b @ ur house @ 6. Good?*
Kylie: *Perfect. See u in a couple days.*

She smiled weakly, wishing she were happier about Ricky's visit, but the heartache over losing Jerry was crushing. Ever since he'd thrown her aside, she'd shed so many tears until no more would come. Her insides were raw as though a winter wind blew right through her skin. The last conversation they'd had mocked her, replaying like an echo. Even though she put on a brave face for her father and friends, and told herself she was better without him, her world crumbled inside her. She craved his touch as she lay alone in her bed, swearing she could smell his familiar clean scent.

Maybe Ricky would be the diversion she needed to put everything in perspective. She'd have to snap out of it, because lamenting over what could have been didn't mean shit. Jerry obviously didn't share the same feelings for her as she did about him. It was over, time to move on. The way he had Wendy in his lap, her breasts jammed against him, told Kylie that he'd already moved on just fine.

She sighed and wrapped her arms tighter around her knees as she stared out at nothingness.

SINCE RICKY ARRIVED the day before, Kylie had been having a great time. She'd been so busy showing him around the area that she didn't have time to obsess over Jerry until the moments when she was in her room, surrounded by darkness and moonlight. It was at those times when she missed him the most. Since they'd had their talk, she hadn't heard from him, and it hurt her that he hadn't even reached out to ask how she was doing. He turned out to be a typical biker asshole—the ones her father had warned her about since as far back as she could remember.

Ricky was staying in one of the guest rooms at her house. Banger and Belle had Baylee design a huge house, so there was always plenty of room.

Running down the stairs, Kylie swung open the front door and rushed to Ricky's car. "Sorry I'm late. I was just finishing up sending a resumé to another job application. I can't believe what a hard time I'm having getting a damn job. You're lucky you can work for your dad's accounting firm. If I work with my dad, I'd be covered in grease." She pulled on her sunglasses.

"I thought you had your heart set on the Wildlife Preserve job?"

"I did, but it's full-time, and I don't want to take it then quit in a couple of months."

"What job did you apply for now?"

"It's sounds very intriguing. It showed up in my e-mail with a few other postings. It still works with wildlife, but it's a small non-profit that brings the injured animals back to health and reintroduces them to the wild. I've never heard of it before, but I'm definitely curious. And the best part is that it's a summer job. It'd be perfect. I'm keeping my fingers crossed."

Ricky placed his hand on Kylie's bare thigh. "I'm sure you'll get the job. You're just too damn enthusiastic not to."

She laughed and shifted in her seat, and Ricky slowly slid his hand away.

After the afternoon movie, they hung out at the mall for a while. Kylie helped Ricky pick out some souvenirs for his parents and siblings. When they walked out of the T-shirt store, Kylie bumped into Marcus. Surprised, she said, "What're you doing here?"

Marcus glanced at Ricky. "Same thing you are. Shopping."

"Yeah, that's right. You live here."

He nodded. "What are you doing with *him*?"

Before Kylie could answer, Ricky put a protective arm around her. "Are you following Kylie? You need to back off and leave her alone. Just because you were in the same class together doesn't mean you're friends."

Kylie shivered when she saw the coldness in Marcus's gaze. He turned from her and stared at Ricky. "It's too *fucking* bad they found you alive." Then he whirled around and marched away.

"Shit. I can't believe he just said that." Kylie looked after Marcus, but he'd disappeared into the crowd. She scanned the area and spotted Axe, who quickly slipped away. She narrowed her eyes. Axe was watching her, which meant only one thing—her dad put a tail on her.

"That asshole better never come near you again, or I'll beat his ass." Ricky's face was flushed and his nostrils flared.

She gave him a quick hug. "Thanks for standing up to him. The guy definitely gives me the creeps. I wish he'd just go away. I'm pretty sure he's going to learn soon not to mess with me, since one of the brothers is tailing us. I guess my dad wants to make sure the weirdo in the purple Corvette doesn't try anything with me. Most likely, Axe has been tailing me since I got home from school or shortly after—"

She stopped mid-sentence, shame and fear crawling down her back. *Axe must've seen all the times I went to Jerry's to spend the night. Dad's going to find out that all the times I said I was going to Margo's or Ginny's house, I was lying out my ass. Shit.*

"You okay, Kylie? You look real pale. Do you need to sit down somewhere?"

"I'm good. I'm just hungry."

"Let's go eat then. I'm hungry too."

For a few minutes, she stood frozen, letting the weight of the situation sink in, mortification spreading through her. She didn't want her dad knowing all *that*. Learning she was seeing Jerry was something she had planned on dealing with if they would've stuck together, but finding out about her overnight visits was something she never would've shared with her dad.

"You sure you're good?"

Kylie leaned against him and nodded. The tightness of his arm around her brought her out of her daze. She looked up and smiled at him while gently pulling out of his hold. "Let's get something to eat," she said, wincing at his disappointed look.

When the hostess showed them to their table at Burgers & Beer Joint, they walked past Jerry, Throttle, Rock, Rags, and Hoss, who were seated nearby. Seeing Jerry made her heart race, but she kept her chin up high as she went by their table.

"Hey, Kylie," Throttle said. "Who's your friend?"

From the tone of his voice, she knew he was ribbing Jerry, and she took a perverse pleasure from it. She stopped by him. "Hey. My friend Ricky is visiting from Denver. We just saw a movie at the mall. What kind of burger did you order?" She felt Jerry's eyes boring into her, but she didn't glance at him once.

"Plain. I'm a simple guy."

"Simple in the head," Rock said, and the other two brothers guffawed.

"Fuck off." Throttle looked at Ricky. "You having a good time with Kylie?"

Kylie bristled. She'd known Throttle longer than she knew Hawk, and he could be a real asshole. Taunting laced his voice, and she didn't want Ricky to be the butt end of one of his stupid jokes. "He is. We gotta go. Later." She tugged Ricky by the hand and they settled down at their table.

"Are those some of the guys in your dad's club?" Ricky looked over her shoulder at them.

"Yeah. The Insurgents own this restaurant, and there're always a few of them eating or drinking here."

"Wasn't one of the guys the one who I met at the spring festival?"

Her heart squeezed. "Uh-huh. What looks good to you on the menu?"

"I haven't looked yet. Just so you know, he's giving me some sort of death glare." He laughed nervously.

"Ignore him. He's a jerk." The words came out harsher than she intended.

"It's hard to do, since he hasn't taken his eyes off our table since we sat down. When you were talking to the older dude, he kept staring at you. I noticed you dissed him. You two fighting?"

She shook her head. "We're not doing anything. I didn't come here to talk about him, okay?"

"Fair enough." He opened the menu. "Tell me what you recommend."

They laughed and talked for a couple hours, and Kylie forgot Jerry was seated just one table behind her. It wasn't until Throttle yelled out, "Bye, Kylie," that she remembered they were there.

She twisted around at the waist and waved at Throttle. Jerry tilted his chin to her, but she paid no attention to him. "See you, Throttle." She turned back to Ricky and the dessert they were sharing.

When they arrived at her house, they were both pretty beat. "I had a real nice time," Ricky said as they walked up the sidewalk under the moonlight. The heat of the day had been replaced by a cool breeze, and goose bumps carpeted Kylie's bare arms. Taking out her key, she quietly opened the door.

"I need to talk with you." Jerry's deep voice startled them both. She spun around and saw him step out of the shadows from the green bushes, now looking almost black against the night's sky.

"Go on," she whispered to Ricky, who walked into the house. She closed the door and ambled down the brick sidewalk to the shadows where Jerry stood. Her heartbeat thumped against her bones, and she was sure he could hear each strike.

"Why'd you ignore me at the restaurant?"

She rubbed her chilled arms and shook her head. "You are too much. I gotta get back in."

He reached out and gripped her hand, her flesh tingling from the shock of his touch. "How've you been?" His breath fanned out over her face, warming her.

"Fine."

"That's good. How long's Ricky staying?"

She gave a half-shrug. "Not sure. We're having a good time, so maybe another week." She knew perfectly well Ricky was leaving the following morning. Even though he wanted to stay, he had to return to work.

"Don't do anything stupid with him."

Her nervous, longing demeanor turned into liquid fire as she jerked her hand out of his. "How dare you tell me what to do. You told me we were finished, and now you're creeping around my bushes spying on me? How fuckin' pathetic!"

Jerry gripped her arm and shook her. "Watch your goddamned mouth. I'm not spying on you. I just wanted to talk to you. I don't like the way you're talking to me. You're fuckin' out of line, woman."

She shoved him back. "I'm not your woman, and I can speak to you any damned way I want. You gave up any claim you may have had on me, so you back the fuck off. And stop telling me what I can and can't do with another man." Her chest rose up and down as she breathed heavily.

He glared at her. "You got a mouth on you. I can tell you're Banger's daughter."

"And don't you fucking forget it." Kylie tossed her head back, sprinted up the walkway, then went inside the house and shut the door. Her body shook from both anger and arousal. Feeling Jerry's closeness and his hand on hers made the spot between her legs throb. She missed him so much and wanted him to fill her up, take her over the edge, and consume her. She hated that her body and mind weren't on the same page; the hurt he bestowed on her told her he was a grade-A jerk, but her body craved him like an addict.

"Everything okay?" Ricky's hushed voice echoed in the foyer.

Slowly, she exhaled. "Yeah."

"Do you have something with him?"

Hanging her head, heavy with thoughts of Jerry, she said in a low voice, "No. I don't." Silence shrouded them then Kylie sighed. "I'm so tired. I'll see you in the morning."

As she lay in her bed, watching the ribbons of moonlight seeping through her slatted blinds, she lifted her hand and smelled Jerry's scent, still on her skin. She'd never have him again. What had happened? She'd been on an all-time high one minute then crushed down the next. She'd let him into her life, and only someone on the inside could have shattered her heart as he'd done with just a few words. Wiping her wet cheeks, she hugged the pillow close to her, wishing it were Jerry.

Chapter Twenty-Six

Kylie waited outside Axe's apartment for a long time until he came out, heading toward his Harley. He whirled around when he heard her call his name. "Hey, Kylie." His eyebrows rose. "Whatcha doing here?"

"I know my dad has you following me. I spotted you at the mall. I'll say you're good because I didn't notice you until the day before."

Axe stared at her, stone-faced.

"Since you've been on my ass, you must know Jerry and I had a thing for a bit. And that's why I'm here. I don't want you telling my dad that I spent many nights at Jerry's apartment."

"Kylie, you know I can't do that."

"Hear me out. It was in the past. Jerry and I aren't seeing each other anymore, so what'll be gained from telling my dad about it? I'm asking you as a friend not to do it. There's no reason to upset my dad."

Axe blew out a long breath. "Fuck. I can't lie if he asks me."

"I'm not asking you to lie. I'm asking you to omit that part of your report. Please?"

He groaned and rubbed his hand on his chest. "Fuck. Okay, I won't say anything, but if he asks me about you and Jerry, I gotta tell him the truth. Fuck, Kylie, he's my president. You know how that goes. You've been around this your whole life. You're asking too much from me."

"I know, and that's why I'm not asking you to lie. Just don't bring it up first."

He nodded slowly. "Okay, but if he asks me, I'm telling him what I've seen. You better be prepared for that."

"I can deal with that. Thanks. I owe you big time." Kylie shifted her weight from side to side.

"So, you and Jerry are really done? I'm surprised. I thought you two were really into each other. Fuck, he's been talking about you for years."

"Well, I guess we got it out of our system. Fantasies are usually better than the real thing. I gotta go. Thanks again." She sauntered away and slid into her car. Axe started his Harley and took off. Kylie felt calmer knowing her dad may never find out, but a sudden onslaught of loneliness captured her. Ricky had left that morning, and the last thing she wanted to do at that moment was go home. She took out her phone and called Margo, and the two friends made arrangements to meet up in an hour.

As she sat in The French Bistro waiting for Margo, she opened her e-mails, her pulse racing when she saw one from the non-profit wildlife rescue. She opened it and adrenaline shot through her when she read they were interested in setting up an interview with her. They'd asked her to pick some of the available dates they'd listed, so she hurriedly typed back her response, choosing an interview date for the upcoming Friday. When she clicked "send," she crossed her fingers.

About fifteen minutes later, Margo came in and Kylie told her about the interview. She and Margo had been friends since she could walk. They'd lived in the same neighborhood and had shared all the joys and pains of growing up. They'd attended all the same schools, and when Kylie had left for college, the two girls had cried until Banger told them if they didn't stop, either Kylie would stay home or Margo would go to college. Her father's gruff voice and bewilderment at dealing with the two teenagers had made them laugh, and soon their tears of lament had turned to ones of merriment.

Margo never had an interest in studying beyond high school, so she took a job at the local shipping and packaging company. She seemed happy with working and partying.

"You doing okay?"

"Not really, but I'm forcing myself to get over him. I think it's harder because I've been crushing on him for quite a while. I was always insecure about screwing him. He's definitely used to way more experienced women than me."

"That shouldn't matter if he cares for you." Margo stirred a packet of artificial sugar in her iced tea.

"Right, but the point here is that he doesn't care for me. He told me that in so many words. I was just a good time for him, and now he's bored. Fuck, I even bought a book on how to please a man so I could learn some new things and get better at it."

"You did? Can I read it?"

Kylie giggled. "Sure. I was going to try some of the stuff on him, but then the fucking asshole broke up with me."

"I don't think he really wanted to. He probably thinks he's doing you a favor, and then you've got your dad who would scare the hell out of the devil." She laughed.

"Maybe, but he's still an asshole, and my head aches from thinking of him too much. Let's talk about you coming up to see me during Labor Day weekend. We'll have so much fun."

The two women laughed and talked while the black-haired man watched at a distance, his eyes lingering on Kylie's mouth, aching to kiss it.

BANGER CLOSED THE garage door and entered the house, hoping Belle hadn't seen him. He'd been thinking about her most of the day as he sat in his office at the clubhouse, and when he started writing her name instead of his on some documents he was working on, he decided to call it a day and head home. Kylie was hanging with Margo, Emily was at work at the hair salon, and Ethan was at baseball camp, so he'd have some much-needed alone time with his wife. Excitement coursed through him, and it still amazed him how affected he was by Belle. She was the constant sparkle in his life.

When he came into the kitchen, she was cleaning string beans by the sink, the loud beats of Creedence Clearwater Revival filling the room.

He padded softly over to her and wrapped his arms around her large belly. At seven months, Belle was huge. She'd complained to Banger about how big she looked, but he loved every inch of her; to him, she was the most beautiful woman in the world. He couldn't stop rubbing her stomach, loving how it felt whenever their baby kicked.

Belle jumped and squealed when he held her close. "You scared the crap outta me. Why are you home so early? You feeling all right?" Concern clouded her eyes.

He pulled her closer to him and nuzzled her neck, kissing the spot he knew made her weak in the knees. "Been thinking 'bout you all day. I wanted to spend some time with you without all the kids around." She pushed back and wiggled against his ass, his dick firming immediately. "You keep that up, woman, and we're gonna end up in the bedroom."

"I'd like that, but since the kids aren't here, we don't have to hide in our bedroom." She turned around and palmed his hardness, pushing him toward the table. After she pulled the chair out, she settled herself down. "Now, let's see if I can fix what you got going on in your jeans." She slowly unzipped his pants as he sucked his breath, his hands buried in her thick curls.

Keeping eye contact with her, Banger watched as Belle placed his dick into her mouth, sucking the underside of his head just the way he loved it. He was so damn horny that he almost blew in her mouth, but he gently pulled her back. "I want inside you, woman."

Belle stood up, turned around, and placed her hands on the table. Since she'd entered her third trimester, sex standing up or doggy style were her preferences since it relieved her back and pelvic pain. Banger reached around and fingered her wet clit before he pushed his hardness into her. Her soft moans turned him on and he slid into her heat. Careful not to thrust too hard or deep, he rocked back and forth, loving the way her fleshy ass bumped against him. As he stroked her bundle of nerves, he felt her silky walls tighten around his cock, and he knew she was close. He let himself go, and when she came, yelling and squealing, he followed with feral grunts. They stood like that for a few minutes before he bent over and kissed her, then pulled down her dress and helped her sit on one of the chairs.

"Damn, woman. You fuckin' know how to please your man." He winked at her as he shoved his dick in his jeans.

She smiled. "Be good and get me a bottled water. I'm parched. You made me scream too much."

He handed her the water and sat on the chair next to her. "You have a good day today?"

"It was just okay until you got home." She drank a large gulp of water then looked at him, a hint of concern glazing her face.

"You feel okay?" He instinctively placed his hand on her belly.

She nodded.

"Something you wanna tell me? You got that look on your face."

Belle pulled herself up, opened the desk drawer in the nook they'd made for it in the kitchen, and took out a book. Without saying a word, she handed it to Banger. He looked at the hardback, titled *Drive Him Wild: Knowing How to Pleasure Your Man*. With a quizzical gaze, he said, "You want me to read this? You want me to pick out the things I want you to do?"

Belle took a deep breath. "It's not mine. I found it under Kylie's mattress when I put clean sheets on her bed earlier today." She pressed her lips together and stared at him.

For a while, Banger just held the book, staring at it but not really comprehending what Belle was trying to tell him. Then a deep heat flushed through his body, his muscles tensing, his teeth grinding. "What the fuck? This trash is Kylie's?"

Belle nodded, even though it was a rhetorical question. Banger blew out of his chair and threw the book across the room. His face was red as he pounded his fists against the table, the steady thump of its legs against the stone tiles filling the space between him and Belle. Whipping out his phone, he dialed Axe. "I fuckin' want to see you at the clubhouse in ten minutes."

"I'm in the middle of fixing a carburetor on an old Harley. Can we make it in an hour?"

"You now got nine fuckin' minutes."

"On my way."

He shoved the phone in his back pocket. "I gotta go."

Belle walked over to him and hugged him. "Please don't overreact to this. I showed you because you asked me to keep an eye on Kylie this summer, but I want you to remember how it was to be young and curious about sex."

"If she's fucking who I think she is…" He slammed his fist down on the table again.

"You raised her well. You have to give her credit for knowing who is right for her and who isn't. These are *her* feelings for a man, not yours."

He cracked his knuckles and looked at her, his expression tight. "Enough. I gotta go." He kissed her quickly on the forehead and went out to the garage, slamming the back door. Jumping on his Harley, he peeled out of the driveway and rushed to the clubhouse, adrenaline pumping through his body.

"What the fuck's been your problem for the last few days? Shit, you've been acting like a bitch who has PMS," Throttle said to a glum-faced Jerry as they leaned against the bar.

"Maybe he's in love and she can't stand him," joked Rock.

"Maybe the two of you should shut the fuck up before I bust you in your mouths." Jerry turned away from them and stared at the back wall behind the bar as his two brothers guffawed and ribbed him more. Ignoring them, his thoughts drifted to Kylie, as they always did. Seeing her with Ricky the previous Saturday night had driven him crazy. When he'd seen her enter Burgers & Beer Joint, he'd been blown away at how beautiful she'd looked, and when she'd passed his table, her familiar scent drove his dick into overdrive. He'd been fucking miserable since he'd told her it was over. The truth was he didn't want it to be over. He wanted her in his life—always had.

All the hookups he'd had since he first had sex back in high school were superficial—a collage of one-night stands, nameless faces, and pleasure induced encounters. Nothing was real until he saw her, but she was young and off-limits, so he watched her grow from afar, burying his desire in easy pussy and booze. Then she was grown up but still off-limits, but the desire he had for her had grown until it was too big to contain. He'd finally succumbed to it, loving every minute of being with her.

The first time he'd taken her, he'd seen her reaction—beautiful and raw. The times they'd spent pleasuring each other were more real to him than anything in his life ever had been, and he'd felt her like the beating of his own heart. Even though he'd pushed her away, the tie they forged was still molten, and he knew it always would be.

As he brought his beer up to his lips, it flew out of his hand. Startled, he turned around, his gaze falling on Banger's red face and pulsating vein above his temple. Instantly, Jerry's stomach hardened as he stepped back, squinting.

With his finger in Jerry's face, Banger screamed, "You fuckin' sonofabitch! I told you never to touch my daughter!" He slammed his fist into Jerry's face, making him stumble back further. Then Banger punched him in the stomach and Jerry dropped to his knees. He kicked up, aiming for Jerry's chin, but Jerry grabbed it and pulled him down. Banger recovered and, with the agility of a mountain lion, pounced on Jerry, pummeling him over and over. "You fucked my daughter, you goddamned piece of shit! Don't ever get near her again!"

The front door swung open, and Jerry looked out of his swelling eyes to see Hawk come in, dash over to them, and pull Banger off. Banger swung his fist at Hawk but he ducked.

"Calm the fuck down! What the hell's going on here?"

Banger jerked away from Hawk, nostrils flaring, chest heaving. He started to go back to Jerry, but Hawk held him back, and Jerry breathed a sigh of relief. "Throttle, Rock, help Jerry to his feet," Hawk ordered.

Two pairs of strong arms set Jerry upright, but then he jerked away.

From the stack of napkins on the bar, he grabbed a few and placed them against his bleeding mouth and nose.

"Get the fuck outta my sight, you sonofabitch! Turn in your goddamned patch! You're out of the Insurgents."

Behind Banger, Jerry saw Axe lower his head. Jerry didn't harbor any ill feelings toward his brother. He was doing what an Insurgent always did—giving loyalty to the brotherhood and the president. Throwing a quick head tilt at Axe, he wiped his hand on his jeans, debating on whether to leave as Banger requested or wait to see if he'd cool down.

"Why the fuck are you still here?" Banger snarled.

In a calm voice, Hawk said, "The bylaws don't forbid members from having relations with any of the members' family." He placed his hand on Banger's shoulder, but he shoved it away. "You know we'll have to call church. Just because Jerry is going out with Kylie isn't grounds to throw him out of the club."

Jerry was grateful Hawk was there to be the voice of reason.

Banger glared at Jerry and Hawk. "He's isn't 'going out' with my little girl, he's *fucking* her!"

"That's not true. I'm not just fucking her. I care a lot about Kylie." Jerry stuffed the bloodied napkins in his jeans' pocket. Banger growled. "I know I should've manned up and talked to you about going out with her, but I didn't think you'd let me date her. So I thought—"

"You're fuckin' right I wouldn't have agreed to you going out with her. You've fucked every whore in the club *and* outside of it. You fuck two and three women at a time. You think I want my daughter with a man like that? What, you were bored with the whores so you decided to stick your cock in my daughter?" Banger lunged at him again, and it took both Hawk and Rock to hold him back.

"It's not like that, Banger."

Throttle came up behind Jerry and whispered in his ear, "Shut the fuck up, dude. You're making things worse for yourself. Fucking tell him you screwed up, take the punishment, and leave Kylie the hell alone."

Ignoring Throttle, Jerry looked Banger in the eyes. "I broke it off with her because I know I'm not good for her."

"The asshole got something right," Banger hissed.

"But that doesn't mean I used her. I have strong feelings for her. Very strong. I lo—"

Banger growled and tried to go for him again, and Hawk said, "Jerry, it's best you get your ass outta here. I'll let you know when we have church on this. In the interim, stay the hell away from the club."

Jerry nodded. As he walked past his brothers, they shook their heads, some muttering what an asshole he was to fuck the prez's daughter. Pushing open the large door, he entered the bright sunlight, the hot rays burning but not able to warm him. He'd lost his brotherhood and his woman, but it was the heartbreak of losing Kylie forever that crushed him; it felt like cement drying in his chest. He pulled his Harley onto the open road, and for the first time since he'd started riding, the peace and sense of freedom he always experienced eluded him.

Chapter Twenty-Seven

After Jerry patched his face and cleaned up, he sat on his balcony smoking a joint, ignoring the fifth call from Wanda he'd received in the past thirty minutes. He punched his thighs as frustration coursed through him. How the fuck had he allowed himself to make such a mess of things? He'd betrayed his president and broken Kylie's heart.

Wanda's right, I'm no good. Fuck!

Over the years, his mother had made it a point to tell Jerry he was a loser and a no-good brat, and when he was taken from her and placed with foster families, they continued the litany of what a piece of shit he was. And after all these years, he had to agree with them. He was the only one in the club who disrespected the prez, and the only one who'd fucked his daughter. Before Axe and Jax hooked up with their old ladies, they used to check Kylie out plenty once she hit eighteen, and Rags, Rock, and half a dozen other brothers always ran their eyes over her rack and ass whenever she'd come to the clubhouse. But they kept their distance, knowing not to go near her and insult the president.

Not Jerry, though. Nope, Jerry was just plain no good.

He stubbed out his roach and shoved his vibrating phone in his pocket. Wanda fucking got on his nerves, and he wasn't in the mood for her. Earlier that day, he'd told her he'd be around in the early evening, so why the hell did she have to keep calling him? He made his way to the pharmacy to pick up her meds. She was so goddamned addicted to the painkillers; he couldn't believe her doctor continued to prescribe them as frequently as he did.

When he walked into the trailer, Wanda was in her recliner watching TV, holding a Scotch in one hand and a cigarette in the other while the oxygen tubes in her nose made audible puffs of air every few seconds. It was fucking classic. Jerry went directly to the medicine chest in the bathroom and placed her medication on the glass shelf.

"Can you bring me one of them pills?" Wanda yelled over the TV.

"Haven't you heard booze and pills don't mix?"

"It's for later. I have trouble getting outta this damn recliner, so I want it near me in case the pain gets to be too much."

Shaking one pill in his hand, he walked over and set it down on the plastic TV tray that was always next to her. On it, she had the remote, a few tabloids, her reading glasses, a pill box, a pack of menthol cigarettes, a flask, and several empty glasses. He flopped onto the small couch.

"What the hell happened to you? Did you get in a fight?"

"Something like that. Where's Kelsey?"

"She's got a new boyfriend who has some bucks. She's with him most nights."

"Does he live in the trailer park?"

"No. He lives somewhere in town."

"Where did she meet him?"

"Not sure."

"What's his name?"

"I don't know."

"Fuck, Wanda. Don't you think you should know what your eighteen-year-old daughter is up to? Do you know anything about this guy?"

"I know he comes over here and is nice to me. A helluva lot nicer than you are. And he gives your sister and me money without a fuckin' attitude."

"Whatever." Jerry *really* wasn't in the mood. They both sat watching the television, his mind on Kylie as always. He wondered if Banger had gone home and confronted her. They should've been dealing with this together, but there he sat in a broken-down trailer with Wanda, who was killing herself with booze and cigarettes, and Kylie was all alone. *Fuck!*

The screen door squeaked open and he turned his head just as Kelsey came inside. She wore a short spandex skirt and barely-there tube top, and she teetered on four-inch heels as she walked past him. She definitely looked like one of the party girls who hung out at the club on the weekends.

"Why the hell are you dressed like a slut?"

"Why the hell do you think you can ask me that?"

Ignoring her question, he said, "You can't be going out like that. Where've you been?"

"Out with my boyfriend. And it's none of your business how I dress. He likes the way I look."

She wobbled to the kitchen, and that's when he saw all the angry red marks across her upper thighs. "What the fuck are those marks on your legs?"

Kelsey pulled down her skirt in a vain attempt to hide them. "I scraped them across a wood bench," she said, turning around to face him.

"Bullshit. Your new boyfriend do that shit to you?"

"No. Look, no one asked you to come in here acting like my fucking dad or something. Leave me alone. I'm tired." She placed a can of pop against her mouth and drank.

"Leave her alone. She's a slut, but at least she's bringing in some money." Wanda lit up another cigarette.

Kelsey laughed, her eyes flashing as she looked at her mother. "You're right. I am a slut and a cunt. I'm my boyfriend's slut."

"What the hell you talking about? You're fucked in the head," Jerry said.

She ignored him and went into her room, slamming the door behind her. He shook his head and went to her bedroom door. "Your boyfriend got a name?"

"Mark."

The gasp was audible through the door. "What's wrong?"

"I wasn't supposed to tell anyone. See what you made me do? Now I'll be punished. Leave me alone."

Strains of anger curled around him. "You letting him do that kind of shit to you?"

"Leave me the fuck alone!"

Jerry stood by the door. "Let her be. Come sit with me," Wanda cackled.

Slowly, he walked into the living room, pissed that Wanda had fucked them all up. "You need to take better care of Kelsey. She's fuckin' outta control, and you're her goddamned mom. Fuckin' act like one."

"She don't pay no attention to me. What can I do? I'm sick. She should be helping me out, not whoring around. I'm the one no one cares about. All you think about is her. What about—"

He opened the screen door. "Where you going?" she asked.

"Home."

"You got some money for me?" Greed lit up her eyes.

"Ask your daughter's john. You're pimping her out, aren't you?"

With Wanda cussing up a storm, Jerry jumped down the porch stairs and straddled his bike. In his peripheral view, he saw a glint of gold and he whipped his head around. Nothing. Sitting still for several minutes, he strained his ears to pick up any sounds that may be amiss. Nothing. Only the muffled voices from television sets, and the moans from fucking. Just a usual evening at Cedars Trailer Park. He turned his Harley around and headed back to his apartment.

Chapter Twenty-Eight

When Kylie pulled into the garage, she was surprised to see her dad's Harley parked there already. Glancing at her phone, she wondered why he was home at four o'clock. A tightness formed in her stomach and she hurried inside, thinking something may have happened to Belle and the baby. She walked into the kitchen and saw her dad seated at the table, his normally cheerful eyes icy and hard.

"Hi, Dad," she said as she opened the refrigerator and took out a bottle of orange-flavored water. "Is Belle okay?"

"She's fine," he replied curtly. "Sit down."

"What's wrong?"

"Sit down," he ordered.

Complying, she pulled out a chair and plopped down, scanning her father's face. He didn't look too happy; in fact, he looked downright pissed. *Oh, shit. He found out about Jerry. Damnit!* Their blue gazes locked, and he took out a book he had in his hands under the table and slid it toward her. "This yours?"

Looking down, her stomach dropped and a deep red flush crept across her cheeks. *Oh, fuck.* She was mortified that her father knew she had such a book. She nodded.

"You fucking Jerry?"

Kylie's impulse was to lie, but she suspected her dad already knew so she didn't want to add insult to injury. In a low voice, she said, "I did. We aren't together anymore." She kept twisting her hands and squirming in her chair. How had he found the book? She kept it under her mattress. Then a single, brave thread of anger slid up her spine. "You searched my things. How could you?" Her look accused him.

"I didn't do shit. Belle was changing the sheets on your bed and came across this under your mattress."

"She had no right to be in my room! I didn't ask her to change the sheets on my bed."

"She's been doing it since you've been back from school and you haven't complained. Anyway, this isn't about that. That's a separate issue you can bring up with her. Don't fuckin' cloud the matter. The question I have is why did you disobey me and take up with that sonofabitch?"

From the glare in her dad's gaze, she knew not to avoid the question. She shrugged. "I don't know. I liked him. I've liked him for a long time." She picked at her cuticle. "I didn't mean for things to get out of control. I'm sorry I disappointed you. You don't have to worry about me and Jerry. We're through."

"Did the sonofabitch break your heart?" A smidgen of softness entered his voice.

She shook her head. "No." *The sonofabitch crippled it and brought darkness and loneliness where there used to be light and togetherness. He destroyed me.* The silence spread between them as they sat lost in their thoughts. After several minutes, she asked in a small voice, "Did you do anything to Jerry?"

"I fuckin' kicked his ass, and would've done more, but Hawk pulled me off the asshole. I want his goddamned patch, but we're having church on it, and I know I'll be down-voted. The fucker has been a good member, for the most part. But this shit I can't forgive. I know the condition of him staying in the brotherhood will be to never see you again, but from what you're tellin' me, you two are through with each other, so it doesn't matter."

Hot tears formed behind Kylie's eyes. The thought of never seeing Jerry again was unbearable. Even though she knew it was silly, she'd held out hope that he'd come back to her and sweep her off her feet, professing his undying love. Now that the club would issue the ultimatum of keeping the patch only if he forgot her, she knew any hope of reconciliation was lost forever. Her breath hitched and she looked at her dad, knowing he'd see her brimming eyes.

"Honey, I know you're a young lady and you want to be with a man. It's natural. I knew this day would come, and I was hoping it'd be with someone you met at college. I'm pissed because you disobeyed me. I know Jerry. He likes women too much, and he'd never be faithful to you. He's always with Wendy or Rosie. You don't want a man like that."

When he said Wendy's name, she winced, the image of her straddling Jerry's lap, her breasts practically in his face, flashing in her mind. Her dad was right, of course, because Jerry had already broken her heart.

"But I don't trust him staying away from you."

"Why?" She recalled his indifference and icy demeanor when he'd admitted he didn't want her anymore.

"Because he made his feelings known to me, like that was gonna change my fuckin' mind." His face flared red again.

"What did he say?"

"That he cared about you. That what the two of you had wasn't just physical. Can you imagine that fucker telling me that? I don't care what he says; I don't want him near you ever again."

As Banger rambled on, her heart soared. Jerry had said that to her dad? Why didn't he tell her how he felt?

"Kylie. You listening to me? Jerry's full of shit, and I don't believe his lies. All he wants is sex, and he gets it all the time with the club whores. I don't ever want to hear his name in my house or coming from your lips. Do you understand?"

She nodded, but her heart was too happy to let her dad's words upset her. Jerry cared for her and that's all she needed to know; the rest would fall into place. Banger stood up then walked out of the room, anger still radiating from him.

Kylie looked down at the evidence that got her into all this trouble. She should just throw the book away, but now that everyone knew what she'd been doing, it wouldn't hurt to keep it. She just needed to find a better hiding place. Anyway, she'd promised Margo she'd loan the book to her. With a heart much lighter than it had been since Jerry had told her it was over, she rose from the table and went to her room.

JERRY SAT IN a corner away from most of the brothers as they discussed what should be done with the man who'd disrespected his president and fucked his daughter. As Hawk once again pointed out, there wasn't anything in the bylaws calling for a brother's patch if he fucked the president's daughter, but the disrespect wasn't to be overlooked.

Back and forth they went, with brothers in Jerry's camp saying he'd proven his loyalty many times over the years, and the others in Banger's camp who couldn't see past his disrespect in disobeying the president's wishes. And all Jerry did was replay every second of every moment he'd spent with Kylie. All he cared about was her; he wanted her more than the brotherhood, and that shocked the hell out of him. He wanted to wake up to her every day with the touch of her fingers on his skin, and he wanted to hold her in his arms every night with the warmth of her lips on his. Love had come to him when he hadn't even wanted or expected it.

"Do you have anything you want to add, Jerry?" Hawk's deep voice invaded his thoughts. Jerry sat up straight and shook his head. "Okay, let's vote. This will be a majority vote, since we have a distinct split."

After all the ayes and nays were tallied, Jerry's patch remained intact by a very narrow margin. When he looked at Banger, the president averted his gaze. Jerry knew it'd be a very long time until he'd earn his trust again. The final edict was that he was never to have any contact with Kylie again, or risk losing his patch forever and enduring a beatdown as a parting punishment. He'd leave the brotherhood in shame.

"Do you agree to these terms?" Hawk asked.

"Yes. Thank you, brothers." Even as Jerry said the words, he knew he'd disobey them. He could never leave Kylie alone; he'd lose his patch gladly just for the chance of being with her again. He couldn't wait for church to end so he could find her and hold her. Together, they'd figure it out. He'd talk to Banger when he cooled down a bit, and he'd show the president how much he loved his daughter.

"Now, on to some other business," Banger said. "We're still trying to locate the fucker in the purple Corvette." Jerry was suddenly extremely focused on the meeting. "Hawk's widening the search and dipping into other states. We've all been on the lookout for this asshole, but no purple Corvette has appeared. I've had Axe watching over Kylie, and he found out that some asshole punk by the name of Marcus Westman has been stalking my girl. He found out some other stuff, but we already know all that." Banger shot a mean look at Jerry. "Anyway, I paid this punk a visit, and it turns out he's obsessed with Kylie, so I had to convince him that wasn't such a good idea."

The club members laughed. "How'd you do that?" Throttle asked as he chuckled.

"A broken kneecap and a promise of more to come if he didn't fuckin' turn his obsession off. The asshole's been stalking her. He thought I was joking around, I guess, 'cause the look of shock as I slammed the tire iron against his kneecap was fuckin' classic." The brothers snickered along with their president. Jerry laughed, admiring Banger's style. He should've done that to the asshole when he'd had the chance in Crested Peak.

"You find out if the two dirtbags in that rat hole your mom lives in are still involved with crank?" he asked Jerry, his voice tight.

"They took off in the middle of the night. They're history. I checked around, and it looks like they blew outta the county."

Banger nodded curtly. "Guess they took our warnings to heart finally. On another note, we found something disturbing. Chigger's left and has joined the Demon Riders to be with Dustin and Shack."

"I knew the sonofabitch had something to do with the information leak regarding the arms deal with the Mexicans. I never believed Tug acted alone," Chas said. Several members grumbled in agreement.

"I worked the fucker over real good, but he never gave Chigger up. Only Dustin and Shack. You gotta admire Tug for that." Rock crossed his arms across his massive chest.

"I don't admire any of those bastards. We were all brothers before some of you were born. Dustin, Chigger, Tug, and I go way back." He looked over at Bones, Gator, and Hoss. "You remember how tight we all were." The three members nodded. "Fuck, our wives were friends, our kids played together, we were fuckin' close. Damn. I can't believe Chigger was tangled up in that." Banger shook his head.

"Maybe Chigger's involved with this shit with Kylie," Jerry said. All eyes turned on him, and Banger glared. "I'm just saying that someone has it out for you, and with Chigger leaving all of a sudden, who knows? It seems kinda suspicious, that's all."

"Jerry's got a point," Hawk said. "I'm definitely checking in the Demon Riders' territory for the vehicle."

"Kylie and her buddy said the guy was young. Chigger's old, and besides, Kylie knows him." Banger leaned against the wall. "I'll admit something doesn't feel right here. I think the Demon Riders do have their hand in this, notably Dustin and Shack."

The rest of the meeting was taken up with administrative accounting in regard to the various businesses the club owned. Finally, Banger's gavel hit the table, announcing the adjournment of church. All members shuffled out to the great area to unwind with their favorite club woman and have a few drinks.

Jerry grabbed a beer, debating on whether he should contact Kylie. Maybe she didn't want to see him anymore. Banger could be very convincing, and if Jerry did pursue her, he knew his president would be a formidable foe.

Axe came up to Jerry. "No hard feelings?"

"Nah. I'd have done exactly what you did. You did the right thing."

"I didn't volunteer shit, but he knew. I don't know how, but he did, and I had to tell him when he asked." Axe threw back his Jack. "You good with never seeing Kylie again?"

Flexing his jaw, Jerry shook his head.

"I didn't think you'd be. Damn, dude. You gotta somehow convince Banger you're the one for her."

Jerry snorted. "Yeah. Right."

Axe clasped his hand on his shoulder. "You wanna play some pool with me and Chas? We got some good money riding on it. Rock and Rags think they're gonna beat us. No fuckin' way."

"I'm not staying. Have a good game." He finished his beer and ambled out to the parking lot. Taking out his phone, he sent Kylie a text.

Jerry: *Hey. How've u been?*

A long pause ensued. When his phone pinged, he smiled.

Kylie: *Ok.*
Jerry: *Ur dad knows.*
Kylie: *No shit.*
Jerry: *U in trouble?*
Kylie: *Ya. U lose ur patch?*
Jerry: *No, but if I wanna keep it, I can't see u anymore.*
Kylie: *Not a problem since we're done.*
Jerry: *R we?*

The pause was longer than the previous one.

Kylie: *Ya. U wanted it that way.*
Jerry: *I wanna be with u.*
Kylie: *U should have told me that b4.*

His pulse pounded in his ears.

Jerry: *I'm telling u now. Can we talk in person?*
Kylie: *What about ur patch?*
Jerry: *Don't care. Want to see and talk to u.*
Kylie: *U can't break my heart & expect me to come running cuz u decide u want me now.*

Jerry: *I always wanted u.*

Kylie: *It's not that easy. I have to think about it.*

Jerry: *Is there a chance?*

Another long pause.

Kylie: *Maybe. Gotta go.*

Jerry: *Later.*

She didn't say no, and he held on to that. They had to be together, because she was the only thing he'd ever done right in his fucking life. He couldn't lose her just when he'd had her. Cursing himself for letting her slip through his fingers, he swore he'd get her back, even if it cost him his life.

Chapter Twenty-Nine

For the past few days, Kylie's dad had avoided her, and when he did bump into her he'd only grunt out one-word sentences. Having him shut her out like that was like a knife gutting her from the inside out. She'd never seen him this angry at her before, and because it pained her, she took it out on Belle, lashing out at her for being a damn snoop. Needless to say, the household was tense, and the only one who talked at dinner was Ethan. He was so excited about his baseball camp, and Kylie was grateful for his idle chatter; otherwise, dinnertime would be more miserable than it'd been since she'd been found out.

The streetlights clicked on as the darkening sky melded into inkiness. The green grass and trees faded into shadows under the night sky. Kylie turned off the ignition and entered the house, her step light and bouncy. She'd just come back from the interview with the wildlife rescue job and she thought she'd nailed it. The woman told her she'd be hearing in the next few days since they had several applicants, but Kylie had a good feeling about it.

She opened the fridge and surveyed its contents, looking for something quick to eat. Since Belle's back had been killing her, Emily and Kylie tried to help out with the cooking. Kylie was used to cooking for her dad after her mother had died, so she didn't mind, but Emily acted like she'd received corporal punishment. Spotting two slices of extra cheese and green chilies pizza, she took them out along with a Diet Coke and sat at the kitchen table.

Since his text a few days before, she hadn't heard from Jerry. She didn't know what to make of it, and she wasn't sure if she trusted him with her heart again. Even though her body craved him in the worst way, her heart was still recovering from the wounds he'd already inflicted. How could she trust a man who'd had a woman on his lap the minute she'd been out of his sight? Her dad had warned her that Jerry wasn't capable of being faithful, and she demanded that much of any man.

Wiping the table, Kylie threw her pop can in the recycling bin and headed to the stairs. The muted volume on the television caught her attention, and she walked into the family room. She saw the back of her dad's head as he sat on the couch watching wrestling. Seeing him alone, watching a sport they used to watch together, tore at her heart. She ambled over to the couch.

He raised his eyes and they settled on her face. Sitting down, she asked softly, "Are you still mad at me?" She heard him sigh. "'Cause if you are, I get it, but it's killing me." Her voice cracked.

He stretched out his arm. "Come here." She scooted over to him, and he hooked his arm around her and brought her head to rest against his shoulder. He kissed the top of her head. "Oh, honey... You know I can't stay mad at you for too long."

She sniffled. "I'm sorry I disappointed you."

"You've never disappointed me. Pissed me the hell off, but never anything more than that." He held her close to him. "How've you been?"

She broke away slightly. "Besides you icing me out, pretty good. I had a job interview today and it went real well. I really want the job." She proceeded to tell her dad all about the interview and what she'd been up to since their fight a few days before.

"You know you don't need to work."

"I know, but I want to. I want to earn my own money. Anyway, I'm the only one of my friends who doesn't have a job, and I'm getting bored."

Banger chuckled, his blue eyes twinkling. "If that's what you want, I'm sure you'll get it. Employers look for enthusiasm too, and you got plenty of that. Where'd you say the interview was?"

"Downtown at the Empire building. I hope I get it." She tucked her legs under her. "Want some company?"

"You're the only one in the house who likes wrestling. I can't get Belle interested in it at all."

"Mom didn't like it either." They both laughed. "I could make popcorn and get you another beer."

Banger smiled widely. "Sold. And get your old man two beers."

Kylie rushed to the kitchen and pulled out two beers from the fridge. As she stood near the microwave listening to the kernels pop like gunfire, she bounced lightly, humming to herself. A warm glow radiated through her.

Placing the large bowl of popcorn between them on the couch, she flipped open her pop can at the same time her dad opened his beer.

"You wanna watch a movie?" he asked as he took a handful of popcorn.

From the sparkle in his eye, she knew exactly the movie he wanted to see—his old standby, *Billy Jack*. The two of them must have seen it a hundred times. Her mom and dad used to watch it, and Kylie knew it'd made him feel nostalgic to watch it with her after Grace had died. The funny thing was she'd grown to love the movie. Without asking which one he wanted, she opened the cabinet and took out the DVD. Resuming her seat, they crunched on popcorn as they waited for the opening credits.

"I love you, honey. I only want the best for you."

"I know, Dad."

As they watched the film, it reminded her of the times when she was a little girl and her daddy took care of everything. For that moment, she relished being that little girl again.

HIS DICK WAS hard as granite as he watched the leather strap mark the tender cheeks of her ass. Having Kelsey wear the long, blonde wig was ingenious. With her hands secured to the bedpost and her ass high in the air, he could imagine it was Kylie he was punishing. She fucking needed punishment for being such a slut with Ricky and Jerry. He hadn't believed the puny college student for one minute when he'd said they were just friends. But the hussy had jilted him for the tall biker. Why did women love bikers? It'd always perplexed him, and even though he'd decided to follow in his father's footsteps, he hated it and the whores who hung around the club.

"I've had enough, Mark. Can you stop?" Kelsey's teary voice irritated him.

"Shut the fuck up, cunt. Didn't I tell you that you aren't to speak until I give you permission? You slut. For that disobedience, you get another five lashes." He loved the sound of the strap on soft flesh. The man couldn't wait to hear it on Kylie's ass.

By the time the tormentor finished, Kelsey was a sniveling mess of angry red marks and welts. He walked over and untied her. He'd let her rest for a bit. The last thing he wanted was to wear her out; his fun was just beginning.

"Why do you like to hurt me like that?" she asked as she wiped her wet cheeks.

"That's how I get off. You agreed to it a while back, remember?"

"I didn't know what I was getting into. I thought you just wanted to tie me up and give me a few swats on the ass. I've had that done by guys lots of times." She giggled while she rubbed her wrists where the restraints had been minutes before.

Disgust coursed through the black-haired man's body. "You really are a slut, aren't you?"

She shrugged. "Want a beer? My mom bought some yesterday."

"With my money or your brother's?"

"I dunno. Probably Jerry's, 'cause he was here a few days ago. So, do you want some?"

"Okay. Do you want to continue with our arrangement?"

"You still paying me, right?"

A curt nod of his head.

"All right, but if you're gonna be too hard with the strap like you just were, it's gonna cost more. My mom can't believe I have such a rich boyfriend." She wrapped her arms around his tapered waist. "You got something good for me?"

What a fucking meth head. "That's for later."

Kelsey smiled, revealing stained teeth from her on-and-off love affair with crystal. "Come on. We can have the drink with my mom. I know she wants to see you."

"All right, but we'll only take a twenty-minute break. You don't want to make me mad, do you?" A razor-thin edge of danger laced his voice. "Lead the way."

They entered the room, and he saw Wanda light up a cigarette. He hated the hacking woman and couldn't wait to snuff out her last breath. His fingers itched to do it right then. *Patience.*

"How's Kelsey treating you?" Wanda asked as she took the beer from her daughter's hand.

"Fine."

"You like it rough, huh?"

With wide eyes, Kelsey looked at him, and she held up her trembling hands. "I didn't tell her anything. I obeyed you just like you told me to."

"She didn't tell me shit. I can hear what you're doing in there. If I wasn't hooked up to this damn oxygen, I'd join you." Wanda laughed.

What a fucking vile woman. I'm going to enjoy killing you. "That's funny, Wanda."

After twenty minutes, the man stood up, prompting Kelsey to jump off the couch. As they walked to her bedroom, he heard Wanda call out, "Have a good time."

"We will." He closed the door.

Two hours later, the sheets drenched in blood, Kelsey lay face down on the mattress, her face unrecognizable. He pulled out the speculum he'd used to sexually assault her after he'd raped her over and over, choking her until he climaxed hard. Placing his torture devices in his black bag, he sat on the cheap wooden chair near her bed, smiling. His excitement had been at an all-time high that night. The maltreatment of Kelsey had been intensely gratifying, and he could only imagine how he'd feel when he had Kylie in his possession.

In the madman's world, punishment rape was the way to avenge acts committed by members of a girl's family, like a brother or father. Jerry had fucked Kylie, so in the twisted mind of the murderer, his sister had to be raped. Things got out of hand, and her murder wasn't intended, but he couldn't control himself. The more Kelsey whimpered and cried through her gag, the more he wanted to hurt her. Of course, deep down, he knew he was bullshitting himself; a dark, dangerous part of him wanted to choke the life out of her, then unleash his fury on her lifeless body. He loved every second of it.

And now he'd choke the life out of Wanda. He figured he'd be giving Jerry a bonus with that death. He shouldn't, especially since Jerry had stuck his cock in *his* Kylie, but he couldn't really blame him. Kylie was tempting as sin, and she should've controlled the situation with Jerry; after all, men were weak to a woman's pussy. He'd have to teach Kylie a lesson, but he wouldn't disfigure her face as he had Kelsey's. Kylie was too pretty, too precious. Maybe he'd keep her, even though retribution required he kill her for the sins of her father. He wondered if she liked rough sex.

Smiling, he went to the bathroom and stepped into the shower to wash off all the blood. After putting on a clean set of clothes, he strode out to the living room where he noticed Wanda's head back and mouth open, a thin line of drool trickling from the corner. He picked up the faded orange throw pillow and stood next to her. As if she sensed something, he watched her eyes flutter open.

She cleared her throat and shifted to sit straight. "You want something?" Her sleep-bleary eyes peered at him.

"I wanted to say good-bye." He reached over and turned off her oxygen tank.

"What the fuck are you doing?" she gasped.

With a flat, cruel smile, he placed the throw pillow firmly over her face and ignored her panicked thrashing as her ability to breathe lessened. With a steady hold on the pillow, and his knee pressed against her stomach, he made it near impossible for Wanda to take a full breath. Slowly, she went limp, and he presumed she'd lost consciousness. Placing the pillow back on the couch, he took out the duct tape he'd had Kelsey purchase for their sex play, wrapping it over Wanda's mouth and nose after binding her hands and legs tightly with it. Then he sat on the couch and waited until the occupants in the other trailers went to sleep. He depended on the darkness to allow him to slip away undetected.

As the trailer park slept, he crept away, a feeling of accomplishment coursing through him.

And very soon, Kylie would be his. At last.

Chapter Thirty

The following morning, Jerry arrived at the trailer amidst a swarm of badges and yellow tape that looked like streamers after a wild party. Face taut, he walked up to a guy in a suit who acted like he was in charge. "I'm Wanda's son. What the fuck happened here?"

The detective's gaze lingered on Jerry's cut. "Do you have any identification?" Jerry handed him his driver's license, which he reviewed before handing it back to him. "We need you to go inside and identify the bodies. The one in the back bedroom is pretty bad, but from your affiliation, I'd guess you've probably seen worse."

Jerry ignored his comment. "I'm ready." He followed the badge up the stairs he'd taken so many times since he'd become reacquainted with his mom and sister. He entered the living room, his eyes immediately going to the recliner as they always had. Wanda looked like she was dozing except for the duct tape wrapped around her mouth and nose. His gaze skimmed down to her tightly bound hands and feet and he ground his teeth together, his body growing hot. Even though she had plenty of faults, and never gave a shit about Jerry or his siblings, Wanda didn't deserve to die like that.

"Is that Wanda Kenyon?"

He jutted his jaw and nodded. "Yeah. That's her."

"I'm sorry," the detective offered while Jerry stared at the lifeless body of the woman who'd given birth to him. "Another woman was found in the bedroom."

Jerry knew the detective would lead him to Kelsey's room. When he walked in, the savagery of the attack shocked him. *What fuckin' animal does this to an innocent woman?* She lay face up, although she didn't have a face, just tissue and bone mashed together in a congealed, bloody pulp. Her body was bruised and swollen, and he averted his eyes from its nakedness, looking down at her feet. The familiar red rose tattoo right above her ankle punched him in the gut, and a lump formed in his throat. He swallowed hard then cleared his throat. "It's my sister."

The detective raised his eyebrows. "You sure?"

"I know my own fuckin' sister. It's her." Jerry scanned the room, and he noticed scratch marks on the headboard that he hadn't seen when he'd dropped by a few days before. Glancing at her thighs, he saw the angry whip marks covered in bruises and his blood turned to ice, his instinct telling him the guy she was dating was responsible for the carnage.

"When's the last time you saw your mom and sister?" the detective asked as he flipped his notebook open.

Jerry scrubbed his face with his hand. "A few days ago."

"Did you get in a fight with either of them?"

He narrowed his eyes. "What the fuck does that mean? I came over to drop off Wanda's medication I'd picked up for her." Their relationship was such that there was always tension between them, but Jerry wasn't going to tell the fucking badge anything more than what was necessary in finding the fucker who'd murdered his family.

"Where were you last night into this morning?"

"At the clubhouse. Pretty sure you know how to get there."

The badge paused, then scribbled something in his notebook. "Did your sister have a boyfriend?"

"Yeah, but I don't know shit 'bout him except he gave her money and was into real rough sex."

"Did your sister tell you that?"

"Nah. I saw the whip marks and the way she was dressed. He liked the hardcore shit."

"Do you know his name?"

Jerry shook his head. He remembered Kelsey had told him when he'd been over a few nights before, but as hard as he racked his brain, he couldn't recall. "You done?"

The heavy-set detective nodded. "Stick around. We may have some more questions. We'll release the bodies in a couple days." He handed Jerry a card. "Call the medical examiner and let him know which mortuary you want them sent to after the autopsy and forensic tests."

Jerry shoved the card in his front pocket and walked outside, grim-faced, his fists clenching and unclenching. He'd find the bastard who did this, and when he did, he'd make sure he suffered more than Wanda and Kelsey. He rolled his bike away from the crime scene, then hit the throttle clutch and sped away from the trailer park.

A WEEK LATER, the small church overflowed with people attending the funeral. Jerry recognized several faces from the trailer park, and he knew Wanda and Kelsey weren't friendly with half of them. What was it about horrifying, gruesome deaths that attracted so many onlookers? He was flanked by his brothers, and he felt their strength and comfort while the minister spoke about the afterlife.

Jerry's gaze fixed on Wanda and Kelsey's coffins. A picture of Wanda when she'd just turned twenty-one was the only one he could find, and it rested next to her coffin, her smile weak, her eyes glazed. Kelsey's picture was next to her white box, trinkets, single-stemmed flowers, and small stuffed animals encircling it. They paid homage to a girl whose life had been cut too short.

After the funeral and burial, the club held a reception for Jerry and the brothers. The old ladies had prepared steaming mounds of hot links, beef brisket, and two roasted turkeys with all the fixings. Belle handed him a plate of food. "Go on and eat something."

"Thanks, Belle, but I'm not hungry. I do appreciate it, though." He gave her back the plate and went to the bar to down a double.

Many brothers came by, clasping their hands on his shoulders, gripping his arms, or pulling him into bear hugs. Each time a brother gave his silent support, pride in being an Insurgent spread through him.

"Fuck, man. This must be tough," Axe said as he placed his hand on Jerry's shoulder.

"Yeah. Wanda was a shitty mom, but she was blood, you know? And Kelsey… Fuck, poor Kelsey."

"Chas, Rock, Jax, Throttle, and I agreed that if you need our help in tracking and killing the bastard who did this, you can count on us."

Jerry smiled. "Thanks, man. I'm gonna need your help, because this fucker's not getting away with what he did."

Then he saw her, her blonde hair a striking contrast against the black fabric of her dress. Their eyes locked in the room full of people, and she walked straight over to him. With her pale lips trembling, she leaned down, a tendril of hair grazing his arm. "I'm so sorry for your loss." Her lips brushed against his cheek and her familiar scent hit him in the groin, then Kylie was gone before he could say anything.

As the well-known strains of *Stairway to Heaven* played over the speakers, the cigarette and weed smoke curled around, and the heat of all the brothers in one place made the room seem smaller. Not able to stand the stuffiness, he slipped out into the parking lot and walked away from the club to the creek that rushed behind it. Jerry sat back on his haunches, throwing pebbles into the clear water. A twig snapped behind him, and he leapt up and turned around, his gaze falling on Kylie.

"Hey," she said softly.

"Hey." He wanted to run and embrace her so hard that she'd never be able to get away.

"Are you doing okay? Do you need anything?" She took a few tentative steps toward him.

I need your tenderness, your laughter, and your softness. "I'm okay. It was too stuffy in there. I couldn't fuckin' breathe."

Kylie nodded. "Too much smoke." She walked closer until she was in front of him. "Can I give you a hug?"

Smiling, Jerry stepped forward and hooked his arm around her waist, bringing her close to him. He cradled her face between his hands while he gently kissed her on the lips. She pressed into him, sucking lightly on his bottom lip then drawing his tongue into her mouth. They tasted, nibbled, and sucked each other; there was a subtle urgency about it as their kisses became deeper and more passionate. In that moment, it was like time paused, and they were the only important people to each other.

After several minutes, Jerry broke away and nibbled on the side of her neck, his voice muffled by her soft skin. "I've missed you so much, babe. I hated pushing you away."

She pulled back slightly. "Why did you?"

He shook his head. "I didn't want you to quit school and change all your plans for me. I didn't wanna be responsible for you fuckin' up your life. And the whole thing with your dad. I didn't want to be the cause of your grief."

"And you wanted to be with other women."

He held her tightly talking into her hair as he stroked it. "No way. The only woman I want to be with is you. Nothing happened with Wendy the day you came to the clubhouse. I staged the whole damn thing to make you see that I wasn't good for you."

"Shouldn't I have the chance to decide that?"

He sighed. "I've never been as miserable as I've been without you." He tangled his hand in her hair and pulled it back, capturing her lips. "I love you so much, Kylie, and even if I have to give up my patch, I only want you. You're worth everything to me." Then he kissed her hard, digging his fingers into her soft flesh while images of his sister flashed through his mind, bleak sadness juxtaposed with hope and happiness. The dichotomy of life crushed down on him.

"I love you too. And I'm so sorry you lost your mom and sister, and in such a horrible way. I really am." Her voice broke. "I'm here for you. You're not alone. I'm here to listen, support, and just hold you." She caressed his cheek with the back of her fingers. "I know it'll take time to work out your feelings, and you'll want space. I just want you to know you can always depend on me."

Squeezing her, he whispered, "I know, and I'm lucky I have you."

Her quiet presence comforted him, and it washed away some of the guilt he felt for failing to help his sister throughout her short life. Wanda and Kelsey were gone, and life went on.

He buried his face in her hair, swallowing the lump in his throat.

Chapter Thirty-One

"So, what time are you guys going to be back?" Kylie asked her dad as he sat on the wicker rocker on the front porch.

"We should be back by six or so. Belle wants to buy some baby stuff, and then I'm taking her to another doctor's appointment. I gotta stop by the club first to do some work."

Kylie's stomach dropped, and she strained to keep her voice steady. "So, you're coming back to pick Belle up?" *Please say no. Jerry's going to pick me up in twenty minutes.* He'd called her the previous day telling her he wanted to see her and spend the day with her. Kylie knew Belle and her dad were planning to be out all day, so she made plans for Jerry to pick her up. But Belle was taking her sweet time in coming down, and her dad had just sprung the stopping at the clubhouse plan on her. Her insides twisted and churned.

"No, she's coming with me. Addie, Cherri, and Doris are gonna be there, and Belle's crazy for Paisley and Hope. She's got some things to discuss with Doris 'bout the October rally. Belle's stepping up to the plate nicely on her old lady duties." Banger smiled.

"That's great." *What the fuck is taking her so damned long to slap on some lipstick?*

"Everything going all right with you? You seem nervous."

Steady. He can read you. "I guess I'm a little nervous about starting my new job."

"You'll do fine. You want me to take you?"

She had to laugh at how protective her dad was with her. "No. I'm not going to my first day at school, but thanks for asking.

"If you change your mind, let me know. Now where in the hell is that woman?" Banger stood from the chair, opened the screen door, and yelled, "Woman, we gotta go."

Kylie saw Belle come down the stairs and say, "What're you yelling about? Do you want to switch bodies so I can see how fast you'd be ready being eight months pregnant and having to pee all the time?" Kylie smiled; Belle didn't take much shit from her dad.

Banger grabbed Belle's hand, pulled her close to him, and then kissed her. "Let's go, beautiful." He helped her down the front steps and they made their way to the SUV parked in front of the house. "See ya." He waved to Kylie, and then they were off.

Not five minutes after her dad and Belle drove away, the pounding sounds of a powerful Harley engine invaded the cul-de-sac. A rush of adrenaline shot through her, and she placed her hands against her fluttering stomach as she watched for Jerry on his bike. Sure enough, he rounded the corner, and the sight of him took her breath away: dark sunglasses, black skull bandana on his head, blue jeans hugging corded legs, and a white sleeveless T-shirt showing off ripped arms covered in ink. *Holy fuck. He's gorgeous.*

She met him at the curb as he pulled up, her tanned legs showing how much free time she'd had since summer break started. He yanked her to him and kissed her hard and deep, releasing a million tingles through her.

"Get on," he said. She hopped on behind him and snagged him around his waist. She brushed her fingertips against his toned muscles and shivered at the thought of seeing him naked. With a jump, the bike roared out of the neighborhood.

The road he took when they'd left Pinewood Springs was a familiar one. It led to Evergreen Lake, a favorite place her mom and dad would take her to when she was little. She hadn't been back to the lake since high school when one of the football jocks had taken her there, hoping to do more than gaze at the stars. Kylie had often felt like the football players dared each other to take her out to see which one would score with an outlaw president's daughter. She hadn't been interested in any of them because none had compared to Jerry.

As they rode on the narrow, one-lane backroads, tousled blonde ribbons whipped about her face like straws in a wisp of air. The sky was clear and blue, the air as soft as a kiss. To the left of them stretched a bright, grassy valley where rainbow-colored flowers dazzled in the whispers of summer. They rushed by the big pines, and the soaring mountains were covered with a rug of trees and yellow, pink, and blue wildflowers.

Jerry stopped the bike near a large lake, silver in the bright light of the noon sun. Flashing green and blue dragonflies hovered above it, and the water gently lapped the shore. He helped Kylie off the bike and drew her in, his lips hungrily seeking hers. His kiss was like the spark of a match, igniting all her nerves. As his hands slid down her arms, resting on her exposed belly, her nerve endings snapped and sizzled. With her fingers, she traced his biceps and tattoos, loving how his taut skin bulged over his muscles.

Jerry tugged away, then lifted his T-shirt over his head, his tanned skin glistening under the hot sun. As he draped his shirt over the seat of the Harley, the muscles of his back drew her in, and she couldn't drag her eyes away from him. He turned around and chuckled when he caught her gaze. "Like what you see?"

Red painted her cheeks, and she nodded as she cast her gaze to the lake. "I wonder if it's cold." The small ripples on the glassy surface looked inviting.

"Probably. Let's try it."

"I don't have a swimsuit, and I don't want people seeing me buck naked."

"Wear your sexy underwear. You can dry it while I fuck you after we take a swim."

"Fuck me? *Here*, in the open? What if someone's around?"

"I know somewhere more private." He hopped on one foot as he shook out of his jeans. His black boxer briefs clung to his strong, firm ass, and the nice big bulge in front. Kylie licked her lips, imagining how he'd make her feel when he was inside her. "You comin'?" he asked as he walked to the water's edge.

Kylie slipped off her halter top, then wiggled out of her skintight jeans, leaving her in white lace bra and matching panties. She kicked off her short biker boots and joined Jerry, who was wading into the lake.

Gripping her wrist, he pulled her close to him then picked her up in his arms. "Don't you dare!" she squealed. He chuckled slowly and warmly, reminding her of honey. "I mean it. Don't throw me in the water." She tried to be stern, but giggles escaped from her.

Nuzzling his face against her hair, he said, "What're you gonna do about it?" His eyes twinkled mischievously, and she knew she was so screwed; he had every intention of throwing her in.

"I'm gonna smack you hard if you do."

"Oh, yeah? Then what?"

"Kick your ass."

Jerry shook his head. "Baby, you're giving me a lot of reasons for why I *should* do it. I'm picturing you wet from head to foot, wrestling with me. Damn."

Then he did it. He tossed her into the lake, the water rushing around her as she popped her head through it. The coolness was refreshing, and she splashed at Jerry, who was laughing his ass off. She swam away from him and he came after her, playing "catch me if you can" under the scorching sun.

When he caught her, he crushed Kylie against his heaving chest, his hardness poking at her through his soaked boxers. With a hand behind her head, he drew her to him and devoured her mouth with deep, sweeping strokes of his tongue. An ache danced through her breasts and between her thighs, her pussy throbbing wildly. Hooking her arms around his neck, she fused herself against him, currents of delight electrifying her body.

"Fuck, you make me feel good, babe. I've never felt this way with any woman." He nipped the side of her neck squeezing her breast, her nipple punching against the sheer fabric of her bra. "Kylie, what have you done to me?"

She sighed when he whispered her name. As he trailed his kisses to the front of her neck, a soft moan escaped from her throat, and he murmured, "I fuckin' love the sounds you make. They hit me right in my cock." He held her hand and slid it down to his hardness, rubbing it with her palm. "That's what you do to me every fuckin' time." He nibbled on her shoulder and neck.

Kylie loved that she could turn him on so completely, and she gained confidence knowing that Jerry wanted to be with her and not one of the club women. She'd believed him when he told her he hadn't had any other women since the first time he'd come to Crested Peak. How close they'd grown since then. Beneath his hands, her skin trembled as he slid them up her rib cage, and she took a deep sharp breath.

"You're in my blood, babe, and you stir some deep, dark desires in me, but you also calm the storm in my life. I fuckin' love you." His voice was molten and warm, and a deep shiver ran from her head straight down to her heated pussy.

When Jerry glided his hand inside her panties, his fingers exploring her swollen lips, a wave of warmth filled Kylie, rushing to every corner of her body—her curling toes, her aching nipples, her throbbing mound. Every inch of her was saturated with desire. She tilted her head up and met his smoldering gaze through hooded lids. Then she smiled wickedly and tightened her hand around his hard, pulsing shaft, moving it up and down, her index finger stroking the underside of his smooth head.

"Fuck," he whispered at the same time she whimpered through parted lips, their breaths mingling.

His large hands skimmed up the sides of her body, their light touch leaving goose bumps in their wake. With a fluid gesture, he unhooked her bra and sucked her hardened nipple. When she moaned, he growled, "I need you."

No longer caring if anyone was around, Kylie wrapped her legs around his waist and peppered his face with feathery kisses. "I need you so bad." She threw her head back, her body arching, and he licked the hollow spot between her collarbones.

"I'll pull out right before I come," he rasped. Then he slid her panties off and shed his boxers.

"I'm on the pill. I started it a couple weeks ago. Just in case we got back together." She didn't share that it was when her dad had told her Jerry's feelings for her. In her heart she'd hoped they'd work it out, and she was thrilled to be back in his arms. "Are you clean? I mean, you've screwed so many club women…"

He brushed her lips with his. "I always used a condom. I checked out great. I can't wait to really feel all of you." He bent his head down again and sucked, licked, and bit her tits and red buds. As he kissed her deeply, he held her up, and she wrapped her legs tighter around him.

Kylie felt almost weightless in the water, her large tits bobbing up and down, the ripples of water over her nipples making her stomach tingle.

"Your tits look even better in the water, if that's even fuckin' possible," he said huskily. He rubbed her clit until she tightened her legs even more. "I want you to come while I fuck your sweet pussy."

With his hand, he guided his dick inside her, and in seconds he filled her up, stretching her even more than he'd done before. He rocked in and out, and the water caressed her as it hit against her clit. Throwing her head back, Kylie pushed her tits forward as she stared at the cloudless blue sky, her skin on fire despite the coolness of the water. Jerry sucked her nipples as he bounced her up and down on his stiff cock.

"My dick feels so fuckin' good inside you. You're mine, Kylie. All mine. Your tits, your pussy, and your ass belong only to me. You and I are connected, and no one's gonna fuck with that." He grunted as he bounced her harder, the water lapping around them.

Jerry's possessive tone warmed her straight to her core. And when he squeezed her ass cheeks and pushed his finger a small way into her puckered hole, her body exploded as wave upon wave of crashing pleasure covered her, her cries echoing in the valley, bouncing off the pine trees. Gasping, she buried her head in the crook of his neck, then felt him stiffen. A low, guttural moan pushed through his lips, his breath ghosting the side of her face.

"Fuck, Kylie. Fuck. Fuck!" His words were low and hoarse, and they washed contentment over her. He hugged her close to him, and she could hear the beating of his heart as he came down from his climax. He pulled back and kissed her shoulders. "That was unbelievable. I've never done that before. We're gonna have to come to the lake more often." His deep chuckle soothed her.

Knowing she was the first woman he'd ever made love to in the lake made Kylie feel fuzzy and cuddly all over. He'd been with so many women that she'd thought he'd done it all, but finding out this was something he'd done only with her made it that much more special.

"We should get dressed," he said softly against her hair.

"Do you have your boxers? I can't find my panties and bra."

"I'll buy you some sexy new ones." He winked at her.

She laughed. Losing her underwear was so worth the orgasm he gave her, and the closeness they'd shared. They walked out of the water and quickly dressed. Even though sex in the lake was fucking fantastic, she didn't want anyone to see her. Fastening the snaps on the back of her halter top, she looked down and saw the material clinging to her breasts.

"Without a bra, I look like a slut," she groaned.

She shook her head when Jerry leered at her chest. "I love the way your tits look. Damn, you look hot, but I don't want any guys staring at you when we go for lunch." He went over and took something out of the saddle bag on his bike. "Here," he said, handing her a black T-shirt. "Wear this. You can keep it."

She slipped on his shirt. It was miles too big for her, but she loved it and decided it would be her nightshirt from then on. "How do I look?" She twirled around.

Jerry's gaze was as soft as a caress. "Beautiful. Come over here."

She walked to him and he cocooned her in his arms. "I love you so much," he said in a low voice.

"I love you, Jerry." Tears glistened in her eyes, and it was as though her heart would burst from happiness and love. He was her soulmate, and no matter what her dad said, she'd never leave him.

They broke away when they heard the distant voices of a man and woman. "Let's go get lunch. I'm starved," Kylie said. Jerry kissed her deeply, then helped her on his bike. They drove out of the valley with the sun shining on them, her arms hooked tightly around her man.

KYLIE STAYED ON the porch until she couldn't see Jerry anymore. Her body was still tingling from their lovemaking and all the wonderful things he'd said to her during their day together. She'd have to convince her dad that she loved Jerry and wanted to spend time with him. The thought of never seeing him again or feeling his body next to hers made her break out in a cold sweat. Surely her father could understand; after all, he'd once been young and in love with her mom.

The coolness from the air conditioner washed over her as she stepped into the foyer. As the days crept into July, the heat bounced off the pavement, even lingering in the shadows of nightfall. She ambled to the kitchen in search of a cold drink.

"Oh," she said when she saw Belle sitting at the table. "I thought you were at the doctor's office." Panic threaded around her, and she hoped Belle hadn't seen Jerry dropping her off.

"No, I postponed it until the end of the week. The heat is too much." Belle lifted her leg and rested it on the chair opposite her. "Did you have a nice time with Jerry?"

Kylie blew out a long breath. "Are you going to tell Dad?"

Belle shook her head. "No. I think you and Jerry are good together, and he obviously makes you happy. You've been on a high for the last few days." She wiped her forehead with a napkin. "You do have to have a long talk with your father. Explain how you feel. He'll understand."

"No, he won't. I tried that, and he wasn't even listening to me. He's made up his mind."

"Well, you don't have to do it tonight, but you do have to do it before you go back to school. You'd be surprised how understanding your dad can be when he wants to."

Kylie plopped down on the kitchen chair. "I know that, but in this case, he doesn't want to be understanding. Anyway, I'll figure it out."

Belle smiled then shifted in her chair. "I'll try and soften him up too. Maybe you can talk to him after the baby is born. I suspect he's going to be nothing but a big softie when he lays eyes on his son."

Kylie laughed. "You're devious, and so right. How're you doing? Did you get Dad to agree to be with you in the delivery room?"

"After a long battle, I can proudly say I won. His butt is in there holding my hand."

"I have to see that. I never would've thought he'd agree to it. Good job."

"It was one of my better moments. Anyway, it's hard to say no to a pregnant woman who is super hormonal." Belle pushed up from the table. "I'm going to rest for a while. I'm so damn hot at night that I have the ceiling fan twirling on high, the AC at sixty-eight degrees, and a small portable fan directed at me. Your poor dad has taken to wearing a sweater to bed at night. He can't wait for the baby to be born."

Kylie laughed along with Belle. When she'd left the room, Kylie checked her e-mails, eager to see whether she was offered the job at the wildlife rescue or not. When she saw a message from them, she crossed her fingers and opened it. After scanning the contents, she raised her arm high in the air and yelled, "Yes!" She'd been offered the job and was beyond thrilled. The day she'd spent with Jerry had been magical, and now it culminated in her finally having a job. It didn't get much better than that. She quickly sent Jerry a text.

Kylie: *I got the job!!!*

Jerry: *Fuck yeah!*

Kylie: *So happy. :)*

Jerry: *When do u start?*

Kylie: *This Thursday. I had a great time with u.*

Jerry: *Me 2. Maybe u can come over tonight? After 11?*

Kylie: *2 risky. Better not.*

Jerry: *I want u, babe.*

Kylie: *U had me all day. :)*

Jerry: *Want 2 fuck u all the time. Never get enough.*

Kylie: *Sweet talking won't change my mind. ;)*

Jerry: *Tomorrow then.*

Kylie: *I'll let u know.*

Jerry: *Not asking. I'm telling. Tomorrow night.*

Kylie: *Tomorrow. We'll talk. My dad just came home. Bye.*

"Hi, Dad," she said as Banger came into the kitchen. "Want a cold beer?"

He nodded while smiling. Ever since her mom had died, she'd run to the kitchen when she'd hear his powerful Harley pulling into the garage. She'd always offer him a beer, and then they'd sit down at the table and talk while he had a drink. That'd been their way of staying in touch with each other during her high school years.

"Belle's upstairs resting." She reached out and touched his hand lightly. "She's fine, it's just the heat. It's bad enough if you're not pregnant, but I can't even imagine having to endure it in her condition. She told me you're in the freezer every night."

Banger chuckled. "Freezer, my ass. I'm in the middle of the fuckin' South Pole. Shit." He gulped down his beer. "How you been doing?"

"Great. I got the job at the wildlife reserve. I'm super stoked!"

"That's great, honey. I'm happy for you."

"I had a good feeling about it when I went in for the interview. It's going to be such a cool job. I start this Thursday. I'll be glad to have something worthwhile to do."

"Is this the big one off the highway?"

"No, this is a non-profit animal rescue. It's very small, but they're growing and they work with all sorts of wildlife. It should be fun."

"Good for you." Banger rose from his chair and threw his can in the recycle bin. "I'm gonna go up and check on Belle. You staying home tonight?"

"Yeah. I thought I'd make a big salad with a ton of stuff in it, and we can order pizza. It'll just be the three of us, since Ethan's over at Luke's and Emily is with her boyfriend. Sound good?"

"Sounds great. In a couple of hours?"

"Okay."

Banger left the kitchen, and Kylie wondered if she shouldn't go over to Jerry's later that night. Deciding it was a good thing for him to miss her she walked to the reading room, a tall glass of iced tea in her hand, and settled into a cushy chair to read her mystery novel.

Chapter Thirty-Two

Jerry sat in the chair next to the detective's desk, staring at the heap of files littering it. He hated being there; he and the badges had never had a good relationship. He glanced at the clock on the wall, steam starting to come off him when he realized how long he'd been waiting for the fucking badge. Sick of wasting his time, he rose from the chair and ambled toward the door.

"Hey, Mr. Kenyon, wait up." Jerry turned around and saw the pudgy detective hurry up to him. "Sorry I'm late. We had an emergency. Come on back. I have some questions I need to ask you, and I want to give you an update on your family's murder."

Jerry scowled and followed the detective back to where he'd been sitting for at least twenty minutes. He stretched out his legs, his hands resting on his thighs.

"I don't know if you remember my name, but I'm Detective Knop." The man extended his hand, then took it back when Jerry stared at him impassively, his hands still on his thighs. "Want one?" he offered, opening the top of a donut box.

"What do you wanna ask me?" Jerry said.

Brushing the crumbs off his desk, Knop pulled out a file from under a stack of other cases and opened it. Rummaging through it, he took out several pieces of paper. "We got some information on the boyfriend your sister had been seeing right before her murder."

"What's the fucker's name?"

The detective leaned back in his chair. "We don't know his name yet, but we got something of a description. Maybe you can let me know if you ever saw him hanging around the trailer park."

"Maybe. Ask the questions. I gotta go somewhere soon." Jerry was still pissed that Knop made him wait around. The only reason he was there was to find out what the badges knew so he could track the motherfucker down and make him suffer for what he did to Wanda and Kelsey.

"It seems like your sister took up with a guy about two weeks before she was murdered. The neighbors saw his car parked in front of your mother's trailer practically every night since they started dating. You see a bronze Buick Lacrosse parked around the place in the last two weeks before your mom and sister died?"

Jerry shook his head. "What's the year?"

"From the pictures we showed the neighbors, I'd say it was a 2006 or 2007. The neighbors said it was a dark maroon, and the guy would blast loud music whenever he came by to pick your sister up. He also flashed around a lot of money. He'd have a wallet he'd take out as if he were counting his bills for something, then he'd knock on their door."

"Never saw the car. What does he look like?"

"A lot of the neighbors didn't get a good look at his face—he usually wore a hat pulled down low. They said he had black hair and always wore thick gold-framed sunglasses, even at night."

A sudden coldness hit Jerry and he jerked his head back. In that moment, he knew the murders were meant as a message from the fucking asshole in the purple Corvette who'd stalked Kylie in Crested Peak. The madman was basically telling Jerry to leave Kylie alone, and he'd punished him for not listening by killing Wanda and Kelsey.

"You know someone fitting that description?" the detective asked.

Jerry shook his head, his shock turning into white-hot rage.

"You sure? You looked like something clicked for you just now."

"Don't know anyone like that. Any leads on who he is and if he's still in Pinewood Springs?" *The fucker is in Pinewood, and Kylie's in danger. I gotta let Banger know.*

"We're still investigating."

Anxious to get to the clubhouse, he leapt to his feet. "Let me know if you find anything out. I gotta go." Not wanting to raise the badges' suspicions, Jerry sauntered at a leisurely pace out of the police station, swung his leg over his Harley, and took off in search of Banger.

KYLIE TURNED UP the hard rock station louder as she swung onto Miller Street, her body buzzing from excitement. She'd been working for the past few days in the office for the non-profit job she'd wanted and was anxious to go to the wildlife rescue and work with the animals. A desk job hadn't been her idea of a good time. She thought she'd be stuck filing for eight hours until the woman, Mrs. Morris, told her the previous day that Kylie would start training at the reserve. Mrs. Morris said she'd be working with the director, Mr. Austin, four other assistants, and a veterinarian. Kylie could hardly contain herself, she was so elated.

Checking her GPS, she veered off Miller Street and picked up Highway 32. She was definitely riding high on the thrill of her new job and her adorable Jerry. Each time she thought about him, her lips would tingle and shivers skated across her skin. He was so awesome, and he loved her. He'd even said he'd deal with her dad, but Kylie had told him to lay low for a while. She knew her dad better than anyone, and Jerry riding in on his chrome steed to proclaim his love for her wouldn't sit well at all with Banger.

As she drove, she noticed steam coming out of the front of her hood. Kylie glanced at the temperature gauge. It was approaching the red mark. *Shit! What the hell is going on?*

She pulled off to a side road and killed the engine. Popping open the hood, a cloud of steam billowed out, and when she looked on the ground she saw the lemon-lime color of coolant puddling under her car. The last thing she needed was car trouble on her way to work. What kind of an impression was she going to make on the director?

She scanned the area looking for Johnnie, the newest guy her dad had assigned to follow her, but he was nowhere to be seen. Did she lose him? Her dad would be super pissed when he found out the prospect couldn't tail an almost twenty-year-old girl. Taking out her phone, she began to call her dad then remembered he was in church, so she called her employer.

"Pinewood Springs Wildlife Rescue," Mrs. Morris answered.

"Hi. This is Kylie, and I have an overheated car. I'm stuck off Highway 32. I'm going to try and find someone who can give me a ride, but I wanted to let you know I'll be a little late for work."

"Are you in a safe place?"

"Yeah. I pulled off the highway just after the Ward Road exit. I'm really sorry about this. I can't believe this is happening. My car is basically brand new."

"It's all right. I can have Mr. Austin pick you up."

"Oh, no. I don't want him to come get me. I swear I can find a friend to help me out."

"It's no bother. He just left and will be driving right by you. I'll give him your location and he should be there very soon."

"Okay. Thanks a lot." Kylie placed her phone in her tote and leaned against her car. The heat from the sun was starting to warm everything up, even though it was fairly early in the morning. Soon she heard the crunch of tires over dirt; she looked down the road and saw a dark blue SUV headed toward her. She smoothed down her hair and stood away from her car.

The SUV stopped in front of her and a young man she'd guess to be in his late twenties stepped out. He had blond hair and brown eyes and wore cowboy boots, blue jeans, and a western-style shirt.

"You must be Kylie. I'm Steven Austin," he said in a heavy accent. It sounded Southern to her, but she wasn't quite sure from which region.

"Hi. I'm so embarrassed about all this. I was just driving down the highway on my way to the reserve when all this steam started coming out of the hood of my car. I pulled over, took a look, and I think it's the radiator."

"Let me see." He bent under her hood, looking inside. "Yep, it's the radiator all right. Looks like it sprung a leak or something. Your coolant is all over the place, except where you want it to be." He flashed a big smile.

"I can't believe this. I've only had the car since last September. This is insane."

"It happens. We'll leave it here and I'll take you to work. You can call someone to deal with this."

"Okay, great. My dad will know what to do. He's in a meeting, but I'll call him during my lunch hour." Mr. Austin opened the door for her and she swung her legs in then settled on the seat. "You have a nice car," she said when he slammed the car door shut.

"Thanks. You from Pinewood Springs?"

"Yeah. I know you're not. You have an accent, but I don't know from which state."

"Texas." He smiled widely, his brown eyes piercing hers.

"I love Texas barbecue."

"Me too." He laughed.

As the car rambled on, they chatted about music, and she told him about the best restaurants in town, the tourist places he couldn't miss, and the best hiking trails in the area. Then, out of the blue, he asked, "Do you have a boyfriend?"

Taken aback, she nodded.

"He's a lucky man. I have a girlfriend, but she's not as pretty as you are." He glanced at her, his eyes lingering on her chest, making Kylie extremely uncomfortable.

She looked around and noticed they hadn't jumped back on the highway. "Are you taking a shortcut?"

He nodded. "There's major construction going on the highway, so I found this detour. It beats just sitting and waiting in the snail-paced traffic."

"I'll have to remember that for tomorrow." She glanced out the window as the dust from the road seeped in through the vents, sticking in her throat. After swallowing several times, the dry spot was still there.

She coughed, hoping that would work, but it didn't. She coughed again, and soon she had a coughing fit. She rummaged through her tote, cursing for having forgotten to bring a couple bottled waters.

"You okay?" he asked in a long drawl.

Shaking her head, tears running down her cheeks, she choked out, "Do you have any water?"

"I don't. I have cough drops in the glove box." He leaned over to open it, but Kylie had beaten him to it.

She saw a bag of cherry-flavored drops and took it out, hurriedly unwrapping one of the candies and popping it in her mouth. The cool menthol calmed her throat, and she sniffled as she tried to keep her nose from running. She placed the bag back in the glove box. And then she saw them: a pair of gold-framed sunglasses with mirrored lenses.

As she stared at them, time froze, and the only thing she was conscious of was the roar of her blood as it rushed to her head. Kylie looked out the window and realized the road Mr. Austin just turned on was in the opposite direction of the wildlife rescue. Slowly, she turned to face him, her heart thumping. His eyes were cold and dead, and ice ran through her veins. *It's* him. *Fuck! Don't you dare panic.*

He reached over her, his hand brushing her knee, and grabbed the sunglasses. He put them on, and memories of him watching her, trying to seduce her into his car, and hurting Ricky pierced her brain like jagged pieces of glass.

"This is better, isn't it, Kylie?" His Texan accent was gone.

Terror gripped her like a vise, and she frantically felt for the door handle, but it was missing. A ghastly pallor spread over her face. *I'm trapped with a psycho. Where the fuck is Johnnie?*

"I knew you'd eventually take a ride with me, Kylie. You see, it's all a matter of patience."

"Who are you, and what do you want from me?"

A single finger trailed down her neck to the top of her breasts, and she heard him suck in his breath. "I think you know what I want, Kylie. Before we have some fun, give me your phone."

"My phone? Why?"

He plastered a flat smirk on crooked lips. "You can't be serious. Now give me the fucking phone." His steely eyes made her flinch.

She dug in her purse, pretending to look for it while she coughed loudly. She turned on another phone she carried, hidden in the lining of her tote. Her dad had given her the second cell and told her it was only to be used in emergencies. No one had the number except for her dad, and she was the only one who had the number to his emergency line, as well. Since Kylie was the daughter of an outlaw MC's president, Banger made it a priority to make sure she could contact him if she were ever in trouble. He'd installed a tracker app, and he made her keep it in the lining of all her purses. He'd even insisted she sew a second pocket on the insides of her pants. Right then, she silently thanked her father for his paranoia.

"Here." She handed Mr. Austin her phone and he stopped the vehicle, opened the window, and threw it on the ground. He then ran over it several times. "That should make your dad crazy. Imagine him not knowing where his precious little girl is. Imagine him staying up nights wondering if you're safe. Serves the bastard right,"

"My dad did something to hurt you or someone you loved, right? Is that why you want to hurt me?"

He smiled cruelly at her. "Something like that. We'll have plenty of time to talk." Then he gripped the steering wheel and continued driving away from Pinewood Springs.

Chapter Thirty-Three

"The sonofabitch is in Pinewood Springs. He's been under our noses all the goddamned time!" Jerry pounded his fists on the table. "He fuckin' killed my sister and Wanda. We gotta stop him before he grabs Kylie."

"Calm the fuck down!" Banger glared at Jerry. "I'll handle Kylie. You say the purple Corvette fucker is the one who killed your family?"

"Yeah. He started dating my sister to get back at me for being with Kylie." Jerry ignored Banger's flaring nostrils. "He did the same shit to Ricky. He thought the kid had something with her, so he beat the hell outta him, thinking he'd killed him. With me, he wanted me to know what it's like to lose something dear, and that's why he killed Kelsey and Wanda. He wanted me to pay for being with Kylie."

"Quit fuckin' saying that. You're not with Kylie." Banger rubbed his face hard.

"He thinks I am, and that's all that matters." Jerry smashed his fist into the palm of his hand. "We gotta find him before he hurts her."

"I got Johnnie tailing her." Banger turned to Rock. "Go in the other room and call him to make sure everything's good."

Hawk stood up. "I finally traced the purple Corvette. It was a pain in the ass because it was a salvage purchase, and originally the car was blue. Anyway, it's registered to a Mark Dudley in Brainerd, Minnesota. Demon Riders territory."

"Fuck! I know the sonofabitch," Banger said. "That's Tug's boy. Shit, I haven't seen him since before Kylie was born. Fuck! Where the hell is Rock?"

Axe jumped up to find him, and just when he opened the door,

Rock walked in, his lips pressed together.

"Well, what did Johnnie say? Has he seen anyone trailing my little girl?"

"He's not answering his phone."

A somber silence fell over the members. They all knew that if Johnnie wasn't answering the phone, it was because he *couldn't*. Something was very wrong.

Banger furiously dialed Kylie's number, cussing loudly when it went straight to voicemail. He reached in his back pocket and took out another phone, fiddling with it as Jerry looked on. "Fuck, she's moving, and she's getting further away from Pinewood. The fucker has her. Fuck!" The pounding of Banger's fist reverberated off the walls of the meeting room. "We gotta find her before he…"

Hawk clasped the president's shoulder. "We'll get her. We need to organize and spread out. We know which direction she is going in, so I'm gonna put you in teams…"

Jerry tuned Hawk out; all he could think about was that his Kylie was in danger and he had to help her. He couldn't let that animal do to her those unspeakable things he'd done to his sister. "I'll help track Kylie."

"Like hell you will!" Banger roared. "You'll stay here in case we need some computer help."

"Fuck no! I'm going after Kylie, damnit. I love her."

"Man, this isn't the time," Hawk said.

"It's the perfect time. Kylie and I love each other, and if you wanna beat the shit outta me and take my patch away, go right ahead and do it, Banger. I'd give up everything for her. And whether you like it or not, I'm finding Kylie." Jerry stood, shaking with rage under his brothers' startled gazes.

"I don't have time for your shit when my girl's in trouble," Banger snarled, "but I *will* beat your ass when this is all done, boy. Let's get moving."

The brothers listened as Hawk gave instructions, and Jerry took some time to rein in his anger; he knew sloppy mistakes were made when emotions ruled. He had to be cold and calculating, especially when he gutted the bastard who had his woman.

"Kylie went to work this morning. Axe, you've been trailing her for the past couple of months. Did you see anyone else around her?" Banger leaned against the wall, his shoulders slumped.

"Just that punk, Marcus Westman, and you took care of that. I never spotted anyone else. Someone should go see if she's at work. She's been going to the Empire Building, room 317 for the past week. Maybe her boss knows something."

Banger nodded. "Let's get over there. The sooner we handle this shit, the faster we find her. As I remember, Tug's kid was all kinds of messed up. Once when Tug brought his family to visit me and Grace, I caught the bastard hurting Gracie's cat, Sparky. I blew my top and told Tug about it. He went ballistic and started to beat the shit outta the kid. I had to stop him before he killed him. The kid's mom just stood there watching, never once saying a word. I couldn't believe how fucked up they all were. Gracie was pregnant with Kylie at the time, and she was so freaked out by them that I told Tug he could come any time since he was a brother, but he'd have to leave the family drama behind.

"Then I heard years later that Mark had joined the Demon Riders, and Tug was pissed as shit at him. He saw it as a betrayal." Banger wiped the sweat off his brow. "And then Tug went along with Dustin and Shack and ended up joining the Demon Riders and became their goddamn mole. Tug came into our club as nothing more than a fuckin' snitch. I still can't get over he stabbed me and the brotherhood in the back like that. He was an Insurgent for over twenty years. Fuck. Chigger must've told Mark we killed his dad." Banger clenched his fists. "His dad knew the risk of being a goddamned snitch, and now his son's out for blood, and he's using my Kylie to get it. What a fuckin' coward. Damnit!"

"I'll head over to the Empire Building and see what I can find out. I'll call you and let you know." Axe moved to the door.

"Jax and Rags, you go with Axe. Let's track this bastard down." Banger pushed himself away from the wall.

They filed out of the clubhouse, their jaws clenched and their gazes steely; the seriousness of the situation was not lost on the brotherhood. The plan was for Jerry to go with Hawk and Rock, but he wanted to be the one to kick the fucker in the balls, so he told them he'd follow with his truck. He tried not to think about how scared Kylie must be; he didn't dare risk losing his cool, not yet. Jerry couldn't let himself feel the worst of his rage until he had blood he could spill, and that meant he had to find Kylie in time. He just couldn't lose her.

Chapter Thirty-Four

HER STALKER SHOVED Kylie on the worn-out mattress in the living room. He'd taken her to a dilapidated cabin, and judging by some of the dusty personal items on the mantel, she suspected it belonged to him, or at least to someone in his family.

"Are you going to tell me your name?" Kylie crossed her legs, furtively searching for a possible means of escape.

He had been staring at her since they'd come in, the hunger in his gaze making her shudder. Slowly, he inched over to her then sat next to her, the mattress sagging under his weight, a blond wig discarded on the floor. In the sunlight, she saw him clearly—black hair down to his collar, flat brown eyes, a strong jaw, and some acne scars around his cheeks. He looked to be about twenty-nine years old, medium build, taller than she was but not quite as tall as most of the men she knew.

She jumped when his fingers skimmed over her forearm. "You're so beautiful. I knew your skin would be soft. I pictured it that way many times." He curled his arm around her shoulders and forced her close to him. "I want to feel your lips."

"No, please," she protested, but he made her turn her head. He pressed his mouth against hers, pillaging it with his thick tongue.

She gagged and twisted from him, wiping him from her lips with her palm.

He raised an incredulous brow. "You'd rather have your fuckin' Insurgent on your mouth? You know, when I first saw you at the university, you were like a glowing angel, so pure and innocent. I didn't think you'd turn out to be such a slut. Fucking Ricky and Jerry." He brought his face inches from hers. "Well, cunt, I want what you've been giving out so freely." With a fierce grip, the black-haired man yanked her head to his and kissed her. "Fuck!" He raised his hand and wiped the blood where she'd bit him, then backhanded her hard. "You like playing rough? I can definitely accommodate you."

Kylie scooted away from him but he grabbed her, forcing her down on the bed. Hovering over her, he put his mouth on hers again. She drew up her knee and slammed it right into his balls. He cried out and rolled off her, and she leapt up and made a dash for the door. She heard him rush behind her, and she whirled around and ducked when his fist came up to smash her face. She sprang up and kicked high, her foot landing against his jaw with a crack. The unexpected blow stunned him and he fell to his knees. Wildly, she tried to open the door, but there were too many damn locks. Picking up a lamp on an end table, she smashed the window with the base, the glass shattering.

But as she began to haul herself out the window, something hard plummeted against her skull, and blackness reigned.

JERRY ANSWERED HIS phone as he followed Hawk's SUV in his truck, headed away from Pinewood Springs.

"What do you got?" he asked Axe, his eyes fixed on the vehicle ahead of him.

"The whole job was a fuckin' scam. Shit. I shoulda investigated it, but it looked legit with a secretary and all."

Jerry's blood ran cold. "Did you talk to the secretary?"

"No one was there. It was dark. We had the super open the door and the office was empty. I bribed him to show me the lease, and it was rented for a month only by a guy named Steven Austin. We know that was a fake name. The asshole went to a lot of trouble for this. I shoulda looked deeper into it. But Kylie was going to so many interviews, and all the others were legit. Shit."

"Don't blame yourself. Banger didn't suspect anything funny about it, either. Who would? Did you ever locate Johnnie?"

"Yeah. He was in his usual place outside Banger's. He got out of his car because he heard low music from the bushes. He went to see what it was and found a CD player buried nearby. That's the last thing he remembers before waking up with a big knot in his head. I was just able to get a hold of him a few minutes ago. Seems like the fucker ambushed him. Johnnie feels like hell for having this happen on his watch."

Jerry breathed out. "I can't let anything happen to her. I gotta find this guy and kill him. If he hurts Kylie, my life will never be the same."

"I know, bro. Kylie is special to us all, but for you, it's worse. When Baylee had that psycho after her, it turned me into a madman. I couldn't stand the thought of something bad happening to her."

"Yeah. I gotta get to Kylie before it's too late, man."

"You will."

Jerry put the phone back in the cup dispenser and gripped the steering wheel. *Fuck. Where did this psycho take her?* He drove on, small dust clouds from the road rising up behind his rear wheels as the morning sun beat down.

KYLIE OPENED HER eyes and winced as pins-and-needles pain bloomed in her head. She tried to rub it, but realized she couldn't—she was tied to the bed, each wrist firmly secured to the bedposts. Her legs were also tied, and she darted her eyes around the room, spotting her kidnapper sitting on a chair opposite the bed, staring at her.

"I'm disappointed in you. You shouldn't have done what you did to me, but then you're Banger's daughter. I guess I was dazzled by your soft skin, your luscious tits, and your innocent eyes. But you're just a piece of Insurgent ass, aren't you?"

"You talk real big. Who the fuck are you? How do you know my dad?" She pulled at the ropes to test them.

"They're very secure. You're not going anywhere. You don't remember me because you were still in your mom's belly when I came to your house with my mom, my dad, and my brother. My dad was an Insurgent, and he and your dad were buddies."

"Who's your dad?"

"Correction, sweet one. It's who *was* my dad. Tug."

Kylie blinked at him. "Uncle Tug? He's your dad? Then why are you doing all this shit? He used to take me on rides around the neighborhood when he'd come visit my mom and dad. I don't remember you, though. I do remember my dad saying Uncle Tug had two sons. Are you Mark or Pete?"

He laughed dryly. "Mark, and you wouldn't, because he didn't hang around his family. My dad preferred the Insurgents to his children, and the club whores to his wife. When he did come home, he acted like the meanest badass around. He used to beat the shit out of me and my brother. He'd tie us up in the garage. He'd put a beam up, throw a rope over it, and tie us up by the wrists. Then for the hell of it, he'd pull on it until only our toes would be touching the ground. He'd strip off our clothes and beat the shit out of us with a paddle, a whip, a belt. You name it, he used it."

"How awful," she gasped. A wave of nausea washed over her and she shuddered. She couldn't comprehend how a parent could inflict such cruelty upon his children.

"I bet your dad never beat you once, did he? Your beautiful, soft flesh hasn't been marked, has it? I bet it'd look so sexy with bright red lashes on it." He licked his lips and his eyelids fluttered.

She noticed his bulge was bigger than it'd been when she'd come to. "If your dad was so mean to you, then why are you mad at *my* dad? Shouldn't you be mad at yours?"

"I'm here for my mother. Even though he beat her to a pulp more times than I can count, she stood by my dad and loved him. Loved him more than her sons. Can you imagine that? She'd close the door and go up to her room when he inflicted his torture on us."

"Please untie me. I promise I won't try anything. My wrists are so sore. I didn't know who you were when I kicked you, but now I do. We're connected through the Insurgents." Kylie hoped she sounded convincing. She couldn't let this madman do what she feared he wanted to do. She'd seen the black bag on the end table when she regained consciousness, the handle of a whip hanging out of it.

Mark stared at her, his eyes roaming over her body. "I think you are the most beautiful and perfect woman I've ever seen. I should've killed you three months ago, but I wanted to touch you. I want to fuck you."

"You should've just come to me. I would've welcomed you. Our dads go way back. They're buds."

Then his softness morphed into evilness. "Your fucking father killed mine. He tortured him then let him die slowly—I know it. My mother is still crying over him."

"My dad wouldn't do anything like that, especially to Uncle Tug. Maybe he just left."

"No, he didn't just run off," he sneered. "Chigger told me what they did, and I have to vindicate his death. You know the rules of our world. The bitch pays for the sins of her father or brother." He rubbed his hands over his face then cradled it in them. "I just didn't plan for you to be so special." He groaned then stood up and walked over to the black bag on the table.

Kylie's eyes widened when she saw the paddle, whip, very large dildo, gag, and various clamps for God knows what. Deep shivers shook her body as she tried to quell her rising fear. She had to get him to untie her; that was her only chance.

He walked back over to her with a few of the clamps in his hands. "These will hurt, but they will also give you pleasure." He stared down at her intently. "I do want to give you pleasure, Kylie. I care very much for you. I have to punish you for fucking Ricky and Jerry, but I'm only doing it because I love you. I don't want to hurt you like I did that biker's cunt sister."

Kylie's stomach plummeted to her feet. This fucking madman had killed Jerry's sister and mom? *I have to get him to untie me.* "Please let me give you pleasure too."

Mark jerked his head back.

"I want to feel you as much as you want to feel me. Please let me wrap my arms around you."

He paused, then shook his head. "Each mark I make, each thrust of my cock in you, will please me." He slowly unbuttoned her blouse. "Your skin is like velvet. I knew it would be."

Kylie twisted her body to avoid his touch, and he rasped, "I like watching your body writhe. Fuck. You're all mine now, Kylie. No one's here but you and me."

"I'm going to lose it. I really have to go to the bathroom. You can come with me if you don't believe me, but I have to go. Otherwise I'll wet the bed, and that's not too sexy, is it?" She prayed he wasn't into body fluids.

"You sure you have to go?"

She nodded, her heartbeats strumming.

For a long pause he stared at her and she met his gaze, unflinching and defiant. Finally, he leaned over and untied her arms then her legs, his eyes never leaving hers. She shook out her wrists and ankles to get the feeling back in them. "Thank you," she whispered, and from the way he smiled, she knew she'd scored some sicko points with him.

She went into the bathroom and shut the door behind her. "I'll just be a minute." She turned on the water and splashed some on her face, wincing when she saw her swollen reflection in the mirror. There was no window in the bathroom; she had no idea how she would escape this psycho who was hell-bent on some twisted form of retribution. Maybe she should succumb to him. He seemed taken with her, so maybe he'd let her go.

"Are you almost done?"

"Yeah." She wiped her face with some toilet paper and opened the door. "Is there anything to drink? I'm very thirsty," she said sweetly. If she could just keep him talking, maybe her dad would figure out something was terribly wrong, especially when she didn't come home, or when Johnnie didn't answer his phone. She was convinced that Mark had done something to the prospect.

"Do you like Coke?" he asked.

"I love it." She smiled, and he came over and kissed her softly on the lips. That time, she didn't bite him; she let him enjoy the kiss while she strived to gain his confidence.

He walked to the refrigerator and took out a Coke for her and a Coors for him. He handed her the can and she sat down in one of the chairs near the fireplace. He took one opposite her. "What happened to Mr. Austin? Did you hurt him?"

He laughed. "There never was a Mr. Austin. I made it all up. I hacked into your Facebook and e-mail accounts and saw you were crazy for the wildlife stuff. I pretended to offer you the job. Frankly, Kylie, I was disappointed you fell for it so easily. I'm sure your father taught you to be less trusting."

"Who was Mrs. Morris?"

"An actress I hired. She needed the money, and I told her I was creating a movie. She has two small kids. She didn't give a shit what I was doing, as long as I paid her as promised."

"Clever." *What a fucking nut!*

"I'm sorry I have to kill you. I don't want to. I'd love to keep you for myself, but it's a fucking shame when the children have to pay for the sins of their fathers."

"Yeah." She nodded, the Coke giving her the much-needed sugar boost her body craved.

Mark rose from the chair, narrowing his eyes. "Come on, it's time I show you a different world of pleasure." She glanced down at his crotch and saw his erection tenting his pants.

"Okay," she said softly, noticing a poker nearby.

When Mark turned his back and took out some other items from his black bag, she grabbed and swung the poker, slamming it down hard between his shoulder blades. He cried out then spun around, his eyes bulging, spittle forming at the corners of his mouth. "You fucking cunt!" He charged at her.

With agility, she moved out of the way and he stumbled on top of the bed. She knew she had to kill him; if she didn't, he'd do awful, sick things to her before he snuffed out her life. She raised the poker and brought it down again, but Mark rolled away at the last second. Furious, he rushed her again, screaming obscenities. Kylie ran to the broken window, but he yanked her back to him by her hair. "You will be severely punished for what you did." He dragged her to the bed, holding her arms securely at her sides.

In a desperate move, she threw her head back hard, hitting his Adam's apple, and he moaned, releasing his hold on her. She sprinted away, grabbing the poker again, and that's when she saw the gun. She stopped in her tracks.

"Get the fuck over here or you're dead," he hissed. "And put the fucking poker down."

At first, she felt resigned, but then she figured he was going to kill her anyway, so she might as well die before he savagely raped her. "I'm not doing shit. You want to kill me? Then fucking do it." She held her ground.

"It's too bad I couldn't fuck you alive, but I'll still enjoy you when you're dead." He lifted the gun and she closed her eyes, tears stinging them as she thought of her dad and Jerry.

Pop! Pop! Pop! The noise was deafening, and she opened her eyes to see the shocked look etched on Mark's face before he fell facedown on the floor. Then she saw her dad, Jerry, and Hawk in the doorway behind the bed. She ran to her dad and hugged him while she stared at Jerry, tears of relief flowing down her cheeks.

Hawk went over to Mark's body and nudged him onto his back with the toe of his boot. He whistled low. "Fuck, Kylie, you didn't need our help. You fuckin' kicked this bastard's ass."

She smiled weakly, but she knew if they hadn't come in, she would've been the body on the floor, not her kidnapper. Part of her felt sorry for the troubled young man whose father taught him nothing but pain and violence. But then she thought of Ricky's broken body, and the savage way Mark had murdered Kelsey and Wanda, and she knew he wouldn't have stopped until someone stopped him—until the Insurgents put him down.

Banger went over to the body and stomped his boot on Mark's face, cussing up a storm. Kylie collapsed into Jerry's arms, and he held her close as she shook like a leaf, her teeth chattering. She caught her dad's gaze as she clung onto Jerry then Banger cleared his throat. "Let's get the fuck outta here." He turned to Hawk. "You and Jerry take care of this. Come on, little one." He held out his hand and Kylie pulled out of Jerry's embrace and took it. Her dad wrapped his arm around her trembling body. "You're gonna be okay. It's all over now."

Leaning her head on her dad's shoulder, she walked out into the sunlight; the darkness had finally passed.

Chapter Thirty-Five

THAT NIGHT, KYLIE sat with her father on the front porch, watching the fireflies spark in the night. A cool breeze washed over the heat of the day, and the crickets sang in the swaying branches of the oak trees. Kylie sat with her knees against her chest on the wicker bench on the porch. Her dad sat on the rocker, smoking a joint, his blue gaze fixed on her.

He uncrossed his leg and cleared his throat. "Did the fucker touch you?" His voice was barely a whisper.

She shook her head. She didn't want to talk about her ordeal just then. The important thing was that Mark was dead. He'd never hurt another woman again.

"You tellin' me the truth?"

"Yes, Dad." She took a deep breath. "He was Uncle Tug's son."

"I know."

"He told me you killed Uncle Tug. Is that true?"

Banger didn't answer. He just blew out a stream of smoke from his joint.

"Is it, Daddy?"

He slowly nodded, and Kylie's stomach dropped. "Why?"

"It was club business. That's all you need to know."

Kylie knew club business meant her dad would never tell her why he killed one of his oldest and best friends. It didn't stop her from being disturbed by it, though. "How could you have done that?"

"It's never easy hurting a brother, especially a brother who was a longtime friend. Your Uncle Tug wasn't the man you think he was. You trust me don't you?"

She nodded.

"Then you know it was necessary and for a good reason. Your trust in me tells you that."

"That guy said Uncle Tug used to beat him and his brother. I don't know if that was true. Uncle Tug was always so nice to me."

Banger reached over and held her hand. "Tug had a sadistic streak in him. I'd say Mark was telling you the truth. He raised a son to be as sadistic as he was. Life always catches up with us. They both got what was coming to them. I'm just happy you're safe and he didn't touch you."

"I'm okay. I always know the risk in being your daughter, but I wouldn't trade you for the world." She brought his hand to her lips and kissed it.

"I could never ask for a better daughter. You make me proud. I'm just fuckin' sorry you had to go through the shit you did because of me."

"It comes with the territory. I never blamed you once, so don't start feeling like this is your fault. He was a sicko. I want to move on from this."

They sat quietly for a long time, listening to the crickets, the buzz of mosquitoes, and the rumble of cars passing their house. It was finally over, and all Kylie wanted to do was head over to Jerry's apartment and spend the night wrapped in his arms. She wanted to tell her dad about how much she loved him, and that they wanted to be together with his blessing, but she didn't think it was the right time. Right then, she knew her father wanted to spend some quiet time with her, to know she was safe and protected.

After a couple of hours, they went inside and Banger engaged the alarm. They climbed the stairs, and before they went in opposite directions to their rooms, he tugged her to him and hugged her tightly. "I'm so fuckin' happy you're safe, little girl." He kissed the top of her head.

"I love you, Dad." She embraced him tightly. Then they parted, each of them going to their bedrooms, closing their doors.

AT FIVE IN the morning, Kylie heard a flurry of activity outside in the hall. She leapt from her bed and threw open the door, seeing her dad's arm around Belle as he helped her down the stairs.

"What's going on?" she asked.

"The baby's coming," Banger said, his face taut and pale.

Kylie's hand flew over her mouth. "Oh, no. Are you okay, Belle? What do you want me to do?"

"Stay calm. I already got your dad freaking out on me, so don't you start. I'm going to be fine. I just need to get to the hospital. My water broke, and my contractions are coming pretty quick." Belle smiled at Kylie, her eyes bright as she took unhurried, careful steps.

"I'm coming too." Kylie turned around to go back in her room to change.

Belle shook her head. "No. It's going to be some time until the baby comes. Tell Ethan and Emily, and then you can all come in a little bit."

"Woman, stop talking and keep walking," Banger snapped. "I gotta get you to the hospital."

Kylie caught Belle's eyes, and both women burst out laughing. "I'll get everyone together and we'll be there in an hour. Dad, call me if the baby starts coming out before I get there."

He nodded and whisked Belle out the door. Kylie rushed to her room to shower and change before waking up Ethan and Emily.

Two hours later, Kylie sat in the waiting room, staring blankly at the pictures of rolling waves and idyllic sands hanging on the walls. Across from her was a rack containing health, women's, and celebrity magazines. A television hung in one corner, the volume turned up too loud, which irritated the hell out of her. Ethan sat two seats down from her next to his sister, munching on a bag of peanuts while Emily yawned and sipped on coffee.

"How long is it gonna be before I get to see my brother?" Ethan asked.

Emily shrugged and yawned again. Kylie smiled weakly. "We don't know. It could take a short time or a really long time." She fixed her gaze back on the door leading to the delivery rooms.

When the third hour rolled in, the delivery room doors opened and Banger walked out, his eyes twinkling and a huge smile on his face. Kylie leapt up and ran over to her dad. "Is he here?" she asked. Emily and Ethan rushed over.

"You all have yourself a healthy nine-pound, three-ounce baby brother. It was fuckin' something to see. Never thought I'd like seeing it, but it was awesome. Just fuckin' awesome."

Kylie hugged her dad, and Emily said, "When can Ethan and I see Mom?"

"We can all go up now. She's in her room with Harley."

Emily stared at Banger. "You got my mom to name my brother after a motorcycle?"

He smiled, nodding.

"How the hell did you do *that*?"

"The delivery room for the name." He and Kylie laughed while Emily scowled and Ethan jumped up and down excitedly.

"Come on. Let's go," Banger said, and the three children followed him down the hospital corridor.

Seeing her little brother made Kylie's heart swell; he was so tiny and so perfect, with his crop of dark brown hair and tiny hands. She was instantly overcome. "You and Dad made a beautiful baby," she said to Belle.

Ethan had his head on Belle's stomach and she stroked his hair with her fingers. "I can't believe how short my labor was. This pregnancy was a breeze." She grasped Emily's hand.

Emily kissed her mom on her cheek. "The baby's beautiful, Mom. I hate his name, though, so I'm gonna have to come up with a nickname."

Kylie leaned over and hugged Belle. "I love the name, it suits him."

Emily rolled her eyes. "Figures."

They visited with the new mother for a while, but after seeing how exhausted Belle was, Kylie told Emily and Ethan it'd be best to let her and the baby rest. Belle's doctor wanted her to stay in the hospital for two nights, so they'd have a chance to come back later in the evening to visit with her and Harley.

Later that night, Kylie heard her dad's footsteps as he shuffled across the tiled floor in the kitchen. When she heard the fizz of the beer can as it popped opened, she smiled and set aside her book on the end table next to the couch. She waited for him to come into the family room. When he entered, he looked happy, but exhausted.

"How're Belle and Harley doing?" she asked.

"Both sleeping soundly when I left." He took a gulp of his beer and laughed. "He's so fuckin' small. I remember when you were born, you were all pink with a tuft of yellow hair. Tonight brought back a lot of memories. Fuck. I can't believe I've got a son."

Kylie leaned over and kissed her dad on his cheek. "You did real good, Dad. He's adorable, and you're going to be just great with him like you are with me. Mom would be proud."

Banger looked at her, his eyes glistening. "I think she would. I know she was in that delivery room laughing her ass off to see the president of an outlaw club nearly choke when he saw the baby's head coming out. Damn." He took another swig of beer.

"I'm so glad you were in there. I think it's totally cool that dads are part of the delivery. I know Belle was happy you were there."

He chuckled. "The way she was cussing, I thought for a while she regretted her decision, but then the nurse told me it was the pain and to just go with it. I kept helping her and stroking her arms and wiping her forehead. She's an amazing woman." He fixed his gaze on Kylie. "I'm happy you're coming around to accepting Belle. She's a fine woman, and your old man is crazy about her."

Kylie nodded. "I know, Dad. I've become used to the idea that she's your wife, and we actually have had some nice conversations over the past couple of months. And I see how happy you are. Whenever she comes into a room, your whole face lights up. I love seeing you that way. I would never take that away from you by being snarky with her. And I know you want me to be happy too, right?"

"Sure, baby girl. I've always just wanted the best for you."

Kylie debated whether it was the right time to tell Banger about her and Jerry, but she didn't want to deflate the high he was riding on. There was time. She leaned against his shoulder and listened as he recounted the birth of his son.

Chapter Thirty-Six

Three weeks later

B ANGER STOOD IN the middle of the great room, holding Harley and swaying back and forth as he sang along softly to *Sister Christian* by Night Ranger. The old ladies chuckled under their breaths as they ran around, making finishing touches to the party the club was throwing for Belle and Banger. Kylie grinned as she walked by her dad, making her way over to Addie to see if she needed any help. Her dad had proven he was nothing but a big old softie, kissing, hugging, and carrying Harley every chance he had, and Belle loved it because it gave her time to rest. Her baby brother had brought a gaiety to the household, and even Emily smiled more than Kylie had ever seen her do.

"Start bringing out the salads," Addie said while she smoothed down the blue-checked tablecloth on the banquet-sized table. "Emily, if you're not going to help, then can you please watch Paisley and Hope? Cherri's in the kitchen warming up her chili, and I'm too busy to keep my eyes on the kids."

"What about Chas and Jax? They should be watching their kids instead of drinking beer."

Addie, Cara, Baylee, Doris, and Marlene stared at the young woman for a second, then burst out laughing. "Yeah. Right. Like that's gonna happen."

Emily walked over and scooped Hope up in her arms, then tucked Paisley's hand in hers. "It just seems like the workload for these parties is very unfair. Why do we always have to do all the work? The men in this club need to bring their asses into the twenty-first century."

"Most men need to do that," Cara said, smiling. "I can't tell you how many Thanksgivings, Christmas Eves, and birthday parties I've been to where the women planned, cooked, and cleaned up for the event." She shook her head then placed the rolled napkins with utensils on the table.

"Yeah, you're right, Cara. I can't remember a Thanksgiving where Ruben helped me with the dinner. And afterward, all the men are glued in front of the TV watching football while the women tackle the dishes and greasy pans." Doris pulled her hair back into a ponytail. "It's just the way it is. If you think too hard on it or try to change 'em, you'll go fuckin' crazy."

The women laughed, but Emily twisted her mouth. "I won't put up with that from any man. He either helps with the food and dishes, or he doesn't eat. Are you with me on this, Kylie?"

Kylie shrugged. "I know what you're saying, but I don't think men are going to change. I mean, we do the cooking, and they do the protecting. I love knowing my man has my back and would fight to the death to keep me safe."

"Your man? Are you holding out on us, Kylie?" Baylee said.

Kylie turned a bright red. Damnit. How could she let that slip out? She shook her head and opened up the large bag of pretzels Cara had given her to put in the bowls strewn across the tables. As she filled each one, she stole glances at Jerry, and each time she did, he met her gaze. How she longed to go over and kiss him in front of everyone. Jerry was right—she had to tell her dad. Jerry had wanted to come over and do it many times over the past three weeks, but her dad had been so happy with Harley and everything, she didn't want to see him angry.

"How's Harley doing?" she asked, standing next to Banger.

"Sleeping. Damn he's fuckin' cute."

She smiled and ran a finger gently over her brother's tiny hand.

"Don't even think about helping," Addie said loudly, causing Kylie to turn toward the table that had begun to fill up with food. She saw Belle holding a big pot of something, the steam dancing above it. "I'm not joking, Belle. Give me the pot of beans and go sit down. This is a party for you, Banger, and Harley. We've got everything under control."

Belle began to protest when Banger's baritone voice rang out. "Woman, come over here. Your man needs you."

Emily sighed and rolled her eyes while she played with Paisley and Hope.

Kylie moved away when Belle came over, and Banger hooked his arm around her and kissed her on the lips. The couple stood close together with Harley in the president's arms. As Kylie watched her dad, Belle, and her brother, a wave of longing came over her, and she yearned to be with Jerry in the way her dad was with Belle. She shuffled toward the kitchen to see if the old ladies needed any help.

"You can place this dish on the table," Cara said as she handed Kylie a huge Pyrex pan. "Be careful—it just came out of the oven."

Kylie breathed in the aroma. "Smells delicious. What is it?"

"Eggplant parmesan. I made it for one of the barbecues last summer and all the guys wolfed it down, not realizing it was eggplant. It was too funny. They thought it was chicken or something. You know, if I would've told them it was eggplant, they would've made a face and not tried it. So for the members, it's chicken parmesan."

Kylie laughed. She loved that Cara always brought a tasty Italian dish to family parties. She placed the dish on the table just when Addie went over and turned off the music. "Food's on." The sound of barstools and wooden chairs scraping against the floor filled the room as the brothers eagerly made their way to the food table.

Kylie grabbed a plate and stood in line, then turned around when she felt someone's leg brush against hers. "Hey," Jerry said huskily. Tingles ran through her. "You cook any of this?"

"No." She licked her lips.

"You're gonna have to cook for me sometime. You know how to do it, right?"

She nodded, then placed a large scoop of potato salad on her plate. "Do you?"

"Nah. The microwave is my stove, and the phone is my cook."

She giggled "Do a lot of takeout, huh?"

"Yeah. Am I gonna see you later?" he whispered.

She nodded. "Try the chicken parmesan. Cara made it, and it's so good." She smiled mischievously. He took a large portion.

Kylie was thrilled that Jerry was sitting at a table with Axe, Baylee, Jax, and Cherri. Since the old ladies were there, her dad would be cool with her sitting with Jerry. Everyone talked, laughed, made toasts to the new parents, and ate too much. Kylie looked around the room and was filled with a deep sense of family, loyalty, and closeness that only the MC could provide. They were a family who struggled, cried, laughed, and partied together. Each of their worries was shared by the whole club. When Kylie was in danger, they all jumped to help her. The enormity of their love and respect for one of their own always blew her away.

After they'd devoured all the food and the women had washed and put away the dishes, some of the brothers played pool while others sneaked off to have some fun with the club whores who'd been relegated to their rooms. Club girls and old ladies never shared the same space at the same time. It was just the way the Insurgents' world worked, and everyone knew their place and respected it.

Jerry sidled up alongside Kylie. "Where's your dad?"

"I saw him go out to the back porch. He's probably smoking a joint. Why?"

He grasped her hand and pulled her behind him to one of the small rooms off the hallway leading to the back porch, closing the door behind them. "I wanna talk to him."

The hard edge in his voice made her stomach lurch. "You can't be serious. Now isn't the right time."

"When is the right time? You've been telling me that for too long. You're not gonna tell your dad, are you?"

"Of course I am. I told you I'd do it. I know my dad better than anyone. You have to trust me on this."

"I get that, babe, but I'm the man and I have to tell your dad. I love you and want to be with you. You love me and want the same thing. It's simple." His gaze lingered on her mouth. "Give me your lips."

Before Kylie could say or do anything, Jerry captured her mouth with his and kissed her deep, her insides melting as they always did when he kissed her. He crushed her to him, his hands cupping her ass, and she forgot that her dad was only about twenty feet away. All she could do was *feel*: tingling nerves from his touch; butterflies fluttering in her stomach; soft, warming strokes.

"I'm so in love with you, Kylie. I can't fuckin' stand it anymore." Jerry sucked her neck gently.

"I love you too," she murmured.

The door flew opened and Ethan and Jack stumbled back. "We didn't think anyone was in here. Whatcha doin', Kylie?" Ethan asked.

"Just hanging with my friend. You know Jerry, right?"

Ethan scrunched up his face when he looked up at him. "Sure. I thought he was your boyfriend."

"No. Why would you say that?"

" 'Cause I am." Jerry put his arm around her shoulders.

"See?" Ethan turned to Jack. "Isn't this the room your dad told us the baseball and mitts were?"

"I think so." Jack said, his eyes darting around the room.

"They're in the small room in the gym downstairs. You know where it is, Jack," Jerry said.

"Oh, yeah." His face lit up. "Come on, Ethan." The boys rushed away, their footsteps loud on the stairs.

"Come on," Jerry said to Kylie, then stepped out of the room, and her heart thumped wildly as she followed him to the back porch.

They caught Belle and Banger kissing, the moonlight streaming through the screened windows, bathing the couple. Kylie glanced at the loveseat and saw Harley snuggled under a yellow blanket in his baby carrier. Banger pulled away and raked his gaze over Kylie and Jerry standing so close together.

"Sorry, Dad. I didn't know Belle and Harley were with you."

He narrowed his eyes, his gaze fixed on Jerry. "What are you doing back here?"

Kylie saw the apprehension on Belle's face as she sat down next to her baby. "We just needed some fresh air."

Jerry took a few steps forward. "Actually, I wanted to talk with you."

Here we go. Kylie's stomach was in knots. Banger lifted up his beer bottle. Jerry gripped her hand, and she saw her dad's beer freeze in midair. *Shit. Now all Hell's going to break loose. Damnit.*

"What do you wanna talk to me about?" Banger asked, his voice a low growl.

Jerry rubbed his hands on his jeans. "About something very important."

Banger furrowed his brow. "Go on."

Jerry fixed his gaze on Banger's. "I'm deeply in love with your daughter. I'm asking you permission to date her properly. I know you don't like me, but before you jump to conclusions, you have to know that I would never hurt or cheat on Kylie. I'll always respect her and give her the life, love, and attention she deserves. She loves me too, and it's important that you're okay with our relationship."

There was a tense, awkward pause. Then Banger stepped forward. "You done?"

"I love her," Jerry repeated.

"So you both been seeing each other behind my back again? Did you forget about the agreement you made at church 'bout never seeing or being with Kylie if you wanted to keep your patch?"

"I didn't forget. I tried, but it was no good. If I have to choose, I'll lose my patch. Kylie is my life."

Kylie noticed her dad's eyes grew wide for just a second when Jerry told him he'd take her over his patch. A warm, fuzzy feeling radiated through her, and she squeezed his hand. "Dad, I know you told me to stay away from Jerry, but I love him. Remember when you told me you wanted me to be happy and—"

Banger turned his hard gaze on her. "You fuckin' disobeyed me."

"How can you expect two people who love each other to stay apart?

Why would you want to see your daughter miserable?" Belle said softly, reaching out to grab Banger's hand. He turned to her, and Kylie swore she saw tenderness pushing away the steel in his eyes. "What if someone told you to stay away from me? Would you?" Belle touched his cheek with the back of her hand. "Well, would you?" Banger pressed his lips together and shook his head.

"And grandpa wasn't crazy about you when you were going out with Mom, but you pursued her anyway, and you guys got married despite what grandpa said," Kylie whispered, cringing at the way her dad glared at her.

"I'll treat Kylie like a princess her whole life."

"Her whole life? What the fuck you talkin' about? She's not even twenty yet. She's not getting hitched."

"I'm with her until she tells me to go away, and then I'll still be with her."

Banger looked at Kylie, and she forced herself not to look away. "You really love him, or is this some crush shit you got going?"

She shook her head. "No, Dad. I really love Jerry. I think I always have."

He blew out a big breath. "I purposely kept you away from the hardness of this life. I sheltered you so you wouldn't come and tell me what you're tellin' me now. Fuck. I didn't want you to end up with a biker."

"How couldn't I? You were the best mentor and role model in my life, and you were a biker. It's in my blood, Dad."

He chuckled. "Yeah, I suppose it is." He ran his hand through his hair. "If I say no, are you still gonna see him?"

She looked down. "Yes," she said softly.

"Figured as much. I just don't want you hurt. I want you to be happy and have a good life."

"I'm happy with Jerry. It's time I start making decisions about my life. You have Harley to protect and coddle now."

"I'm here to make sure she's happy and safe." Jerry put his arm around her.

Banger shook his head. "I don't give a fuck if you're sixty damn years old, you'll always be my little girl."

"I know, Dad. I wouldn't want it any other way."

Banger waved his hand. "Come on over here."

Kylie slipped out of Jerry's arm and went over to her dad, who hugged her tightly. Over his shoulder, she saw Belle grinning. Kylie winked at her then kissed her dad on his cheek. "Thanks for being the best dad ever. Harley's so lucky to have you as his father. And so am I."

Banger drew back, and Jerry stepped in to fill the space. "I will treat her well," he said.

"You're fuckin' right you will."

"How long are you guys going to stay?" Kylie asked.

"I'm tired to the bone." Belle stood up and placed her hand on Banger's shoulder. "You ready to go?"

"Yeah." His gaze stayed fixed on Kylie and Jerry. "You comin' home tonight?"

Feeling funny, she nodded. "I'm not ready to leave yet. I'll probably be late."

"You watch her, you hear?"

"Always." Jerry met Banger's piercing stare.

Sighing, he grabbed the baby carrier in one hand and Belle's hand in the other. As they left the room, he looked over his shoulder. "I still gotta decide 'bout the patch. You disobeyed the brotherhood, and even though you explained why, your loyalty belongs to the club. I'll let you know."

"Do what you have to do."

When Banger closed the door behind him, Kylie whirled around. "They can't take away your patch! That's a crock of shit. I'm going to tell my dad not to do it."

"You're not gonna say anything, babe. This is club business, and I disobeyed the condition of keeping my patch."

"I'll feel awful if this goes badly for you."

Jerry shook his head. "This has nothing to do with you. Don't own this. I knew the consequences, and I didn't care. I only want to be with you. If I had to do it all over, I wouldn't change a thing." He pressed her against him, and placed his hand under her chin, tilting her head back. "You're so fucking beautiful, and you're mine. Don't ever forget that."

She grasped his biceps, digging her nails deeply into his flesh. "And you're mine."

"Forever, babe," he rasped, then devoured her mouth. Kylie melded into him, loving how their bodies fit so well together.

She clasped her arms firmly around his neck, welcoming his hot tongue as it plunged into her mouth, and her body tingled with desire and elation. She finally had all of him, and she was exactly where she wanted to be.

Chapter Thirty-Seven

One month later

"IF I EVEN catch you *looking* at another woman, I'll beat your ass. You treat my daughter with the utmost respect or I'll fuck you over good." Banger had his finger in Jerry's face.

Jerry wondered if he'd gone completely insane asking Kylie to be his old lady. With a father like Banger, he should've just headed for the hills. But his sweetie was too precious and lovable, and he was willing to put up with Banger's scrutiny for the rest of his life if it meant having Kylie next to him forever.

Jerry still couldn't believe Banger hadn't kicked his ass yet. He'd been positive that after all the shit with Mark had died down that the president would've made Jerry's suffering his next priority. At first, Banger had given him the evil eye whenever Kylie wasn't around, but Banger had grown less hostile toward him over time, and Jerry figured he was growing on the president. In about thirty years, Banger may actually *like* him.

"I'd never disrespect Kylie. You know that, Banger."

"You're fuckin' right you won't, 'cause if you do, you'll have *me* to reckon with."

Belle's voice filtered through the screen door. "Let them get on their way, honey."

Banger gave Jerry the evil eye for the umpteenth time, then smiled at Kylie and retreated into the house.

Jerry scrubbed his face with a hand. "Fuck. You're dad's gonna ride my ass for the rest of my life. Does he ever get over things?"

Kylie flashed him a sly grin. "Nope."

"That's good to know," he muttered with a wry smile of his own. "I won't expect things to change."

She laughed. "He'll soften up when he gets more used to us being together. He didn't think you were going to ask me to wear your cut so soon." She pressed into him and whispered in his ear. "I'm so happy that you did. I'll wear it with pride."

"I love seeing you wear my patch. The shit Banger's putting me through is worth it, if I can have you." He brushed his lips against hers.

She smiled and drew back slightly. "You're coming to Margo's barbecue." As was her habit, she wasn't asking him—she was telling. He chuckled. She was just like her old man.

"Then we can go for a swim in the lake?" he asked.

"You're always thinking about how you can get into my pants," she murmured in his ear, her breath warm against his neck.

With one movement, Jerry held her securely in his arms, his lips skimming over hers. "Damn right. I think about it all the time." He squeezed her ass, loving the way she squealed.

"You gonna miss me when I go back to school?"

"You know I am." He regretted insisting that she go back to college in the fall, but he knew it was important to Banger that she finish her education and secure her degree. She'd be the first one in his family to have graduated from college. Jerry didn't want to take that away from her, or from his president. Hell, knowing how much fulfillment it would bring to Kylie's life made it important to him too. "Of course, my ass is gonna be there every weekend, and the only one you'll party with is me." He kissed her deeply.

"I don't know if I can do it," she whispered. "I'm gonna miss you too much."

"It's only for two more years. We can do it, baby. Then when you come back, we can get hitched and start having babies."

"Wait a minute there." She pushed him back a little. "We've got a while to go before you make me a baby machine. I want to work and have some time for us."

He loved teasing her. He wanted the kids, the house, and the sexy wife, but they both had time for that. All he cared about was that she was his. And he was still in the Insurgents. Life couldn't get better than that.

Jerry had laid to rest his guilt over not protecting his sister. He'd been a small boy the first part of her life, and he'd lost her before he even became reacquainted with her during the last part of hers. What ate at him, and he suspected always would, was that Kelsey and Wanda had been killed because of him. His love for Kylie had done them in. How could he have ever known that would happen? He wished he could have prevented the murders, could've made the fucking sociopath pay for what he'd done. Dying almost instantly of a few gunshot wounds seemed too damn merciful a fate for him.

"So, you gonna stay with me when you visit? I'm living off campus with Taylor, Ari, and Mary next year."

"I know, and I'm with your dad on not liking that one bit. You gotta watch yourself."

"I do. I have the biggest room," she said as she ran her finger under his T-shirt, her nail making a trail upward. She grazed his nipple and he jerked.

"Fuck, babe. Your dad's right inside."

"I didn't think you were such a prude." Her laughter was like a familiar song, and it warmed him. All he could do was smile. "Now, let's go back to your place so we can relax a little bit before we go to Margo's."

"You're a wicked little minx, and I love it," he breathed. "Let's go." He walked down the porch to his Harley, and with Kylie's arms around him, he took off. He loved the way she held him so tight, her warmth pressed against his back. He'd never wanted a chick on the back of his bike, but with Kylie, it was different. But then, everything had always been different with her. From the first time he'd noticed her, he was hooked. She was his soulmate, and he couldn't even begin to imagine not growing old with her.

They scrambled up the stairs and made out in the elevator until the door opened on his floor. Inside the apartment, it was cool and dark, like a cocoon. He picked her up and carried her to his bedroom, her giggles hitting him in the groin.

When he stripped down to his boxers, he slowly undressed her, her smoldering gaze pulling him in like it did every time. Bending down, he kissed her deeply then massaged her tits. God, he loved them; they fit into his hands perfectly, and they were so damn soft and luscious. If he could only touch one thing on her body beside her sweet lips, it'd be her tits. And the way she moaned when he licked her nipples to marble-hard beads hit him in the cock every time.

"I love you, honey," she gushed as he nipped the underside of her tits.

"I love you, babe." And he'd never stop loving her. She was the blood in his veins and the air he breathed—she was his everything.

His hands and mouth explored every part of her, connecting them through touch and passion. Then he trailed his tongue down her velvety skin until he settled between her legs. He sniffed deeply, breathing in the aroma of her arousal. As she whimpered, writhed, and gasped, he brought her to higher levels of ecstasy than he ever had before. With one hard roll of his hips, he entered her wet heat. He thrust in and out as they clung to each other, fused together by their raw passion and lust, never wanting to let go. She screamed when he stiffened then released his thick streams into her clinging core, and he collapsed on top of her, loving the way she smelled after coming.

Jerry rolled off and drew her close to him, nestling her under his arm. They lay in the dim-lit room, the AC gently blowing over their sated bodies. In that moment, Jerry knew he'd finally found the calm to the storm that had been brewing his whole life.

It'd been simple. He loved her, and she loved him.

And they were never letting go.

The End

Make sure you sign up for my newsletter so you can keep up with my new releases, special sales, free short stories, and other treats only available to newsletter readers. When you sign up, you will receive a FREE hot and steamy novella. Sign up at:
http://eepurl.com/bACCL1

Visit me on Facebook
facebook.com/Chiah-Wilder-1625397261063989

Check out my other books at my Author Page
amazon.com/author/chiahwilder

Acknowledgments

I have so many people to thank who have made my writing endeavors a reality. It is the support, hard work, laughs, and love of reading that have made my dreams come true.

Thank you to my amazing Personal Assistant Amanda Faulkner who keeps me sane with all the social media, ideas, and know how in running the non-writing part smoothly. So happy YOU are on my team!

Thank you to my editor, Kristin, for all your insightful edits, excitement with the Insurgents MC series, and encouragement during the writing and editing process. I truly value your editorial eyes and suggestions as well as the time you've spent with the series. You're the best!

Thank you to my wonderful beta readers, Kolleen, Paula, Jessica, and Barb—my final-eyes reader. Your enthusiasm for the Insurgents Motorcycle Club series has pushed me to strive and set the bar higher with each book. Your dedication is amazing!

Thank you to my proofreader, Amber, whose last set of eyes before the last once over I do, is invaluable. I appreciate the time and attention to detail you always give to each book.

Thank you to the bloggers for your support in reading my book, sharing it, reviewing it, and getting my name out there. I so appreciate all your efforts.

Thank you to Carrie from Cheeky Covers. You put up with numerous revisions, especially the color of Kylie's fingernails and the tattoos until I said, "Yes, that's the cover!" Your patience is amazing. You totally rock. I love your artistic vision.

Thank you to the readers who support the Insurgents MC series. You have made the hours of typing on the computer and the frustrations that come with the territory of writing books so worth it. You make it possible for writers to write because without you reading the books, we wouldn't exist. Thank you, thank you!

Jerry's Passion: Insurgents Motorcycle Club (Book 6)

Dear Readers,

Thank you for reading my book. I hope you enjoyed the sixth book in the Insurgents MC series as much as I enjoyed writing Kylie and Jerry's story. This rough motorcycle club has a lot more to say, so I hope you will look for the upcoming books in the series. Romance makes life so much more colorful, and a rough, sexy bad boy makes life a whole lot more interesting.

If you enjoyed the book, please consider leaving a review. I read all of them and appreciate the time taken out of busy schedules to do that.

I love hearing from my fans, so if you have any comments or questions, please email me at chiahwilder@gmail.com or visit my facebook page.

To hear of **new releases**, **special sales**, **free short stories**, and **ARC opportunities**, please sign up for my **Newsletter** at http://eepurl.com/bACCL1.

A big thank you to my readers whose love of stories and words enables authors to continue weaving stories. Without the love of words, books wouldn't exist.

Happy Reading,

Chiah

THROTTLE'S SEDUCTION

Book 7 in the Insurgents MC Series

Coming August 23, 2016

Throttle, Road Captain of the Insurgents Motorcycle Club, likes his women willing, stacked, and no strings attached. His life and needs are simple: riding his Harley, bedding as many women as can fit in his bed, and scorching his throat with whiskey.

The tall, rugged outlaw is a magnet for women who love life on the wild and dangerous side. They know not to expect anything from the tattooed biker but sheer pleasure.

Life couldn't be better.

Until he meets Kimber. The black-haired mechanic at Hawk's bike shop. What the f@#k? In his world, the only thing a woman should do on a Harley is spread her pretty legs wide.

She is sassy-mouthed, aggravating, and not his type at all. And he doesn't need any woman—let alone a chick in mechanic coveralls—messing with his head.

It's a shame all he can think about is doing nasty things to her on his motorcycle.

Kimber Descourt has had to fight to be accepted in a man's world, and she is not a quitter. Always attracted to the bad boy biker, she has had her share of unfaithful, jerky boyfriends. Swearing off all bikers since her last boyfriend made her his punching bag, she's content with working on Harleys, taking a few business classes, and being blissfully alone.

Then she meets Throttle.

He's a cocky, chauvinistic bastard. Oh yeah… he's also incredibly handsome, built, and sexy as all hell. He's exactly her type. She should run far away from him, but her body wants him in the worst way.

They say opposites attract, but when a hardened biker and a tough free-spirit ignite, their world combusts. Will their differences bring them together or pull them apart?

In the midst of Throttle and Kimber's tug of war, a Peeping Tom has been creeping around Pinewood Springs watching ladies behind the shadows of the night. He spots Kimber Descourt and is drawn to her. And he's beginning to grow bored of just watching....

Can Kimber put her pride aside and ask for Throttle's help? Is Throttle ready to let the feisty mechanic melt his icy heart?

The Insurgents MC series are standalone romance novels. This is Throttle and Kimber's love story. This book contains violence, sexual assault (not graphic), strong language, and steamy/graphic sexual scenes. It describes the life and actions of an outlaw motorcycle club. If any of these issues offend you, please do not read the book. HEA. No cliffhangers! The book is intended for readers over the age of 18.

Excerpt

THROTTLE'S SEDUCTION

Note: This short excerpt is a ROUGH DRAFT. I am still writing the story about this bad boy. It has only been self-edited in a rudimentary way. I share it with you to give you a bit of an insight into Throttle's Seduction.

PROLOGUE

ANNIE LOFTIS AND her parents arrived home from spending a lovely evening in Clermont Park listening to the free concert and watching the sky light up from the fireworks display. It was a perfect August night: clear sky with thousands of twinkling stars, a light, cool breeze carrying a subtle whiff of jasmine, and crickets chirping in the trees and shrubbery.

When they entered their home, eighteen-year old Annie rushed to her room to check out her emails and chat with her friends on facebook. She'd graduated from high school two months before, and she'd decided to work for a year before heading out to college. Happy that her two best friends decided the same thing, she looked forward to a year of hanging out, no studying, and earning more money than her after school jobs had while she'd been in high school.

Her parents, Julia and Kurt, had long gone to bed by the time Annie turned off her computer. Slipping off her cotton top, she unfastened her bra. The man, hidden by the shadows and the bushes sucked his breath in sharply. Although her curtains were pulled, her silhouette danced about like a shadow puppet on a rice paper screen. Her young, pert breasts were outlined perfectly, and the man held his breath, his pants growing tighter, as he watched her slip on her nightgown then turn off the light.

He stood there for a long time, watching and waiting. Waiting until the cul-de-sac fell asleep, waiting for the pounding in his ears to stop, waiting for his chance to make his move. And when the sliver of moon lit a path to Annie's opened window, he crept like a lion on the prowl, his sneakers silent on the lush grass. The gleam of the blade from his pocket knife flashed briefly before he cut the window screen.

He'd been watching her for over a week, getting to know the habits of the household. He'd even sneaked in a few days before when the family had gone to a cousin's house to celebrate a birthday. The man wanted to familiarize himself with the layout of Annie's room. On that night, he'd taken one of her pretty, lacey bikini panties—the white ones with the baby pink bows all around. They were so sexy, he couldn't help himself.

The intruder knew that Annie had a large hand painted trunk to the left of the window so he had to be careful to avoid it lest he wake her up. With the screen cut, he pushed himself up. He was an athletic fellow, worked out in the gym a lot and watched what he ate. In a couple of movements, he was standing in Annie's room hearing her soft breaths as she slept. He inched closer to her double bed, her coconut scent wafting up to his nostrils. A soft smile spread over his lips; Annie was so adorable and young. She had all the innocence and idealism of youth. He'd watch her come and go with her giggling girlfriends, and it almost made him wish he was eighteen again so he could date her.

She stirred in her sleep, a small whimper escaping through her slightly parted lips. He froze. He didn't want her to wake up, not yet, he wasn't ready for that. Like a statute he stood, not daring to move a muscle until the deep sounds of her breath assured him she was sleeping heavily. Then he stood next to her bed, looking down at her while he reached in the pocket of his hoodie and took out a roll of duct tape. The rip of the tape bounced off the walls in the quiet room, and Annie stirred again, this time her eyes fluttering open. Bleary sleepiness was soon replaced with bugling eyes fraught with terror, but before she could cry out, he'd secured the tape firmly across her mouth. She thrashed in her bed, her arms flailing, her legs kicking, but she was no match for him. In a matter of seconds, he'd subdued her, her hands taped together as well as her feet. Small whimpers attempted to break through but the tape caught them and kept them on the surface of her lips. Wetness dampened her cheeks, and in a show of empathy, he brushed the tendrils of hair clinging to the side of her face then wiped away her tears.

"I'm not going to hurt you," he whispered as his eyes slowly ran down the length of her, lingering at her rounded hips, then came back to her frightened brown eyes. "You're beautiful," he murmured.

Annie tried to scoot away from him when he caressed the length of her body with his hand. It felt cool to the touch as he slid his fingers over her cotton nightgown, the one with little unicorns and half rainbows. When his fingers touched her bare thigh, she whimpered again and shook her head furiously.

"Shh, little one. You don't have to be afraid. I'm not going to hurt you. I just want to see your panties." He pushed up her nightgown and gasped loudly when his gaze fell on her white bikini undies with tiny purple polka dots. "How perfectly beautiful." Without hesitation, he reached out and touched the side of her panties, loving the way the fabric felt on his fingertips. Pushing her nightgown up further, he stopped just under her breasts. "Do you have a matching bra?"

She nodded, her gaze wide. The intruder glanced at her closed door. The urge to see her in her bra and panties was too great. He took out his pocket knife and a sting of sadness pricked his skin when he saw the fear in her eyes. "Look, I'm not going to hurt you. I want you to put your bra on. I won't touch you. I just want to see you. Okay?"

She nodded, a tear rolling down the side of her face toward her ear.

"If you try to scream or anything, I will hurt your parents. If you do as I say, you and your parents will be all right. Do you understand?"

Again she nodded. He slowly helped her sit up then he carried her over to her dresser. He cut the tape from her hands and watched as she rummaged through the first drawer. He spotted a pair of yellow checked panties and grabbed them, stuffing them in the pocket of his hoodie. He'd use them when he returned to his place, when he remembered how pretty Annie was with her perky breasts, soft hips, and in her purple polka dotted panties.

Annie pulled the matching bra out. He told her to put it on, and she turned her back and slipped it on. The man escorted her back to the bed, secured her hands again, this time above her head, and posed her while he took pictures of her in her underwear. After snapping about sixty pictures of her in so many provocative poses, he stopped and leaned against the bed. The tightness in his pants was too much. He was harder than he'd been in a long time. Stepping up his voyeurisms and visits into pretty women's homes when they were out, had proved to be very effective.

Unzipping his pants, he exposed himself to Annie who promptly squeezed her eyes shut. The man didn't care. He didn't need an audience, he was perfectly content to make himself come into her yellow gingham panties. After several grunts, he spilled his sperm into her undies, making sure to keep it contained. With his head thrown back, eyes closed, his body slowly returned to normal. When he opened his brown eyes, his gaze fixed on hers. He smiled widely then pushed his limp dick into his pants and zipped them up.

Taking out his pocket knife he approached Annie, who tried to wiggle away from him. Leaning down, he kissed her gently on the forehead. "Thank you. I appreciate what you did for me tonight." He cut off the tape from her hands. "Wait until I go then you can get up and do what you have to do."

In two long strides he was at the window, slipping out. By the time he reached his car around the corner of the cul-de-sac, he heard Annie screaming. He hummed under his breath, switched on the ignition and disappeared into the darkness of the night.

Chapter One

THE STACKED REDHEAD slipped her lips around Throttle's stiff dick, and a jolt of pleasure zapped him. "Fuck," he murmured as he buried his fingers in her thick, curly hair.

"You like that, baby? Mmm...I love the way you taste."

He chuckled and decided it was going to be a fun afternoon with this sexy redhead and her blondie girlfriend who was rubbing her big tits in his face, begging him to suck her hard nipples. Of course he'd have to oblige, after all, the two women had agreed to come to the clubhouse to have a bit of fun with him. He'd met them at the Rusty Nail, a biker bar where a good game of pool with a side of fucking was the norm. All the back rooms were taken so he'd asked the two chicks to come to his clubhouse. They couldn't drive fast enough. They were definitely biker groupies—women who loved biker cock and wanted a taste of the dark and dangerous life for a night or two.

Throttle was fine with that. New pussy was always fun, and if they proved to be as adventurous as he though they would be, he may even let them spend the night with him. He normally didn't do overnights, not even with the club whores or hoodrats, but sometimes he'd make an exception and let a woman or two share his bed.

Damn, the redhead gave good head. He placed his hands on each side of her face and thrust his hips forward, plunging harder and deeper into her throat while he sucked the blonde's pink nipples. The blondie's rack was big and high, just like he loved it. The blondie pulled away and gave him a deep kiss, her tongue plunging into his mouth, mimicking a dick in a pussy. He pushed her away. He didn't go in for that kind of shit, didn't like a woman who was too aggressive in taking control.

"What's the matter, honey? I'm just showing you what I want your dick to do to my pussy."

"I'll get there. Right now I'm enjoying the way your friend's sucking my cock. Show me how you can eat her out, sweetheart. I fuckin' love to see that." Throttle pushed her away and she scooted down and went by the redhead, who parted her knees. The blonde slid in-between her friend's knees, flat on her back, spread the redhead's wet lips apart then started lapping away. Seeing her pink tongue play with the redhead's slick sex made him blow hard, his come shooting down the woman's throat. It was fucking awesome. He leaned back and watched the blonde play with the redhead's clit as she licked off all the come from his shaft. Life was just too good sometimes.

The women's moans filled the room as they pleasured each other, and his length grew hard as he saw them sucking and finger fucking each other. Throttle crawled over to the blonde and pulled her off of her friend pushing her on her back as she squealed in delight. Placing her ankles on his shoulders he rammed his hardness into her wet slit and pumped it in and out while the redhead sucked on her friend's hardened nipples. Throttle pushed his finger into the redhead's pussy and finger fucked her as he slammed in and out of her friend.

"That feels so good, Throttle," the blonde moaned as he rode her rough.

He wished he could remember their names, but all he was really interested in was the blonde's rack and the redhead's ass when they were making conversation at Rusty's. He knew from the moment their eyes landed on his they wanted to fuck him, and he was more than willing to give the women a treat.

Women flocked to Throttle, and, even though he was known as a cold-hearted bastard, they still wanted to spend time with him even if it was for only a quick screw. At six feet, with long brown hair, brown sugar eyes, a perpetual five o'clock shadow, and a sculpted physique, women usually drooled over him. The fact that he was a player and could be a cocky jerk didn't deter the women. With a defined jaw, straight nose, a lopsided grin that melted a woman's panties, and colorful tats curling around ripped arms and shoulders, Throttle had no shortage of women. In all of his thirty-five years, he never met a woman who he couldn't bed. And it suited him perfectly because, he wasn't about to chase any chick. Hell, *they* chased him. If a woman started that princess bullshit, well, he was onto the next one without even a glance backward. That was the lifestyle he loved; easy pussy and the more the merrier.

Just when he spread the redhead's ass cheeks positioning his hardness to enter her puckered hole someone banged loudly on his door. He let out a frustrated sigh, "I'm busy here. Come back." He pushed onward.

"Open up. Banger's got something he needs you to do." Rock's baritone voice cut through the door.

"Can't it wait for fifteen minutes or so? I got something I'm doing here."

"Make him go away," the blonde pouted as she kneeled behind him and played with his balls.

"I'm fuckin' tryin', sweetheart."

"So you want me to tell Banger to wait?"

That one question proved to be the perfect cock blocker. "Shit." He pushed back with his feet and stood up scooping up his jeans from the floor. "Sorry ladies, my president is calling.

The two women, flushed with arousal, looked confused. "You're going? *Now?*" the redhead asked as she sat up and leaned against the headboard.

Sighing, a deep sense of regret coursing through him, he nodded. "Yep, and you both gotta get your asses outta here. Like now."

"Don't you want us to wait until you get back?" the blonde said as she squeezed her tits.

He groaned. "I don't know what I have to do. I don't like people in my room when I'm not here."

"We're not just *any* people. Right? Can't you bend your rules?"

"Baby, you too are some hot chicks, but there's plenty of hot pussy around here. Now get going. Dress up fast. I gotta go."

The women cursed under their breaths but put on their clothes while throwing dirty looks at Throttle. "You said we could party with the brothers tonight."

"That's the way it goes. Go back to Rusty's you won't have any problems finding another biker who's horny. Leave your numbers. I'll call you when we have a big party. Sound good?" He walked over and squeezed the blonde's tits and the redhead's ass. The women laughed then wrote out their numbers and walked out with him.

Rock smiled broadly at Throttle, his hungry gaze checking out the two women. "Sorry to have disturbed you, but you know how it is when the president wants something."

"No worries. Hey, these two chicks still want to party. You doing anything?"

Rock's black eyes lit up as he shook his head. Throttle leaned in. "The redhead has lips for sucking and an ass made for fucking, and the blonde's pussy is tight and her tits are damn big." He winked.

"What're you two guys whispering about?" the redhead asked, batting her eyelashes.

"My brother here, Rock, he's the Sergeant-At-Arms of the club, and he was telling me how hot he thinks you two are."

"Are you telling us the truth? You're really the muscle of the club?"

"Yep."

Throttle shook his head, marveling at the way the biker groupies acted like the officers of an outlaw MC were like gods or something. "He *loves* pleasing women. You think you can take care of my brother while I'm away? If you're still here when I get back, we can have a foursome. Would you like that?"

The women's eyes shined and as Throttle stood before Banger's door ready to knock, the two women, tucked snuggly under each of Rock's arms, waved to him, telling him to hurry back as they disappeared in the stairway. Laughing, he knocked on the door.

"Come in," Banger's voice boomed.

Throttle walked in and stood in front of his president who was seated behind his desk. "Rock said you wanted to see me?"

"Yeah. I need you to go over to Hawk's shop and see if he's done with my Harley. He's had the bike for over a week, and I'm getting fuckin' antsy to ride it."

Banger pulled me away from a luscious ass to check on his goddamned Harley? Is he fuckin' serious? "You can't get a hold of Hawk?"

Banger narrowed his eyes. "If I could, I wouldn't tell you to go over to his shop, would I? He's not at the shop, and he's not answering his phone. Probably in some damn country club tasting the food for their upcoming wedding. Fuck, he's turning into a real pansy-ass." Banger and Throttle chuckled. "Anyway, I want to go on the charity poker run next week, so I need my damn bike back. I've got a ton of shit to do here." Banger waved his hands over the papers scattered on top of his desk.

"Sure, I'll go. You want me to call when I'm there?"

"Yeah. Let me know what's goin' on with my Harley."

"That it?"

"Yeah."

"Cool. Later." Throttle ambled out of the office, stopping to have a quick beer then he jumped on his bike. Why he couldn't finish fucking that sexy piece of ass *before* he went on this errand was beyond him. Remembering that the two women would still be at the clubhouse when he returned, he revved up his engine and blasted out of the parking lot, eager to finish quickly so he could have some fun with Rock and the sexy girls.

Chapter Two

WHEN HE ENTERED Hawk's shop, a blast of cold air slapped him in the face and he sighed in relief. It was damn hot outside, and he looked forward to the cool nip in the air that autumn always brought to the high mountains.

A lanky teenager sat behind the cashier's counter, his head bent down his fingers flying over the keyboard on his phone. Throttle recognized him as Banger's nephew; he'd seen the kid at a couple of barbecues he'd gone to at Banger's sister's house. "Hey, do you know anything about Banger's Harley?" Throttle looked through the closed door's glass window at the bays.

The teenager raised his head and smiled. "Hey. Your name's Throttle, right?"

He nodded and drummed his fingers on the counter. He wanted to finish up fast so he could get back to the horny chicks he'd left at the clubhouse. "So do you know what's going on with your Uncle's bike?"

"Not really. Hawk just asked me to watch the place and check customers out while he was gone. He said he'd be back in a couple of hours."

"I got somewhere I need to be. I'll ask one of the mechanics."

"That's a good idea."

Throttle clenched his jaw in exasperation and headed to the bays. When he stepped into the repair area, oil and gas fumes curled around him. He loved the smell, it always made him think of the ride and the wind wrapping around him. Damn, being on his bike, going a hundred, was better than sex most of the time. It was total freedom, and when he was soaring, it was like an out-of-body experience. He'd never found anything in the world that compared to it.

"Hey, Throttle, what brings you here? You got problems with your 1250?" asked Dwayne. He was the manager of the shop, and he'd been working for Hawk for nearly ten years.

"Nah, my baby's good. Banger sent me here to see if his bike's almost ready. He's going crazy without it. Besides, he's got a poker run coming up soon."

Dwayne wiped his brow with a dingy cloth and jerked his head to the right. "I think it's almost done. Go ask the mechanic."

Throttle walked over to the third stall and saw a short, slight mechanic, bent over Banger's Harley, turning a wrench. The mechanic's back was to him, and Throttle noticed a full sleeve of tats and slightly rounded hips. Hard rock blasted from the radio on the shelf next to the stall. Surprised someone so slight could handle a powerful bike like Banger's, he stepped a few steps forward and said in a loud voice, "You almost done with this bike?" as he turned the radio down.

The mechanic spun around, and Throttle's eyes widened when he realized that the dude was a chick. "Uh…sorry, I thought you were the mechanic. Get the guy who's fixing this bike to come here. I need to talk to him."

She looked confused. "What? I'm fixin' this bike. Is it yours?"

Fuck, I don't have time for someone playin' a joke on me. I bet Banger and Hawk are in on this. "Look, darlin', I got something I gotta do, so I don't have time to play this out. Be a nice little girl and bring the tech. Now."

Her blue eyes flashed, and she placed her hands on her hips, her chin jutted out. "I'm the tech, so fuckin' deal with it. And I'm not 'darling' or 'little girl', I'm Ms. Descourt. The bike will be ready tomorrow by five o'clock. I'm replacing the alternator. It took a while to get the part in." She smirked. "You can close your mouth now."

"You're the fuckin' mechanic that's been working on the president of the Insurgents MC's bike? I don't think so."

She laughed dryly. "I don't remember asking you what you thought.

I'm busy so move it outta here. Hawk will call Banger and let him know." She turned around and cranked up the radio, the hard rock beats reverberating off the walls.

Throttle narrowed his eyes, anger crawling over his skin. The bitch had a mouth on her, and she was pretending to be a mechanic. There was no fuckin' way Hawk hired a chick to do a man's job. No way the VP would have a chick with a wrench near any Harley. Throttle stormed over to Dwayne and motioned him to follow him back into the shop.

When the heavy metal door closed, Throttle said, "Who the hell is fuckin' around on Banger's bike? Man, aren't you watching what the shit's going on in the bays?"

Dwayne scrubbed his face with his fist. "Whoa, there. What the hell are you talkin' about? I have a damn good mechanic fixing his bike."

"You have a bitch fixin' his Harley. What the fuck?"

Dwayne burst out laughing. "Is that what this is all about? Kimber's a damn good mechanic. You know how picky Hawk is, so he wouldn't have hired her if he didn't think she'd do a good job."

"Hawk hired her? There's no way I want her near my bike if it ever needs fixin'. What the hell do chicks know about fixin' bikes?"

"Kimber's better than some of the younger guys we have for the summer."

Before he could answer, the metal door banged open and Kimber walked in, throwing a smile at Dwayne and a grimace at Throttle. She slid between the two men, then walked up to the counter. "You got some cold bottled water, Patrick?" She propped her elbows on the counter and rested her chin on her hand.

"Yep." The teenager bent down then stood up and tossed a large plastic bottle at her.

She straightened up and caught it and grinned at him causing his cheeks to redden. "Thanks." She unscrewed the top and took a long, deep drink. Throttle watched the way her shoulder-length black hair spilled out from her baseball cap. The tips of her hair were colored a bright pink. He hadn't noticed how snug her blue coveralls were, especially around her small hips and firm ass. She glanced at him. "What the hell are you lookin' at?"

Hot sparks rose in him. "Not you that's for fuckin' sure." He turned to Dwayne who had a goofy smile on his face, one that Throttle wished he could smack off. "I'm outta here. I'll tell Banger that his bike will be ready tomorrow."

"It will." Kimber wiped her mouth with the back of her hand. Amid the grease on her fingers, a splash of neon purple filtered through. One of her arms was covered in colorful tats of flowers, butterflies, and crosses. It seemed that the chick always went for the frilly shit.

"I wasn't talkin' to you."

"You should've been since I'm the one working the bike." She tossed the empty bottle in the trashcan across the room, and, much to Throttle's chagrin, it made it in. Smiling smugly she brushed past him and went back to work behind the metal door.

Throttle's Seduction coming August 23, 2016.

Chiah Wilder's Other Books

Hawk's Property: Insurgents Motorcycle Club Book 1
Jax's Dilemma: Insurgents Motorcycle Club Book 2
Chas's Fervor: Insurgents Motorcycle Club Book 3
Axe's Fall: Insurgents Motorcycle Club Book 4
Banger's Ride: Insurgents Motorcycle Club Book 5

I love hearing from my readers. You can email me at: chiahwilder@gmail.com.

Sign up for my newsletter to receive updates on new books, special sales, free short stories, and ARC opportunities at: http://eepurl.com/bACCL1.

Visit me on facebook at:
www.facebook.com/Chiah-Wilder-1625397261063989

Lightning Source UK Ltd.
Milton Keynes UK
UKHW021837251020
372208UK00018B/360